MADAME PRESIDENT

The Unauthorized Biography of the First Green Party President

Imagine if we had a Green Party President on September 11, 2001

Mark A. Dunlea

Big Toad Books

Visit our website at http://nys.greens.org/rachel for more information about the Green Party and other issues addressed in the book.

Printing 2004

Library of Congress Cataloging-in-Publication Data

Dunlea, Mark A.
Madame President: The Unauthorized Biography of
the First Green President / Mark A. Dunlea
ISBN 0-9749274-4-9
LCCN 2004091393
1. Dunlea, Mark A. 2. Fiction-United States

Printed and bound in the United States of America

Big Toad Books

ABOUT THE AUTHOR

Mark Dunlea has been an activist since he was a student at Rensselaer Polytechnic Institute in 1972, helping to found the New York Public Interest Research Group. As a student, he was active on a range on environmental and consumer issues, including the bottle bill and solar power. His lawsuit, <u>Dunlea v. Goldmark</u>, is the landmark Freedom of Information case in New York.

Upon graduating from Albany Law School, he became a community organizer for ACORN in the South and Southwest working on utility, health care and neighborhood issues. In 1979, he helped organize the 200,000-person No Nukes rally in NYC.

Upon returning to Albany, he became active in the Citizens Party, running for Congress in 1982. His report, "The Financial and Environmental Dangers of Garbage Incineration," helped convince environmentalists nationally to reverse their position and oppose garbage incineration. Mark became active in the peace movement, convincing Albany County to declare itself a nuclear free zone. He helped found the Albany chapter of the National Lawyers Guild.

Mark helped managed the 1984 Citizens Party presidential campaign for Sonia Johnson, who became the first independent candidate to qualify for federal primary matching funds. In 1985, he and his wife, Judith Enck, built their own passive solar home in the hills of Poestenkill in an intentional ecological community with six other families. That is where they live with their son, Reed.

Also in 1985, Mark became the Executive Director of the Hunger Action Network of New York State, a statewide economic justice group working with food pantries and soup kitchens. He has worked through HANNYS on issues such as raising the minimum wage, corporate accountability, welfare rights and sustainable agriculture.

In 1991, Mark organized the first statewide meeting of the Green Party of New York State. Later that year, he was elected as a Green to the Poestenkill Town Board. In 1998, the Green Party obtained official ballot status in New York through the Gubernatorial candidacy of (Grandpa) Al Lewis.

Working with Ralph Nader, he helped stopped the $1.1 billion corporate welfare giveaway to the New York Stock Exchange in 2001.

Mark is active in the community media movement, helping to found the Hudson-Mohawk Independent Media Center. He also hosts a weekly public affairs radio show on WRPI, Troy NY.

CONTENTS

PREFACE

September 11, 2001 was a tragic day for America.

The media proclaimed that the world changed forever that day.

America missed an opportunity to use the tragedy of 9/11 to build a better world, to respond to the murder of more than 3,000 people by seeking to build a world dedicated to peace and justice, not one dominated by an American global empire that rules by military might.

Like most viewers, I was overwhelmed with grief and horror as we watched the towers collapse with an unknown number of victims inside. My heart went out to those courageous individuals who looked into the face of death, ran to rescue others and never came back. For a moment in time much of the world was united in sympathy for America, giving us an opening to provide leadership to create a world that reflected values of justice and democracy. Unfortunately, our own leaders followed a much different path.

The night before September 11, I sat down with a friend to discuss the need to include a "terrorist act" in my novel to illustrate how a Green president would respond to violence differently from the two existing parties. Seven hours after I went to bed, the shocking events, and the American response to them, were beyond anything I could have imagined.

For those who have waited for answers as to who was responsible for 9/11, the efforts by our top leaders to prevent the truth from coming out is disturbing. More than two years later, most basic questions about these murders remained unanswered, blocked by the Bush administration with a compliant Democratic Party. Meanwhile, we have invaded Afghanistan and Iraq, killed tens of thousands of civilians, curtailed civil liberties here at home and awarded huge tax cuts and increased corporate welfare to large campaign contributors.

MADAME PRESIDENT: The Unauthorized Biography of the First Green Party President, is an alternative history. It makes two major historical changes.

First, the voters and the Electoral College, not the US Supreme Court, decide the 2000 presidential election. A Green ends up becoming vice-president because the Democrats need their handful of electoral votes to select the Democrat as president. The Democrat dies — under mysterious circumstances of course — and the Green becomes president.

Second, a Green is president on the day that two airplanes fly into the World Trade Center.

The seemingly fictional nature of the 2000 presidential election was too comical and tragic to ignore. The Republicans nominate a failed businessman whose only qualifications seem to be his father and his willingness to serve as the spokesperson for corporate interests. The Democrats, after eight years of a booming economy that still leaves tens of millions hungry and homeless, challenge the Republican family dynasty by running their own family dynasty candidate to replace the incumbent who has become the staple of late night talk show jokes for his sexual activities and his lying.

The son of the former director of the CIA is anointed in an election decided by his brother blocking blacks from voting and with a butterfly ballot that confuses elderly Jewish voters into voting for an anti-Semite. The nation is transfixed for a month as Americans discover that we don't count every vote in an election. The Supreme Court overturns established court principles to stop the vote counting and seat their preferred candidate. The Democrats fail to fight in Florida, in the courts, in Congress or in the streets, for their nominee yet label Ralph Nader and his minimal vote as the spoiler.

Given the absurdity of the above plot line, it didn't seem too far-fetched to propose an alternate result to the 2000 presidential election — one that follows the constitution and ends up with Rachel Moreno as the first Green Party president after the death of the incumbent.

This book imagines what would have happened if a Green was president on September 11.

I wanted to write a book to share my life experiences as an organizer with those just starting out. Saul Alinsky's *Rules for Radicals* had been an inspiration to me thirty years ago when I was trying to figure out what it meant to be an organizer and how to do it better. This book covers many of the key movements for justice in the US over the last two decades.

We need to learn from the successes and failures of those who have gone before us. Strategies and tactics are more often recycled or modified than invented. Yet if there is one message I have for new organizers, it is to avoid being limited by the observation that "we tried it before and it didn't work."

Ecotopia, the ecological utopian novel by Ernest Callenbach, had also inspired me. I wanted to provide not only a vision of a different world, but also some ideas on how such a world could be created.

After three decades of organizing and agitating, I admit to being more of a cynic than an optimist. Like most progressives, I am better at critiquing the failures of the present system than in figuring out how to overcome the powerful interests that benefit from it. I am still in search of the blueprint for a peaceful, joyful revolution that will liberate the planet and its inhabitants, that allows us to live cooperatively rather than competitively, that seeks to lift up all beings to their highest potential.

I have often remarked that since no single approach to fundamental political and economic change has a realistic chance of success against the forces of corporate America, one should be open to all progressive initiatives because one never knows what ultimately will be successful.

All the approaches I have tried — lobbying, education, demonstrations, electoral politics within the Democrats and as a third party, community organizing, coalition building, building alternative economic institutions — provide hope while facing significant obstacles.

The debate, the struggle between reform and revolution, between pragmatism and idealism, is a never-ending one.

Dreams, not logic, will create a better world. Lardi-dah

If the 21st century is to be the time of the green revolution, when corporate rule is replaced by a cooperative-based economy, where the need to preserve the planet overwhelms the desire to strip it for short-term profit and pleasure, when people power and democracy overcome the rule and power of the few, how will this happen? Will some ecological crisis, such as global warming, so clearly threaten the survival of the human species that change will be forced upon us? Will a new global village arise out of the ashes of a world war fought over oil, water or religion?

I believe that leaders are more of a reflection, a byproduct, of history than they are the principal protagonists. I do not believe that the election of any one individual, no matter how well intentioned or courageous, will by itself change the system. Nor do I believe that we have a real democracy in America or in the world, or that those who do have the power and the wealth would respect democratic choices that curtail their position. But I believe that a leader of vision and courage is often needed at the right moment to allow new paths to open.

I believe in Margaret Meade's observation: *"Never doubt that a small group of thoughtful committed citizens can change the world, indeed it's the only thing that ever has."*

I thank my wife Judith and son Reed for their support and inspiration as I wrote this book. I thank all the people that I have known over the last thirty years that have been willing to stand up for justice, to challenge the status quo, to dream of a better world.

Thanks to Carl Arnold, Dave Smalley, Sally Cass, Mimi Czjaka Graminski, Claudia Ricci, John Warren, Rudy Stegemoeller, Victorio Reyes and Jamie Matzdorf for their support and help with this book. I thank Michael Pelly, Martin Ping, Fred Munson, Ralph Nader, Medea Benjamin, Al and Karen Lewis, Joel Kovel, Barry Commoner, Sonia Johnson, Masada Disenhouse, Howie Hawkins, Karl and Steve Breyman, Gary Bowitch, ACORN, Greenpeace, the Green Party, Ralph Nader, NYPIRG, Earth First!, ACT UP, Public Citizen, Indy Media Center, Hunger Action Network of New York State and all the peace, environmental, economic and social justice activists for who they are.

Mark A. Dunlea
March 11, 2004

ONE

CHANGES

August 2001

Rachel gave up trying to fall back to sleep and slipped out onto the veranda, wrapping the bathrobe around her. She'd been tossing in her sleep recently, not getting much rest. She left her feet bare, running a brush through her shoulder-length black hair. The city was almost quiet. The birds sang their greetings, the sky still gray in the few remaining minutes before sunrise. The flowers in the hanging pots began to stretch out their petals to catch the first rays of sunshine.

Rachel leaned over to pick one of the dying blooms, and sensed movement in the yard below. She retreated, settling back into the wicker chair, one of the first personal items she had moved in, rocking slowly. She pictured herself spending the day with her large straw hat and faded jeans, sitting in her garden pulling weeds while listening to her favorite community radio station. She knew, however, that such tranquility wouldn't be hers for quite some time.

Behind her she heard Wynn stretching in the bed, trying to avoid waking up. Rachel had always been a morning person, while Wynn preferred working late into the night. She closed the French windows and climbed back into bed, pulling him close while gently kissing his neck. He retreated to the far corner, pulling the blankets more tightly around him. She halfheartedly tried to convince him to join her in a morning shower, perhaps her most guilty pleasure. After a few minutes she gave up.

A quiet tap on the bedroom door announced that it was time for her first meeting. At least one good thing about her new job was that she didn't have to worry about preparing breakfast. Cooking should be a production; breakfast was too short to do it justice.

Wynn was still asleep as she strode down the hallway. The guards snapped to attention. She gave them a quick smile. Her breakfast guests stood as she entered.

"So gentlemen, what have we messed up today?" she asked, pouring herself a large glass of orange juice.

Facing her were Secretary of State Robert Darling and National Security Adviser Frances Walls. CIA Director Winston Solomon was "too busy" that morning to join them.

Darling was the power player among the national security team, a certified war hero. As an 18-year-old airplane mechanic in the Pacific, he led the fight against a squad of Japanese soldiers that had attacked his unit's makeshift landing strip. This won him the Congressional Medal of Honor. After the war he had entered West Point, graduating with honors, the first African-American to be selected Regimental Commander of the Cadet Corps. He continued his meteoric rise up the career ladder, the Army only too happy to push him along and show him off as their success story in integration. He made friends easily, combining intelligence and ambition while being every bit the soldier.

Retiring as a two star general, Darling then entered politics. He spent two decades in Congress, half the time as Chairman of the Senate Armed Services Committee. For the recent general election, the Democrats had put Darling in charge of mobilizing both the promilitary and black constituencies for the ticket, which included fund-raising.

The crowning moment of Darling's career was when Harrington appointed him the first black secretary of state. In his own mind, he would be able to act as a check on Harrington's more liberal positions, especially when the president would want to appease the Europeans. Darling viewed himself as being in charge of the nation's defense, though technically that wasn't part of his job description.

The secretary of state was still in shock, indeed denial, over the idea that he would be reporting to Rachel.

Sensing Darling's reluctance to respond, Walls jumped in. A former Harvard professor, he'd parlayed his wife's generous campaign contributions to Harrington into his appointment. He was considered the lightweight of the foreign policy team, the errand boy who'd write position papers while Darling decided matters.

"The Israelis and Palestinians are fighting again. The Palestinians claim that a woman in labor lost her baby because a roadblock prevented her from getting to a hospital. Several young Palestinian boys were injured on their way to school. The Israelis are charging that the Palestinian security forces looked the other way when the Hamas shot some rockets into an Israeli settlement. They're threatening to cut off water supplies to the territories if Arafat doesn't halt the attacks. Various groups are making their usual litany of threats," stated Wells.

Rachel took a long sip of coffee. She'd have to make sure that they switched to Fair Trade coffee. She made a note on her palm pilot to replace the paintings on the walls of the meeting room. Too many old white guys. Maybe some pictures of Elizabeth Cady Stanton and Susan B. Anthony. Or Harriet Tubman and Mother Jones. Some labor art posters.

Rachel swiveled her seat to look directly at Darling. Darling was impeccably dressed as always, sitting erect with military precision, his salt-and-pepper hair neatly cropped. It was time to make a few points with the secretary.

"Bob, let's tell Arafat and Skolnick, the Israeli Prime Minister, that I'm planning to cut off all American funds if they both don't stop the shootings. Tell them I want to use the money instead to build some day care centers, public housing, schools, some water mains. We could build a lot of stuff for ten billion. Tell them I'll dedicate a sewer treatment plant in their names."

Rachel knew that he preferred being called Mr. Secretary but she wanted to establish the new pecking order.

Darling took a deep breath, letting it out slowly. He knew Rachel was playing him, but he was galled that he had to waste time with this impostor who knew nothing about the real world of foreign policy.

"Now, President Moreno, as I'm sure you realize, such threats will be both ignored and laughed at. Starting with Congress. Let's not forget that the real victims here are the Israelis. If you want to stop the violence, tell Arafat that he either has to rein in the Palestinian terrorist groups or it's time for him to go," Darling replied.

Rachel cut Darling off. "Bob, I realize that you think the Greens and I are knee-jerk lefties who just mouth pro-Palestinian rhetoric. But I strongly support the right and fact of Israel's existence. It's just that I equally support the right to a Palestinian state. Both sides have their faults."

Rachel walked over to the window to look out. The guards outside stiffened.

"Growing up," she continued, "I believed that World War Two was a 'good' war, a war where America intervened to save the Jews from the Holocaust. Only when I was older did I learn that stopping genocide was relatively low on our reasons for intervening. So I understand Israel's paranoia and why they care so little about world opinion when they think their survival is at stake."

"I understand," Rachel added, "the conventional wisdom that it's in our national interest to side with Israel. But we've funded them for our own military and strategic interests rather than for any concern about Israel's well-being. And we only began paying lip service to the Palestinians when the Arab world showed they were willing to use oil as their weapon."

"If we're going to stop the violence," Rachel told him, "we've got to be even-handed. We have to support justice on both sides. That means dealing with economic issues that are critical for the Palestinians — land ownership, access to water, the refugees," Rachel added.

Darling had to jump in, a bull responding to the red flag. "Rachel," he lectured, "America supports Israel because they share the same values that we do. They believe in democracy and the rule of law. It's the Israelis who've come back to the peace table time after time, even after some horrible acts by the Palestinians. They're surrounded by enemies who are ready to pounce at the first sign of weakness, either by Israel or us. The Israeli leadership has shown incredible restraint."

Rachel wasn't finished. Walls wondered if they would notice if he slunk out of the room.

"Bob, let's not waste time on a history debate. There are more than enough bloody hands on both sides. But far more Palestinians have died than Israelis, and the Israelis are by far the more powerful of the two. It's Israel which is the occupying force," Rachel said, sounding more angry than before.

"The Palestinians want to know what sins they have committed. They're not the ones who committed genocide during World War Two." Rachel purposely turned up the volume. "The Palestinians have endured decades of harsh military occupation, their own version of apartheid, a system of constant humiliation and economic deprivation. Even Palestinians who live in Israel proper are denied the right of equal citizenship," Rachel added.

Darling did little to disguise the disdain he felt for the Palestinian leadership. Or for Rachel.

"Madame President, the Palestinians are merely pawns used by the various Arab leaders who find it much easier to whip up passions about Israel among their citizens than it is to deal with their own shortcomings. Like many other Arab countries, the Palestinians suffer from a lack of democracy, which results in widespread corruption among their leaders. Arafat never takes any action until things escalate into a crisis. Once that pressure point is dealt with, he slides right back into the same disastrous behavior, giving Hamas and the others free rein to kill," Darling said in exasperation, a vein in his forehead throbbing.

"Let's be real," Darling countered. "Israel wants peace. A lot of Arabs want to wipe Israel and its citizens off the face of the earth."

"And are you in a position to be changing American policy by yourself at this moment?" Darling challenged, reminding her that Harrington was still in a coma. He prayed that the Congressional leaders would figure out how to resolve this succession mess.

Rachel smiled. "We all have our roles to play, Bob. Let me worry about presidential prerogatives and powers. You listen to what the White House decides." She wondered how Harrington had dealt with Darling.

She tried to soften her demeanor. "Mr. Secretary, I condemn all violence, whether it's by the oppressor or the victim, but the oppressor bears more guilt. Israeli citizens have been wronged by terrorism. But Israel also uses terrorism. And state violence is almost always more destructive than terrorism carried out by individuals or underground groups, because they simply have more firepower. The US is the one paying for Israel's firepower," said Rachel, as Darling noticeably stiffened.

"Our attempts to broker a deal over the last two decades have not been successful," Rachel concluded. "Enough is enough. I want to send both sides a clear message that it's not going to be business as usual during my administration. I want to start by having the State Department reach out to the grassroots peace groups in the area."
She would call the American ambassador to Israel to make sure he got the message, rather than just an earful of complaints about her from Darling.

Rachel looked up at the clock. Only fifteen minutes had elapsed since they had come in. She hoped the rest of the meeting would be quick and uneventful. She had more than enough problems on the domestic front and didn't need any more foreign policy crises.

"So what else needs fixing?" Rachel asked.

It wasn't going to be an easy day.

"We've got a situation in Nigeria," stated Wall. "A half-dozen Chevron employees have been taken hostage, including two Americans. The insurgents claim the company has been destroying their farmlands, as well as recently starting a fire that burnt down several homes. The company says the fire started when local people were trying to siphon off some oil, which happens all the time," stated Walls.

"We need to be prepared to use any force necessary to get the American hostages out alive," Darling added.

"Of course we have to get the Americans out safely," Rachel responded testily, "but do you have any concerns about the local residents? Doesn't it bother you that once again the world sees us sending in the cavalry to rescue yet another American company that has gotten into trouble from siphoning off the wealth of a third world country? Or it is okay since Chevron uses their oil dollars to pay off the military regime to crack the heads of anyone who dares to question what is going on?"

"Nigeria has made a lot of progress in establishing civilian rule and expanding democratic participation since President Obasanjo took control," Darling curtly responded. "Chevron has lawfully paid for the right to extract the oil. They're doing the hard work of making sure we get the oil that keeps the American economy strong."

"I am not willing to pin a medal on Obasanjo yet as a champion of democracy," Rachel replied. "And my guess is that Chevron is more concerned about their profits than they are about their patriotic duty."

Chevron had been involved in a similar incident in 1998, when protesters occupied one of their offshore oil platforms. Chevron flew in the Nigerian Navy and Mobile Police, who shot and killed several unarmed civilians. Rachel also knew that Chevron had donated 100,000 US dollars to help pay for the Democratic Party's recent national convention. They had donated even more to the Republicans. Just buying some good will from both sides. Hedging their bets.

Rachel told Darling to "make it clear to Chevron and the Nigerian government that we need to avoid the loss of any more lives. Tell the local people that we're prepared to seriously investigate what's happened and to hold those responsible accountable. Let them know I'm willing to send my own personal emissary if they release the hostages."

"Keep me and Sophie informed," added Rachel.

****

"The suits didn't look very happy when they left," observed Sophie when Rachel arrived at the Oval Office.

"I doubt they're ever going to look too happy. We need some names for replacements," Rachel said, taking the folder that her chief of staff handed her. "Darling is such an arrogant sonuvagun. America is the all-knowing, all-powerful, benign ruler and savior," Rachel added, shaking her body, trying to cast off his spell. "He gives me the shivers."

"Could you have someone figure out who are the peace and community activists we should be talking to in Israel and Palestine?" Rachel requested. "Also, do we have someone we could name as our personal envoy? I doubt that Ambassador Gargano is going to be able to convey my sentiments accurately."

"I'll check," Sophie said. She paused. "Anna called. She's on her way to Nigeria and urgently needs to talk to you about some hostage situation. She sent you some information by e-mail."

Rachel lit up at hearing Anna's name. Anna was an old friend working in Africa on women's economic development issues. They hadn't talked in a few months. Anna was someone who jumped feet first into a situation and asked questions later.

"Also, various Green Party committees, officials and members urgently want a meeting with you," Sophie added. "Lots of meetings. Some are sending demands and threatening protests if the meetings don't happen yesterday. They all want to know where their offices will be in the White House."

Rachel loved the Greens' enthusiasm and beliefs but decried their obsession with process, their tendency to be a debating society. Their concept of grass roots democracy often seemed to mean that each member felt a need to be consulted about every decision.

"Good. We could use some colorful protests in front of the White House. I hope they bring puppets and lots of costumes. Maybe they'll let Tommy do a skit. He loves protesting me," Rachel responded.

Tommy was her 23-year-old son, a professed anarchist and committed slacker, or so Rachel argued with him. Tommy had moved to DC when she became vice-president, and was living the grand life of being the first son while pursuing music and activism. He had managed to put together an impressive network of young women to assist him.

"One of the things the Greens aren't happy about is the group you're convening to develop the program for your administration. They think that's the Green Party's responsibility. I reminded them that there are plenty of Greens involved," Sophie added.

Wynn had walked in during the conversation. "Make sure they realize we're starting with the Green platform," he interjected.

"We're just fleshing out the details, adding things like timelines, costs, the names of people who can do the work," Wynn continued. "We're bringing in additional people because we've got to expand our base. We can't rely on just the 10% who voted Green. Hopefully we can agree to make it a priority to build the party at the grassroots level in the next four years, taking our message door to door."

Rachel had pulled in a number of Green Party leaders as her kitchen cabinet when she became vice-president. She would be expanding that now. Barry Frost, Sandy Alvarez and Ray McDaniels were the core. Frost was the renowned consumer and environmental activist who'd been the Green Party presidential candidate. Alvarez and McDaniels were the two Greens in Congress.

Rachel and Wynn had worked closely with McDaniels back home, helping to organize the "Battle in Seattle," the landmark antiglobalization protest at the World Trade Organization summit where corporate and political leaders gathered to negotiate the terms of "Free trade."

Alvarez had been elected from New Mexico, where for two decades she had been running health clinics and social programs in poor rural areas.

She had done surprisingly well in her first race for Congress in 1996, pulling more than 15 percent of the vote. A Republican had won that election by a few percentage points over the Democrats. When the Democrats accused her of being a spoiler, of helping to elect a Republican, Sandy replied that "our electoral system elected the Republican. If we want to make sure that the candidate with the broadest base of support wins, we should use IRV."

With Instant Runoff Voting, voters rank candidates by order of preference. If no candidate wins a majority in the initial count, the votes for the lowest-ranked candidate are redistributed to those voters' second choice. This process continues until one candidate wins a majority, thus ensuring that the candidate with the broadest base of support wins. It also allows voters to vote for whom they wanted, rather than worrying about the "lesser of two evils" approach to elections. "Oh, I really like candidate A, but I hate candidate B, so I'll vote for candidate C who I don't really like but at least has a better chance of winning than candidate A."

IRV enabled Alvarez to win in 2000 even though she had a lower vote total than the Republican on the first round.

Rachel had also hired Greens as part of her vice-presidential staff. She would be looking to place more into the federal government now that she was president.

****

Rachel pulled up Anna's e-mail message on her computer screen.

She'd met Anna Brown through her healthcare organizing in the Bay Area. Anna had been working in Africa and South America the past couple of years, assisting women to set up work collectives the dealt with everything from clothing to pottery to computer assembly, helping to control both production and marketing. It was their one hope of escaping from abject poverty. The alternative was working long hours for pennies in local sweatshop that sold to the multinationals such as Wal-Mart and Nike. Anna had been attending a regional women's economic development conference in Nairobi when the hostages had been taken in Nigeria.

"Dear Rachel. Sorry I have not sent congratulations sooner. What an inspiration for the world. The news hit here a few days ago. Keep your head low and women close," said the e-mail.

"I'm leaving for Nigeria in a few minutes. I'm sure you know what type of lousy living conditions are foisted on the locals so the oil barons and their political and military puppets can get rich stealing their oil. There was an Ogoni woman at this kick-ass women's empowerment conference in Kenya, Ayesha Anyanwu, you'd love her, she has this great melodic voice, and a smile that could melt butter. She received a call about what was going down. She asked me if I knew anyone in the American government that could help save their butts. When she found out that I knew you, she begged me to fly back with her."

"Ayesha says that Chevron threw around a lot of money a few months ago upgrading the roads. The truck traffic has been much higher ever since. Something's going down. The company goons are more jumpy than ever recently. Local labor and environmental activists are disappearing left and right. Some pretty gruesome stuff," Anna wrote.

"You've got to save these people," Anna pleaded. "Send in those god-damned Marines, get some use out of their misguided testosterone."

"Love and best wishes. Give my best to Tommy and Wynn. Make me proud. XXX. Anna."

Rachel skimmed the background information from Anna, most of which she was familiar with.

The links between the oil companies and Nigeria dated back to British colonial rule. While Royal/Dutch Shell Oil had long been the dominant player in the oil-rich Nigerian delta, four American companies — Chevron, Exxon-Mobil, Texaco and BP Amoco — also operated in the area. Oil accounts for 90 percent of Nigeria's foreign exchange and more than 80 percent of federal government revenue.

The first commercially viable oil strike in Nigeria had been on Ogoni land in 1956. Since 1992, the Movement for the Survival of Ogoni People in southeastern Nigeria had campaigned against the "environmental terrorism" of their homeland by the oil companies. Along with other local tribes, they formed the Chicoco movement, named after the rich soil of the delta, to reclaim their lands. International attention finally turned to the struggle following the military rulers' execution of Nobel Prize-winning poet and Ogoni activist Kenule Saro-Wiwa along with eight others in the mid-1990s. With the reestablishment of civilian rule, their plight had once again faded from international attention.

Rachel typed a formal response, sending a copy to Sophie and Darling.

"Dear Anna:

"Thanks for the update. I hope you will be my personal representative in this matter. Please let the Ogoni know that I support their right to live on and enjoy their own land, and that I pledge to work with them to get them fair treatment. I hope that as a sign of good faith they will release the hostages as soon as possible. If this is done, I will personally guarantee the safety of anyone involved in the protests. Please contact me or my chief of staff, Sophie Kretsky, if you have any problem obtaining the cooperation of American representatives in Nigeria."

Rachel appended an additional note for Darling. "You're responsible for Anna's safety. As my personal envoy, please extend to Anna all appropriate courtesies, including access to our briefings and meetings. Anna has full power to investigate what is going on. Please let me know when our representatives have made contact with her."

****

Sophie opened the door to the Oval Office. "Madame President, the honorable Barry Frost," she announced, escorting in a tall, trim man with a mane of thick gray hair. His suit jacket as always was rumpled.

Frost had headed the Green presidential ticket in the recent election, with Rachel running for vice-president. When the two major parties finished in a virtual tie, the ten Green electoral votes had been used to elect Harrington, the Democratic candidate, as president. As part of the deal, the Electoral College had elected Rachel vice-president.

Ten days ago Harrington suffered a heat attack. He was in a coma, brain dead, with no possibility of recovery. So far no decision had been made to disconnect him from the machines. While the power of the presidency had been transferred to Rachel under the 25th amendment, the situation was still fluid, with Harrington's appointees still running most of the government and wondering what they were going to do about Rachel. Rachel had become more assertive in recent days as it became clear that Harrington was not going to recover.

Fortunately, Rachel had insisted on a larger than normal staff when she accepted the position of vice-president, arguing that she was the junior partner in a coalition government. Tension within the White House had increased in recent days, with her vice-presidential staff assuming more and more of the key duties. Boxes were piled everywhere as staff were being shunted in and out.

As vice-president, Rachel had used her staff to develop a green agenda for many of the issues that the Harrington administration was dealing with — as well as for some they were ignoring. She was now convening a group of 100 policy experts and community leaders to develop a "Blueprint for America."

Rachel got up to give Frost a big hug. As always, Frost stiffened as she enveloped him.

"It's so good to see you, Barry," Rachel said, letting him escape. "By all rights you should be the one sitting here," she added.

"That's nice of you to say Rachel but we made the right decision," Frost said. "Harrington would've driven me crazy. I knew the Democrats were underestimating you and besides, you're the one with the people skills needed to work this job."

"Well, any position you want, it's yours," she said. "Pull up a seat. I want your input on this meeting I'm putting together," Rachel said.

Frost surprised her by focusing on the process of putting the plan together rather than on the content. Frost was an acknowledged public policy wonk. Organizing he normally left to others.

"You need to show that it won't be business as usual in Washington. Use the process to broaden your base, develop some grand themes for your administration. Hold some town hall meetings around the country after you have a first draft. Add capability on the White House website for the public to comment," Frost remarked, fidgeting with his horn-rimmed glasses.

"Your honeymoon with Congress and the media isn't going to last long," Frost warned, "assuming you even get one. Be careful what issues and fights you focus on first. Don't be like Clinton, picking an issue like gays in the military where he alienated both sides without a real victory," he observed.

"Focus on a few critical issues where the public will back you against Congress and the special interests. Be the people's champion. Things like healthcare, minimum wage, prescription drugs, maybe energy or global warming," Frost added.

"I have two other main points of advice," he continued. "First, have someone quickly pull together a list of the top level administrative appointments you can make without the need for confirmation by the Senate, such as the deputy commissioners who really run the agencies. With no Green base in Congress, it's these appointments that will end up being your biggest legacy — the thousands of administrative decisions on everything from parks to pesticides to trade rules to social services that you can make without Congressional approval."

"Put your best people in these positions," Frost told her. "Make sure they're already running the place before you put forth any names for Cabinet positions. That way they can't veto them. Unfortunately, you won't be able to get really good people past the Senate confirmation. And I would ask all of Harrington's appointees for a letter of resignation, starting with the Cabinet. You may not need to use them, but you have them if you need them. If they balk at key staff appointments, show them the door."

"You should also pick an attorney general who'll have a passion for prosecuting corporate criminals. Particularly ones who have been using campaign contribution as their get-out-of-jail-free card. Harrington's guy at the Justice Department, Solcraft, is still running around trying to make it easier for corporations to rip us off," Frost remarked. Solcraft had been chair of Harrington's campaign fundraising committee.

"Harrington is paying back his contribution big time," Frost noted," rewarding them across the board on taxes, liability, environmental protection, consumer rights, corporate welfare — they're practically lining up at the front door for their goodies. The more money they steal, the bigger the photo. They have no shame. The line stretches all the way down Pennsylvania Avenue."

Frost hardly needed to convince Rachel of the need to go after such criminals. Corporate crime had been a staple of her campaign speeches.

"While the politicians from the two major parties claim they want to be tough on crime, they never seek to prosecute corporate criminals who steal far more money and kill far more people than street criminals," Rachel would tell the crowd. "Ford Motor Company was never held criminally liable for killing more than 500 persons in Pinto accidents when they knowingly decided not to spend eleven dollars fixing each gas tank, deciding it would be cheaper to settle the resulting damage lawsuits."

The Pinto was a bone of contention between Frost and Wynn. When Wynn was a student in Albany, he'd volunteered to pick Frost up at the airport to drive him to a speech at a local college. He ended up borrowing a friend's car at the last moment, showing up with a Pinto. Frost had questioned Wynn's sanity, refused to get in and had taken a taxi cab instead. The story had made it into the twenty-fifth anniversary edition of *Mother Jones*.

Rachel had cited plenty of other examples of corporate criminals during the campaign. "Companies that still dump toxics into water bodies, knowing it'll kill living things, including humans. Companies that deny drugs to poor people by price gouging. Companies that view it as a competitive sport to maximize the money they extract from government contracts, always on the prowl for new ways to stuff their pockets by evading the law," Rachel told the crowds.

Frost told her, "You need to find someone who'll bring in a lot of eager beaver consumer and public interest advocates who'll be willing to take these companies on, who won't be worrying about getting a job with corporate America after they leave. Let's have a new version of the FBI's ten most wanted. Educate the public, issue by issue, on just how big these corporate crooks really are, sparking the outrage needed to win fundamental change," Frost added.

Rachel was always amazed at Frost's fervor, even though it was probably the hundredth time he had made a similar speech.

Pacing around the Oval Office, Frost examined the memorabilia. It was still Harrington's office. Frost was most interested in an autographed picture of the world champion Yankees.

"Well, there's one person I know with the requisite passion," Rachel observed. "When should we send your name to the Senate?" Rachel asked.

Frost perfunctorily dismissed her suggestion. "Didn't I just tell you to avoid picking losing fights? I'll find you some names that I think we can slip through," he said.

"Any company you have in mind to go after first?" asked Rachel.

"It would be a tough nut to crack, but General Electric has a rap sheet that would put Al Capone to shame. They'd probably tie you up in court for years though," Barry replied.

"So Barry, tell me," said Rachel. "Let's say I do go after GE. What would be the most important points to hit? Politically speaking."

"Oh, where to start," Frost sighed.

GE was a major corporate polluter, having dumped PCBs and other toxics across America, across the planet in fact. It had also repeatedly pled guilty to defrauding the Pentagon, operating unsafe nuclear reactors and for workplace safety violations.

"To get popular support, I'd highlight the fact the GE has slashed its US workforce by almost half since 1986, while its stock value has skyrocketed. Community after community in America watched as tens of thousands of their workers were laid off, killing other local businesses from suppliers to diners. Whole communities crumbled, while GE globalized its operations by shifting production to low-wage countries overseas. GE has even forced its suppliers to move out of the country if they hoped to continue their relationship. That is what I would highlight in the press."

****

Senate Majority Leader Jonathan Deutsche from Maine was fuming. He couldn't believe that after winning a hard-fought election, the Democrats were turning the Oval Office over to a Green who knew nothing about politics. He'd argued with Harrington that giving away the vice-presidential slot was a dumb deal, a big mistake.

"He should've offered Rachel EPA, not VP," he'd complained to anyone who would listen.

Harrington could be on life support for weeks, months, who knew how long? Deutsche's staff had been researching the 25th Amendment, which deals with the transfer of power when a president is incapacitated,

The Democrats had also been doing some research on impeachment. You needed to know what aces you had up your sleeve. Presidents could be impeached for the vague standard of "high crimes and misdemeanors." Most constitutional scholars felt this meant threats to the state, but the House had used a much weaker standard in impeaching Clinton for lying about having oral sex with an intern.

Deutsche's staff had uncovered an outstanding charge against Rachel in the DC courts from a civil obedience protest at the Capitol a decade ago. At the time, the Capitol police had told her she could go home to San Francisco and not worry about anything. They would drop it from their system if she didn't get pulled in for anything else in DC during the next twelve months. It was something they might be able to use if they were desperate.

Deutsche's first step would be to reason with Rachel, appeal to her sense of fairness. Since she was thrust into the presidency completely unprepared, she might be looking for a graceful way to bow out. Threats would come later.

But if she resigned before a new vice-president was sworn in, the presidency would go to the third in line of succession, the Speaker of the House, Republican Frederick Wilson Baker III of South Carolina, an old-fashioned wheeler-dealer. Rachel would be a nuisance, but Baker would be real trouble for the Democrats.

Sophie ushered Deutsche into the Oval Office.

Deutsche gave Rachel a quick hug and peck on the cheek, pausing a few seconds to take her hands into his, and give her a meaningful, if not altogether reassuring, look.

"Rachel, I'm sure this unfortunate tragedy is a major blow for you. I want to let you know how much we have appreciated the grace you have shown in the last week in filling in," Deutsche began. "How are you holding up?"

Deutsche was a career politician, having never lost an election in his 30 years of campaigning. He had started off as a town selectman. After a decade, he had moved into the state Senate, then into Congress and finally the US Senate. Competency rather than charisma had elevated him to the Majority Leader position. He was known as a straight shooter, someone whose word you trusted. He also was known as someone who didn't suffer fools. He was used to getting his way.

"Thank you, Senator, for all your kind words. This is a trying time for all of us. Our prayers go out to Mrs. Harrington," Rachel said, indicating for Deutsche to take a seat.

"I'm doing okay, not great" Rachel admitted. "You feel the enormity of this office, all those people counting on you. Fortunately you feel the love and support of so many Americans. It makes you want to do the right thing. I'm sure you feel the same calling, Jonathan," she said.

"A new sense of the world comes to you," Rachel went on. "You see new solutions and paths that weren't there before. I pray for the strength and wisdom to be up to this challenge. I'll need to rely on people like you, Jonathan, to help me in my efforts to serve the American people," she said, laying it on thick.

Deutsche wasn't amused.

"Okay, Rachel, okay, I guess we can get beyond the small talk. You're moving somewhat fast, considering the president isn't even in the ground. Let's remember that it's the Democrats, not the Greens, that won the presidency."

"You're here because of a glitch in the Constitution," he went on. "We can't allow that glitch to subvert the democratic process. As a Green, you're familiar with how coalition governments work since the Greens in Europe are in several of them. The party with the highest number of votes gets to name the head of government. If the leader of the senior party resigns, dies, leaves office, whatever, the major party gets to name the successor. It's called democracy, something you and your party like to proclaim that you have a monopoly on. Well, we're not seeing a commitment to democracy here."

Rachel chose her next words — and emotions — carefully.

"Senator, the Democrats didn't win the election, Harrington did. And to win, Harrington needed me to be vice-president so he could get the Green electoral votes. I would be the first to say we don't have a very democratic electoral system, but that's how our Constitution works. If you want to argue about fairness, you can't choose which part you want to comply with and which you ignore," said Rachel, doing her best impression of playing hardball with the boys.

"Harrington was the Democratic candidate," Deutsche replied. "People voted for him because he was on the Democratic line. The Democrats got the highest vote total for president."

"But not a majority, and you needed the Greens to win," responded Rachel. "You argue that I got to be VP because the Electoral College is a quirk. Well, there are a lot of quirks in our Constitution. Sure, when it was written two hundred years ago, it was a major step forward in the concept of democracy. It was written, however, by and for the wealthy, many of them slaveholders. You might remember," she added, "that women, for instance, were excluded from this democracy, as well as people who were tenants or couldn't read. The purpose of 'quirks' such as the Electoral College was to protect the interests of the wealthy against the general population."

"Our Constitution has changed as society has changed," Deutsche pointed out. "Women do get to vote. We did abolish slavery. We still have the most open society of any country. The Democrats won the election."

"Under our present system," said Rachel pointedly, "we elect individuals, not parties. The law of succession is clear. If you want to propose some constitutional changes, I have several I'd be happy to discuss for the next election cycle — starting with proportional representation, where you vote for parties rather than individuals."

"If what you're asking is when we should hold a funeral for President Harrington to clear up the issue of succession," she added, "I respect the right of Mrs. Harrington to make that decision. I have no intention of rushing her."

Deutsche's anger was rising. "Look, Harrington gave you the vice-presidential slot to avoid a constitutional crisis over an election he *and* the Democrats clearly won. He was gracious enough, too gracious in my opinion, to give the Green Party an opportunity to work with us to promote some issues that both parties agree upon. We do you a huge favor and now you want to grab the White House because Harrington has a heart attack. Are you going to sit there and argue that is democratic?" he asked.

"May I remind you, Jonathan, that I *am* the vice-president?" said Rachel. "The Constitution is quite clear on the right way to proceed here."

"Rachel, one only gets credit for doing the right thing when it's against your self-interest. Right now you're acting like the typical self-serving politician grabbing power. Be honest, you're not qualified to hold this position and the American people will pay for your shortcomings. You have no experience running a government, let alone one this huge and complex. You've got to do what is best for the American people," he added, crumbling his napkin into a tight ball.

Deutsche shifted to a conciliatory tone. "Rachel, in the interest of fair play, you should support the idea that the Democrats select the next president. We can certainly arrange it so you get renominated for vice-president. And we'd be willing to consider some changes to the Electoral College, possibly even that Instant Runoff Voting that you and the Greens are always clamoring for."

Rachel took a deep breath and counted to five. Not for the first time she wished that Frost had accepted the vice-presidential slot. She doubted that Deutsche would even be having this discussion with Frost. Or any other man for that matter.

"I must have missed some meeting, Senator, since I don't remember any European-style coalition government being created after the recent election. There haven't been any negotiations between Democrats and Greens about policy objectives," Rachel stated.

Most of Rachel's work in the first eight months of the administration had been of the ribbon-cutting nature. Harrington had occasionally consulted with her but usually ignored her advice.

"Nor do I recollect receiving a 'thank you' from you for your position," she added. "Without the Greens pulling progressive voters to the polls, the Senate would still be in the hands of the Republicans. And there's a damn good chance you'd have lost the vote in Florida and the presidency without our intervention. The president's responsibility is to serve the people of this country. I will do the best job I can," Rachel said bluntly.

"You and the Democrats control the Senate, the Republicans got the House, the Greens have the White House," she pointed out. "I'm ready whenever you are to sit down and hammer out a program for the next four years," Rachel said. "What would you say to a national unity approach to the Executive Branch?" she suggested, hoping to move on. "Each of the parties would name some prominent members to the Cabinet, work together to form a consensus agenda. This might help us break the gridlock that has paralyzed Congress in recent years."

"Rachel, what I hear you saying it that if we allow you to keep the Oval Office, in exchange you'll fire most of the Democrats in the Cabinet, and allow the Republicans and Greens to put their own people in, expecting the Democrats in the Senate to rubber stamp their confirmation," Deutsche snorted.

This was even worse than she'd expected. Maybe it was time to bring Sophie into the meeting.

"The Democrats say they agree with the Greens on issues like healthcare for everyone, clean air, living wage jobs, even curbs on corporate power. But you never actually do it, even when you have the votes," Rachel pointed out.

Deutsche replied, "Excuse me, but we did pass campaign finance reform —"

"You always have an excuse," Rachel interrupted, "as to why now isn't the right time for real change. Meanwhile, the Democrats are paid handsomely every step of the way by the same corporate interests you claim to be fighting. The American people have a once in a lifetime opportunity to enact real democracy. I'd be betraying the oath I swore to the American people if I refused that challenge," Rachel concluded.

"Let's put our cards on the table," Deutsche said.

"I thought we already had," Rachel snapped back.

Deutsche plowed ahead. "The Twenty-fifth Amendment to the Constitution deals with a dead president, not one in a coma. The document you signed transferring power had a two-week expiration. True, that's not in the Constitution," he admitted reluctantly, "but Section Four requires a majority of the principal officers of the executive department to sign off on the transfer of power, and you don't have that yet. And if there is a dispute, then Congress has twenty-one days to resolve the matter, and your party has a grand total of two votes there."

"Your read on the 25th Amendment is a bit of a stretch, Senator," Rachel responded. "Once power is passed to the vice-president, you need to have the incumbent sign a document reclaiming it. Sadly, that's not going to happen here."

"I know that you haven't forgotten that the Republicans have more members in Congress than you do," Rachel reminded Deutsche, "which is why Harrington had to deal with the Greens in the first place. If the Cabinet members hold up the paperwork, things could get messed up pretty quickly, and I don't think the voters will look kindly on the Democrats for putting partisan concerns ahead of the good of the country."

"Even if you broker a deal with the Republicans," she added, "you're probably going to lose in the Supreme Court. Yeah, I realize the Justices are political appointees who tend to do what they're told in cases like this, but do you really think the American people would sit still for such a blatant disregard for the Constitution?" asked Rachel.

"Rachel, even if you were to grab the presidency, you're not going to have much input into what passes Congress and you can damn better believe that both parties will be working to ensure you're a one-term fluke. If you survive a term," Deutsche noted.

Deutsche couldn't believe this woman, this Green, really believed she was qualified to run the largest economy in the world, the most powerful military. *She should be back teaching some political science class at a community college. God damn it Harrington, what did you get us into?*

With great effort, Deutsche calmed himself. "Be realistic. Strike a deal while you can. Let's agree on a few issues to work on, like universal healthcare. We'll give the Greens two additional Cabinet positions. We'll reappoint you vice-president and promise this time to consult you about decisions. We'll also let you make a substantial number of appointments to the federal agencies," Deutsche conceded.

"It's time for you to join us, Rachel," he went on. "I don't understand why someone as bright as you wants to waste your time with a bunch of tree huggers who have a hard time even agreeing on what tree to hug. Take the little power you've got right now and trade it in to win some things. You handle it right, you can write your own ticket once you're out of office. Mess it up, and you'll end up out in the cold," warned the senator.

"Jonathan, from where you're sitting, I'm sure your proposal makes all the sense in the world," Rachel replied. "But the need for a revolution is not a campaign slogan for me, it's a core belief. We can't allow global warming to go on, we can't keep throwing chemicals into the environment and into our bodies. We can't continue to allow a few people to be rich while billions lack food and water. We can't keep propping up third world dictators who kill their own people while multinational corporations rob them blind."

Rachel walked around to sit on the front of the desk. "I don't care whether it's the Democrats or Republicans that are in power, the corporations will still call the shots and everything on the planet will continue to be just some numbers that some bean counter will factor into his spreadsheet. The American people are going to have the opportunity to make some real changes," Rachel said firmly.

She reached out to touch Deutsche's shoulder before continuing. He visibly flinched.

"Jonathan, I hope you and the Democrats will work with me. You know that the system is messed up. The Democrats haven't been able to change it. The Greens are your best chance to get what you loudly proclaim you want," she argued.

Deutsche got up to leave. This had been a waste of time.

"Rachel, the American people are not going to believe that it's fair that a party with less than 10% of the vote gets to run the country," he told her. "You also underestimate the power of those nine Supreme Court Justices to resolve political disputes involving the Constitution."

Deutsche was not smiling when he departed. He kept his statement to the waiting press unusually short. He made a point of referring to Rachel as vice-president.

****

Visiting the following day was Frederick Wilson Baker III, Speaker of the House of Representatives from South Carolina.

Freddy Baker was an old-fashioned politician. He remembered your name, showed up at every firehouse dinner and funeral he could. Delivering pork for his district was ahead of ideology. He had a picture of Huey Long hanging on the wall behind his desk.

Baker excelled at the hand-to-hand combat needed to rise to the top of Congress. Though he was more intelligent than most of his opponents gave him credit for, he had what was known as street smarts. A born hustler, he knew what buttons to push to get the votes he needed. He had a memory like an elephant and kept track of where the bodies were hidden.

"Sophie, has the Speaker shown up yet?" Rachel asked, pushing the intercom button on her phone.

"He just entered the building. Should be here in about three minutes."

Sophie Kretsky had been a suburban soccer mom before that was a campaign focus group. She began to notice that a lot of women in her suburban Philadelphia neighborhood were coming down with a rare form of cancer. Dismissed by public health officials as a kook, she discovered that her subdivision had been built on top of an illegal toxic landfill. She fought for five years to get the state environmental bureau to take action.

Sophie's husband stayed around for three more years. He admired her for what she was doing but couldn't stand having his world turned upside down — he hadn't married an activist. She'd gone to meetings many nights running, requiring him to pick up childcare responsibilities that he wasn't used to. Moreover, he wasn't comfortable playing second fiddle to a woman frequently in the public eye. His buddies at work never stopped ribbing him about her.

Sophie had relocated to DC to start a national environmental group training local housewives and community activists to fight to clean up local toxic sites. Wynn had worked for her for a couple of years and had urged Rachel to hire her as chief of staff for the vice-president, though Rachel didn't need much prodding.

Sophie came into the Oval Office to get Rachel to sign some papers. She looked like she was ready to resume smoking cigarettes, looking for something to do with her hands. Rachel made a note to order some lollipops.

"You sure you're up to meeting alone with Baker? My skin crawls whenever I'm around him. Makes we want to take a shower. I can hang out in the room to give you protection," offered Sophie.

Rachel laughed. "I'll be fine with Freddy. I often find it easier to deal with people whom you know you disagree with, because there's less bull about you both being on the same side," Rachel said.

The secretary announced that the Speaker had arrived. Sophie left to show him in.

It was difficult to tell who was play-acting more.

Rachel was effusive in her greeting. "Mr. Speaker, so good of you to give me a few minutes."

The Speaker as always seemed a little out of breath. "Rachel. My condolences. Such a shame, such a young man. We'll all miss him," he said in his soft, pleasant accent.

He moved on quickly. " Have you decided when you're goin' to bury him?"

"Mrs. Harrington will make that decision, in her own good time. Please, Mr. Speaker, take a seat. Care for a drink? Some Wild Turkey on ice?" Rachel almost purred.

"I see someone has been doing their homework," Baker said as he deposited his ample body in the chair. "Nice place you have here. Haven't seen it in awhile. The few times I talked to Harrington, it was a quick phone call. He wasn't a man that enjoyed the 'social' aspects of politics, at least not with me."

"Well, I hope you'll feel free to drop by often while I'm here, Mr. Speaker," Rachel responded.

"Nice of you to say that, Rachel. And please, call me Freddy. By the way, I saw Jonathan on the newscasts after he came out of your office yesterday. He didn't look too happy," said Baker.

"I'm sure he was just upset about President Harrington. He's having a difficult time adjusting," Rachel responded, trying to avoid sounding too sarcastic.

"I'm sure he's Rachel," said Baker. "Yes, I'm sure he is. Probably havin' almost as much difficulty if I had ended up behind that desk rather than you. So, what do you have in mind for this little talk between new friends?" he asked.

Baker wasn't quite sure yet what to make of Rachel. He had learned not to underestimate his opponents, a mistake many had made with him. He assumed she was clueless about the nuts and bolts of governing, but she had a warm, winning personality that appealed to voters, especially women. She was self-assured, bright and, as far as he could tell, she wasn't interested in using the office to feather her own nest. A potentially dangerous combination. Always harder to horse-trade with someone who really believed their job was to save the world rather than appeasing the various special interests.

"I have to admit, Freddy, that I've never been much of a card player. Maybe I'll have to take it up now to keep up with you boys," said Rachel. "I'm asking for your help. Not just for me but for the good of the country," she said, delivering her best sales pitch. "I know that sounds corny, but this is a difficult moment for everyone. The nation is in shock over the loss of the president. Congress was already paralyzed with gridlock. Now we have a third party at the table. For me, or anyone else, to get anything done, there needs to be an accommodation with you and the other House Republicans. So I'm interested to hear what you'd like to see happen."

Baker reached into his pocket to pull out a cigar, noticed the lack of ash trays and the frown on Rachel's forehead, and decided against it.

"Get government off everyone's back, Rachel. You do-gooders," he chuckled. "Your idea of savin' the masses is to pass yet one more law to regulate yet one more perceived problem. But the only thin' that changes is the number of laws the little guy has to obey and the amount of taxes you turn over to the government."

Rachel refused to take the bait.

Baker took another sip before continuing. "For starters, we need to pump money into the economy. Some tax cuts for businesses, maybe repeal the alternate minimum tax, a more business-friendly attitude from the administration. It's businesses that put Americans to work, put food on the table. With the increased competition from China, third world countries that pay their workers peanuts, we've gotta take the handcuffs off American companies. Of course, some government contracts for some of our depressed areas, like my district, would also be helpful," Baker offered.

Rachel took her time responding.

"Well, Mr. Speaker," Rachel said with a smile, "you certainly know I won't just turn over this country to the robber barons — they've been in control long enough. But I am open to discussing the Republicans' involvement in some form of a national coalition government. Give your party, uh, a couple of Cabinet positions. Maybe Secretary of Treasury, or the Commerce Department, make Wall Street feel a little more comfortable. I'd give you the opportunity to nominate people for my administration, some independent types, people of integrity and dedication to public service. People who are willing to look for new solutions," Rachel said.

Baker wasn't sold. "Rachel, you're gonna have to do better than that, a whole lot better. Heck, we're talking about the presidency here. Eventually, you're gonna have to jump into bed with either us or the Democrats. If you strike a deal with the Democrats, they're gonna insist that they be top dog, at best throw you a few bones. We woulda given you a better deal than what you got from Harrington if you'da thrown your electoral votes to us. Don't blow it a second time."

"With us," Baker continued, "you come out much stronger — you get to keep the presidency. If you and I come to an agreement on a package of legislative proposals, some for us, some for you, I'll get 'em through the House and we'll just need to pick up a few of the more independent types in the Senate. Sweeten the pot a bit," Baker offered.

There of course was a price. "But you gotta make it worthwhile for us — at least the vice-presidency, and half a dozen Cabinet positions, including a few big ones. We'd need you to support some key pieces of our program, pieces that the Greens ain't gonna be happy about. It ain't like my members gonna be jumping for joy just at the opportunity to tweak the Democrats. A lot of them think you and the Greens are worse — Marxists in drag: green on the outside, red on the inside."

Rachel wasn't ready to buy.

"Mr. Speaker — Freddy — I'm prepared to make some concessions but not as much as you're asking. I may need you but you need me as well," Rachel pointed out. "The president has the power of veto, and you guys don't have a good track record of getting two-thirds of your members in both houses to agree on much. The Democrats seem primarily concerned about beating your brains in at the next election. I'm more concerned about getting a few things done to make life a little better for the average person."

The Speaker finished his drink. "For a novice, you ain't a bad poker player," he said, trying to butter her up. "But I still don't think you got an ace in the hole. But how's this? In the near term, we're probably willin' to help prop you up, long as we get some concessions. Watchin' Jonathan get steamed up is one of my pleasures in life. But Rachel, you and I both know that the price of our cooperation goes up the longer it takes to strike a deal."

Baker stood up to leave. "This is not intended as a threat, but I'm sure you realize that if the Democrats and Republicans unite on removing you, it will happen so fast that your head will spin. You can't play us off against each other forever; you're gonna have to make some hard choices if you want to survive."

Baker offered a final piece of free advice. "No matter how morbid this sounds, until Harrington's in the ground, you could face a constitutional challenge from the Democrats. It's in your interest to arrange Harrington's funeral as soon as possible. It's also in your interest to take as much time as you can before nominating a vice-president. With me next in line in succession, the Democrats will be in no hurry to get rid of you."

Rachel walked him to the door.

"Politics is a game to me, Rachel, but it's a game I care a lot about. We all believe in our hearts that we're doin' the best to help people. Just have different ways of gettin' there. I have learned not to make political fights personal. Life's too short and there are too many unexpected curves and corners. I expect, Rachel, that you'll face a difficult road. You're gonna have to learn how to keep your head down a bit, for your own sake. The country can't afford to lose a second president so soon," Baker said in departing.

****

Anna called soon after she arrived at the hostage site in Nigeria.

"Anna, it's so great to hear from you," Rachel said. She spent a few minutes catching up.

"Are you getting cooperation from the American officials there?" Rachel asked.

"They have this sour look on their face whenever they see me, but they respond ok long as I yell at 'em every so often," Anna said. "Kinda fun to watch 'em jump. But they ain't helpin' much in resolving this mess."

"What's the situation there?" asked Rachel.

"It's freaking tense, just waiting to blow," Anna replied. "Two dozen Ogoni are inside the Chevron compound. They're pretty scared. Got six oil workers with them, all foreigners, including the two Americans. Kicked all the local workers out, didn't wanna have to worry about keeping tabs on them since no one would give a damn about them anyway. It's a zoo. Hundreds of local residents are taking shifts blocking the entrance — workers, grandmothers, children, couple of priests. Everyone's scared the people inside are gonna get massacred."

"Have you been able to talk to the hostages? Are they okay?" asked Rachel.

"They're fine, just nervous as all hell. Haven't slept much in the last two days. Ayesha vouched for me with the locals, so they let me inside. Both the hostages and protesters are afraid that Chevron will send in some Rambo wannabes to attempt a rescue and get everyone killed. "

"How did this happen?" Rachel asked.

"The villagers discovered the hacked-up body of one of the local leaders who'd gone to complain about the fire that burnt down a buncha homes," Anna replied. "That was the last straw. They've been complaining for years about all the pollution, the crap thrown into their water, the loss of farmland. They just started marching on the plant to demand that something finally be done, that a real investigation take place."

"They'd also heard a Green was now president of the US," Anna confided. "The Greens are weak in Nigeria, but they've been supportive of the Ogoni, so the locals assumed you'd take their side. I told them you'll back them to the hilt."

"I hope you haven't been promising them I'll send in the Marines," Rachel asked nervously.

"Or course not," Anna, replied indignantly. "Okay, well, maybe a little bit. But I told `em I'd have to talk to you first."

"Anna," Rachel yelled.

"Don't have a cow," Anna interrupted. "Just pulling your leg a little bit. But let me finish telling you what went down."

"At the beginning, they just planned to sit in front of the gate until someone showed up to negotiate," Anna continued. "But when a representative from Chevron regional headquarters showed up, all hell broke loose. The company's thugs began shoving people, there was a lot of confusion and yelling, the crowd surged forward, broke open the gates, and took the guards' guns after beating them up. They barricaded the gates and only let out the local workers.

"An hour later the company's security forces began to pull up from other facilities in the area, along with every other local police, military and thug paid for by the oil company. That really turned the foreign workers into hostages, because the locals feared getting shot or worse at any moment."

"I'll call the head of Chevron," Rachel said, "reinforce with him the need to resolve this without any more killing. I'll push him to agree to negotiations, tell him that I need to see a plan about how they're going to improve things for the locals. I'll make sure a similar message is passed on to the Nigerian government. But don't be making any promises on my behalf," she warned, "especially about the use of troops."

"I promise," said Anna, "but some American troops would calm things down real fast. You wouldn't need a lot. How 'bout a flyover of some American jets, wave the flag a bit?"

Rachel told Anna to call back with regular updates. She then had Sophie get the Secretary of State on the phone to give her an update from his end.

Darling had not been happy to receive Rachel's message about Anna. "Madame President, this is a job for professionals," he told her. "Otherwise, we end up getting people killed. And our first priority is to make sure that the American hostages are released safely."

"Apply whatever pressure you feel is needed on all sides to make sure this thing gets settled peacefully," Rachel told him. "And make sure you keep Anna in the loop."

Both Baker and Deutsche backed up Darling about the hostages.

"Bottom line, you can't lose any American lives," Deutsche told Rachel. "If you do, you've got to immediately make them pay a high price for doing so; everything else is secondary. And don't use it as an excuse to bash American corporations or expect a huge payment of American tax dollars to buy our way out of the situation," said Deutsche.

"I'll get our people out," Rachel told him, "but we also don't want American businesses or the Nigerian government killing any more local residents. Nor do we want to keep wasting our tax dollars pulling American companies' butts out of the fire after they mess up by running roughshod over local people. When this is over with, I'd like to see some ideas from Congress about how we avoid such messes in the future."

****

Rachel had been putting off meeting with Mrs. Harrington.

She'd spent some time with the First Lady in the first few days after her husband had been found on the floor of their White House quarters, stricken by a coronary. Had it been anyone other than the president, he probably would've been buried by now.

The Secret Service had convinced Rachel last weekend to move into a bedroom in the White House to make their job easier. Mrs. Harrington still occupied the presidential quarters, though she'd been spending most of her time at her husband's side at the hospital, along with her two adult daughters and other family members. The pressure on her to pull the plug had been growing. The nation needed a sense of closure.

Patty Harrington had never shared her husband's passion for politics. Many suspected that part of his attraction to her had been her family's fortune, which had certainly come in handy during his initial campaigns for public office. She was also devoutly Catholic and was known to follow her church's teaching on many issues, including the definition of life. Pulling the plug was not her inclination.

Several of Mrs. Harrington's relatives and old friends were with her in her quarters when Rachel was escorted in. Rachel spent a few minutes offering her condolences before the rest departed to allow the two women to talk alone. Rachel took a seat on the couch next to Mrs. Harrington.

"Patty, you know that if you or your family need anything, you just have to ask. And if you need someone to run interference for you — with the hospital or the media or the Secret Service — just let me know," Rachel said, trying to draw strength for the next few minutes.

Patty mumbled a few words of appreciation. She was still in shock.

This was awkward. Maybe it was still too soon for this conversation.

"Patty, I am so sorry for you and Phil," Rachel said, trying to figure her way through this. "I would like to talk to you as one wife to another. I know you're feeling a lot of pressure to make a decision about Phil. And I won't hide the fact that the sooner you do, the sooner it would make my life a lot easier. But the important thing is doing what you feel is right for you and your family. Please, don't feel rushed."

Mrs. Harrington leaned forward and gave her a hug, She began to sob. Then the words came pouring out.

"Rachel, I appreciate your understanding. Everyone sees him as the president. I see him as a husband. The last ten years or so, it just felt that everyone else owned him. I didn't enjoy the traveling like he did, flying into a city for a few hours to meet with campaign contributors, political supporters, making promises," Mrs. Harrington rambled on.

"Don't get me wrong," the First Lady added, "I was very proud of him, and wanted to help him to do what was best for the country. But I decided to spend as much time at home as possible, raising our kids, taking care of the family business. I was looking forward to his retirement after the presidency, so that we could spend time together. And now he's laying in that hospital bed, with all those wires and tubes and doctors and nurses running around, with the Secret Service everywhere and the media and the satellite trucks camped outside. And everyone is waiting for me to write the final line," Mrs. Harrington sobbed.

She tried to compose herself. She used her handkerchief to wipe her eyes, blow her nose. Rachel waited.

"When I sit there holding his hand," Mrs. Harrington continued, "I feel his presence. He seems at peace for once. In some ways I feel like I've been closer to him in the last two weeks than I've been in years. I don't want to say good-bye, but I don't want him to be a spectacle either. I won't lie to you. The Democrats are pressuring me to keep him hooked up, because it gives them some time to figure things out. I don't have anything against you personally, but they keep on saying that the presidency is something Phil worked for all his life, that and the Democratic Party, and that I have to think about what he would want in this situation."

Rachel felt guilty about adding pressure on the First Lady.

"Patty, the politics will work themselves out. They always do. Maybe you should think about moving him to a place where you can get some privacy. Maybe take him home. Or bring him here to the White House," Rachel told her.

Rachel gave Patty a long hug before she departed.

As Rachel left, a young Hispanic woman in a housekeeping uniform came up to her. "Madame President, I just wanna say how much I admire ya. I be very proud to work for ya. The country will have good hands. We need a strong señorita, a mother, make things better."

The young woman reached out and clasped her hands. Rachel smiled, though it was strained. "Why thank you, I appreciate that. I'll try to do my best. What's your name?"

"Jennifer Garcia, ma'am."

"Well, Jennifer, have a good day."

Jennifer had discreetly passed her a small piece of folded paper. Rachel read it when she got back to the Oval Office: "When President had attack, he was in bedroom, not hallway. Someone with him."

****

When Rachel got back to the Oval Office from her meeting with Mrs. Harrington, Sophie was on the phone with Anna. Rachel put her on speakerphone.

"Anna, how are the talks going?"

"The Chevron representatives are calling the shots," Anna told her. "They claim the kidnappers are just hooligans shakin' `em down for money. Chevron is arguing they're already paying enough to the local tribes. All the usual crap about how they hire local residents as truck drivers and security. The Chevron people want a military solution to this — throw in some stun grenades and tear gas — just overwhelm the locals."

"What are the Ogoni saying?" Sophie asked.

"Let me put Ayesha on. She can speak for them a lot better than I," suggested Anna.

"Thank you, Madame President, for helping us," Ayesha said.

"Our people demand that Chevron leave," Ayesha continued. "We feel local people should control the oil supplies. We know this won't happen — Chevron and the central government are too close. But we want Chevron to stop poisoning the drinking water, harming the fishing and farms. We want to stop the beatings, no more killings. We want much more of the oil revenues to go for local development. For schools and healthcare."

Anna added, "The Ogoni also want two representatives of the Chicoco movement on the Nigerian Human Rights Commission. They want the commission to investigate what's being going on at the refinery."

Ayesha said some of the women were considering disrobing in protest. "To see a naked woman is the most shameful thing for my people. They'll do anything to avoid it. Chevron won't care, but it will shame their tribal liaison. Even the national government representatives will not like it," she told them.

"So what," asked Rachel, "are the nuts and bolts of Chevron's latest negotiating positions? I assume they're also arguing that they need to deal with the duly elected national government and that the Ogoni's dispute is an internal Nigerian matter that they can't interfere with?"

"I see you've read this script before," Anna replied. "Well, Chevron argues that shakedowns are a daily occurrence out here and a line needs to be drawn at hostage-taking. They accuse the Ogoni of sabotage. They admit to some problems in the past but claim they've been corrected, that they're doing the best job possible. Yadda yadda yadda. They even claim," Anna added, "that they're willing to relocate the locals out of the area to reduce their exposure to oil-related health problems," Anna added. "That's going over like a lead balloon."

"The Nigerians saying anything worthwhile?" asked Sophie.

"The Nigerians take their cue from Chevron," Anna replied.

"Any information on why there's been such an increase in truck traffic?" asked Rachel.

"Chevron says its just because the roads are more passable at this time of year," Ayesha responded. "So they've stepped up production. But we've seen a lot more of President Obasanjo's men visiting. We assume to collect their money. It could just be the usual corruption, buying off the generals. Or it may be to buy votes in the upcoming elections that Americans have demanded. No offense meant, President Moreno," she quickly added.

"No offense taken, Ayesha. About what I expected," sighed Rachel. "I'll ask the Department of State to push for an accounting from Chevron. I don't know if the IRS has any jurisdiction, but it wouldn't hurt to rattle their cage. Maybe call the Chevron CEO in for a meeting. Shareholders don't usually like to hear that they're paying for bribes and graft, even though they probably assume it's part of the cost of doing business."

"Anna, Ayesha, the longer this hostage situation goes on," Rachel continued, "the more likely that military force will be used. Would the Ogoni be willing to release the hostages if the Human Rights Commission came to the facility and agreed to begin a formal investigation?" Rachel asked.

"If there was also a guarantee of safety, I think they'd be relieved to let the hostages go," replied Anna.

"My people worry," Ayesha added, "that once hostages are free and everyone leaves, they'll be pulled out of their homes and killed."

"I'll see what we can do but there are limits to my power," Rachel said. "I can't wave a magic wand and cure Nigeria's problems overnight. The oil companies have a lot of support in Congress. I'll talk to President Obasanjo directly to let him know I expect him to personally guarantee the protesters' safety if they release the hostages unharmed."

Rachel called Secretary of State Darling to mobilize his people to press the Nigerian government and Chevron Oil for a resolution.

He continued to complain about amateur diplomacy and interfering with his department.

"If you don't like what I am doing, you are free to replace me," he said in a huff.

"I realize that, Mr. Secretary. Like all of Harrington's appointees, please make sure to send over your letter of resignation in case I need it.

In the meantime, make sure that Chevron and Nigeria are clear about what we want. And by the way, there's a limited number of times you'll be able to play that threat, so you just wasted one." She disconnected the call without a good-bye.

To his credit, Darling helped resolve the situation. Chevron agreed to pay for two new health clinics, as long as the payment went directly to the government and not the Ogoni. Chevron denied that they were diverting funds to anyone.

When Rachel got President Obasanjo on the line, he gave her a long lecture about the need not to interfere with the internal politics of Nigeria. Rachel patiently listened, and then covered the four objectives she'd prepared. She suggested that it might be in the interests of both countries if America withdrew all economic support from Nigeria until such internal crises were resolved so the US wouldn't be seen as interfering. She then commiserated with the challenges involved in trying to move to a true democracy, offered to meet with Obasanjo personally some time in the near future, and got him to sign off on the deal she'd discussed with Anna.

The hostages were released two days later to a representative of the Human Rights Commission. The commission agreed to accept two Ogoni representatives as "observers," allowing them to sit on the panel and ask questions of witnesses.

In announcing the successful release of the hostages, Rachel stated: "I would like to thank the Nigerian government for working with our negotiators to secure the release of the American workers. It is important that American companies doing business in foreign countries act as good ambassadors. We trust that Chevron and other oil companies in Nigeria will continue to take steps to ensure that their stay there helps improve the quality of life for local residents. My administration will develop a code of conduct for American companies operating in foreign countries," she added, "that I trust our business leaders will readily embrace as our economic ambassadors."

****

Over a dinner of smoked salmon and asparagus, Rachel asked Wynn to take the lead in organizing a People's Summit in conjunction with the upcoming World Trade Organization meeting. Scheduled to take place in a few months in Alberta, Canada, it would bring together corporate and political leaders from throughout the world to negotiate the terms of Free Trade. The meeting essentially pitted North and South against each other on questions such as development, labor rights and environmental protection.

The last gathering in Genoa, Italy, had seen the heavy use of police force. Several protesters were killed. Ever since the very large antiglobalization protest in Seattle in 1999, which Wynn and Rachel had helped organize, the police had sought to deter protesters with escalating security measures. In answer, the protesters had grown more spirited and determined.

"Wynn, I think I found a job for you. It'll help keep you occupied. I know you wanna be a productive and groundbreaking First Husband," Rachel said, giving his knee a squeeze.

"Rachel," Wynn replied, wary of her tone, "you know I already have a job. One I like."

When they moved to DC, Wynn had gone back to working for Greenpeace International, helping out with media.

"I think you need to resign," Rachel suggested. "Too much chance for someone to yell conflict of interest. It's not like we need the money with my new salary. Besides, here's an opportunity to expand your horizons. Being First Husband could be a lot of fun.".

"Yeah, except a lot of people think First Husbands should be seen and not heard. I'd like to have the option to publicly protest whenever I think the government is messing up. No offense Rachel," said Wynn, getting up for another beer.

"Very funny, Wynn. Feel free to send me a personal e-mail whenever you disagree with one of my decisions," Rachel replied.

"Don't worry, I will," Wynn said. "Long, detailed ones."

Rachel wanted the People's Summit to develop a counteragenda to what the corporations and WTO were proposing. "This job is right up your alley. You'd pull together proposals, reach out to get opposition groups involved, figure out how we're going to pay for it all. You'd negotiate with foreign governments and the groups planning to protest to get them all to sit down together," Rachel explained. "Leave the corporations home."

"The WTO summit is less than two months away, Rachel. This type of gathering takes a good year to put together," Wynn argued, pouring Rachel another glass of wine. Two was usually more than enough to get her in the mood.

"Aren't you the one who tells me when you need the impossible done, hire a good organizer?" Rachel teased. "It's time to see if you can live up to your reputation, Wynn. Give them a year to plan, they'll take a year to argue. Get a core group of people together, come up with a proposal in the next week, send it around for some quick feedback, then have me endorse it. We can always add a few things along the way if a good idea pops up. People have to be ready to seize opportunities, and they're not always going to have the leader of the free world in their back pocket."

"How do we convince them that it's not just a diversionary tactic to keep them from shutting down the WTO or upsetting the negotiations?" Wynn asked, getting more interested.

"The protests at these meetings are more about media than anything else," Rachel argued, "trying to have an impact on world opinion. If they want to protest, they can go ahead. It's not like the corporate or government leaders are responding to the protesters' agenda." Rachel felt somewhat guilty for saying it aloud.

"How they hell are you going to convince other governments, especially the G8, to meet with the enemy?" asked Wynn.

"Oh ye of little faith. I think I can convince some countries," she continued, "particularly the European Union, to at least have some level of participation. Certainly observers, if not full delegations. We are the US, remember."

"This gives us an opportunity to put the WTO on the defensive," Rachel contended. "So what if the summit itself will be window dressing? We can use it to push our message and develop some proposals for change." Sensing continued resistance, she added, "Besides, the more important thing as always is how we follow up on it. That'll be your job as well. This is just a beginning, not an end point," she pleaded.

"Why do I feel," said Wynn, "like I'm suddenly out on a very precarious limb?"

TWO

WYNN: COMING INTO ARIZONA

August 1978

A bad twenty-four hours was getting worse.

The hot Arizona wind rising over the desert hills was a sand blaster. The views were spectacular, but Wynn Harris was in no position to appreciate them as he whipped around mountain curves on the back of a Harley motorcycle at 85 miles an hour, his knees almost touching the pavement, arms clutching a guy whose only words to him had been, "Hop on."

He trusted that the dude who'd picked him up after his car broke down knew what he was doing. Wynn's depression over the demise of his long-time companion, Amanda, and its financial implications, outweighed any immediate concerns for his personal health.

Wynn had volunteered to move to Phoenix to open up Arizona for the community organizing group he worked for — part of their 20/80 plan to organize 20 states by 1980 so they could launch a People's Party in the 1980 presidential election. If a candidate raised $5,000 in each of twenty states, then the federal government would match contributions through the primary.

Arizona had seemed a good choice during the middle of the Iowa winter — for three months in a row the temperature never got above 32 degrees. Wynn's main recollection of that winter in Des Moines, besides doorknocking for hours every night in the bitter cold, was using Amanda's emergency brake to try to stop the car when the foot brake failed to hold on the snow.

"They say you're a local when you view 19-degree weather as a spring thaw, an occasion to walk around with your jacket open," Wynn had written home to his parents. All he knew about Arizona was seeing the Sun Devils football team on TV play in 80-degree sunshine in December. "It seems like a good place to spend the winter," he told them.

Warning bells suddenly went off when he passed the "Welcome to Arizona" sign. *Hey,* he thought. *Isn't Barry Goldwater, the darling of the John Birch society, still the US Senator from here? Maybe I should've done a little research.*

Goldwater had been the conservative Republican presidential candidate in 1964 against Lyndon Baines Johnson. His rallying cry: "Extremism in the defense of liberty is no vice, and moderation in the pursuit of justice is no virtue." The Democrats responded with a TV ad of a little girl counting daisy petals, changing over to a nuclear blast countdown, to highlight that Goldwater couldn't be trusted with his finger on the nuclear button. Out of the ashes of his failed crusade emerged the conservative movement two decades later that captured the Republican Party and catapulted Reagan into the White House.

Wynn thought about Goldwater when the Interstate suddenly disappeared, becoming a narrow two-lane that slowly wound its way through small towns one block wide. They were little more than a collection of motels, bars and convenient stores desperately clinging to both sides of the road. Everywhere else in the country these towns had died off when the interstate had passed them by. *This Goldwater must have a lot of power,* Wynn mused. *This might be a tough state to organize in.*

He kicked himself for not taking the three hundred dollars offered by Jim Spencer, his favorite backyard mechanic. "The body ain't worth nuthin, but I could use the engine for parts." Jim, his flaming red hair tied into a ponytail that reached half way down his back, had looked skeptical when Wynn told him he was going to drive the VW bug to Arizona. Wynn declined his offer, rationalizing that "I'll just have to spend most of the money getting to Phoenix anyway, and when I get there, I'll have to buy another three-hundred-dollar car."

"Suit yourself," Jim said, patting Amanda's rump good-bye. "Don't push her too hard on the way out."

Wynn dropped down through the Texas panhandle to avoid straining Amanda over the Rocky Mountains. It didn't work. "Clutch stopped working — it won't let me get outta gear," he told the cop when he slowly rolled through a stop sign in a sleepy town outside Amarillo at one in the morning. "I got everything I own in the back seat and front trunk, and I barely got money for gas to get there, let alone for repairs. I've didn't stop because I'm not sure I can get it moving again." He sounded so pitiful the cop waved him on without a ticket.

At four am, Wynn finally had to pull over for some sleep on a butte overlooking Albuquerque. When he woke up shortly after dawn and tried to start the bug, the gas pedal was so rusted it broke off. By chance, an old trailer parked across the way had a sign on it: welding $15 hour. "That'll be fifteen dollars," the welder had said, holding his hand out after spending five minutes reattaching the pedal.

When Wynn couldn't get the car in gear, he asked the welder if he could take a look. "Sure. That'll be another fifteen."

But I get an hour of your time for fifteen bucks."

"Nope, you get me to do a job for you for fifteen an hour, and this is a different job." After a few minutes of crawling under the car he told Wynn, "Yup, looks like your clutch is broke. Nope, I can't fix it."

Wynn had to use the rest of his cash, along with a personal check that he insisted wouldn't bounce but did, to have Amanda towed and a new clutch installed. He slept next to his car at a rest stop that night and was hoping to make it into Phoenix the next night.

His engine had seized coming down the mountain passes from Flagstaff. It was 110 degrees in late August, the asphalt was melting and there wasn't a town or building in sight. He expected the vultures would be circling overhead shortly. Instead they were waiting for him up ahead.

The motorcyclist left him at the first crossroad, about fifteen miles down the interstate, in what appeared to be the middle of nowhere. A run-down dusty garage, with a shiny new tow truck, a few chickens, a mean-looking dog and lots of old junkers dominated the immediate landscape. Water looked expensive at that place.

He was never sure what the dispute was, or how serious they were about inflicting bodily harm, but their negotiations over the retrieval and repair of Amanda did not go well. Perhaps they thought VW owners were subversive. They wanted either 250 dollars to tow it — 180 more than he had — or they'd keep the title and give him a week to come back and reclaim his stuff. They mumbled something that sounded like the N word and he might have muttered under his breath some observation about rednecks. Fortunately, the Doberman halted at the property line.

As fate would have it, a pickup truck was just chugging around the curve as he ran out of the garage. It was headed up the hill with a bunch of young people with tie-dye shirts and beers in their hands lolling in the back. They good-naturedly waved him along as he ran after the truck. It had a No Nukes / Stop Palo Verde bumpersticker next to a few Grateful Dead ones. Two guys helped haul him up. "Hop aboard," they called out. "Plenty of room. Looks like you're in a hurry."

His lifelong possessions were in the opposite direction, as was Phoenix.

"Hi. I'm Bret," said a hippie with long, blond, stringy hair and a few days' growth of beard. "This is Sue and that's Bill and Denise. Grab yourself a beer out of the ice chest." Backpacks and sleeping bags were scattered about the back of the truck. Wynn found a space to squeeze into.

"Thanks. My name's Wynn. Wynn Harris. I sure appreciate the ride. Where you headed?"

"We're going to a festival up the road at Arcosanti, a solar city this Italian architect is building out in the desert. It's supposed to be all futuristic, lots of glass," said Brett.

"Arcosanti is a model for how we should live in the future, using the sun, working *with* the planet rather than against it," Sue explained. "This weekend they're having some music, food, crafts, environmental groups, a little of everything. Raise some dough to help them keep building," she added, giving Wynn a big smile. Sue was in her early twenties, with long brown hair parted in the middle, held down with an Indian headband

Denise picked up a brochure from a stack in the cab and handed it to Wynn. He read: "Arcosanti was inspired by Buckminster Fuller and other technological utopians. Developed by Italian architect Paolo Soleri, Arcosanti is based on arcology, a combination of architecture and ecology, where the built and the living interact as organs would in a highly evolved being. It's designed to have many systems work together, with efficient circulation of people and resources, multiuse buildings and solar orientation for lighting, heating and cooling. Greenhouses provide gardening space for public and private use, and act as solar collectors for winter heat. It'll eventually house about 7,000 residents, a self-contained, sustainable community."

"Who's the dude driving?" Wynn asked, accepting the offer of a second beer. Boy, was Arizona hot. If it was like this up in the mountains, what must it be like down in the valley in Phoenix?

"Some guy name Pete," Brett replied. "He's helping out driving performers back and forth between the airport in Flagstaff and Arcosanti. He picked up us hitchhiking."

The truck lurched as a jackrabbit darted away from the road.

"Well, I'm moving down to Phoenix for a job but blew an engine on my car about fifteen miles back. Know anyone who's going to be at the festival that I could bum a ride with that way?"

"We live in Flagstaff, so we're headed in the opposite direction," said Sue. "Dunno where Mike is headed, didn't have much of a conversation before we piled into the back. But there should be plenty of people headed down to Phoenix."

There was a long line of cars and trucks as they pulled up to Arcosanti. Pete waved to one of the volunteers directing traffic and pulled onto a side road that led to a back entrance. Everyone clambered out.

"Enda da line, folks. There's a suggested donation of ten bucks for the festival to raise some bread to help build the place. You're already in, so it's cool if you can't afford it, but every bit helps the cause. I could use a hand or three lugging equipment over to the stage," said Pete. Pete was in his early twenties, with a New Jersey drawl, skinny but all wiry muscle, his dirty blond hair tangled like a crow's nest.

An attractive woman in her thirties with massive auburn tresses climbed out of the front seat holding a guitar case. Wynn was startled when he noticed the name on the case: Ronnie Faith, the well-known blues and rock singer. She thanked Pete for the ride. The others in the back dug into their pockets, pulling out some change and crumpled bills, which they handed to Pete.

Wynn introduced himself. "Hey Pete, my name's Wynn. Appreciate the ride. I'd be happy to help unload the stuff. You work at this place?"

"Just volunteer when I can," Pete said. "I live down in Tempe, just outside Phoenix. I get up here about once a month or so. I really dig what they're tryin' to do, showing how you can live in a city but have a minimal impact on Mother Earth. They're doin' some cool stuff with solar panels and windmills, energy conservation, things like that. I noticed ya were moving pretty fast coming out of the garage. Any problem?"

"Not too much," Wynn said, helping Pete unload the truck. "Just the usual redneck racist stuff combined with wanting an arm and a leg to deal with my car. Hey, any chance I could grab a ride with you? I'm moving to Phoenix for a job, but coming down from Flagstaff my car decided to ride off into the sunset."

"Was that your bug I saw alongside the road?" Pete asked, wiping his brow with a bandanna. Wynn nodded. "Bummer. Sure, you can catch a ride. Probably headed back midafternoon tomorrow. I'm sure you can score a ride earlier than that if you're in a rush. I got an extra sleeping bag you can borrow tonight. Got a place to crash in Phoenix?"

"Not really," Wynn said. "I'm going to be organizing for a new community group. I have a couple of possibilities, but nothing firm yet about a place. Us organizers tend to live by the seat of our pants. Figured I'd stay at a shelter at a church or grab someone's couch for a few nights till I find an apartment or something."

"Well, we always got people crashing at my place. Rent it along with a friend from Jersey. We call it the Hostel for Wayward Youths. Gotta couple couches, and a big front yard for tents. If you wanna watch the stars, gotta nice flat roof you can lay out on. Doesn't rain much around here. The roof is often drier than the yard, since they have this crazy old canal system where they irrigate neighborhoods. Can't ever figure when the water is goin' to be pushed through," Pete told him. "You're certainly welcome to stay for a few days, and if you can throw a few dollars in for rent, well you're welcome to stay until you can find your own place."

"That's mighty generous, Pete," Wynn said thankfully.

"Well man, whatever you wanna do is cool. Hey, Ronnie looks like she needs to check in. Mind grabbing that amp?" Pete asked.

Wynn caught up with Pete and Ronnie as they made their way backstage, and introduced himself.

"Ms. Faith, I'm a huge fan of yours," said Wynn. "I know you won't remember but we met briefly when I did voter registration at a concert you did at the Palace in Albany a couple of years ago. We got to say hello backstage after the show."

"Sure I remember. You're the one who I'm sure registered the most people that day. Only I can't remember your name," she said with a smile.

"It's Wynn."

"Well, Wynn, I knew that," she said with a wink to Pete. "It's your last name I forgot."

"Harris," Wynn stammered, finding it difficult to carry on a conversation for some reason. "Ms. Faith, how'd you end up playin' at this event? Seems a little off the beaten path."

"A musician friend of mine, John Small, asked me. He helped start this organization called Musicians United for Safe Energy, or MUSE. You might have heard this great song he wrote called 'Power' about the need to develop solar energy? I like to do as many benefits as possible. It's the way I give back some of the good things that happen to me."

"That's great of you to do that, Ms. Faith," Wynn said.

"Call me Ronnie," she said. "Wynn, that's an unusual name. Did your momma name you after anyone in particular?"

"Depends who you talk to. My dad says it was after a friend he met during the war. My mom said it was really for the wind, you know, the air. Said she got the idea from a book by Pearl Buck called *The Reed*. It's about a Korean guy who took all the blows that society and god and the king rain down on people like him. Like a reed, he bent but didn't break when the wind blew, sprung right back up when it stopped. Like the way black folks somehow manage to survive here in Amerikka. I guess she thought that *Wynn*, for *wind*, was stronger than *reed*," Wynn added.

"Well Wynn, I hope you live up to your momma's expectations," smiled Ronnie.

The festival was an eclectic mixture of hippies and carpenters, college professors and students, Mexican and Native American workers. Booths hawked crafts of every type — pottery, jewelry, clothing, colored sand in glasses, musical instruments. There were literature tables from every progressive cause imaginable. And composting toilets, solar panels, wind generators, alternative healing spaces.

Wynn kept seeing people walking around carrying funky handmade signs saying, "Need a Ride to Rainbow." Wynn asked a young women what Rainbow was.

"The Rainbow Gathering's next week over in Apache National Forest, 'bout three hours from here in the White Mountains. People from all over the place come together as the Rainbow Nation to recharge ourselves, celebrate life. You get naked, commune with nature, do drugs if you want, attend workshops, help out in the communal kitchens. It takes place every year in a different national forest far away from anyone — real wilderness. There's lots of dancing in circles, spiritual stuff, like praying for peace. You should check it out," she said, smiling.

"My name's Heather. Heather Butterfly." She picked up the hem of her long skirt to reveal a butterfly tattoo on her ankle, set off by a dancing ankle bracelet.

"Some people see Rainbow as a revival of the Ghost Dance of the Plain Indians from the end of last century." She then began a well-practiced recitation: "When the earth is ravaged and the animals are dying, a new tribe of people shall come unto the Earth from many colors, classes and creeds, and who by their actions and deeds shall make the Earth green again. They will be known as the warriors of the Rainbow," she intoned. "That's us."

****

Pete detoured back up the interstate for one last visit to Amanda, sitting forlornly along the side of the road, helping to pile Wynn's stuff in the back of his truck. Pete even offered to find a chain to tow the car down into Phoenix, but Wynn said "Forget it. I'm sure it'll cost more money to put in a new engine than it's worth. Let the garage grab it for spare parts. It'll make their day." He tore the license plates off, gave a eulogy for Amanda, and hung a message from the rear view mirror: "Warning, explodes for rednecks."

Pete slid a bootleg tape of the Grateful Dead from a New Year's Eve concert at the Fillmore into the tape deck, which was precariously hanging below the dashboard, wires sticking out. It sounded a little slow from repeated play.

"So, you seem to be a bit of a Dead Head," Wynn observed.

"Some people would say that, though not true Dead Heads. Growing up in Jersey, I caught maybe a couple dozen shows, mainly up at the Garden. Did a couple of road trips to see them. Got maybe 50 tapes. They're the only band that allows you to tape their concerts. I enjoy the scene. It's like an extended family reunion with a mellow buzz. Speaking of a buzz, can ya pass me that rolled up cigarette in the glove compartment," Pete asked.

"So how come everybody I meet from Jersey is into the Dead?" Wynn replied as Pete lit up.

"Must be all the toxics in the water. It either fries your liver or opens up your mind, brings you to a different level of reality. The music is great, they do at least a three-hour show, and everyone treats you like a long-lost friend. I dig the scene in the parking lot before the show, everyone selling something, food, clothing, pipes, trying to score enough to move on down the road to the next gig. How about you? Ever done the Dead?" He offered Wynn a toke.

"I have to confess, I've yet to have the pleasure," Wynn replied, coughing. "Speaking of Jersey, I'm much more of a Springsteen fan. I'm also into reggae, people like Marley, Peter Tosh, Jimmy Cliff."

"So Wynn, what's your story? Where ya initially from?"

"I grew up in Brooklyn," Wynn replied. "My dad was in the Army during the war, then did construction. Became the super at the apartment building we moved into when I was ten. My mom teaches seventh grade English. Both my parents were active in the local Baptist church. My mom sometimes took me to NAACP events, my first political events. Mainly, they raised me and my older brother, Ward."

"Then the Vietnam War came along. My brother and a lot of guys from the neighborhood got drafted. He got shipped over when I was a freshman in high school."

"So how did your dad feel about the whole thing?" Pete asked.

"My dad wasn't really big on the war, but he was big on the military, felt they had treated him right, treated blacks right. He though it was our duty to go if we were called."

Wynn paused, looking out the window at the shadows on the desert floor as it whizzed by.

"Got a knock on the apartment door one day," Wynn said, the pain still present. "Got himself killed six months after he got there."

"My brother coming home in a body bag is what made me political. I got real mad at the government, paid a lot more attention to what was going down. Started going to antiwar protests, which my dad didn't like. Checked out the Black Panther Party, read books by Huey Newton and Bobby Seale, the autobiography of Malcolm X," Wynn said.

"Hey man, I don't want you to take this the wrong way, but as a black dude, weren't you already aware how screwed up the system was?" Pete asked.

"Sure," Wynn replied. "But now I was seeing how the whole thing fit together. It made me aware of how systemic racism is, not just by individuals but by institutions. How hard it really is to escape from it. And then I came to see that if anything is bigger than racism, it's the pursuit of the almighty dollar."

Heading into the final stretch of his trip had Wynn in a talkative mood.

"So how'd you end up an organizer?" asked Pete.

"With all the arguments I began to have with my dad about the war, I decided to go to college upstate, even though CUNY would've been free. My parents always said that I could be a doctor, lawyer or preacher. I don't have the stomach for blood, and I never liked sitting in church much on Sundays, so I signed up for prelaw. Thought I could be the next Thurgood Marshall, win cases like he did on school desegregation," Wynn said.

"The first semester at Albany State, I went to a speech by this guy Barry Frost. He takes on the corporations on behalf of the small guys. Sounded like the type of thing you're supposed to do when you're prelaw. He's another guy that connects the dots. Talked about abandoned housing, redlining by banks, insurance companies, developers and politicians, corporate polluters, automobile and oil companies," Wynn explained.

"Frost challenged us to start a local chapter of a student group called the Public Interest Research Group. PIRG for short. It was also a good way to meet girls, plus they had lots of parties with free beer. I spent a summer driving a school bus around to county fairs talking about environmental issues and consumer rip-offs. We stood out like a sore thumb, especially me with my black skin. A lot of nasty comments under people's breath. Just kept smiling and asking them if they want to ban the can, no, not your fat white ass sir, I mean the bottle bill, a five-cent deposit on cans and bottles. Want to buy a button?" Wynn continued.

"I went to Albany Law School because they had a PIRG chapter, plus I could finish earlier. Law school was a mistake. All about brainwashing, training you to be amoral so you could defend your client no matter how sleazy or rotten they were. This one guy finally stands up, says he's tired of debating whether the little old lady or the railroad company should win the lawsuit — we have to help the little old lady. He never came back for his second year," Wynn told Pete.

The Dead tape came to an end. Pete asked him to find something in the glove compartment. Wynn put on a Gil Scott Heron tape.

"So how'd you make your escape?" Pete asked.

"I found out organizing was a lot more fun than the law. And I felt good about myself for doing it," Wynn replied.

"PIRG started this community organizing project with some former United Farm Workers, you know, Cesar Chavez's group. They organized in low-income neighborhoods around housing issues, like redlining."

Pete interrupted. "What's redlining?"

"That's where banks refuse to give mortgages in poor neighborhoods because they claim it's too risky. Which makes it hard for people to sell. They and the real estate brokers play the neighborhood like a yoyo, driving the prices down, pressuring long-term residents to 'get out while you still can,' selling to absentee landlords who neglect the properties, driving even more people out. Once they've broken the neighborhood, they get the politicians to give them federal housing funds to gentrify, selling to yuppies and raising the rents, pushing the low-income tenants out."

Pete opened the last beer. Wynn declined his offer to share. "So had did you bring the banks to their knees?" Pete asked. "I never get anywhere trying to argue with a bank, even when it's clear they screwed up."

"They had lotta creative ways. We'd get the parents to bring their kids with us to a bank and demand a meeting. Tell 'em we wanted to know why they refused to give loans and mortgages in our neighborhoods. If they told us they didn't think anyone could see us, we give out graham crackers to the kids. They'd sit down and ground the crackers into the carpet. We'd just shrug our shoulders and say 'what can you do, they're just kids. Hey, you found anyone to talk to us yet?' We'd start singin' songs, sometime there'd be TV cameras, pretty soon the police would show up, we'd have good ole time arguin' and givin' speeches," Wynn said.

"Eventually some bigwig would agree to meet, but only a few of us. Of course all of us would troop into their big, fancy conference room and begin negotiating. It was impressive how much money they forced the banks to lend into the neighborhood," chuckled Wynn.

"When I graduated, I went to work for CAN, Community Action Network, 'cause I heard they were the best. They're an offshoot of the National Welfare Rights Organization. Follow the techniques developed by Saul Alinsky, pretty much the guru of community organizing. He wrote the organizing bible, *Rules for Radicals*. He preached direct action, directly confronting the person who had the power to make the decision, get right in their face with a lot of people. Alinsky wasn't into spending time lobbying state legislators who were bought and paid for by the rich and the corporations."

"Alinsky stressed the need to focus on a single target that symbolized all that was bad about the opposition. Do actions that were fun, that made people laugh but which also got across the point you were trying to make. Make life unbearable for your target until they gave in," Wynn added.

"Hey, Wynn, I'm going to pull off the road up ahead. I feel the call of Mother Nature. Besides, I always like to take a few minutes to watch the sunset," said Pete. The sunset, as usual, was spectacular, as if God herself had retired to Arizona and painted every evening with wild swirling splashes of oranges, purples and reds.

"What I like about CAN is they build bridges between people, especially black and white," Wynn continued. "They always make sure they organize black neighborhoods right from the start. You organize a white neighborhood first, black second almost at the same time, then no arguments, already integrated before any questions asked."

"So what about you, Pete? How'd you end up in Phoenix?" Wynn asked.

Pete lacked Wynn's gift for gab — he was a man of few words. Pete had grown up in a Catholic family of eight kids in a small working class town on the New Jersey shore. His father was a machinist and union supporter, his mother was an artist who scraped money together by teaching art classes for kids and restoring old furniture.

"Us kids early on mastered the art of driving our parents insane. We never did anything *too* bad," Pete said, "but we certainly did enough to draw the wrath of the nuns at school. We quickly graduated to making life difficult for the rather dull-witted and slow-footed police officers hired by the town to make the tourists feel safe during the summer. We'd do little things, like pour super glue into cop's car doors."

"When I graduated high school three years ago, my friend Steve and I jumped into an old van to head out to California. Unfortunately, it broke down in Phoenix when we were visiting a friend from Jersey, so we ended up staying here. One day we stumbled on this funky old vacant house about a mile from the university in Tempe. We tracked down the owner, this wacky economics professor, and wangled a deal to clean up the place in exchange for a few months of free rent. We're still there," Pete said.

It turned out that the house was one of the first solar houses in America, with a retractable roof that moved by turning an old sailing ship wheel. Unfortunately the roof no longer moved but there was still this amazing 360-degree mural around the opening in the ceiling of the mountains surrounding Phoenix. Pete also found it amusing that the huge house next door was the official residence of the president of Arizona State University.

Pete made enough to get by working on and off as an auto mechanic, or helping Steve paint houses. He preferred to spend his time working with community groups, particularly the local food coop and antinuclear group. He also took an occasional class at the university.

"By the way, Pete, this truck sure smells like French fries. What did you do, spill some down the seat and can't get them out?" asked Wynn.

"No, this truck runs on vegetable oil. I pull up every few weeks to McDonald's for a fill up. They give me their used oil," explained Pete.

"You're pulling my leg," said Wynn in disbelief.

"Nope. I've always been interested in how to make cars less environmentally damaging. Okay, bikes are better, but not everyone's gonna ride one. I spent a couple of years tryin' to figure out how to redesign a carburetor to get 100 miles a gallon. Started out in my shop class in high school," Pete told him. "This was how I was gonna make my fortune."

"The principle is quite simple. Right now, a car is very inefficient.

Less than 50 percent of the gas goes to powering the car. My solution is to modify the carburetor, combusting the gas a second time, greatly increasing its efficiency. What sucks is that every time I figure it out, someone else already made the discovery and got a patent on it. Some car company then promptly bought it to stop it from going to market. That's capitalism for you. Make money by forcing everyone else to waste money and harm the environment," commented Pete.

"I haven't given up," Pete continued. "But since I wasn't getting anywhere with my ideas about regular gas, I decided to switch direction and bought a diesel truck so I could run it on processed vegetable oil, basically biodiesel. Works fine — the original design for diesel was to use vegetable oil. And the emissions are much cleaner compared to gas."

"So what are you going to do?" Wynn laughed. "Develop a fleet of trucks to promote McDonalds? Driving up to a fast-food joint for a fill-up doesn't seem too practical," remarked Wynn.

"You're right about that," said Pete. "The first time I pulled up, the guy at the local McDonald's thought I was nuts. But I got him hooked. He said he'd give it to me as long as I signed a waiver that I wouldn't sue him if the engine blew up. Now they call me up if the supply's gettin' too large. I have to process it before I can use it to run a car, but it ends up costing me a whole lot less than regular gas. I don't have the processing system perfected yet, it's still pretty labor intensive, but I am gettin' close."

****

Pete let Wynn borrow his car to get to work on Monday. Pete was working with Steve this week and would be sharing a ride anyway.

Wynn told Pete that CAN would lend him 300 dollars to buy another car, since having one was a condition of employment. Not only did you need a car to be an organizer, "you wanted a big one, a boat, so you could stuff it full of members to bring to events."

Pete said not to worry, old junkers were his specialty. "I've even gotten a few of my cars into a movie — *Used Cars*, with Chevy Chase. Ever heard of it? Its climax was driving a mile-worth of old junkers across the Arizona desert. I'll get ya a car for 200 dollars tops, good enough to drive around town for a couple of years." Wynn told him to try to make it American. "The union guys tend to get a little uptight if you show up driving a foreign car."

"That's why you need an old car," Pete said. "Buy a new American car, the only thing American on it is the brand name. Open the engine and half the time there's Japanese writing on the engine block. Built overseas, assembled in Ohio, financed by multinationals."

Before leaving the house, Wynn called Father O'Riley, his main contact, to set up a meeting. CAN's organizing in Arizona was being funded by the Catholic Church through its national Campaign for Human Development. CHD was putting up 30,000 dollars to bring CAN to Arizona. That may not sound like much, but when you paid your organizers only 3,200 dollars a year, reimbursed them two cents a mile for using their cars, and expected them to scrounge for things like office equipment and furniture, 30 thousand went pretty far.

CAN embraced the principle of paying poverty wages to organizers. New staff were told, "When you make so little yourself, you can look people right in the eye when they say they're too poor to join and tell them, I know what it's like to be poor. We need you to join." Living in poverty made organizers experience the same realities that poor people did. Like not having enough money to fix your car. Or having to live in run-down neighborhoods.

CAN often rented big old rambling houses in one of the neighborhoods they organized, allowing the staff to live upstairs for 35 dollars a month. It saved money for the organizer while keeping them close to work at all times. In CAN, 12-hour days, seven days a week were the norm, the only time off being from 6 pm Saturday night to 1 pm on Sunday. No wonder that some compared CAN to a cult — CAN staff claimed cult members were allowed to have more fun.

Wynn spent the morning doing a "windshield survey," driving around the city looking for problems. You often looked for neighborhoods near downtown or business districts where people could get cheap rents or mortgages in exchange for putting up with a lot of noise, garages, factories and bus fumes. He wanted neighborhoods with vacant lots and abandoned houses.

The first neighborhood Wynn had organized was in Fort Worth. The work had not gone well initially. It certainly didn't help that most of the residents were Mexican-American, with Spanish their mother tongue, Wynn was able to say hardly more than a few words. Texas was also a hotbed of racism, and Wynn had often been cursed at from passing cars. There were lots of neighborhoods and bars he was warned to keep out of.

Walking up to strangers and asking them for money to join a group didn't come naturally to him. Every day for the first month he had sat down in his organizing neighborhood and thought about quitting, asking why was he wasting his time here.

He told Pete, "Fortunately for my organizing career, CAN sent me into a classic impoverished community, exploited by one and all. Straight out of a John Steinbeck novel. The neighborhood was cut off from the rest of the city on every side — an interstate, a major city street, a shopping mall. The fourth side was a steel factory that operated around the clock, shutting down only on Sunday evenings for six hours for maintenance. The rest of the time the pounding was nonstop, with toxic fumes spewing all over the place. The men would pour out of the factory for their half-hour lunch, and jump into their cars to barrel down the local streets to buy a sandwich and a six-pack of beer before dashing back to the blast furnace. A couple of weeks before I got there, a young girl was killed by one of the speeding cars. Nothing much happened to the driver."

The houses were small and rundown. Many lacked flooring. The streets looked like an auto repair shop, rusted cars sitting on jacks.

"If I couldn't organize that neighborhood, I couldn't organize anywhere," Wynn told Pete. "All I needed was the sound track for the movie, it was so bleak. After doing office work for six hours, I knocked on doors for five hours every evening, asking people to join. Everyone said they'd have to think about it. After the first three weeks, I had almost no members. I'd sit on the curb every afternoon thinking about a career change.

"I don't know how, some combination of growing frustration and desperation, afraid to admit failure, but after three weeks I cracked some psychological barrier. Over the Labor Day weekend I signed up 20 members, dues and all. An organizer had been borne," Wynn told him.

"How did it turn out?" asked Pete. "Was it a success?"

"Well, at the first community meeting a month later, a hundred people jammed into a small church, so that was a success. But then I got blown away when so many of the neighbors stood up and demanded more police protection. I mean, this was a dirt-poor neighborhood, and cops protect rich people. I had come to view police as the enemy. They constantly harassed me and the other brothers. In fact, when I first got to Texas, they threatened me with arrest — twice — on the first day. For petitioning in the parking lot of a supermarket. I was trespassing on private property, they told me.

"But these people wanted to feel safe in their homes. They wanted the police to protect them. So that's what we worked on. You work on the issues that matter most to people," Wynn added.

Another organizing lesson Wynn had absorbed was how physical boundaries impacted upon neighborhoods. "Neighborhoods that are near the city line always have problems. They remember to collect the taxes but forget that you're also entitled to services," he told Pete and Steve one evening. "Even the dogs know about the city line. When I organized in Denver, the stray dogs would move from one side of the street to the other depending on whether the city or county dog warden was driving around."

"Rivers are also good targets for organizers," Wynn added. "Communities start around rivers for transportation, but as they grow, the more affluent move up the hill. The poor get stuck with the flooding, the smell, the factories, the sewage disposal plants."

Steve had a harder time than Pete in absorbing what organizing was. For the first few weeks he kept asking Wynn, "What do you do for a living again? Hand out leaflets door to door? Is this some type of advertising gimmick?"

Pete came up with an old white Chevy station wagon. It sounded like it had gravel in the transmission. He promised it was good for at least another 30,000 miles or so, even though it already had 150,000. "They don't make them like this anymore." Wynn readily agreed.

Nicknamed White Lightning, its only major problem was that it had the type of gearshift that could "jump" out and become disengaged. He became quite adept at scrambling out at stoplights, crawling under the car, reengaging the gear and jumping back in before the light turned green. A bargain for 200 bucks.

Wynn bought a map to help identify neighborhoods for further research. One promising area was just south of the river in South Phoenix, surrounded on the three sides by undeveloped land.

When he found a problem, he'd park the car and doorknock half a dozen houses. "Hi. I'm with a new community group in town called CAN. I couldn't help noticing the abandoned house down the block. Do you have any concerns about that? Has this city been willing to do anything to get it fixed?" Wynn would ask.

When he checked out South Phoenix, he discovered that all the roads across the river except one ran through the riverbed. Apparently it wasn't supposed to have water. He discovered that part of the riverbed had been turned into a major dumping ground. Garbage was piled everywhere — plastic bags, abandoned cars, oil drums, you name it. His heart beat faster. Garbage was always a great organizing tool.

The vacant areas on the map turned out to be farm fields, primarily cotton. There were about 500 homes in the neighborhood. It was a poor community, many of the small houses in need of paint. It seemed mostly to be Mexican-American. He found out later that they worked mainly in the factories just the other side of the river, on the surrounding farmland, or as day laborers. The yards were hard-packed dirt. There were plenty of run-down cars and trucks. Chickens, kids and dogs roamed everywhere.

Wynn drove slowly through the streets, waving hello to everyone. A number of the houses ran a little food store in the front. A commercial strip wound along one side of the neighborhood, mainly auto repair shops and a couple of hard-looking bars. To the outside eye, it was a tough neighborhood. One waiting to be organized.

After discovering the garbage dump, Wynn began to systematically doorknock the neighborhood. Fortunately, there was usually at least one member of each family who spoke English.

Wynn went to the public library to copy pages from the city directory, a telephone book in reverse, where residents' names and phone numbers were arranged by street address rather than alphabetically.

On a manual Smith-Corona typewriter, he typed up three sets of labels, using carbon paper between each set. One set of labels would be kept for the office records; another would be used for a mailing before the first meeting; the final set went onto three-by-five index cards, which he took with him when he went doorknocking. The cards allowed him to ask for people by name, making him less like some door-to-door salesman. He also used the cards to keep track of the responses, writing down any issues they mentioned, creating a little bio on everyone.

"Hi. My name is Wynn. I'm helping to start a new community group called CAN. CAN is neighbors working together to solve local problems, anything from getting vacant lots cleaned up or more parks built, to citywide issues like healthcare and funding for affordable housing. One problem some of the neighbors have mentioned is all the garbage piled up in the riverbed just north of the neighborhood. They say it smells really bad in the summer, especially when the wind is blowing the wrong way, and it attracts bugs and rats. Who knows what's being dumped there? I was hoping I could have a few minutes of your time to see if you have any ideas about things we could get improved in the neighborhood."

Most people were willing to talk for a few minutes, though they usually stood at the door rather than inviting him in. Getting in was always a goal; it made it much more likely that people would agree to join. Pretty much everyone agreed right off the bat that the garbage was a problem. Quite a few doubted that anything could be done: "City hall don't care 'bout people in this neighborhood."

"Well, they might not care about you right now, but they will when you get organized," Wynn told them. "The people who made up the saying that you can't fight city hall are the ones who work there. Our only power is in numbers. It's one thing when one or two neighbors call up to complain; it's another when dozens get together. That's what CAN is all about — getting the community organized. City hall will pay attention if we bring them down here and make them face 50 or 100 people, make them smell that thing, with TV cameras stuck in their face" said Wynn.

CAN's goal for each organizer was to get at least one family a day to sign up as a member. Wynn was able to average two. Most neighbors said they wanted to think about it but would try to come to the first meeting.

Wynn asked the neighbors if there was ever a problem with the river washing out the roads that ran through it. "You gotta be new around here," they told him. "Three times in the last year all the roads, other than the bridge, washed out. The politicians told us this would only happen during a fifty-year flood. Seems like we're having a lot of fifty-year floods. Last time the roads washed out, it cost me an extra hour each way to get to work. Took 'em three months to fix it. It was a royal pain in the ass."

Several decades previously, the federal government had built a hydroelectric dam east of Phoenix. The lake behind the dam has now filled up. With a major rainstorm, the excess water was released down the riverbed.

Wynn also discovered that people were having problems with the pesticides sprayed on the cotton fields. While the spraying had been going on for years, something was different this year. "The planes fly just a few yards from the houses. Big white clouds fall over our yards. You try to stay inside when you see them spraying," Maria Theresa Perez told him. "This year, people are getting sick."

Maria told Wynn, "I'd be willing to have my neighbors over to talk about doing something, as long as my husband says it's okay." Wynn made a tentative date for his first organizing committee meeting in Arizona.

THREE

A BLUEPRINT FOR AMERICA

Late August 2001

Wynn glanced up from his computer screen as Rachel returned to their private quarters after a long day at the office.

"Hi, darling. Saved the world today?" he asked.

Rachel threw herself down on the couch and put her feet up.

"I did my best. But it's an uphill struggle. I want to focus on issues like healthcare and housing, global warming. Seems like the world wants me to focus on the thirty-year bond market and a cut in the capital gains tax," she said.

"Well, here's something to warm your heart — the newest report from United for a Fair Economy. Pay for CEOs rose a whopping 571 percent during the last decade, while the working stiff got an extra 37 percent. Now get this. If the minimum wage, which was a measly three dollars and eighty cents an hour in 1990, had grown at the same rate as the pay of CEOs, it would be twenty-five dollars and fifty cents today.

"What will really warm your heart is CEOs did best when they laid off a thousand or more workers — they were able to soak up an extra 80 percent. And in honor of you, the 30 highest paid male CEOs earned thirteen times more than the 30 highest paid women CEOs," Wynn chuckled to himself. "Ain't America great?"

"Why don't you just e-mail a summary over to congressional leaders? I'm sure they'll jump right on it. Any idea what's for dinner?" Rachel asked.

Economic justice was one of those issues that Congress preferred to jaw about rather than take action on. The minimum wage was a favorite ruse. The Democrats dutifully demanded a one dollar increase over two years, the Republicans predicted doom and gloom for small business, both parties raked in campaign contributions from the competing sides, but somehow they managed to adjourn every year with no results.

One of Rachel's standard campaign riffs was to call for a maximum wage. "The minimum wage would be set at some percentage of the maximum, say one-tenth," she said provocatively. "That way doctors, lawyers and real estate developers would have to lobby Congress for an increase, rather than home healthcare and fast-food workers." FDR had proposed a maximum wage during the forties. Not surprisingly, it went nowhere.

****

Rachel had arranged for the Blueprint for America symposium to convene the following weekend at Camp David.

It was an ambitious undertaking. Sessions were held on the environment (air, water, wetlands, biodiversity), healthcare, energy, housing, education, science, food and agriculture, education, civil liberties, racism, women's issues, labor, tax policy, the economy.

"We can't solve all the country's problems immediately. Solving half of them in the first ninety days would be great," Rachel said to laughter in her welcoming remarks Friday night. "Feel free to lay out the long-term vision, but we need the steps to get us there. Give me your priorities. Respond to the likely objections. I don't want to just throw more money at issues. I want a different path. I want to green America. We'll set up committees to continue the work, but we need to start somewhere. Be bold. Make a difference."

Rachel found that her presence served as a distraction. She excused herself to work on her first speech to the nation to be delivered the following Tuesday.

Wynn sat in on the session on affordable housing.

Marcia Hanratty of the National Coalition on Low Income Housing argued for increased support of public housing. "The US, unlike many countries, heavily relies upon private home ownership rather than public housing. Congress has poured billions into supporting private home ownership, starting with allowing homeowners to deduct the interest payments on their mortgages. The federal government spends four times as much money on the mortgage deduction program than on public housing, with most of the benefit going to the upper middle-class. This tax subsidy also artificially inflates housing prices by twenty percent, since buyers are willing to pay more for the house because of the tax deduction. The higher prices hurt both tenants and homeowners who can't use the interest deduction."

Going after people's tax deductions on their homes probably isn't our wisest first step thought Wynn. *We don't need to start off with a fight with the soccer moms.*

"Funding for public housing has been cut in half over the last two decades," added Bill Norman of the Affordable Housing Coalition, "with almost no new construction. Only five million Americans live in public housing and it's often poorly constructed with high energy costs, and concentrated in poor and unsafe neighborhoods. Communities resist new low-income housing projects, fearing they'll attract 'undesirables,' driving housing prices down. People of color still face significant discrimination in their housing options, resulting in economic segregation."

The panelists called for increased funding for public housing, with more emphasis on smaller, scattered-site projects, along with requiring communities to accept some public housing in exchange for federal revenue sharing.

Wynn was particularly interested in the presentation by Cynthia Cartwright, a Green, who spoke in favor of funding, including tax incentives, to develop intentional communities, such as community land trusts, cohousing, urban housing cooperatives, ecovillages and student coops.

"Such housing builds a sense of community and promotes environmental preservation." Cartwright noted. She also supported "requiring all new housing to take advantage of solar power, with high levels of energy conservation. At a minimum, require houses to face the sun. But we should also promote active uses of solar for hot water and electricity, and support geothermal heating and cooling. Developments should preserve as much green or open space as possible, clustering the houses together."

Cartwright explained that community land trusts keep housing affordable by eliminating speculation on the value of the land; the trust owns the land while individuals own the buildings. Land trusts often have additional restrictions on the property to promote environmental conservation and energy conservation.

"What's cohousing? I haven't heard of it before," Wynn asked Cartwright after the session.

"Cohousing started in Denmark. It's similar to a condominium in that they're privately owned, clustered living spaces and shared land. It goes further, though, in creating common spaces, such as kitchens, dining rooms, gardens and recreational spaces, allowing the houses to be smaller. Why should every family buy a lawnmower or a pool? Families build a strong sense of community, sharing chores and even meals if they choose to."

"Ecovillages are a form of cohousing, with greater emphasis on the environment. They feature recycling, carpooling and the elimination of pesticides," Cartwright added. "The common land is where you put your organic garden and park, the swings for the kids. They use conservation easements to permanently protect the common land from development. You design your water use, energy and waste disposal systems to be as environmentally friendly as possible."

Rachel rejoined the group to lead the Saturday afternoon plenary on the military budget.

"In his farewell address, four decades ago, President Dwight Eisenhower stated, 'this conjunction of an immense military establishment and a large arms industry is new in the American experience. The potential for the disastrous rise of misplaced power exists and will persist.' President Eisenhower also observed that 'every gun that is made, every warship launched, every rocket fired signifies, in the final sense, a theft from those who hunger and are not fed, those who are cold and are not clothed."

"America never restored our military budget to a peacetime level after World War II," Rachel continued. "During the 1980s, President Reagan increased military spending to such a degree that he incurred more debt than every president from Washington to Carter — combined! One reason he did this was to force the Soviet Union into economic collapse. I want to make sure that our military spending doesn't force us into the same economic collapse.

"I would like to see you address two major areas of concern. First, what are our legitimate defense needs? Our military's role should be to protect this country, not to be the world's bully. We spend more on the military than the next ten largest countries combined, and most of those countries are our allies. We shouldn't be spending tens of billions of American tax dollars to protect Europe against a land war with the Soviet Empire; it makes no sense. We must change our military strategy to reflect the security needs of the new millennium and leave the last century behind."

"How much can we cut military spending to make available funds for domestic programs? How do we take the research and development dollars we're using to develop more lethal weapons and instead invest in making our civilian economy stronger — building better cars, electronic equipment and renewable energy systems?" she added.

"The second area of concern is how to focus our national security agenda on resolving the economic instability facing third world countries. That's what a panel convened by President Reagan identified as our biggest national security threat. How can our country best assist third world countries to meet the needs of their people?" she asked.

"Poverty and a lack of resources feeds the growing divide between rich and poor, which in turn inflames ethnic, religious and social tensions. This leads to more outbreaks of armed violence by both nations and terrorists."

Shortly before the conference broke up, David Smythe, one of the Green Party's national cochairs, got a few minutes alone with Rachel to express some concerns.

"Rachel, I'm getting tons of e-mails asking why the Green Party isn't playing more of a role in the transition," Smythe said, wasting no time. "You had a lotta people here this weekend who aren't Greens. Hell, probably half of 'em, maybe more, voted for Harrington. Bunch of academics, probably haven't organized a demo in their lives."

"Looked and sounded to me like a Green Party event," said Rachel. "You couldn't turn around without tripping over a Green. Everybody started with a copy of the Green Party platform. If the Green Party national leadership doesn't like anything we come up with, just pass a resolution vetoing it. But that means the national party, not every caucus, subcommittee, or discussion group."

"But it shoulda been just the Greens meeting here this weekend, deciding what your administration, *our* administration, is gonna do," Smythe replied. "We're the ones who ran you for office. You wouldn't be here without us."

"Who's trying to kid who here?" Rachel asked. "Wynn and I've been with the Greens long enough to know what the score is. Hey, there were tons of Greens who did a lotta work on my campaign, and I appreciate each and every one of 'em. But we both know it was Frost who raised almost all the money, and it was his people who collected most of the signatures to get us on the ballot. Most of the people who voted for us were voting for Frost, not the party. I wish the Greens were stronger, but we're still learning how to walk," Rachel reminded him.

"There ya go, dissing the party. Just like every other politician. Once you're elected, ya'll forget —"

"Excuse me Dave, let's not waste time here," Rachel cut in. "How 'bout you give me a few days to get on my feet before you start hollering over all the bad things I'm doing? I'm a Green, and intend to govern as one. I hate to be the one to break the news to ya Dave, but there ain't enough of us. We can't be worrying 'bout who didn't vote for us this time. We gotta focus on getting them to vote for us next time," Rachel asserted.

"But you gotta act now," argued Smythe, "before they gang up and kick you out. Issue an Executive Order or something, close all the nukes, get our troops outta Colombia, the Middle East, free some political prisoners."

"You gotta get real about what we're facing here," she said in exasperation. "The president isn't a dictator. I can't just snap my fingers and change the world. Like with nuclear power plants. Something called the Nuclear Regulatory Commission oversees, and for some reason I don't think the Dems and Republicans on the commission are gonna shut 'em down just 'cause I tell them to. And Congress ain't gonna roll over just 'cause I tell 'em the Greens passed a resolution. *We didn't win the last election.* We've got to broaden our base, educate people about what we're tryin' to do, mobilize folks to support our agenda. That's what we were starting here this weekend.

"Don't waste your time arguing with me," Rachel added. "Hit the streets and preach the revolution to the masses." *Just like you're always arguing we should do,* she thought.

The weekend did wonders for Rachel's spirits. In DC she felt surrounded by power brokers who regarded her as the sister from another planet. The conference provided an alternate reality, her reality, a reality based on making a better world. These were the people she needed to be surrounded with on a daily basis. She told Sophie to followup with the participants to figure out how best to keep them involved, and consider who should be offered positions within the administration.

The Blueprint for America was an ambitious agenda. When asked to comment on the Blueprint by the press, Senate Majority Leader Deutsche said, "It has some good ideas, but too much of it is pie-in-the-sky stuff. Besides, it will cost way too much money to implement." The Republicans dismissed it. "It's pork for the greenies, your standard left-wing manifesto. They just want Green bureaucrats to tell the rest of us what to do while tearing down business."

****

Rachel delivered her first national televised address on Tuesday night, August 14, 2001, from the Oval Office. Sophie had suggested that she wait until after Labor Day so more people would watch, but Rachel felt it was important to reach out to the country sooner.

As the minutes clicked down to the broadcast, Rachel breathed slowly and deeply, seeking to create an inner peace. As always, her stomach had butterflies but she knew these would disappear as soon as she started talking. She invited an audience of staff and friends to the Oval Office so she could feel that she was talking to real people rather than the television camera.

"Good evening. It is with a heavy heart that I address you. President Harrington remains in a coma following his heart attack. Our medical experts offer no hope of recovery. There are no words that I can say to make up for the loss of Mrs. Harrington and her family. I know that all Americans join me in offering our prayers and condolences.

"I find myself thrust by these tragic circumstances into new responsibilities. It is a humbling experience. I was very honored when President Harrington offered me the position of vice-president as a way to allow our country to move forward at a time when the electorate was divided. President Harrington sought to use this unprecedented coming together of two different political parties to do what he thought was best for the American people. I can seek to do no less than what President Harrington set out to accomplish — to build unity among all segments of our society.

"In the last few days I have met with the leaders of both the Democratic and Republican parties to ask them to join me in putting together a government of national unity, to put aside whatever differences we have in this time of tragedy and challenge. I need their help to do what is right for our country.

"Tonight, I ask you, the American people, to join in this effort. I pledge to work very hard to bring our government and country together. I will work closely with the representatives of the other parties, welcoming and listening carefully to their proposals. I will strive to find our points of agreement. I am asking the Democrats and Republicans to join with the Greens in having each party name their best people to the cabinet so that we all share the responsibility of realizing the full potential of this great country.

"I ask each of you listening tonight to do the same in your communities. There is no limit to what we, the American people, can accomplish if are we willing to tap our unlimited potential. I hope that we can open the doors of city halls, school boards and state houses, and welcome our neighbors to hear what they have to say and to ask them to join with us in building the future that we wish to leave to our children and grandchildren.

"I know many of you are curious about me and the Green Party. We welcome your inquiries. The Greens share the common-sense values that are important to all of us: a commitment to grassroots democracy, peace, justice and ecology. The Greens understand the importance of jobs that pay a living wage while helping to improve our quality of life. We also understand that we have only one planet and that it is our responsibility to ensure that we leave our future generations with air that they can breathe, water they can drink, and soil that will grow healthy food.

"I have recently convened a conference of community leaders from across the country to start the process of developing a Blueprint for America. The Blueprint will guide my administration in expanding access to healthcare, strengthening our schools, creating living wage jobs that protect our environment, and in making our communities safer. We will make copies of this plan available shortly in local libraries, schools and on the web so that you can provide your input. My administration will convene local meetings across the country to hear your ideas about how the plan can be improved.

"My administration will strive to give *every* American the opportunity to participate in the American dream. We have the resources and talents to make that happen.

"Thank you. Good night."

The pundits were generally subdued in their reviews. While privately many of them dismissed Rachel as naïve and doubted her ability to survive the political infighting that was sure to come, the media recognized their responsibility to give the acting president the exposure that her position required.

The media would take out their knives in the future. For tonight, they were content to limit their criticism. Ralph Henning of CBS remarked: "Admirable objectives, but she remains a leader in a very difficult town without a base of support in either house of Congress." Many pundits were openly skeptical of the Green Party, inviting Rachel to distance herself from them. "To govern, she needs to show that she is willing to find a middle path," intoned Simon Baxter on the "Washington Roundtable."

****

Sophie had followed up on the note from Jennifer Garcia, the housekeeper. Her report to Rachel the morning after the speech was troublesome.

"Jennifer says that the day Harrington had his heart attack, the housekeeping staff was told not to go to the personal quarters after five. She says that wasn't that unusual — sometimes Harrington and his wife just wanted privacy. But Mrs. Harrington was out of town. Jennifer said she snuck back in 'cause she'd forgotten her purse. She heard Harrington and a woman, talking in one of the bedrooms. Pillow talk is how she described it," Sophie told her.

"The next day, when she went into the bedroom to clean up, the sheets had been replaced and items on the dresser rearranged. As far as she knows, no staff member was supposed to have been in that bedroom before her, though of course anything is possible in the pandemonium after the heart attack. She also found a woman's earring on the floor, which she gave to her supervisor. According to the reports I've seen, Harrington was alone when he had the attack. His chief of staff found him lying in the hallway when he went looking for him after he didn't respond to his calls," Sophie said.

"Sophie, set up a meeting with Bill Thompson for late today."

"Who's Thompson?" Sophie asked.

"The Director of the Secret Service," said Rachel. "Been pestering me for a meeting to go over security details. I'm sure he's been planning to lecture me 'bout all the things I can't do anymore. I got a few questions for him."

****

Sophie ushered in Thompson. He was a big, powerful man. He was beginning to show a bit of a paunch, without the sleek muscles he had twenty years earlier as a field operative.

"Madame President, thank you for taking the time to meet with me," said Thompson, a man used to being in control. "There's just a few details I need to go over with you about some added precautions we need to establish now that you're in the Oval Office."

Rachel motioned him to join her on the couch. Sophie remained in the room, leaning back on the front of the presidential desk. Rachel let Thompson drone on for a few minutes about the protective cocoon he wanted her to live in.

"Bill, I get the point," Rachel summed up. "Never go anywhere, never go outside, never look out the window, never meet with anyone whom you haven't screened. Bill, why don't you just leave the folder with me? I'll read it over later tonight and let you know tomorrow which half I won't be following. One thing, though, Bill — you're not going to continue to use *greenbean* as my code name. How about *sunflower* or *rose* or anything a little more cheerful? Even *cactus* I like better than *greenbean*."

"We should be able to handle that, Madame President," replied Thompson without a flicker of reaction.

"You can call me Rachel, Bill, if you want, at least when we're alone. I'm not used to being addressed by title."

"I'm sorry. No, I can't, Madame President."

"Have it your way," Rachel shrugged. "However, there's something that I need you to help me with. And I hope we won't be playing any games. It's very important that on this one, I hear the truth and only the truth and I hear it right from the start, not tomorrow or next week. So take your time in answering, because a lot depends on it."

Thompson didn't do a very good job of keeping a blank face, clearly interested in what she was going to say next.

"I've received some information that raises some doubts about the exact circumstances of Harrington's heart attack. I was hoping you'd clear up the confusion. I'd like to hear your version — the complete, accurate version," said Rachel, the smile gone from her face.

Thompson rubbed his chin a few times before answering. "Madame President, the job of the Secret Service is to protect the president," Thompson explained, carefully choosing his words. "To do that job, we need to be allowed to be there when the president lets his —," he quickly caught himself, "or her hair down. It's not our job to report on, or to judge, what the president is doing. It's our job to keep the president alive."

Rachel spoke slowly and deliberately. "Bill, who was the woman with the president when he had the heart attack?"

"I personally have no evidence as to the identity of anyone who was with the president when he had his heart attack," Thompson responded, stiffly clasping his hands across his knee.

"Mr. Director, I'm going to ask this question just one more time. And while I hope your future career does not depend upon this one answer, you do need to stop playing games," said Rachel through clenched teeth.

Thompson ran his hand over his crew cut.

"And look me in the eye when you answer," added Rachel, which snapped Thompson to attention.

The Director of the Secret Service took a deep breath. "Madame President, you've asked me to be truthful," he finally said. "President Harrington, over my objections — and I do hope you won't do the same — had a habit from time to time of declaring an exclusion zone around the private quarters. When he did that, he required the Secret Service to establish a perimeter and keep everyone out, including us. It's possible during this period for someone to move from certain parts of the White House into this area without being observed — especially when we're instructed not to observe. We don't like it but believe it or not, we do take orders from the president."

"Mr. Hughes, Harrington's chief of staff, found the president lying on the floor unconscious," Thompson continued. "Hughes contacted the medical emergency alert team first, us second. When the Secret Service entered the private quarters, the only people there were Mr. Hughes and President Harrington, in the hallway."

Rachel was rapidly losing her patience. Her voice had an edge to it. "Mr. Thompson, you've had a fine career of distinguished service to our country. I'd hate to see you end it prematurely. We both know that the Secret Service knows more than what you put in the report. Who was the woman, what was she doing there, and why wasn't this reported? And while you may need some flexibility in respecting the privacy of the people you're protecting, that doesn't apply when your client, in this case the president, ends up dead. This is your last opportunity to come clean before I dismiss your entire detail and launch a full-scale outside investigation."

Thompson took a few minutes before he answered. *Why did I listen to that idiot Hughes?* he asked himself. Almost imperceptibly, his body began shaking, a combination of anger and guilt.

"Her name is Paula Marshall, an executive with one of the pharmaceutical companies."

"Which one?" Rachel interrupted.

"She was a vice-president for Governmental Relations for Noventis. Marshall has a long relationship, both professionally and personally, with the president. She'd been a major fundraiser during the campaign —"

Rachel cut in again. "Was Harrington still having an affair with her after he got elected?"

"That's a little unclear."

"How unclear?"

"Phone logs show she'd called him a number of times. However, he called *her* only twice," Thompson responded. "Including the day of the heart attack."

"And what has Ms. Marshall told you?" Sophie interrupted. "A jealous lovers' quarrel, a fight over Harrington breaking off the relationship?"

"Not according to Marshall," responding now like a witness on the stand. "She understood that their relationship had to change now that he was president."

"How did you know that?" Sophie asked.

"Well, okay, that's her line," Thompson conceded.

"What else did she say?" Rachel prompted.

"Harrington had wanted some company that evening and she was glad to oblige. While having sex, he suddenly grabbed his chest and fell over. She became hysterical when she couldn't get any response from him, grabbed the nearest phone and asked for Hughes, whom she knew pretty well, blurting out that the president had become sick, come quick. According to Hughes, he was there in less than three minutes flat. He says he called emergency medical services as soon as he saw Harrington." Thompson paused. "Though the gap seems longer."

"How long?" Rachel demanded.

"Five, maybe ten minutes. We're not entirely sure," he admitted.

Sophie slammed her hand on the desk.

"Great. Just great," said Rachel.

"Listen, it would take longer than three minutes for Hughes to figure out what to do, check Harrington, see if he could revive him." Thompson responded. "He'd have to get Marshall calmed down, get her cleaned up, tidy the place up, and then move the president before the paramedics arrived."

"Those few minutes might have saved Harrington's life" Sophie noted.

"Not according to the docs…" he mumbled.

"And isn't that what's known as cleaning up the crime scene?" Sophie finished.

"What else does Hughes say?" Rachel asked.

Thompson was sweating bullets now. "He told Marshall to get out of the White House as quickly and discreetly as possible. Harrington has arranged a way for her to come and go without her visit being logged in. Hughes moved the president out to a couch in the hallway, which is where my agents and the medical team found them. The president was unconscious, but breathing. We put him on a stretcher, carried him out to the garden, and took him by helicopter to the hospital."

"Don't you think these little details were worth reporting?" Rachel asked.

"It is … certainly not one of the proudest moments of my career," he replied grudgingly.

"Look, the important fact was that the president had a heart attack," Thompson said, struggling to regain his composure. "We were focused on keeping him alive. We wrote the reports up that you have seen based on our best information at the time," Thompson replied.

Rachel stared hard at Thompson. After a brief pause, Sophie said, "Yesss?"

"There was no reason to investigate further," Thompson gulped, "until one of the doctors pulled me aside the next day to tell me there was evidence that the president had recent sexual activity and could I shed any light? I went to Hughes, who, after a fair amount of evasion …"

"Similar to this performance?" Sophie threw out.

"… admitted what had taken place," Thompson continued. "We interviewed Marshall, took some tissue samples to confirm she was the one who'd been with Harrington. The doctors confirmed her story, so to speak — no marks or evidence of any abuse on his body."

"Is that all?" asked Rachel.

"Come on," Thompson said with barely concealed exasperation. "The bottom line is he had a heart attack while committing adultery. Hughes strenuously argued that it wouldn't do either Harrington or the country any good to share the sordid details. I agreed. Hey, politicians fool around, it happens all the time in DC.

"Hughes was chief of staff, so we left it to him to figure out how to handle it. We'd already written our report; the essential facts were correct. It was a political problem at this point, not one for the Service to deal with."

Rachel was trying to avoid losing her temper. "I assume you realize she may have a motive for killing him or at least hurting him if he wanted to break off the relationship, or she was trying to blackmail him — and so on?"

"There's no evidence she was trying to harm him," Thompson argued defensively, picking at his pant legs. "Having sex is not usually a sign of discord. Hughes confirmed the president was still fond of her. She was a professional lobbyist, been around politics a longtime, she knew the ground rules for this type of relationship. She sought help as soon as Harrington was in trouble. She's remorseful, has no apparent motive, and we haven't found anything out of the ordinary to indicate that it was anything other than the continuation of a long-term affair," Thompson argued.

"Bill," Rachel said after a few moments, "I'm going to need every file, every report, everything you have on this situation. I'm going to need statements from everyone who was in the president's quarters. And I'll tell you this much. I'm not sure yet where I'm going with this but I'm very unhappy to finally *begin* to hear the real story about the president's attack more than two weeks after it happened."

"That's all for now," Rachel said, dismissing him. "But I'll be bringing in some new people to conduct an investigation. I want every Secret Service person who had any involvement in this cover-up pulled from the job for the time being, starting with you. Sophie will accompany you back to your office to gather up the reports you already have."

FOUR

ORGANIZING IN PHOENIX

Wynn had his usual butterflies before the first organizing committee meeting. Despite all the doorknocking and phone calls, he always fretted that no one would show up, that local residents would feel he was just making up all the problems that seemed so obvious to him.

His fears were unfounded, as usual. Eight people crowded into Maria and Juan's living room. The house was small and tidy. A crucifix hung on the wall behind the couch. Juan pulled in several chairs from the kitchen.

After introductions, Wynn gave a quick history of CAN. He explained why CAN was starting a chapter in Arizona, and outlined the organizing needed to hold a successful first community-wide meeting in a month.

"We need to talk to all the neighbors before the first big meeting in four weeks," Wynn explained. "This needs to be the biggest thing to ever hit the neighborhood. We need to get everyone talking, build excitement and momentum. We want to get as many of the neighbors to join as possible. We've got to make sure they have a sense of ownership in the group, ask everyone to volunteer to do something, no matter how little.

"Tonight, we're establishing an organizing committee — the OC — to pull the first meeting together. Y'all need to sign a letter that we'll mail to each neighbor. The OC also picks the issues to discuss at the meeting. Some of you will need to help run the first meeting. Since this is the first CAN meeting in Arizona, a CAN member from another state will come to explain CAN. But we'll need some of you to talk as well," said Wynn, trying to get everyone excited.

"But Wynn," said Maria, "you talk real well. You'd be best to lead the meeting. I mean, you're the one starting this." The others nodded in agreement.

"Maria, Jose, you all talk just fine," said Wynn. "This is your organization, not mine. CAN has a rule that its members, not the staff, speak for the group in public. The politicians and media need to hear from local people, the ones directly impacted by the issues."

"You call what CAN pays you a job?" Juan scoffed. "Wynn, I could get you a position on the factory floor tomorrow that pays twice as much for half the hours."

Wynn pushed on. "We don't need to decide on speakers tonight, but we should start focusing on a few issues to present. We need to pick an issue that we can win right away, so we can make the neighbors believe in the power of organizing. It's easiest if this is something that the city is already supposed to be doing. That way we don't need a new law or city council decision, we just need to convince the bureaucrats to do their job. Something like getting a vacant lot cleaned up, boarding up an abandoned house, or getting the garbage out of the river bed."

"We should also start thinking about a bigger issue to work on, one which will take longer to win. We can start researching it now, figure out what solution we want to push. Maybe getting another bridge over the river that doesn't wash out every time it rains. Now Maria, you mentioned that you and other neighbors have complaints about spraying from the cotton fields?" Wynn asked.

Maria was in her late thirties, with a full figure from having five children, several of whom peered around the door frame to see what was going on. She stammered at first, not used to talking in public with everyone looking at her. But she quickly got excited and began to talk faster. Her husband encouraged her.

"We've lived here thirteen years," Maria said. "There's always been problems with the spraying but it's been much worse this year. The plane's supposed to stop spraying before it reaches the houses, so the chemicals don't come down on us. But most times the pilot waits till the first house, and then cuts the spray off. In the past, sometimes you got a headache. This year, it seems like they're using a different chemical, smells like onions. My stomach's been sick a couple times. Some neighbors even threw up," Maria reported.

"Last week, our dog died," Maria said, her eyes tearing up. "He was a good dog. Never bothered anyone, real friendly. He was old, just liked to lie in the sun. But he crawled under the house and wouldn't move. I had one of the kids climb under with some water, but he still didn't move. He was dead the next day."

Another neighbor, Belinda Gamez, spoke up. "A couple pregnant women have gotten sick a lot, a lot worse than just morning sickness. One woman miscarried. And there's been quite a few other animals that died — chickens and a couple of pigs. My brother used to work for one of the farmers, so he called him up. The farmer said they were using something new, Bold Star or something. The farmer said he'd remind the pilot to turn off the spray before the houses. It was better that week, but the next week, it was the same thing."

Wynn jumped in. "We should look into is. Maybe there's a government agency that tracks what pesticides are sprayed, hands out permits. We can try to find out what this chemical is. Maybe find someone at a college or government agency to explain it. Who's willing to help?" Wynn asked.

A young woman, Rachel, who had come with her young son, volunteered. "I'm taking some classes at the community college. I took chemistry last semester. I could ask my professor."

"Thanks, Rachel, that's great. Belinda, would your brother be willing to ask the farmer some follow-up questions? Maybe meet with him," Wynn suggested.

"I can ask," Belinda replied.

"We need to be careful," said one of the men. "These are local farmers. Most barely scrape by. They hire people from the neighborhood to help pick and people need the money." Several others nodded in agreement.

"We all understand the need for jobs," agreed Wynn. It was important that an organizer provide positive reinforcement for concerns raised by the neighbors. "But we also don't want people getting sick. We'll make sure he knows that we're not trying to make him the villain or put him out of business. We just need some information. If the problem is because they're using something new, maybe they can go back to the old stuff. Let him know we want to work with the farmers to solve the situation, keep everyone happy."

Wynn wrote down Belinda and Rachel's assignments in the notebook he carried to keep track of things. "We should also do a survey of health problems people are experiencing. I'll write up a one page questionnaire, show y'all a copy, see what other questions you can think of. We can include it in the mailing we send out for the meeting. But we'll get more neighbors to fill it out if we go door to door with it."

"Okay, that was a good first meeting," Wynn said, wrapping up after an hour and a half. "It was great that Maria and Juan let us meet here tonight. Does anyone else want to host the meeting next week?"

Maria looked over to Juan, who nodded. "It's no problem meeting here," she said. "This way we can keep an eye on the kids. If it's all right with everyone, we can meet here again."

"If you're sure we wouldn't be imposing, that would be great," Wynn said. "How 'bout everyone try to bring one or two neighbors next time?"

Wynn stopped Rachel on her way out the door. "It's great that you volunteered. I don't think we've met before."

"My son is a friend of Maria's son. You must've stopped by my house when I was at school. There was a flyer in my door. I mentioned it to Maria and she invited me over," said Rachel.

"I'm glad you were able to make it. Maybe I could stop by some time to talk about what research we need to do?" suggested Wynn.

"Sure. I work at the supermarket Friday evening and Saturday morning but I should be home the rest of the weekend."

****

Living with Pete and Steve in the Hostel for Wayward Youth was an adventure.

While CAN organizers subscribed to the motto, "work hard, party hard," that usually meant drinking a lot of beer on Saturday night and maybe going out dancing somewhere. With Pete and his friends, partying was performance art, seven days a week.

Pete and Steve burned the candle at both ends. They usually managed to somehow drag themselves out of bed each morning to get to whatever job they had at the moment. But having a good time was what they lived for. Steve was the ringmaster, though he and Pete both had a knack for picking up friends in odd places. Ralph and Laurie were two of their closest friends, fellow Dead Heads with an artistic streak. Steve told Wynn, "I met Ralph when he stopped me from walking off with the toilet paper from the restroom at the garage where he worked. A couple of hours later, he and Laurie were sprawled on our living room couch grooving to the Dead."

"You wouldn't believe these guys I'm living with," Wynn told Mary Halliday, his replacement in Iowa, when she called with a question. "When things are slow, they head down to the ice cream parlor and order a few cones. They stick them on their foreheads and parade around on the sidewalks near the campus as Coneheads, in honor of the Saturday Night Live skit. Or they go to the laundromat and climb into the dryer to spin around. Or organize a party by wheeling a shopping cart with a keg of beer around town, inviting everyone they meet along the way back to the house."

"Pete's great," Wynn added. "He volunteers for everything — the antinuclear movement, Native American causes, Amnesty International, cleaning up vacant lots. Before we hit our favorite jazz bar on Saturday night, Pete helps mop the floors and restock the shelves at the food coop. Last Sunday morning, he dragged me out to paint the local child care center," Wynn said.

Wynn didn't have a lot of choice about joining in the circus. The house was small, with two tiny bedrooms, a small living room, a kitchen, and an enclosed porch they used for storage. For the first month, while he looked for somewhere else, Wynn slept on the couch. This meant waiting for everyone else to crash first. He began taking naps in the office before hitting the doors. Rents were high everywhere, especially on CAN's salary, and since they enjoyed each other's company, they eventually cleaned out the porch to make another bedroom.

There was almost always someone extra camped out at the house — friends on their way to somewhere else, friends they had just met earlier in the day, guests too tired to drive home. The rule was, if you stayed more than three days, it was time to start contributing to the rent. Many did.

The second week after he moved in, Pete, Steve and Wynn went out to "The Dive," a seedy Tempe bar catering to the college crowd. They were aghast to discover that Coors was the only beer on tap.

"Coors!?" they screeched in unison at the bartender. "The only draft beer you have on tap is Coors?" they said in disbelief.

"How can a place called The Dive only sell Coors?" Wynn asked. "Don't you know that they discriminate against gays, they're antiunion, they spy on their own workers, they're antichoice? They even fund Republicans," Pete added.

"Hey, I'm just the bartender. You're welcome to come back during the day and talk to the manager. It's beer, it's wet and it's cold. If you don't want a draft, we got plenty of bottled beer."

"I'm am organizer," said Wynn. "I can't risk being seen drinking beer in a Dive that only serves Coors. We're going to have to take our business elsewhere. What time did you say the manager comes in?"

Their outburst had more of an impact on the bartender than he let on. A few weeks later they heard The Dive had switched to Budweiser. They dropped by for a celebratory draft.

A woman was tending bar. Wynn asked her, "Last time we were in you had Coors on tap. How come you dropped?"

"The owner hit the roof when he heard they discriminated against gays. He's one of them," she replied. "More peanuts?" she asked, grapping the empty dish.

****

Rachel called Wynn at the office to say she had to work till five on Saturday. "Would you mind stopping by a little later? We can talk over dinner if you want." Wynn readily accepted her offer. CAN organizers, with their low pay, made it a habit to drop by members around dinner time.

Rachel's house was typical for South Phoenix, a one-story white stucco building in need of paint. It had the ever-present swamp cooler on the roof, the poor man's air conditioner that cools a house by blowing air through water. Noisy but it helped a bit. A small flower and vegetable garden was in the front yard. A dirt alley ran out back.

Rachel's son answered when Wynn knocked, pushing open the door and wrapping his arms around Wynn's legs.

"Come on in, Wynn," Rachel called from the kitchen. "Dinner's just 'bout ready. Don't mind Tommy. He likes to make everyone feel welcome. There's a beer in the fridge. Or wine, lemonade or water if you prefer."

The house was small, with two bedrooms, a kitchen and a living room. The furniture was second-hand. Toys were scattered everywhere. Wynn got a beer and sat at the kitchen table. Jars of homemade tomato sauce, salsa, jams and hot peppers lined the planks hung for kitchen shelves. On the pantry door was a poster of healing herbs. Bouquets of mint, oregano and basil hung over the window. Rachel took cooking seriously. She waved off his half-hearted offer of help.

Tommy climbed onto Wynn's lap.

"Tommy, why don't you get one of your coloring books and show Wynn how good you are at coloring?" Rachel suggested. Tommy darted out.

"I talked to my professor," Rachel continued. "He said we should check with the Pesticide Control Board. They regulate the use of pesticides. It's their job to keep track of what farmers are using. He said the farmers and applicators control them, so don't expect too much out of them. He also saw a newspaper article a couple of weeks ago that some residents in Scottsdale, you know, that rich community on the northeast side, are complaining about some pesticide from the Indian Reservation."

Wynn was impressed. "Sounds like you've done quite a bit of homework," he commented.

"Not really," Rachel said, wiping her hands on her apron. She took it off before bringing the food to the table. Her long black hair was braided. "I just stopped by his office. He also suggested we contact the Center for Science in the Public Interest. They have an office by the Capitol. He thought they'd be into working with community residents on pesticide issues, giving technical advice."

Wynn opened his notebook. "I drafted some questions to ask neighbors about health problems they're having from the spraying. Maybe you can take a look at it later, see if there are any additional questions you want to include. If you've time, perhaps you could run it by your professor," he said. "I'll give this Science group a call next week."

Wynn drained the end of his beer. He declined the offer of an additional one. He'd wait till he got home to do his serious drinking.

"I'll set up a meeting with this pesticide board, see what they have in their files. I'll ask if they know anything about this Bolstar," Wynn added. "Once I've got a date, I'll give you and some of the other neighbors a call."

"I'm pretty busy weekdays between school, work and taking care of Tommy," Rachel said. "I'll try to make it, but don't count on it. My car isn't running either, which makes it more difficult to get around. Fortunately both school and my job are on the main bus line."

"My housemate Pete fixes cars. He'd probably look at it if you want," Wynn offered.

"That'd be great, but don't kill yourself over it. Gas is so expensive these days — almost 50 cents a gallon — I can't afford to use it much. But it's nice to have in an emergency, like child care. Thank goodness for Maria. We switch off watching each other's kids. Luckily, a counselor at the college got social services to pay for Tommy to attend a child care center 'cross the street from the school," Rachel added, bustling around with a controlled grace.

Wynn was losing himself in Rachel. God, she was beautiful. In body and spirit.

Dinner was refried beans, some chopped-up peppers, onions, cheese and tomatoes, wrapped in a tortilla and smothered with salsa. There was rice on the side and sour cream for the top.

"This is great, Rachel. Are these home made tortillas?" Wynn asked.

"Thanks," Rachel said. "I did make the tortillas. They're not too difficult. I usually make up a batch on Saturday night and keep them for the week. The tomatoes and peppers are from my garden. Haven't had much luck growing onions, though." Rachel grabbed Tommy's hand as he tried to feed his dinner to the cat.

Wynn dug into the food. "So Rachel, would you have time to go with me to talk to some neighbors about joining CAN? It's always easier if I'm with someone from the neighborhood."

"Sure. I'll take care of the dishes later. I can drop Tommy off to play with Maria's kids. It can be pretty hard to talk with the little imp running around."

****

As always, CAN's first community meeting was a rousing success. All it took was six weeks of hard work, knocking on a thousand doors, making several hundred phone calls, sending a letter to every resident and leafleting the neighborhood a few times. The real challenge would come once they started working on a major issue.

The small, neighborhood Catholic church was packed with almost eighty residents on a hot Thursday evening in early August. The overhead fans did little to cool the crowd. Father Suarez gave an opening prayer. Juan ran the meeting, giving an overview of what they hoped to accomplish that evening. He introduced Paul Cort, a tugboat captain and CAN member from Louisiana. Juan translated for him.

"CAN helped my neighborhood win better housing, improve the local school," Paul told the group. "Working with CAN, we found out that you could beat City Hall. It's time to get organized."

Paul's enthusiasm was contagious. People began to dream, to believe that the impossible was possible. The first few speakers were hesitant, and the crowd strained to hear them. But the crowd's power pushed them. They began talking faster and louder.

Several residents gave short presentations about local problems — the garbage in the riverbed, the lack of city services, people feeling ill from the pesticide spraying. When it was time for the audience to speak, the dam broke. A wave of excitement washed over the crowd, which clapped ever louder as one new problem after another was identified, until Juan called a halt. Wynn had told him to cut it off after half an hour or they'd be there all night.

"It's time to vote," Juan said. "Do you want a better neighborhood? Do you want a better life for your children? All those in favor of organizing the Southwest Phoenix Community Action Network, please stand up." The crowd rose in unison. Smiles and handshakes were everywhere

Juan was elected chairperson. Someone who was a bookkeeper was elected treasurer. Rachel was elected secretary. Several people volunteered to be block captains.

Everyone agreed to meet the following week after work at the dump with Richard Davis of the State Department of Transportation. DOT maintained a building-material site there. Their lack of oversight had turned it into a free-for-all for garbage. Wynn gave flyers about the action to everyone as they left, asking them to hand them out to their neighbors. Nearly two dozen new members joined that night or over the weekend as Wynn and the officers made follow-up visits.

An hour before the action the following Thursday, Wynn doorknocked the houses closest to the dump. "Hi. I'm Wynn. I'm with Southwest CAN, the new community group. We're meeting over at the dump with the state at 5:30 to get it cleaned up. Hope you can join us for a few minutes. The more people there, the more likely we'll get something done."

Davis arrived early. A half-dozen residents were on hand — along with a couple of crews from local TV stations. He didn't like seeing the TV. Davis was sweating before he even got out of the truck. The Salt River looked like a disaster area. Garbage, dead animals, broken glass, oil drums and barbed wire were strewn about. The smell was overpowering.

The crowd kept growing. People pulled over on their way home from work, or walked over from the nearby houses, to see what was going on. Kids drove up on their bicycles. Even the dogs came over to sniff.

Two residents who lived near the dump, Dennis Hernandez and Jerry Spalmer, served as spokespersons. "You wouldn't tolerate this in your neighborhood." "How'd you like to deal with the smell or the rats?" "We're taxpayers too. We want this cleaned up," they told Davis.

Wynn's role was to walk around the crowd, whispering in people's ears, giving them a new chant or a demand to call out. "Stop treating our neighborhood like a dump," said Linda Acosta. "Clean it up. No more excuses," cried out Joe Rodriguez.

The police arrived to check out what was going on. Davis was relieved to see the police but their arrival just riled up the neighbors even more. "Why don't you arrest the dumpers?" "Hand out tickets," they told the officers. The cops quickly retreated to the sidelines, happy to leave it to Davis to deal with.

Wynn had written five demands the organizing committee had developed on a large piece of cardboard: clean up the dump; post "No

Dumping" signs; post fines for illegal dumping; ticket violators; and, "I promise to clean up the garbage within one week." To get him to sign them, Dennis and Jerry repeatedly stuck the demands in Davis's face.

Davis made the mistake of saying, "There's no way to know who dumped here. If you catch someone doing it, give us a call or write down the license plate and we'll hold them responsible." Someone piped up, "What if we find their name on a bill or something?" Someone else called out, "Look, here's a bill. Harry Glasser, 2019 20th St. Why don't you give him a ticket?"

A dozen people started rummaging through the garbage, running back to Davis whenever they found something with a person's name or address on it. Wynn got the crowd chanting, "Clean it up. Clean it up."

Two of the television stations went live on the six o'clock newscast. "This is a really bad eyesore. No one would want it in their neighborhood. What is the State going to do to help these people?" the reporters asked, sticking a microphone in Davis' face. Davis squirmed, loosened his tie. "We'll have a state crew out here next week to clean it up. We'll put a fence up after we finish, along with 'posted' signs." The crowd cheered.

The cleanup became a neighborhood celebration. Children and grandmothers brought chairs to watch the dump trucks and front end loaders clean up the mess. They gave lemonade and cold water to the workers. They had beaten city hall for the first time.

Wynn knew that the next fight, over the spraying of pesticides, would be more difficult. The agribusiness and the chemical industries would fight back, with lots of money on the line.

****

Peter worked with the local antinuclear group trying to stop five nuclear power plants that Arizona Public Services, a private utility, planned to build forty miles south of Phoenix.

Pete told Wynn that "in case of the most serious nuclear accident — a meltdown of the reactor core, which would release radioactivity from the exposed plutonium rods — more than one million people would be at risk. Yet the plants were approved by the state Siting Board just minutes after they concluded their one and only public hearing, which lasted the grand total of three hours."

"Two of the power plants," Pete added, "will sell electricity to California. Governor Brown in Sacramento has imposed tough

Madame President   77

environmental rules. By building in Arizona, the utilities plan to get around California's regulations."

As the protests grew in Arizona Brown announced that California would hold its own hearings on the two plants. While the utilities screamed that this was illegal, they canceled the two reactors within twenty-four hours of Brown's announcement.

Emboldened by this victory, the protesters decided to organize a blockade to stop any trucks or heavy equipment from entering the site. While an environmental issue like nuclear power was not normally part of CAN's agenda, Wynn asked several local members for their opinion. While a few were interested in finding out more about the issue, several of them were members of the local steelworkers union, who were hoping to get jobs there. Wynn didn't bring the issue before the CAN citywide Board of Directors, partially afraid that they might vote to support it.

Pete had recruited Ronnie Faith to appear at a local rally the next time she was in Phoenix for a concert. The antinuclear group organized the blockade to coincide with her visit.

Pete had a few of the protesters, his affinity group, over the night before the blockade to finish painting banners and signs. The slogans were: No Nukes, Plutonium is Forever, Solar Power, Don't Poison our Bodies, and Radioactive Waste Lasts 100,000 Years. They also worked on costumes. Pete had found several WWI-type gas masks to wear, along with white plastic suits that painters wore over their clothing.

While most of the protest would be walking on a picket line, holding signs and chanting, several dozen individuals planned to sit in front of the entrance to block traffic. Those planning to get arrested divided into three affinity groups of about ten people each. They would work together as a team during the event, providing emotional support to one another and collectively making decisions in response to anything unexpected from the police or Arizona Public Service.

The affinity groups met in the basement of the local Unitarian Church a few days before the protest to get training on how to do peaceful, nonviolent civil disobedience.

"Avoid arguments with the police and workers," Pete told the group. He had been trained in civil disobedience the year before. "Be polite. Give 'em a big smile even when you're refusin' an order to move. Don't insult the cops. When they say you're under arrest, you can either get up and walk to the police van, or you can go limp and make 'em drag ya. But they may decide to bump your head against the ground if they have to drag you. Cops view goin' limp as a challenge to their authority."

Wynn agreed to serve as a legal observer, writing down what he saw, including names of police officers and company representatives. However, Wynn wasn't sure how he felt about civil disobedience as an organizing strategy.

"One of Alinsky's rules of organizing is you use tactics that community people can relate to, that you never go outside their experience," he told Pete. "Most people haven't experienced civil disobedience. I doubt community people identify with scruffy-looking protesters getting dragged away and thrown into jail. One, people think you're getting arrested for doing something wrong. Second, they're less likely to join future demonstrations 'cause they think they'll get arrested.

"Also," Wynn added, "aren't you concerned about the media just focusing on the people getting arrested and diverting attention from the other protesters? It's like the other couple of hundred people there are just invisible. Besides, why give the government and the police control over your body?" Wynn asked Pete.

Pete was surprised by Wynn's position.

"C'mon Wynn, you should see the value of putting your body on the line when somethin' is wrong. We need to bear witness. The utility companies buy off the politicians and judges. Gandhi and King used nonviolent civil disobedience all the time. We need to make people think — *If people are willing to get arrested, they must be really concerned, maybe I should take a closer look.* There's been a lotta protests where we carried signs or gave speeches. The media either ignored us or buried it in the back of the paper. While I don't wanna give the government control over my body, I sure as hell don't want 'em exposin' me and everyone else to nuclear radiation," argued Pete.

"Yeah, but at least in the civil rights movement, they made sure they had the ministers and doctors out front," Wynn countered. "Everyone tried to look as respectable as possible. And the protest was a direct action to integrate restaurants or bus stations. They confronted the opposition, pushing them to integrate. Plus, they had a couple hundred years of oppression on their side, including a Civil War, with a whole lot of protests beforehand.

"The way you do CD, it seems just a ritual, some form of religious rite. You cross over a line, the police tell you to leave, you don't, they arrest you, they bring you to jail, they fine you, you get out. You're happy and proud you got arrested, but it doesn't seem like anything has changed. Having all those protesters go doorknocking for four hours to talk to real people about why you oppose the plant, or going to the home of the CEO of the utility company to demand that he stop, that would be a lot more effective use of time," Wynn contended.

"Wynn, you've told me you're an organizer 'cause you wanna be able to tell your children that you did somethin' to oppose all the bad things goin' down," Pete responded. "Well, people bear witness, fight back, in different ways. Not everyone feels comfortable goin' up to some stranger's door and strikin' up a conversation. You organize your way, we organize our way. Every blow struck against the empire is a blow worth striking. Who knows which blow will finally cause it to topple?."

Several Native Americans slowly banged a drum as the protesters marched in front of the main gate for an hour. Cops and private security guards were everywhere. Several people stood up and spoke against the nuclear facility. Ronnie led them in singing a few peace anthems, "We Shall Overcome" and "Down By the Riverside." Ronnie's involvement brought out the media.

Unfortunately, the company had rerouted the trucks to the back entrance.

At noon, several dozen protesters sat in front of the gate. The police ignored them, since there was no traffic going in. After fifteen minutes, the members of one of the affinity groups decided to climb the fence. The crowd cheered. Several of the private security guards rushed to pull the protesters down. Guards on the other side began to hit the fence with sticks. One of the protesters fell and hurt his head on the ground. Several protesters got stuck on the top of the fence, with the guards trying to jump up to pull them down.

Things were turning ugly. The TV cameras were rolling. The crowd began chanting, "The whole world is watching", "Leave them alone", "Hey hey, ho ho, nuclear power has got to go."

The police stepped in. Two of the group's lawyers, with Wynn tailing along as legal observer, negotiated with the cops. The lawyers told the affinity groups: "If you want to get arrested, grab the fence. The cops will read a warning. If you don't leave at that point, you'll be arrested."

It took about 45 minutes to go through this routine, handcuff their arms behind their backs, and load them on an old school bus for the drive back to the county jail in Phoenix.

Once the protesters were out of public sight, the guards got surly. They refused to allow the protesters to have any water. Several requests to go to the bathroom were denied. A couple of the protesters were roughly pushed back into their seat when they complained. "No talkin'," yelled one guard. "Save it for the judge."

Personal possessions such as backpacks were confiscated and their contents scattered over the floor "to make sure there were no weapons there." Police made some derogatory comments to a couple of the women: "Are you a man or a woman? You're sure ugly enough to be a man. Guess we'll have to strip search ya when we get to jail to find out."

It took an hour to drive to the county jail. They were kept locked on the bus in an underground garage for about another forty-five minutes. When they were let out, they were forced to walk through a gauntlet of police officers, several of whom pushed the protesters from side to side, shouting "Keep walking," "Look forward," "Watch out where you're going." Treatment improved once they were inside, especially after the lawyers were able to talk to the judge.

Wynn and Steve joined several dozen activists who gathered outside the jail until all the protesters were released, occasionally singing songs and beating on drums. They went to The Dive to celebrate Pete's release.

****

Wynn and Rachel were spending considerable time together.

Rachel was the most active CAN member on the pesticide issue. She tabulated the data from the health surveys. Rachel and Maria went with Wynn to meet with the Center for Science in the Public Interest, who were already working with residents from Scottsdale.

Pete asked Wynn, "Who's this Rachel who keeps calling? Nice voice, very friendly. Why don't you bring her to one of our parties?"
"She's a CAN member, which means hands off. You gotta keep personal and work separate," he replied.

Wynn had left his first serious girlfriend when he joined CAN; he'd been slow to "discover women." CAN's 100-hour-a-week schedule didn't leave time for much of a relationship. He had certainly been attracted to several of the politically aware women who made frequent appearances at the Hostel for Wayward Youth.

Wynn slowly learned Rachel's life story.

"I grew up in Colorado, mainly around Denver. My mom's parents came over from Ireland during the 20s, headed out to Chicago where they had some relatives. My dad was a truck driver. So was his father, who grew up in Mexico but started working as a farm laborer in Texas when he was 14. My father drove a truck between Denver and the Mexican border. Home one day, gone for three, but we had fun when he was around. He got killed when I was eleven — some drunken driver pulled in front of his truck one night. We had a hard time after that.

"My mom mainly stayed home to raise me and my younger sister while my dad worked. We lost our house when he died. We had no insurance, never collected anything from the guy who killed him. We started moving all the time. My mom tried to support us by waitressing, but she got sick a lot, at least partially from depression over my dad. Then she started drinking.

"She got married again when I was fourteen. A big mistake. Harry was a loser. Got drunk a lot, always losing his job. I don't know what she saw in 'im. He used to hit my mom, sometimes me, when he was loaded. It got worse after my stepbrother was born. My mom sort of lost it. Three kids were too much for her, and Harry was no help at all.

"I wasn't the greatest kid either. By the time I was in tenth grade, I was pretty much on my own, arguing with my mom all the time, staying over at my friends' whenever I could. Especially after Harry began showing me pictures from his girlie magazines, putting his hands on me, trying to kiss me. I'd put a chair against the door of the bedroom my sister and I shared, kept a baseball bat under the bed.

"When I tried to talk to my mom, she wouldn't believe it. Harry denied it, said my sister and I misunderstood him, told us to stop parading around in front of him in skimpy clothes and bath towels. Yeah, like we'd ever do that.

"I started smoking, drinking, gettin' high, when I was 15. Hung out with guys I shouldn't have. I stopped going to class halfway through my junior year of high school, moved out permanently when I turned seventeen."

"I eventually hooked up with Danny. Danny was okay just not big on commitment, sort of a tumbleweed. But he was cute, really cute. He played guitar, wrote poetry, sang at protests against the Vietnam War, said he wanted to be a yippie like Abbie Hoffman and Jerry Rubin. He was in his twenties. Everyone loved Danny. He was the life of the party. One day he was goin' to be the next Jim Hendrix, the next day Woody Guthrie. He'd get a guitar in his hand, sing a song, you'd melt.

"He didn't believe in monogamy, which wasn't a big deal to me either, at least at first. Initially he was paying for the apartment, but that didn't last long. He wanted to concentrate on his music, couldn't waste time on these dumb jobs. He was gonna be a rock- and-roll star, and we'd be rich and live happily ever after. I got a job waitressing at this tavern he played at. We didn't have a whole lotta money, but we got by, had enough for the partying.

"Danny ended up in trouble with the law. He sometimes dealt pot on the side, you know buy a pound from someone, keep a couple ounces to party with, sell the rest to friends to cover costs. Sold some to a kid whose parents found out, made a big stink. Danny hired an attorney, beat the rap, but the cops had their eyes on him now.

"Danny decided to move to Phoenix. It's got a big music scene, and he knew someone here putting a band together. I was happy to tag along, ran home one day to pick up some things, gave my mom a hug, told her I'd write. She at least cried for a few minutes. I didn't. Danny and I moved into these two big adjoining houses with some of the guys in his band, sorta like a commune, near the outdoor amphitheater and amusement park. There's a little artist colony over there. It was pretty cool, except too many of the men expected the women to do all the housework and be into free love.

"Fortunately, a couple of strong women lived there who worked on setting them straight, starting with Starr Fire. She was way cool, into crystals and herbs and the desert. She was also a wiccan. She taught me about paganism and the goddess. There's lots of witches in Arizona, attracted by the desert and the large Native American population. Starr helps organize the Annual Witches Ball, which is a big deal around here.

"Then I got pregnant. That didn't go down well with Danny. We had a big fight over whether or not I'd have an abortion. If you asked me before I got pregnant, I would've said, get an abortion. But once I was pregnant, I sensed this life growing in me. No way was I going to terminate it. Danny wanted an abortion. I was willing to put the baby up for adoption but Danny wasn't. Said he didn't want some kid of his out there not knowing who his daddy was.

"Neither of us were interested in marriage. Heck, Danny wasn't even into the relationship. We had a few ugly scenes, very clear he was looking for an excuse to walk. After one fight, he announced he was moving to LA to pursue his music career. I could come if I wanted, but the baby was mine, he wasn't going to take any responsibility. How could he even be sure it was his? At that point I began throwing things. Some of our housemates ran into our bedroom, dragged Danny out. He left town a couple days later. I was six months pregnant.

"Starr made our housemates let me stay, even when I had to stop working and couldn't pay rent. I didn't have any medical coverage, of course, and Arizona doesn't participate in Medicaid. Starr used to drive me over to this free clinic. She also had some friends who were midwives. They taught me how to take care of my body. Getting pregnant triggered my mother gene — my baby was the only thing that mattered. I stopped partying, began to eat lots of fruits and vegetables, got into yoga.

"I had a home birth with a midwife. A bunch of Starr's friends came over. We had lots of candles, chanting music on the stereo, relaxation exercises.

"Danny actually showed up after the birth. One of our housemates called him up and yelled. He hung out for a couple of days. He occasionally sent me a few bucks but he argues that it was my decision to have this baby, not his. I just gave up on him.

"I applied for welfare a couple of weeks after the baby was born. The welfare office wasn't happy with my living arrangement, wanted to know where the dad was, and they said I had to count the income from everyone in the house, which meant I was ineligible. To qualify for some help, I moved into a small apartment in downtown Phoenix, Section 8 housing, pretty run down in a rough neighborhood. I didn't go out much.

"It was tough making a go of it. It was a miserable time, actually. Jobs paid so little, especially with my lack of education, that I wouldn't make anything at all if I put Tommy into day care. You can't believe how much they charge for infant care. Fortunately, I bumped into this caseworker who cared about me. She helped me pass the high school equivalency test, and told me how I could go to school to get a nursing degree. Of course, as soon as she helped me, they transferred my case to someone else — thought she was getting too personally involved.

"I moved to South Phoenix for the cheaper rents. I speak Spanish, at least enough to get by, so I get along fine with the neighbors. Besides, everyone loves Tommy. He has that impish smile he got from Danny. I just hope he doesn't break too many hearts when he grows up."

****

The farmers were using Bolstar, a new pesticide. The Pesticide Control Board didn't require pretesting of new pesticides. Apparently the issue of possible negative health impacts wasn't a priority for them.

Bob Masterson of the Center for Science recommended urging the farmers to adopt "integrated pest management, or IPM, where insect damage is controlled through the rotation of crops, use of beneficial insects, natural biopesticides and cover crops."

Wynn initially resisted IPM. "It's too pollyannaish for a working-class neighborhood. We should just call for it to be banned — people understand that. Talking about bugs taking care of one another is too touchy-feely."

But in later years, he would often say, "My initial opposition to advocating IPM was my one clear political mistake. It shows how the 'radical' solution almost invariably turns out to be the right one, once you study the problem and become comfortable enough to step outside the box."

Rachel invited Wynn over for another Saturday night dinner to review the testimony she and Maria would give at the Pesticide Board meeting the following week. Wynn stopped at the supermarket to buy a bottle of wine and put three dollars of gas in his car. He had sworn he would give up driving once gasoline topped the 50-cent mark.

Rachel made spaghetti, with a sauce using tomatoes, zucchini and peppers from her garden. She was wearing a low-cut Mexican blouse.

"This is great, Rachel. I like your outfit by the way; very attractive." Wynn tried not to gush. "Where's Tommy? Shouldn't we wait for him before we eat?"

"Oh, I fed him already," Rachel explained. "He's staying over at Maria's tonight, playing with Roberto. Thanks for bringing the wine. One little tip, however. It's usually a good bet to try the wine with a cork in it rather than a twist-off cap," Rachel laughed.

"Sorry. I don't buy wine all that much," Wynn said sheepishly.

After catching up on the news about Bolstar, the conversation took a more personal bent.

"What's it like being a black organizer?" Rachel asked. "Like, how do people respond in some all-white working-class neighborhood?"

"Results are what people want to see from an organizer," Wynn said. "Race isn't an issue for the members. People who get active in CAN are interested in fighting the system. They'll take any allies they can find.

"Doorknocking can sometimes be tough, though," Wynn admitted, "especially the first few days, before you get the feel of a new neighborhood. You sometimes run into a jerk that threatens you with a shotgun or sets the dog on you. You learn to look for a few telltale signs, like multiple confederate flags on their truck. But most racists you meet on the doors just shut down. They make it pretty clear they want to you to leave. Occasionally they'll call the cops, report that some guy's casing the neighborhood. It's worse after dark. A lot of older white people don't want to open the door, let alone see a strange black person standing there."

"Don't people blame blacks for ruining their neighborhoods?" asked Rachel. "I hear that kinda talk all the time at the supermarket. Both about blacks and Chicanos. That they're taking over the neighborhood, just throwing trash around and playing music too loud. That they're tenants and don't care about anything."

"Well," Wynn laughed, "they avoid making those comments to me. Except about the tenants. You've got lots of neighborhoods where the only whites left are seniors who can't sell their houses. But if they do complain, they always make sure to say they know someone of color who's hard working."

"Race can become an issue when you confront the target," he added. "They're looking for any way to fight back, any way to isolate the organizer. Race is an easy way to try.

"To tell you the truth, racism tends to be more of a problem when I step outside my role as an organizer. A person of color in America is always conscious of race, while most of my white friends never think about it," Wynn observed. "But I'm sure you know that."

Wynn twirled his spaghetti with his fork. Rachel cringed when she saw the amount of cheese and hot pepper he added. "Don't you even bother to taste it first?" she asked incredulously.

"No need to," Wynn replied. "Always need more cheese, more hot spices. Load it up first, then see how much more you need. Saves time."

Rachel's hand found his as he reached for the bread. "So, tell me Wynn, what do you do for a social life? Found anyone special since you moved out here?" she said coyly, her face beautiful in the candlelight.

Wynn gulped down some wine.

"Kinda hard to have much of a social life with the hours we keep at CAN. I usually just have Saturday night and Sunday morning off. Hang out with my housemates, Pete and Steve."

"Well, it's good to hear you have some boys to hang out with," Rachel remarked, brushing his arm, looking into his eyes. "Ever hang out with women?" she purred.

Wynn moved his arm to grab his glass. "Not recently. Relationships require more time than CAN allows."

"But you don't have any objections to having a relationship with a woman?" Rachel asked, her eyes sparkling. "That's good to hear."

Rachel got up from the table. "Why don't you come into the living room?" she called over her shoulder. "A friend of mine lent me a new record I'd like you to hear. Can you bring the wine? Thanks."

The curtains were drawn in the living room. Wynn had assumed that was to keep the hot sun out. Now he realized it gave a cozy, intimate feel. Rachel lit several more candles, along with a stick of incense. She sat back on the couch and patted the cushion next to her for Wynn to sit on.

Wynn sat down, a little awkwardly, in the far corner.

Rachel leaned over, gently giving him a kiss. Wynn returned the kiss with passion, his body on fire. Then just as suddenly, Wynn came up for air.

"Rachel, we need to talk," Wynn managed to get out.

"Are you sure? I can think of a few things I'd rather do right now." Rachel began to lean over Wynn again. Wynn put his hands up to hold her back. Half-heartedly.

Rachel pulled back. "What's the matter? Is this too fast? Is it Tommy? The race thing?" She smiled, dismissing those possibilities. "Want a different album? Want me to put on something different?" she almost leered.

Wynn was conflicted. He knew he needed to slow it down but he wasn't sure he wanted to stop it.

"It has nothing to do with you. Or with Tommy. He's a great kid," said Wynn, trying not to piss off a woman he was falling in love with.

"CAN has strict rules," Wynn told her, "against getting involved with members. We're told from day one to avoid partying with members, to avoid smoking pot with them, and most of all, to avoid, er, um, climbing in bed with them. There's an old joke that you could tell who the welfare rights organizer was sleeping with by the women who showed up at the meeting. It isn't a very good joke. Rachel, I like you a lot, but there's a line here we shouldn't cross," Wynn said, as gently as he knew how.

Rachel sat back and studied him. "Wynn, I like you a lot too. I'd like to get to know you a whole lot better. You're bright, you're good-looking, though you need some meat on those bones of yours, and you work hard. You treat people with respect, you want to change the world, and you're the most fanatically responsible person I've ever met. And most of all, Tommy likes you, which is critical to me.

"I confess — I look forward to hearing your voice on the phone,"

Rachel told him, folding her legs underneath her. "Hey, I'm not looking for a life-long commitment from you. But I'd like to explore a relationship with you."

Wynn lean over and kissed her, gave her a long hug.

"I'm sorry," he said. "The last thing I want to do is to hurt you, or Tommy. But there's a reason why organizers aren't suppose to have a relationship with the people we organize. We come into a neighborhood, we create a lot of noise and excitement, we pay a lot of attention to people because we're tying to get them involved. Organizers by nature are seducers. But we have to separate the professional from the personal."

Wynn took her hands. Looking into her eyes, he told her, "When you have a relationship with a member, other people in the community being to wonder if you are just an alley cat on the prowl. It can change the dynamics of the group if the staff goes out with a member, especially someone who is a leader. People begin to wonder whether you're doing something because it's in the best interest of the neighborhood or because you want to sleep with someone."

Rachel got up to flip the record. She poured herself another glass of wine. Wynn declined her offer of a refill.

"I dunno what to say," Rachel said, frowning. "I certainly wasn't expecting to be talkin' about CAN's rules rather than about you and me. Could we do that for just a few minutes, Wynn?" she pleaded. "Let's pretend we're just two normal people, chilling out, groovin' on each other, whatever, drinking some wine, hoping for a back rub, maybe something more? Can ya forget about CAN for a moment, Wynn, and tell me what *you* feel?" Rachel implored. "Take the protective armor off for a sec?"

Wynn let out a deep sigh. He started to speak, then stopped. He kissed her hand, then brushed her lips and looked into her eyes. "What I see is a beautiful woman. A wonderful mother. I see someone who I respect and care a lot about. I can't believe I'm even hesitating here. I see someone who cares about others, who wins everyone's trust, who is able to laugh and enjoy life, all those things that are a struggle for me," Wynn said. "But I need a time-out here. This is a problem for my work with CAN. I don't want to betray their trust."

Rachel jumped on top of him, and began to plant kisses on his neck and earlobes. She sat up, with her knees straddling his hips, laughing. "Oh, I just love men who play hard to get. You've got to learn how to follow your heart once in a while, not always your head. Wynn, are you going to let CAN control your whole life, for what, less than 70 bucks a week? Jesus. Wynn, you make them sound like the Moonies or something, can't do anything without asking permission. Yeah sure, there are reasons for rules, and I'm glad to hear that you are committed to not using your incredible organizing skills to seduce every lonely woman in the neighborhood. But rules are made to be broken." She resumed kissing him.

Wynn extracted himself from underneath Rachel. "All good points," he said, breathing heavily. "But I still need time to think about this. And seriously, you need to think about what it means to have a relationship with me. CAN moves its people around quite a bit. There's no guarantee how long I'm going to be in Arizona.

"Let's say this was a wonderful evening, and plan to do something social next weekend," Wynn suggested. "Pete and Steve have been after me to go tubing. I'll play hooky next Sunday. You can bring Tommy if you want. It's safe from what I hear."

Rachel laughed. "Great. A date with chaperones and my son. How romantic."

"Hey, you're the one who brought me here under false pretenses. Where's that testimony we're supposed to be going over," Wynn asked, trying to move on as gracefully as he could.

FIVE

LAYING A PRESIDENT TO REST

A few days after her interrogation of the head of the Secret Service, Rachel asked Wynn to join her when she received the report from Sophie about the woman who had been with Harrington.

"Marshall took a leave of absence from her job at Noventis," Sophie reported. "Many people at work knew that she had a long-standing special relationship with Harrington, even if they didn't know it was sexual, so they assumed her leave was just part of the grieving over losing a close friend."

"The FBI found Paula holed up at a lake cottage that her family owns," Sophie continued. "She was quite messed up, drinking heavily. She talked pretty freely. Apparently needed to confess to someone. Said she'd been expecting someone to show up, assumed that the doctors would've found out right away that there was more to the story."

"So what did she have to say?" asked Rachel.

"It gets a little strange," Sophie said. "She'd pleaded with Harrington to see her. She was upset that he'd been avoiding her. She claimed she understood the reality of him being president, thought she'd be able to handle it, but she cared for him more than she realized. She decided to spice things up with a new wonder drug that Noventis was developing to increase sexual pleasure for both men and women — sort of a his-and-hers Viagra. Something to do with hormones."

Noventis had interests in pharmaceuticals, medicine, animal health, and bio and genetic engineering. It was one of the multinational companies trying to corner the market on life sciences, the "new industrial revolution." In the 20th century, fossil fuels had driven industrialization. In the 21st century, genes would be the new raw resource.

Noventis viewed genes as mere building blocks that could be transplanted from one species to another to achieve results that nature could not — or would not — produce. Noventis wants to sell you genetically engineered drugs to go to sleep, reduce anxiety, provide sexual stimulation, lose weight, reverse hair loss, and provide "cures" for a long list of real or imagined ills.

"How's it supposed to work?" asked Rachel.

"It has something to do with hormones. The woman takes the drug.

In a couple of hours, it causes her to secrete some 'love chemical' in her vagina. The man absorbs it through his penis, and away they go to sexual heaven. She hoped a great time in bed might rekindle the fire in their relationship," Sophie said.

"This thing been approved by the FDA?" asked Wynn. "I've never heard of it."

"Not yet," said Sophie. "It's still experimental. It's been under development for a couple of years, gone through some initial testing, including on humans. Noventis is still trying to figure out the health impacts on women. For men, they're convinced it acts pretty much like Viagra."

"Marshall claims she disclosed to Harrington that she was using a new sex drug, but it seemed like they were already into it really heavy before she tried to mention it. She was also really aroused from the drug, so her focus was on having sex, not talking. She said Harrington cut her off when she began to give him a clinical description of the drug, which would have included what the medical warnings were. This wasn't the first time she'd brought, er, a little something extra to their sex play. Harrington apparently enjoyed it kinky," Sophie continued.

"So what went wrong?" Rachel asked.

"Marshall doesn't know. As far as she could tell the drug worked like it was supposed to, though she hadn't used it before. His hard-on was noticeably stronger. He came pretty quickly but kept right on going. Suddenly, he took a deep breath, grabbed his heart and keeled over. From there her story pretty much matches what we've heard from Thompson."

Sophie continued. "Just like Viagra, someone with a heart condition shouldn't use the drug. Maybe Harrington had a heart problem that he wasn't aware of, or he'd kept it secret, didn't want it to hurt his campaign. Though who knows what other unexpected reactions he might have had?"

"What did she say the company's role was in all this?" Wynn interjected.

"She claims they didn't know she was planning to use the drug. It's still in the testing stage, though they were gonna submit it for FDA approval shortly. She was friendly with one of the researchers who gave her a sample, actually gave her a form to fill out to report on her experience. 'Enjoy,' she was told.

Rachel paced around the room. "So let's see if I understand the situation," she said incredulously. "We have a top executive of a Fortune

500 company, a top campaign fundraiser, committing adultery with the president, using him as a guinea pig for their new sex wonder drug — and no one bothers investigating. In addition to the usual motives for killing in an adulterous relationship, we have motives such as getting a favorable ruling from the FDA on this new sex toy, or government contracts or appointments or who knows what."

Rachel dissected the situation even further. "She claims she gave the president notice of the experimental drug, but he waived disclosure of the medical warnings. We don't know whether the heart attack was a preexisting condition that was covered up, was caused by the sex, was caused by the drug, or was caused by Harrington suddenly remembering the phone call he needed to make to the Russian president or his wife's birthday. The president's chief of staff and the head of the Secret Service then conspire to cover up the details of his death. Am I missing anything?" Rachel almost shouted.

"Just that, as far as we know, his wife doesn't know about any of this, starting with Marshall," Sophie reminded her.

They all pondered this tidbit for a few moments.

"So what do we do?" Sophie asked, breaking the silence. "If we go public with this, we'll destroy Harrington's reputation, humiliate his wife, initiate a criminal investigation of Marshall and possibly Noventis, the president's chief of staff and the Secret Service. We'll probably also throw the religious right and the Republicans into a feeding frenzy over the White House being a den of iniquity and fornication," Sophie noted.

Wynn jumped in. "I don't see how we can avoid going public. You've hit the nail on the head. A Fortune 500 company may have killed the president. It's not our responsibility to protect adulterers from the consequences of their actions. Let's not forget that the person who benefits most from Harrington's death is you. If this information comes out later and we're not the ones who released it, you'll be at the center of god knows how many conspiracy theories and charges of a cover-up. I know you feel some loyalty to Harrington and don't want to embarrass his wife, but this isn't our problem or our scandal. Let's not make it ours."

Sophie agreed. "We can get the information out without tying it to you. We can make it the Secret Service, FBI's or even the DC police's problem. But we can't sit on this. We don't want to let someone possibly get away with murder and we don't want anyone else dying from this drug," Sophie argued.

Wynn added, "We also don't know anything about what kinda

hocus-pocus they used to create this drug. There's a damn good chance it involved genetic engineering, knowing Noventis."

Rachel wasn't ready to make a decision yet.

"I need to talk to Mrs. Harrington," she said. " I hear what you're saying, but I don't want the political concerns to overwhelm the personal. The bottom line is that a man cheated on his wife and apparently died from it. It happens all the time; the only difference here is that it took place in the White House. The wife, as usual, is the biggest victim, left to clean up the mess."

At least she's still alive, Wynn thought.

Then Rachel shocked Wynn and Sophie. "Maybe this is the chicken way out, but I'd like her to make the call on this," she announced.

****

The meeting with Mrs. Harrington was brief.

Rachel struggled to find the right words. She couldn't think of a way to sugarcoat it.

"I'm sorry to have to tell you this Patty, but we've uncovered some new details about your husband's heart attack." Mrs. Harrington visibly steeled herself. "Some of it won't be easy to hear. I've never wanted any harm to come to Phil or you," Rachel said, her voice beginning to crack.

"There are some tough decisions to be made. I think you and the public have a right to hear it. But it's your call. I can do my best to keep it under wraps. If you prefer, I don't even have to tell you," Rachel said.

Mrs. Harrington tried to compose herself. She wanted to trust Rachel, but she felt like she was in the center of a dark storm, leery of everything that was swirling around her. She dreaded hearing which of her deepest fears were about to be confirmed.

"You'd better tell me," she sighed finally.

"We don't know everything yet," began Rachel, "but your husband was intimate with another woman when he had the heart attack. The woman was using an experimental drug that may have caused the heart attack, especially if he already had a heart problem. To find out for sure would require additional tests. It may be possible, but unlikely, to keep the details hidden. Your husband's chief of staff and the Secret Service decided to keep this information secret. There are possible criminal charges against the woman and others. I want you to decide what to do with this information. I will abide by any decision you make. I'm sorry."

Rachel began to weep. Mrs. Harrington sat in stony, stunned silence for a few minutes. She eventually asked, "Who was the woman?"

"Paula Marshall."

Mrs. Harrington nodded, biting her lip. "I knew that Phil had been seeing other women, including Paula, in recent years." Rachel exhaled with relief that Mrs. Harrington already knew. "You put up with it for the sake of the children. Oh, you try to fool yourself that it's the pressure of politics, that he needs someone to tell him how great he is, that he's away from home a lot, that it doesn't mean anything. But it always meant something to me, even when I tried to pretend I didn't see it."

"I read him the riot act last year," she said bitterly, "told him that he couldn't continue, that he was risking too much, not just for me and our family, but for his own career. I thought that being president would be enough of an ego boost. Looks like I was wrong."

Mrs. Harrington let out a deep sigh, pausing to wipe some tears. "But through it all I've never stopped loving him," Mrs. Harrington said, her heart breaking. "And I don't think he ever stopped loving me. Really, I believe that. When he turned his attention to you, it was wonderful. I was just hoping that I would have him again once his term was finished."

Rachel asked softly, "Do you know if your husband had a heart problem?"

Mrs. Harrington nodded her head. "The doctors couldn't agree on how serious it was. He fainted one time — dismissed it as exhaustion combined with the flu. His doctor wanted to conduct more extensive tests, possibly put him on medication, but Phil was never one for doctors. I don't think it was as much trying to hide it from the public as trying to hide it from himself. He said when his time came it would come, there was nothing he could do about it," she said. "In many ways he was such a vain man, never wanting to acknowledge any weakness or need."

Rachel spent some time outlining the various scenarios she saw to handle the situation. She offered Mrs. Harrington words of encouragement and support when she left, along with one departing piece of advice: "Please remember that confronting the truth is usually a necessary step in the healing process." She hoped it didn't sound too condescending but it was a hard-earned lesson from her own life.

The following evening, Mrs. Harrington decided to remove the life support from the president. She gathered the family together for a last visit before the plug was pulled. He was officially pronounced dead an hour later.

Mrs. Harrington alerted Rachel that she was going to inform the authorities about the true circumstances of her husband's attack.

The funeral was presidential but subdued. Mrs. Harrington knew that a firestorm would hit shortly, so she reined in as much of the pageantry as she could.

Many world leaders complained about not having enough time to make preparations to attend. They all wanted the opportunity to size up Rachel and get a few minutes alone to press their favorite causes. Rachel reciprocated by exchanging with as many dignitaries as possible a few words about holding a People's Summit in conjunction with the upcoming WTO meeting. Most evaded responding, offering safe words of condolence instead. She told them that she or Wynn would follow up.

The State Department sought to overwhelm her with the protocols of diplomacy required to receive so many heads of state. Rachel delegated it all to Sophie to keep straight. "Just tell me where I'm supposed to stand and what I'm supposed to do at what time. Make sure they keep it simple. Tell them they're going to have to get used to my style. First and foremost, we are burying someone. The rest will sort itself out."

Wearing a black dress that came well below her knees, Rachel kept her remarks at the funeral brief, speaking as much to Mrs. Harrington as to the country. She tried to prepare them for coming revelations, speaking of "the frailty of all humans, of the need to embrace both the strengths and weaknesses of each of us that make us unique individuals." She included a few personal stories about Harrington from some of his old friends and mentors, stories that illustrated his concern for the well-being of others and the love he had for his family and country.

Mrs. Harrington had decided to bury her husband in the private cemetery on her family's estate.

****

Rachel arranged to have Senator Deutsche join her and Wynn for the ride over to Andrews Air Force Base to see Harrington's casket loaded onto Air Force One for the flight home to California. The internment was for family members only, so Rachel wouldn't be attending.

"Jonathan, thank you for joining us," Rachel said as he entered the limousine. "It's a sad day."

"Yes. Harrington was a good man. I knew him for more than twenty-five years. A great loss. I appreciated the graciousness of your remarks and I know a lot of Harrington's friends and colleagues did as well," Deutsche said. He had served as one of the honorary pallbearers.

Rachel held Wynn's hand as she looked out at the solemn crowds along the roadside paying their final respects.

"Jonathan, there may be some additional news about the president's death in the next few days, depending upon how Patty decides to handle it," Rachel paused. "It could be awkward for a number of people, including Hughes."

She had the Majority Leader's full attention now. He raised his eyebrows, eager for more information.

"Rachel, what exactly are you talking about?" said Jonathan suspiciously, glancing over at Wynn.

"As I said, I'm leaving it up to Patty to decide how to deal with this. I have no desire to harm Phil's memory," Rachel responded.

"What are you talking about?" Deutsche asked impatiently.

"I'm not," said Rachel. "You'll have to ask Patty for the details, but I would leave her alone at the moment. I just feel I owe you a heads-up. I hope that I can work with you and the other Congressional leaders to reassure the public that there is no crisis. In fact, I would like you to consider becoming my vice-president. It'd maintain the Democrat-Green alliance that Harrington put together, and give a sense of stability to the country. There's a lot that we can accomplish together."

The offer was not as dangerous a gambit as it appeared. It was highly unlikely that Deutsche would trade the power of senate Majority Leader for the political limbo of the vice-presidency, especially to play second fiddle to Rachel. However, by making the offer and having it rejected, she'd now have a lot more freedom in finding a second choice.

Deutsche looked like he'd been hit by a one-two combination.

"Well," he said cautiously, "it's not every day that someone asks me to be vice-president, so let me thank you for the offer. My initial reaction would be to decline, but I'm very troubled by what you're saying about the president's death. I'd certainly need to find out far more before I or the Democratic Party can figure out what our next steps are," said Deutsche.

Deutsche decided to give an old effort one last try. "Rachel, you could solve a lot of our mutual problems if you became a Democrat," he propositioned. "It would be very healing for the country. You could create a green caucus within the Democrats if you want. This would settle things down for the voters — they understand the two-party system. You'd be able to move forward with your agenda as part of the majority party."

Rachel could feel that Wynn was about to speak, and placed her hand on his knee to calm him.

"Jonathan, you gave me the courtesy of not rejecting my offer out of hand, and I'll do the same. But the Green Party is here to stay. It's certainly larger than one individual, and personally I think is the party of the future in America. We've had this conversation before, so I won't repeat it. I'll focus instead on the fact that you are willing to look for ways for us as individuals, and as representatives of our parties, to work together. Why don't we give each other some time to think about it?" Rachel suggested.

The limousine pulled up in front of Air Force One. They all got out to pay their final respects.

****

Deutsche decided to ride back with some of the other Senate Democrats to update them on his conversation with Rachel. Wynn could hardly wait to get her back into the limousine.

"You're not serious about joining the Democratic Party?" Wynn blurted out. Rachel leaned over and gave him a quick kiss on the lips, then a longer hug. She smiled at him. "Calm down, boy. No, I'm not thinking about jumping ship. But I have to treat his offer respectfully if I expect him to seriously consider working with me and the Greens."

They turned to the VP nomination. "So, now that's out of the way, who *are* you going to get for VP? I'm sure the Greens want to name someone," Wynn stated, loosening his tie. Rachel loved the way he looked in a three-piece suit. She seldom managed to get him into one.

"Well, I've got my wish list for Santa too," said Rachel sarcastically. "The Greens unfortunately don't control the Senate, which has to confirm the nominee. I should at least offer it to Barry, but he'll just laugh. He knows his nomination is DOA."

"So what are you thinking?" asked Wynn.

"Why don't we tell the Greens we need two lists? One, their wish list, which we'll ignore, the other with candidates who actually have a chance of being approved. Remind them that the VP slot is the most powerful tool we have to broaden our political base. What we need is someone who can fracture the Democratic Party a bit, while pulling in a base of independents. We need to get some political power on our side. It probably has to be someone in Congress, maybe the head of one of the big unions," Rachel stated.

She then added: "I don't want someone who I have to worry about stabbing me in the back. Or someone who just wants to use the next three years to position themselves for their own run for president."

One of Wynn's suggestions was Michael Clark, the congressman from Atlanta. Back in 1984, when Wynn was helping the Citizens Party, Clark had given serious consideration to running on their national ticket. But that was before he was elected to Congress as a Democrat.

"Clark was one of the leaders of the Student Non-Violent Coordinating Committee during the civil rights movement," Wynn observed. "He's been one of the most progressive members of Congress, so the unions and activist groups will be on board. Or you could pick George Lowell, the former editor of the *Texas Observer*. Don't forget, he was elected for a few terms as Secretary of Agriculture in Texas, so he knows how to play politics," he added. "But he's probably too independent to have much support with the Democrats."

Lowell was noted for his quick-witted populism and had been at the top of the dream list for the Green Party in the last few elections. He'd actively campaigned for Frost and Rachel.

Linda Perez of the United Farm Workers was also on the short list. She had a lot of support among labor and progressives, as well as with the Hispanic community. Then there was John Mumfi, former head of the Urban League, who was now in Congress.

****

Many of the leaders of the Fair Trade movement who were challenging the growing power of multinational corporations were skeptical of the People's Summit, viewing it as diverting energy from protests.

"Sure, the Green Party is better than the Republocrats," Kristina Roberts of the Global Fair Trade Movement told Wynn when he stopped by her office to pitch the idea. "But the Greens are still politicians, as you yourself have complained to me. Remember whom you're talking to, honey. Politicians love to hold conferences and pass resolutions while the real decisions get made behind by closed doors with the special interests."

Kristina and Wynn had been an item for a while when Wynn had

thought long and hard about these issues and have pretty detailed proposals. It's our job to try to reconcile the conflicting positions. Our world is changing at an incredible rate. We need new rules, and those rules can't be written by just a handful of large corporations," Rachel argued.

The Prime Minister remained unconvinced.

****

Immediately following the interment of her husband, Mrs. Harrington locked herself in her house and gathered her family close to tell them the news.

She'd held a brief meeting with law enforcement officials shortly after Harrington was declared dead. She gave them twenty-four hours to conduct additional tests on the body before the funeral. Though the hospital had already performed an autopsy, the FBI brought in a new set of doctors to do another examination and preserve whatever samples they thought they needed. The FBI complained about the rush; Sophie told them to comply. She also gave them a list of tests to perform.

The FBI managed to keep the news of their investigation quiet for almost a week. When the press finally got hold of the story, the White House held a briefing to discuss what Rachel had known.

"The president is saddened by these circumstances, but believes it shouldn't overshadow the accomplishments and life of Mr. Harrington," began Paul Johnson, the White House Press Secretary. "When the president became aware of some inconsistencies in the reports, she brought it to the attention of the Secret Service and then to Mrs. Harrington, who then brought the information to the FBI. Since this matter is being handled by the Justice Department, President Moreno intends to allow them to do their work while she does hers. She is aware, however, that a number of mistakes were made by the government's security forces, and her administration will take decisive corrective action."

Johnson had worked closely with Wynn in coordinating media for the anti-apartheid coalition, and until recently had served as press liaison for the mayor's office in DC.

The tabloids and the internet had a field day, identifying various women as Harrington's mistresses, and creating conspiracies involving Rachel, the Soviet Union, China, Iran, the Greens and the drug companies.

The doctors said the relationship between the drug and Harrington's heart attack might never be conclusively established.

Since one of the principals was dead and unable to clarify what type of warning was provided, with Mrs. Harrington's consent Marshall pled guilty six months later to unauthorized use of a drug, receiving a sentence of two to four years. She eventually served a little over a year with time off for good behavior.

The Justice Department initiated an investigation of Noventis to determine whether they were criminally negligent for allowing an untested drug to be used outside of the laboratory. The FDA fined them 3.21 million dollars.

A number of the Secret Service staff were forced to resign. Others from the White House detail were reassigned.

Hughes, Harrington's chief of staff, eventually pled guilty to obstruction of justice, but was let off with a fine rather than jail time. His license to practice law was revoked. He went home to write his memoir.

Rachel found new leadership for the Secret Service.

****

Rachel held her second nationally televised press conference September 5, the Wednesday after Labor Day, to respond to Harrington's burial and the subsequent revelations. The Democrats had surrendered on the issue of succession, not that they had much choice: the polls had swung strongly behind her.

She devoted most of her opening statement to her first major domestic initiative, universal healthcare, the culmination of decades of work. She didn't expect much action anytime soon from Congress, but she'd waited a longtime to put this issue on the table. The Oval Office was overflowing with flowers of congratulations sent by former colleagues.

"Good evening," Rachel said. "Tonight I want to focus on an issue that was key to both President Harrington and me — ensuring that *all* Americans have access to affordable, quality healthcare. I can think of no better legacy to President Harrington than to break the gridlock on healthcare.

"But first, I know that many Americans are concerned about recent stories concerning President Harrington's death. President Harrington was a good man," Rachel continued, "someone who sought to serve his country as well as he could. Like all of us, President Harrington made mistakes. But I hope we will remember his lifelong dedication to public service and his love for our country. I hope you will continue to include him and his family in your prayers.

"One of my first steps as president will be to ask Congress to work with me to make healthcare a right for all Americans.

"This is one issue where most of our citizens agree on the ultimate goal but disagree on how to get there. I have here the universal healthcare card that President Clinton held up to the nation nearly eight years ago. Unfortunately, missing from that discussion was a single-payer healthcare system. We won't make the same mistake this time. No other country has this patchwork of thousands of private insurance companies with conflicting forms, paperwork and bloated bureaucracy. The profit margins of these private insurance companies also greatly increase the costs of our healthcare system.

"We pay far more per capita for healthcare than any other country while still leaving more than 43 million Americans uninsured. We need to eliminate this wasteful system of private health insurance so we can free up the hundreds of billions of dollars that will allow us to expand healthcare coverage. Healthcare should be the right of all Americans, not just another commodity bought and sold on Wall Street.

"A single-payer healthcare system does *not* mean that the government will be telling you who will provide your healthcare. Our healthcare program must guarantee people the right to choose among qualified providers. Single-payer simply means one program pays all bills.

"We also need our healthcare system to focus on keeping us healthy, to focus on prevention rather than trying to cure us after we're sick. This is the main reason why our country's healthcare system doesn't even rank in the top thirty among *all* countries for quality.

"Now, many of our friends and neighbors who work for these private health insurance companies are undoubtedly concerned about job security. I will ask Congress to support a full employment act for those presently working for private health insurance companies, guaranteeing them a job at their present pay for at least three years as we make the transition to a new system. We will provide them with the education and training they need to qualify for other jobs.

"At this point, I will be glad to take a few questions," Rachel concluded. She pointed at a matronly woman seated up front. "Yes, Mrs. Weinstein from AP."

Mrs. Weinstein was the dean of White House reporters, and traditionally was given the first question. "President Moreno, could you outline for us your own role in uncovering the details of President Harrington's death? Do you have any evidence of a conspiracy to murder President Harrington, and are you worried about threats to your own life?" asked Mrs. Weinstein.

"What I know has already been made public. I've been asked by the various law enforcement agencies involved not to comment further publicly while the investigation goes forward. I have no reason to believe that it is other than what we have learned so far," Rachel replied.

"Certainly I am concerned about the possible role of a drug — not yet approved by the FDA — being used on the president, or any other American. I have initiated a thorough investigation of this process. I have also called upon the USDA to review its procedures with respect to approval of permitting genetically engineered foods and other products, and have asked them to impose a six-month moratorium, renewable if necessary, to complete their review," Rachel added.

"Madame President, a follow-up, please. You've mentioned your plans for a unity government several times. A number of leading Democrats have said that unity could best be achieved if you allowed them to select the VP. One name mentioned is Secretary Darling. Any thoughts on that?" Mrs. Weinstein inquired.

"I have consulted the Democrats about a replacement. I am sorry that Senator Deutsche declined my offer, feeling that he could best serve the country in his present position. I hope to be able to let you know about my selection in the near future," Rachel responded.

She took a series of questions about her Blueprint for America, the recent hostage crisis in Nigeria and her relations with the business community. She gave the last question to Jim Diamond of *USA Today*.

"Madame President, haven't the American people already rejected universal healthcare? Hillary Clinton's proposals didn't go over very well with the American public. And aren't you worried that single-payer will be attacked as socialism?" asked Diamond.

"I never worry much about what names people use. I worry more about the substance and results. We guarantee every senior citizen some help when they retire. We call it Social Security and Medicare. Is that socialism? The question is, do we want to provide quality, affordable healthcare to every American? The polls show that the answer to that question is a resounding *yes*. Will it be easy to fashion a program that makes everyone happy? No," Rachel responded.

"I believe that the problem with Mrs. Clinton's approach was that she focused too much on keeping the insurance companies and hospitals and the big money players happy. I am going to focus on how to provide healthcare to everyone at an affordable price. The big money players will be able to figure out how to extract their share of the pot no matter how we put it together. I want to figure out how we ensure that the little people get what they deserve."

"Thank you."

As she turned and strode off the podium, Rachel was relieved that her first news conference as president was behind her, with no apparent blunders.

SIX

TUBING DOWN THE CREEK

They needed two cars and a truck to cart the dozen people out to the creek. Wynn and Pete picked up Rachel and Tommy in the biodiesel truck. They rented inner tubes from a roadside stand, picking up a small tube and lifejacket for Tommy.

Though October was a little late in the year for tubing, the temperature was in the high eighties. They parked Steve's car several miles below the launch site. The first to arrive would drive back to pick up the other vehicles.

The river was shallow, barely three feet in most places, though occasionally there were deeper swimming holes. The water was warm from being heated all summer. The beer cooler got its own tube.

It took three hours to float the two miles to the car. They laid back on the tubes looking up at the clouds and drinking beer — with the occasional effort to tumble someone out. There were two other women besides Rachel. Rachel was dressed in a one-piece bathing suit; she removed off her cutoff shorts before they got into the water. Wynn wore shorts and a T-shirt.

Pete leaned over to whisper in his ear. "Hey man, I dunno, but those legs need *somethin'*. Some sun maybe?" Wynn shoved him away.

Tubing was a great excuse for some serious handholding and touching.

"So Rachel, whaddya want to do with your life?" Wynn asked expansively, a beer in his hand, his feet, butt and elbows dragging through the water.

"I want a better life for Tommy, of course," Rachel replied, rubbing her son's head playfully. Tommy peered over the side of the tube, trying to see fish. They had to find a new game for him every ten minutes or so.

"I wanna get my nursing degree and find a good-paying job. In a few years, I'd like to be able to rent a nice house, with a big backyard for my garden and for Tommy. In a better school system," she said.

"I'd also like to get to the point financially where I don't have a nervous breakdown when the car breaks down or one of us has to go to the doctor. Where I don't have to scrimp on food to pay the rent and utility bill."

"Ever think about having more kids?" Wynn asked. "Getting married?"

"Oh, so now you're asking the big ones," Rachel said teasingly. "Well," she drawled, "I love kids, but it's hard being a single parent. And it's tough 'nough scrapin' up the dough to take care of Tommy, let alone a second child."

Rachel dragged her hand through the water. "I also look around my neighborhood, and see these mothers with three, four, even more kids. I dunno know how they do it. There's always a child implanted on their hip.

"As for marriage," Rachel continued, "you can rest assured that's not somethin' I'm out looking for. Marriage has a habit of turning women into second-class citizens. I sure as hell wasn't impressed by my mom's marriages, especially the second one — or by any of her friends'. Seems like relationships change a lot when people get married. You start taking each other for granted. I don't want to be owned by some guy. Too many men treat their wives as the unpaid servant. 'Give me sex when I'm horny.' Danny was bad that way. I think a couple should stay together 'cause they love one another, not 'cause of a piece of paper."

Tommy was getting restless again. Rachel had brought a rubber duck and boat for him to play with. He wanted to jump out of the tube. They pulled over to a sandy beach so the boy could build a sand castle and splash in the water. Wynn told the others they'd catch up. Pete said they'd wait down river a bit — give both groups some personal space. Tommy was cramping their partying. Time to fire up.

"What about you Wynn? What do you want out of life? Besides the revolution, of course?" Rachel teased as she sat watching Tommy. "Do kids and marriage fit into the equation?"

Wynn thought for a moment. "I'm not as negative about marriage as you are. My mom and dad have a good relationship. They like and respect each other. I like kids, I certainly like Tommy, but there are already a lot of them out there, especially poor ones. I don't feel a need to bring another one into this world.

"Kids are what tear my heart out when I do," Wynn said, surprising Rachel. "You can see their whole future in front of you — you just look at their older siblings. You see them when they're little, especially when they're seven or eight, loving school, looking for any opportunity to ride their bike. They're bright and talkative, excited about life. They run up to see if I've got any leaflets to hand out," Wynn observed.

"Then you see their brothers and sisters who are ten to fifteen.

They're supposed to do their homework in a small, two-bedroom apartment crammed with half a dozen people or more, TV in the corner always on, like some Big Brother. They don't smile as often. And then you see their older siblings, teenagers, droppin' out of school, beaten down, thinkin' they got no future. Having babies, hustlin', being stupid, walking around with all this anger built up inside," Wynn said, not trying to hide his bitterness.

"You organize to rescue these kids, but at times it seems so hopeless," Wynn added. "They're living in these run-down places. The cold wind just blasts through the walls, and all they've got for warmth is an old, decrepit gas heater that looks like it's gonna blow up if the fumes don't kill 'em first. And you know that most people, especially the politicians, have no idea how difficult it is for a lot of people to keep their head above water."

Rachel leaned over her and kissed Wynn, making sure Tommy wasn't looking. "What do you want for you?" she asked.

"Me?" Wynn said, hoping for more kisses, laughing, trying to forget he worked for CAN. "I'm just a pebble cast into the ocean, sending out little circles that die out in a few feet. Sometimes I think I'll organize either till I drop or change the world. Other times, I just wanna climb up a mountain, get away, grow a little food, listen to music and watch the clouds drift by.

"In high school I read about Jean-Paul Sartre, the existentialist. He argued that life is ultimately absurd, and that the only way we can give meaning to it is by doing something for others. So that's what I do. I work to make a better world for people. At the point when I find out I can't do that, I'm outta here," he said.

"Wynn," Rachel said softly. "Do you ever turn it off?"

"Not unless I have too many beers in me," Wynn replied, a little embarrassed.

Wynn helped Rachel put Tommy to bed that evening, reading a book to him while Rachel cleaned up the kitchen. Rachel stuck her head in the bedroom and smiled at them sitting together in Tommy's bed. "Mind if I grab a quick shower? I want to get the sand off of me. You can turn on some music or grab a beer when you're finished." She leaned over to kiss Tommy goodnight.

A few minutes later Wynn passed the shower on the way to the kitchen. "Hey Wynn, I ran out of soap. Would you mind grabbing a bar from the closet and throwing it in? Thanks."

Wynn got the soap. He came into the bathroom, and took off his shorts and T-shirt. "Here's the soap," he said as he stepped into the shower. "I thought I could help ya get rid of the sand. Now where did you say it was?" he helpfully inquired. She shot a quick look toward the door. "Don't worry, Tommy fell asleep."

Rachel smiled as she kissed him. "I assume you've changed your mind about getting involved. Well, at least make yourself useful." She turned around. He did a good job of massaging her shoulders and back. Rachel eventually pulled his hand with the soap in it across her belly. He proceeded to move down to her upper thighs. "Now, if you want to move the soap right about here, just like this, that would be quite helpful," she moaned as his other hand began to caress her taut nipple.

****

The CAN members told the Pesticide Board about the various health problems they had seen. Carlos Lopez told them, "We've collected papers from dozens of people. They had problems like headaches, nausea, diarrhea, bad stomachs and bloody noses. Many animals also came sick or died. We know farmers need to make a livin', and we wanna to work with 'em. But you need to help protect our families and neighbors. We want you to stop Bolstar being used till health studies are done. Thank you for listenin'," Carlos said. Several others told similar stories.

The farm and pesticide representatives on the Pesticide Board were furious that the neighbors had been allowed to speak. "These people have no evidence that problems are a result of pesticides," said George Lomax, one of the chemical company representatives. "We spray all over the state and we never hear complaints. This group is being manipulated by an outside organization who are just a bunch of socialists that don't like businesses."

One of the farm representatives, looking directly at Wynn, added, "There weren't no problems till some smart-ass colored boy came into town stirring up trouble."

The CAN members were stunned. They rose up and started shouting, waving their fingers at the Board members, shaking their heads in disbelief.

"Who are you people?" the neighbors asked. "My wife is sick and all you do is yell that we're commies? We came here politely to talk to you because we thought you'd want to help. Instead all you do is insult us. We are taxpayers. You work for us," angrily responded Joe

Rodriguez.

Dr. Jerry Robbey, the Chair of the Pesticide Board, banged his gavel. "Mr. Lomax, there's no need to call these people socialists. But you're right, this isn't a public hearing. I wanted to give you people an opportunity to say a few words, but this is not the appropriate forum for a litany of complaints. You can fill out a written complaint if you want, and we'll investigate it just like we do any other complaint."

"How long will that take?" shouted Rachel.

"We usually take about six months to investigate and make a determination, if any, of corrective action."

"That's no good. People are sick now," responded Carlos. The neighbors were in no mood to back down.

"That's our procedure. Since there is no other business, this meeting is adjourned," stated Robbey, slamming down the gavel. The seven Board members fled the room.

The CAN members gathered around Wynn to discuss what to do next. "They aren't interested in listening to us. We don't have any money or fancy houses. This is just a waste of time," said several the members.

"If they won't listen to us, maybe they'll listen to their neighbors," said Wynn. "They can run but they can't hide. Time to turn up the heat."

Wynn told them about one of Alinsky's cardinal rules: pick the target, freeze it, personalize it and then polarize it.

Dr. Robbey became the target.

Several weekends later, fifteen of the neighbors gathered up as many kids as they could fit in their cars and trucks and drove over to Robbey's home in a well-to-do area in North Phoenix. The children were dressed in Halloween costumes. The members delivered trick-or-treat packages containing onions, surgical "gas" masks and cotton balls to Dr. Robbey's neighbors. Tommy raced the other children to ring the doorbells.

"Hi. My name is Juan Lopez. I'm chair of the Southwest Phoenix Community Action Network. We're here today because we're getting sick from bein' sprayed with a chemical called Bolstar. It's used to grow cotton. Your neighbor, Dr. Robbey, he is head of the Pesticide Control Board. It's their job to protect people from getting sick from pesticides. Mr. Robbey, he says the Board wants to study the problem for six months before doing anything 'bout it. We need help now. We ask if you'll call Dr. Robbey to tell 'im you want to stop Bolstar from being sprayed. Here's his phone number. Thank you."

Many of the neighbors were sympathetic. "I wouldn't want that to happen in our neighborhood. I'd be happy to call. Would your children like some treats?" Others were less happy but also called. "Hey Jerry, I don't know what's going on, but I don't want those people at my door again. Whatever you need to do to resolve this problem, do it."

Robbey was incensed. He called the CAN office early Monday morning. "I don't know what game you think you're playing, but don't ever bother my neighbors again. I'll call the police the next time you try something like that."

Wynn was expecting the call. "Good to hear from you, Dr. Robbey. Feel free to call the police, but the last I heard it's legal to go trick or treating, even in North Phoenix. Nor it is illegal to picket in front of your place of business, or write letters to the newspaper about you, or leaflet at your church. I'll let you know what we think up for Thanksgiving; maybe some stuffed turkeys. It is illegal, however, to make people sick from spraying them with pesticides. This isn't a game to us. You stop people from getting sick, we stop protesting. Now, when can you come out to the neighborhood for a meeting?"

The neighbors protested at the monthly meetings of the Pesticide Board, at Robbey's office and in his neighborhood. They showed up at a fundraiser for the hospital where he worked. CAN also met with representatives of Governor Babbitt, local City Council members and state legislators.

The big break came from one of the Scottsdale residents, whose college roommate was a producer for the "20-20" TV news program. He convinced him to do a segment on the problem. Several CAN members were interviewed. The newscast prompted the federal EPA to convene an emergency hearing in Phoenix. Finally, in early spring, the Pesticide Control Board voted to ban the use of Bolstar — but only in the two neighborhoods that had complained.

Part of Wynn wanted to keep on fighting, but as a community organizer it was time to declare victory. "Power is a matter of perception," he told Rachel. "The more powerful we appear to be, the easier it is to win things in the future. Right now, we forced the state to give in to our demands. We keep on fighting now, our own members won't be as invested since it won't help them, so they're less likely to turn out for actions. And if we fail to get a statewide ban enacted, we could turn a victory into a defeat, making the group look weaker. Let the Center for the Science continue to push statewide."

****

Wynn continued to organize a new neighborhood every three months or so — and to spend more time, and nights, with Rachel. There were now three other CAN organizers working in Phoenix. CAN began to get a lot of media coverage. CAN made sure their protests provided good visuals and storylines.

CAN decided to tackle healthcare, a major problem for poor people in Arizona. Arizona was the only state that failed to participate in the federal Medicaid program. The CAN researchers on the national staff found a federal program that was supposed to help people who lacked healthcare coverage. The problem was no one knew about it.

"Under the Hill-Burton law, hospitals pay off various federal grants and loans by providing free care to poor people. Of course, hospitals don't tell their patients about it, using the funds instead to write off unpaid bills," Rachel told reporters as CAN protested at a hospital, demanding to see the hospital administrator. "We want the hospital to inform every patient without healthcare insurance about this program."

The TV coverage prompted several ambulance drivers to call CAN to tell them horror stories. "You pick up a farmworker out in Sun City, where all those rich retirees live, the local hospital says they're not in *too* bad of a shape and makes you bring 'em to County General. That's an hour drive away in Phoenix. I've had several patients lose limbs as a result. At least one died."

CAN had a lot of fun opposing the renewal of the franchise agreement between APS, the local utility company, and the City of Phoenix. The franchise agreement gave APS the right to operate within the city. The agreement had to be approved by the voters.

While the city and company treated it as a routine administrative matter, CAN used the vote to pressure APS to adopt Lifeline rates. The Lifeline program provides a small amount of electricity to customers at a nominal rate, allowing poor people and senior citizens to afford to keep their lights and air conditioning on.

"Utility companies overcharge small residential customers," Wynn told the CAN Board. "They impose a high service charge on each customer merely to get the power delivered, then give a huge discount to large volume users. The more you use, the less you pay per kwh. This promotes increased electric usage rather than conservation. The banks and other financial investors who control the utilities like it because building new power plants, especially nukes, requires huge capital investment, which means more interest payments and profits for investors."

Wynn thought of creative ways to torment APS and generate media attention. Rachel led a delegation of CAN members who rolled a wheelbarrow of pennies into an APS office to pay their bills — "not one penny more for high electric bills," they chanted. They wrote new lyrics for the old country song "Sixteen Tons" to spoof APS, building on the chorus that "I owe my soul to the company store."

The City of Phoenix publishes an election guide for voters. Both sides of a ballot issue can write 500 words for the guide — if they pay 500 dollars. CAN members marched into city hall to pay their bills with "Monopoly" money. "Since APS is a monopoly, that means they paid their fee with monopoly money. We want to pay with monopoly money as well." Even the city clerks had a hard time not laughing. After several demonstrations at council meetings, the city voted to allow CAN to include their position included without paying the fee.

Wynn decided to spend more time on his personal life, starting with Rachel. He told the CAN staff that Sundays were now an off day. He confessed to Rachel, "I'm beginning to burn out. I dunno whether the sacrifices needed to work with CAN are worth it. While we win issues like gettin' vacant lots cleaned up or abandoned houses boarded up, we don't make a lotta progress on big ticket issues, like job creation, housing, or healthcare. And the campaign contributors are still the ones making the decisions and getting the biggest slices."

Rachel and Tommy spent considerable time at the Hostel for Wayward Youth. Rachel often accompanied Pete on Saturday evenings to clean up the local food coop. Doing "work" hours gave you a discount. Sundays often involved cooking up large pots of vegetarian chili or ratatouille for the rest of the week. Or they would pile into Pete's truck for protests at the nuke plants, to go to some music festival or to go hiking in the desert.

Steve and Pete gave Rachel and Wynn some time alone by watching Tommy. Once they even managed to sneak away for a weekend hiking and camping trip to the bottom of the Grand Canyon. When they returned and asked Steve and Pete how the weekend went, they explained, "We showed him the finer points of being a man, like using oranges from the neighbor's tree to play baseball in the street."

Wynn and Rachel increasingly debated the balance between politics and personal needs.

"CAN wants to make a better world for oppressed people, but they oppress their own staff," Rachel scolded. "There is nuthin' 'family friendly' about CAN's work conditions. Relationships require time, especially if you got kids. Voluntary poverty may work for priests and nuns but it doesn't work for a four-year-old. Most of your staff burn out in a few months. If you're in this for the long run, you gotta start paying more attention to yourself and the people you love."

Wynn usually defended CAN even though his doubts were increasing. "No one said the revolution was going to be easy. The corporations have tens of thousands, if not millions, of paid staff to make sure they win. We only got a handful of organizers. If you wanna change the world, you have to be willing to sacrifice. Look how many patriots have been willing to sacrifice their lives. We just have to make sure that each free moment we get together is special," Wynn suggested sweetly.

"I don't have too many complaints about the time we spend together, Mr. Harris," Rachel replied, "other than you've gotta learn that stoppin' at the store involves more than a six-pack of beer. It's the time we don't spend together that I'm complaining about. And Tommy wants to see more of you. He's usually asleep before you get off of work."

Rachel also wanted to know where the revolution was. "You talk about the people but the staff do most of the work. Even getting the members to show up for a meeting is a struggle. Their first concern is taking care of their own families, making sure the bills get paid and food is on the table."

Pete agreed with Rachel. "The revolution needs more education, more fundamental changes in people's lifestyles" he said. "It's not enough to just get people to fight the banks or utility companies. You gotta go deeper — make 'em see there are alternatives, that there are other ways to organize the economy and society. We need a revolution of the hearts and minds."

"The first step should be to change people," Pete argued. "People can't control the world yet, but they can control themselves. People have to change their lifestyles to have less of an impact on Mother Earth. They gotta eat less meat so we don't waste so much energy, water and other resources growing cattle. They have to buy organic vegetables so pesticides don't poison them. They have to stop throwing away so much garbage, and start recycling and composting. We gotta create a new economy, build a new society in the shell of the old."

Wynn countered that most of Pete's friends never talked to real people. "When's the last time y'all went doorknocking and talked to someone with a wife and three kids who needs to work two jobs to pay the rent? It's nice for the counterculture to talk about creating a utopia, but most people have to struggle to just stay alive. Droppin' out and hangin' out ain't a viable option for them. You can't create a new world by just talkin' to the already converted. And don't forget that corporate America has a thousand ways they brainwash consumers into adopting the lifestyle needed to create demand for their products, starting with the boob tube."

****

Rachel agreed to chair CAN's political action committee. Electoral politics is an integral part of CAN's strategy to build power for its members. Since electoral politics is about how we allocate power in the US, CAN works on elections.

CAN always looks for new ways for community people to get power. In Arkansas, CAN's home state, it discovered that the Justices of the Peace met once a year to adopt the county budget. It had become a mere formality. But CAN got nearly a hundred members to become Justices of the Peace. This enabled them to make a little extra money officiating at marriages and witnessing signatures. When the day came for the budget to be ratified, the county officials were stunned to find a large crowd of CAN members who had their own ideas about what to spend money on, such as community services and affordable housing.

The CAN members in Phoenix interviewed various candidates running for city council and mayor, asking them to commit to support CAN's issues. CAN did not like the conservative Republican mayor who normally opposed CAN's initiatives. But she was so popular with the power brokers that the Democrats didn't field a candidate, leaving David Moore of the Socialist Workers Party as her only opponent.

The interview with Moore, a young man working in a local steel plant, went well. The CAN members nodded their approval of his answers to questions on housing, utilities, healthcare and taxes. But Moore lost the endorsement when the CAN members asked him about police protection. "The rich get to write all the rules to make sure they stay wealthy," Moore responded. "The police are the tools of the capitalist system. They are there to enforce the oppression of the poor by the wealthy. I would eliminate them."

The community residents, while agreeing with Moore's class analysis, wanted better police protection in their neighborhood. "We don't want people to walk into our homes and steal our TV set. CAN members aren't opposed to the police. We want them to be more responsive to our needs," said Jesse Suarez. CAN voted against an endorsement in the race. It highlighted for both Wynn and Rachel the need to listen to your members.

****

By the fall of 1979, Wynn was terribly confused. He liked Rachel a lot, probably loved her, but felt he was too young to settle down. It also wasn't clear what type of long-term relationship Rachel wanted if any. Tommy was still her prime focus.

That spring, Wynn had slept with an old friend from Texas at one of the quarterly CAN staff meetings in New Orleans. Rachel had been miffed when she found out, overhearing a phone conversation when Wynn returned. "It wasn't like I was keeping a secret, but it didn't seem to call for a news release. I don't remember either one of us talking about a monogamous relationship," Wynn responded. "Kate and I have always been attracted to each other. She's leaving CAN. Who knows when I'll see her again? I'm sorry. If I knew this was going to be a problem for us, I wouldn't have done it."

"You're right Wynn, we haven't made that type of commitment," Rachel said icily. "I don't believe in making demands on the people I love. I just kinda thought we were both at the same place with this relationship. I guess I was wrong."

"Hey, that's not fair," argued Wynn. "I'm sorry I hurt you. You're very important to me. So was Kate. We just thought spending the night together was a special way of saying good-bye to a dear friend. It felt right."

"Oh Wynn," Rachel snapped, "when doesn't sex feel right to a man?"

She cut him off when he tried to offer a few examples.

Rachel forgave him a few weeks later, agreeing that he hadn't actually *cheated* on her, but she still felt hurt.

Wynn knew he wanted to keep organizing, but he had growing concerns about CAN's organizing style. CAN meant well but he felt that the members just ratified decisions already made by staff, especially on big stuff. While CAN insisted that members had to be the public speakers, he felt too often he was merely writing plays for others to perform.

"A lot of the best organizers, the young creative ones with energy," Wynn told Rachel as they laid in bed one evening, "are in the antinuclear movement or on college campuses. I wanna help train them, make them better organizers, take advantage of the lessons I've learned. CAN does a good job of training new organizers — it's like the Marines: we'll tear you apart, then build you back up again. But there's not enough organizers to make the CAN vision a reality. We need one organizer for every ten neighbors we organize, and the burn out rate is too high."

"That's what I've been telling you for a while," Rachel reminded him.

"I'm also thinking about moving back East," Wynn added, "at least for a while" he hastened to add.

"Oh?" remarked Rachel.

"It's nothing definite," Wynn said. "But the West just doesn't seem to have the energy level you feel back East, the need to get involved. Most of the people I've met out here moved from somewhere else. I see why Phoenix is the divorce capital of the country. People move here to escape, to find some space. Building a sense of community isn't high on their priorities. Also, my parents aren't getting any younger and they're starting to have health problems. It would be easier to see them if I was on the East Coast."

"Be sure to let me know what you decide," Rachel told Wynn as she rolled over.

Wynn shared his concerns about the shortfalls he saw with CAN's organizing strategy in a memo with the head organizers in the other nineteen states. The national staff leadership reacted coolly.

CAN never liked to lose staff, especially experienced ones. It was hard to find people willing to work long hours for no money. Seth Lyman, CAN's Chief Organizer, called Wynn to make a pitch to keep him. "If you want to work in a broader coalition, why not help organize the People's Party and the presidential election for CAN? You could start with the Iowa caucuses, which kicks off the primary season. They're in February. You'd be a great lead person there since you've already organized in Iowa, you know the turf."

CAN had sent Wynn to Arizona as part of the 20/80 Plan for the presidential campaign: organize 20 states by 1980, so CAN could raise 5,000 dollars in each of the states and qualify for federal matching funds for its People's Party candidate. While the party's platform was well received by other groups, the unions and black churches that CAN saw as their strongest potential allies were firmly entrenched in the Democratic Party.

CAN had decided to focus on helping Senator Ted Kennedy win the Democratic nomination against President Carter, starting with Iowa.

Wynn tried to convince Rachel to come with him as an organizer.

"Rachel, you'd be a great organizer. You've got much better people skills than I do. I have to work at talking to people. You do it naturally. I'm always getting into arguments even with people I agree with. You give them hugs. You put people at ease, they trust you because they know you care about them as individuals. CAN would hire you in a minute. Or we'll find another organization to hire both of us. We can make it work," Wynn argued.

Rachel laughed at the idea of trying to raise Tommy while moving around working for CAN. "Wynn, if you want to move in here, that would be fine with me. Great as a matter of fact. No strings attached, we'll see how it goes. Tommy thinks you're wonderful. If you're burnt out on organizing, you could easily find a better paying job. Listen, I don't want to tie you down to something you're not ready for. I'm going to stay here to finish my nursing degree. If you gotta hit the road, we'll miss you, and I hope you keep in touch," Rachel said, a tear glistening her cheek. "Let's enjoy the time we have left."

****

Wynn left CAN several months after leaving Arizona. While he helped carry CAN's neighborhoods for Kennedy in the Iowa caucuses, Carter carried the state and was headed for re-nomination. The media and the polls had loved Kennedy, begging him to run. Once in the race, his standing with both rapidly fell.

Wynn took a position as the national field organizer for the Campaign for Safe Energy, pushing to have the Democrats and Republicans adopt an antinuclear, prosolar platform. Wynn's job was to organize protests at campaign appearances by the presidential candidates.

"It was a lot of fun during the early primaries, such as New Hampshire," Wynn wrote to Rachel. "The candidates seemed to be on every street corner. The protesters easily stood out with such small crowds. In the early states, the candidates took questions from the audience. The trick was to be aggressive about asking the first question.

We also handed a list of our questions to everyone in the audience."

Wynn missed a golden opportunity to derail Ronald Reagan's presidency in New Hampshire. He doubted that a second opportunity to so change history — or herstory, as Rachel liked to say — would come his way again.

Reagan, the former B-movie actor, General Electric spokesperson, and ex-Governor of California, was the frontrunner for the Republican nomination. His advisers adopted a coronation strategy, trying to keep him away from the crowds and the media where an unscripted moment might occur.

Reagan didn't campaign in Iowa, which allowed George Bush to spring an upset. His coronation suddenly in doubt, Reagan was forced to hit the campaign trail in New Hampshire, as questions swirled about his advanced age.

Reagan's first appearance was at a "cattle call", where one candidate after another dutifully parades out to give a fifteen-minute speech. The place was packed with national reporters, including several national TV anchors who were noticeably drunk. When Reagan came off the stage to work the crowd for a photo op, Wynn grabbed his hand and didn't let go.

"It was a surreal experience," Wynn told Pete when he called him after the encounter. "There were TV cameras and flashing lights all around us. No matter what I said, Raygun offered stock vignettes about nuclear power. I asked him whether the Price-Anderson Act, which caps how much damages utilities are liable for in case of nuclear accident, violated his commitment to the free market. His response was that he and Nancy received more radiation by flying in an airplane than Jimmy Carter got from walking around at Three Mile Island after the accident."

Wynn's big opportunity came the following weekend.

"The Campaign bused volunteers up from Boston earlier in the day to doorknock about nuclear power," Wynn told Rachel. "Later that evening, we held a funeral for the nuclear industry, complete with a coffin, outside the school where the debate was taking place. Inside, Bush was looking to deliver a knockout punch. After his Iowa victory, he claimed the primary was only a two-man race and debate should only have him and Reagan."

"What was Reagan's position?" asked Rachel.

"He of course wanted to treat Bush as just one of the pack, so he wanted all the candidates in the debate. The format hadn't been resolved by the time the debate was supposed to start. It was chaos. The half dozen presidential candidates milled about arguing among themselves, the media and campaign aides," Wynn said. "I noticed that the security was very light and decided to move the protest inside, hoping to grab the stage before the debate started."

"What happened?"

"Well, I hustled three of the people inside. I told them to open the doors when we marched up. Unfortunately, Jeff Singer, the guy from PIRG paying for the campaign, needed to be convinced. Just as he gave the green light, the Secret Service got their act together. They locked the door and pushed out everyone without a ticket, including our three people. A few minutes later, Reagan grabbed the microphone, said that he had paid for it and they were going to do it his way."

The King had reasserted his leadership. Reagan defeated Bush in New Hampshire, and resumed his march to the Republican nomination.

The other decisive campaign moment was the one debate between Reagan and Carter.

Carter had taken a Rose Garden strategy after the American embassy in Teheran had been stormed, refusing to attend the first debate, leaving the forum to Reagan and John Anderson, a moderate Republican running as an independent.

Anderson did quite well in the campaign, rising as high as 20% in the polls. His campaign collapsed after the League of Women Voters refused to allow him to participate in the second debate. He was also mortally wounded by the lack of federal election funds for his campaign. As an independent, he would only receive public funding after the election if he got 5% or more of the vote. He was at his high point in the polls when he began to negotiate with the banks to borrow money against his election results. By the time the banks and League were finished with him, his numbers were in the single digits and falling.

Wynn found Reagan a surprisingly effective speaker during the campaign. He thought the debate with Carter was Reagan's poorest performance by far. America thought he did great. It wasn't the last time Wynn shook his head in disbelief about how out of sync he was with the rest of the country.

Wynn worked for the Safe Energy Campaign for six months, successfully getting the Democrats to adopt the Campaign's platform over Carter's opposition. "In hindsight, it was a mistake to win so early. It would've been much better to have had a floor fight at the convention. Then maybe the media might have paid attention," Wynn told Rachel.

Wynn moved back to Albany to organize off-campus students on tenants' rights and utility issues. He tried to persuade Rachel to join him — "I've got a great apartment right across from Washington Park, lots of trees and grass. Tommy will love it" — but she declined. "Feel free to visit when the snow gets too deep," she told him.

After CAN abandoned its efforts to create the People's Party, a number of staff left to help start the Citizens Party, an environmentally focused party that ran author and scientist Barry Commoner for president. *The Closing Circle*, his book on ecology, was number one on the New York Times Best Sellers list. Wynn helped with the campaign in Albany. Nationally, the party received less than 1% of the vote.

Seven

September 11, 2001

"Darkness cannot drive out darkness; only light can do that. Hate cannot drive out hate; only love can do that. Hate multiplies hate, violence multiplies violence, and toughness multiplies toughness in a descending spiral of destruction. The chain reaction of evil — hate begetting hate, wars producing more wars — must be broken, or we shall be plunged into the dark abyss of annihilation." — Martin Luther King Jr.

The Day the World Changed

8:53 am, Tuesday, September 11, 2001

It was a beautiful fall day in south Florida. Rachel was in town to give a speech on education to the Florida School Board Association. Before the speech, she was scheduled to read to a class of third-grade students. The event would be broadcast by satellite to schools around the country.

As she waited outside the classroom, an assistant handed her a cell phone. It was Tommy, who was in NYC organizing for Frost against a proposed billion-dollar economic development package — corporate welfare — to build a new trading floor for the New York Stock Exchange with public funds. There was a protest that morning at the New York City Industrial Development Authority (IDA), which was meeting to approve the bonds for the project.

The hearing was due to start at nine. As usual Tommy was running late, having not crashed onto a friend's couch until 3 am. His hair was still wet from a quick shower as he weaved his way through the subway crowds. His fellow organizers were anxiously waiting for him to show up with the flyers. After the protest he was going to help Michelle Williams, who was running in the Green Party mayoral primary taking place that day.

"Hey Tommy, how'd the protest go?" Rachel asked. She was proud that he finally seemed to be getting some focus to his life.

Tommy was short of breath. "Mom, you won't believe this but a plane just flew into the World Trade Center. There's a lot of smoke coming out. Sirens are going off. It's pandemonium."

"Are you sure? When did this happen?" Rachel said, glancing

around to see who might be listening.

"Five minutes ago. I just got out of the subway when I heard a loud bang. Everyone looked up and there were flames shooting out of the building." Tommy exclaimed.

Rachel's maternal instincts kicked into high gear.

"Tommy, get out of there," Rachel told him, using her most authoritative mother voice. "Promise me you'll keep away. If you need help, go to the nearest cop and show him your security ID. Tell him you're the president's son," Rachel cajoled.

"Chill out, Mom. I'll be okay," Tommy assured her, like he was borrowing the car for the night. "It's you I'm worried about. You're the target in the family, not me. I just wanted to make sure you knew what was going on. I know how slow the FBI and CIA tend to be in letting you know what's happening. Bye."

"Wait, Tommy. Tommy, get out of there! Tommy are you still there?" Rachel pleaded. All she got in response was a dial tone. "Damn."

8:57 am

Rachel motioned over Chang, the Chief of her Secret Service detail.

"Alice, a plane just flew into the World Trade Center. Find out what's going on and keep me informed. Just in case, alert Air Force One to be ready to depart to DC. Also, please find someone to brief me on standard procedures in case of a terrorist attack, the short version."

9:03 am

Just as she finished saying hello to the students, Chang walked in and whispered in her ear that a second plane had hit the WTC. Rachel stood up, told the students she'd be right back, and asked the teacher if she wouldn't mind starting the reading.

The Secret Service people were pushing everyone out of the hallway.

Chang told her, "We saw it live on television. A second plane, a large one, hit the second tower. We have to assume it's a terrorist attack. We need to move you to a secure site until we figure out what's going on."

"The only place I'm going back to is the White House," Rachel instructed her. "No argument," she said, cutting off Chang's response.

"The country has been on enough of an emotional roller coaster recently. People need to know that we have things under control, not having their president cowering while we're under attack," Rachel replied.

"Madame President, I don't think that's wise. We have no idea about the extent of the attack. We need to follow our security plan in case of such attacks," Chang argued.

"Alice, if the Secret Service and the military can't protect the White House, you can't protect anything. I'm not going to flee around the country while civilians are under attack. We stand together. Take whatever steps you need to secure the White House and Air Force One. If you need to strap me into the back seat of a jet fighter, do it," Rachel snapped in her best presidential pissed-off manner. "I'm headed to the White House — as soon as I say good-bye to the children."

"And get Tommy on the phone and read him the riot act. Make sure the Secret Service in NYC knows where he is and tell them to put some people on him. Drag him away, if necessary."

As an adult, Tommy was not entitled to Secret Service protection. He had rejected all offers to have someone accompany him. "No thanks. I don't want to be under guard. No offense, Mom, but I don't want you *or* the government knowing what I'm doing 24/7. I don't think my girlfriend would like it, either."

An aide came up and handed her the phone. It was Sophie. She shared Chang's hesitation about flying back to the White House.

"It makes sense to follow the emergency plan. A lot of people spent time figuring out the best response to these situations. We should issue an order to shut down all civilian air flights until we have complete control over what's going on." Sophie said.

"Issue whatever orders you think are needed. Short of using force. For that, you need my specific clearance. Get the Joint Chiefs and NSC together. I'll conference in as soon as I'm back on Air Force One. See you back at the White House in an hour," Rachel said.

9:10 am

Rachel looked like she was about to faint. Chang rushed up to her. Rachel told her, "I'm okay. I just have to sit down for a moment."

Rachel slumped into a hallway chair, facing the school's display case of sports trophies. She buried her face in her hands, rubbing her eyeballs as if to get the sleep out of them. Several photographers took her picture as they were being pushed back by the Secret Service.

After a moment, Rachel stood back up, momentarily rocking on her feet. She waved over Johnson, her press secretary. "Tell the press I'll speak to 'em in about 15 minutes and that we're headed back to DC."

9:14 am

Rachel whispered to the teacher before she sat down to face the children and the TV camera. The teacher hurried from the room.

Rachel smiled at the children but only half succeeded. She thought about when Tommy had sat in her lap being read to.

"Girls and boys, I'm sure your moms and dads have explained to you that sometimes people do bad things. Sometimes adults have arguments, just like when you argue with a friend or brother or sister over a toy. But we all know that it is never right to hurt someone else," she said.

"Unfortunately, today some people were hurt in New York City. We're going to find the people responsible for this, and make sure they can't hurt anyone else. But I want you to understand that no one is going to hurt you, that your moms and dads and teachers are here to protect you. I want you to take care of each other, as well. Can you do that for me?"

The children all nodded.

"I want to talk to you about our justice system. In this country, we follow the principle that you are innocent until proven guilty. That means we need to be careful not to blame a person for something without proof."

Rachel spoke more to herself than the class. "We need to be careful that we punish only those who are responsible, not those who just look like the guilty individuals because they come from the same country or have the same color skin as those who did the bad things."

"I'm sorry, but I won't be able to read to you today as I had hoped. There are some people who need my help right now. I promise to come back in a couple of weeks to finish reading to you. I asked Ms. Johnson to get a copy of one of my favorite stories, by Dr. Seuss, called *The Butter Battle Book*. How many of you have already read it?" About half the hands shot up. "Great. Maybe you can help Ms. Johnson with it in case she has any problems. Now, how about a group hug before I leave?" Rachel asked, opening up her arms.

9:20 am

Rachel's face was grim as she walked out. Chang told her every television channel was covering the attack live.

"Any word from Tommy?" Rachel asked.

"The cell phones stopped working in New York. Either they're overloaded or their aerials were on top of the twin towers," Chang told her as they walked down the corridor to the auditorium. She hesitated before continuing. "Somebody called the White House who had several of the security codes and said that both the White House and Air Force One were next. We already have the problem of not having a vice-president. The Secret Service literally picked up the Speaker of the House and carried him away to a secure location. Your national security team wants you in a secure military installation, not the White House," Chang reported.

"Tell them to protect Baker well, because I'm headed back in Air Force One to the White House. Maybe to New York City. The Secret Service can drive back if they want."

9:23 am

She tried not to lean on the podium for support.

"Good morning. At approximately nine o'clock this morning, two planes crashed into the World Trade Center towers in New York City. The two towers are now in flames and are being evacuated. While we need to be careful before jumping to any conclusions, the involvement of two planes makes it likely that this was a deliberate attack.

"We have taken the precaution of closing all airports and requiring all planes to land until we determine what is happening. Our security forces have been placed on the highest alert. I ask all Americans to cooperate with police and security forces to ensure the safety of all our citizens.

"I'll be returning to the White House to coordinate our response. Our first priority will be to provide whatever assistance we can to those in the World Trade Center. I will be talking to Mayor Giuliani and Governor Pataki in a few minutes to see how the federal government can best help.

"I pledge that whoever is responsible for these horrific attacks will be held accountable, but we need to avoid rushing to judgment as to who the culprits are. We must remember that only a few years ago our initial conclusion as to who was responsible for the bombing in Oklahoma City was incorrect.

"We must remain calm. We must refuse to succumb to the fear and panic that such acts are designed to produce.

"May God bless all those who have been hurt by today's tragedy. May God give us wisdom and courage in responding to this evil.

"Thank you."

Rachel ignored the questions shouted out to her as she climbed into the waiting car. The motorcade sped away, lights flashing, sirens screaming.

9:32 am

Ron Peterson, her military attaché, gave her an urgent report.

"Madame President, we have a flight out of Washington Dulles Airport that is refusing to respond to the air controller. It's supposed to be headed toward LA, but has turned around and is headed back to the DC area. We've taken every step we can to force them to respond. It will be over DC in less than ten minutes. Procedure at this point for a plane hijacked over DC is to shoot it down before it can be used to attack any targets. Do you have any other instructions?"

She stared at him in disbelief. She wanted to hide somewhere.

It was either shoot the plane down or let them kill more people on the ground. The passengers on the Boeing 737 were as good as dead. Her heart went cold.

"I assume they have orders to avoid casualties?" she finally managed to blurt out. "On the ground I mean?" she asked hopefully, begging for this not to be real.

"Yes, ma'am, they do," he responded.

"How many people are on the flight?" Rachel asked.

"We're not sure. We'll still waiting for the passenger list. Probably between fifty and seventy," he said.

She let out a gasp.

"No additional orders," she managed to whisper.

"It's a go," said Peterson into the phone.

9:37 am

Peterson huddled in the corner, fidgeting with his earpiece. "The plane has been shot down," he said to Rachel. "It appears that there may be some casualties on the ground. A building, looks like a farmhouse, may have been hit."

The passengers on the hijacked plane had gotten their hopes up when they saw the F-16 fighter jets pull up alongside. The jets escorted them for over fifteen minutes, darting in front of the plane trying to force it down, but the hijackers ignored it. The fighter pilots waited until the 737 approached a rural area. The passengers watched in disbelief as they fired two missiles. A few died cursing the American government.

9:41 am

Wynn and Sophie got on the phone. Rachel wanted to start sobbing. "We just shot down a plane approaching DC," she said. "Probably sixty, seventy dead, maybe some casualties on the ground. My god. I can't believe it." She willed herself to focus on moving forward, nothing else. "What's the latest from New York, and what have we heard from Tommy?"

"Two commercial airliners were apparently hijacked from Logan Airport in Boston. More than a hundred passengers are presumed dead. Both towers are on fire. They're evacuating but there are a lot of people who aren't able to walk out on their own. We've presumably lost everyone on the floors above where the planes crashed," said Sophie. She paused before continuing. "On an average day, fifty thousand people are in the World Trade Center."

Rachel caught her breath. "Fifty thousand?" she cried, in more pain than ever, her legs going rubbery.

"Fifty thousand. No idea how many of them were actually in the building when the planes hit. A lot of the tenants were in finance, so they were likely to be in early," Sophie said. "As for Tommy, he hasn't called in yet. We're working on finding him."

"Don't worry about Tommy, he knows how to take care of himself. He has a good head on his shoulders," Wynn told Rachel.

"It's going to take a while to get all the planes down," Sophie added. "I'm told that at any one moment there are up to 4,000 planes flying. So far every pilot still in the air indicates everything is okay, but we're scrambling Air Force and National Guard jets."

"Do we know anything about who's responsible for this?" asked Rachel, harshness in her voice.

"No one's taken credit. The military and CIA are pointing at bin

Laden as the most likely culprit but that's just gut instinct. There were no communications or demands from any hijackers," Sophie informed her. "The assumption is that they must have taken control of the planes from the pilots, since no one can imagine a pilot agreeing to use his plane as a weapon, even if they had a gun to his head," Sophie informed her.

Rachel had learned a lot about foreign affairs since she became VP, arranging for extensive briefings. Trouble spots like the Middle East got extra attention, which included meeting with progressive academics outside government, such as Roberta Freed of the Institute for Middle Eastern Studies at Georgetown University.

"Osama bin Laden is a wealthy Saudi," Freed had told Rachel, "who went to Afghanistan in the eighties to assist the freedom fighters — the mujahedeen — in the war with the Soviets."

"Weren't the mujahedeen our allies?" Rachel asked.

"More than allies," Freed responded. "The Carter administration, in July 1979, had begun to secretly fund the mujahedeen to fight the pro-Soviet Afghan government, hoping to draw the Soviet Union into their own Vietnam. Five months later the Soviet Union fell into the trap and rolled across the border, declaring they were intervening because the US was secretly funding the Afghan opposition. Which the Carter administration naturally denied."

"Where does bin Laden come in?"

"His father, Mohammed Awad bin Laden, started as a poor laborer from Yemen. He became close to the royal family after building a palace for King Saud and used his connections to build the largest construction company in the Middle East. Osama, the seventh among fifty brothers and sisters, shared his father's religious devotions. Osama helped finance both community construction and war efforts in Afghanistan.

"The CIA found foreign fighters like bin Laden easier to work with than the Afghanis, who were caught up with intertribal rivalries. Bin Laden and the Maktab al-Khidamar group that he ran became the CIA's primary conduit, through the Pakistan intelligence service, for supporting the guerrilla war against Moscow," Freed continued.

"So if he was our ally against the Soviets, what caused him to turn?" Rachel asked.

"In the late '80s, bin Laden established a new group, al-Qaida, that included many of the more extreme members of Maktab al-Khidamar. Many of these Afghan vets played prominent roles in some of the more violent Islamic movements around the world."

"After the Gulf War in 1990, the US was allowed to keep permanent military bases in Saudi Arabia. As you know, Mecca is the holiest site in Islam. Bin Laden viewed the permanent American presence as heresy. He and many other Muslims saw the US as a decadent regime built on greed and sin that seeks to corrupt and control Islamic countries," Freed explained.

"The chaotic nature of Afghanistan created an ideal place for bin Laden to train fighters. In exchange, he provided the Taliban government with the military training and foreign soldiers needed to keep them in power," Freed concluded.

The US accused bin Laden of a series of increasingly deadly attacks against US military bases and embassies in the Middle East and Africa. In retaliation, the Clinton administration had fired cruise missiles to blow up several of his camps in Afghanistan.

Now someone had targeted the symbol of the American financial empire, the Twin Towers of the World Trade Center, killing thousands of civilians. Whoever was responsible had timed the delay between the two planes to ensure that the TV cameras in the media capital of the world were all watching as the second one hit.

"How the hell did they get past security to hijack the flights?" Rachel demanded.

"We don't know. We don't know whether they sneaked their weapons past the security guards, mainly minimum wage workers without a lot of training, or if they breached security to plant them on the plane before takeoff." Sophie paused. Rachel could hear her talking to someone else in the room.

"Rachel, the Secret Service has begun to evacuate the White House," Sophie said. "They want me down in the secure bunker as soon as we finish this, though they look like they may just start carrying me as we talk."

"What does the military want to do?" Rachel asked, looking at Peterson.

"They're not sure, but they want to talk to you, not me. There are some who want to launch a strike immediately on bin Laden in Afghanistan," Sophie replied.

"Sophie, I'll be ready for the security conference call in fifteen minutes," Rachel informed her as they pulled up to Air Force One. "I also need you to pull together a peace command center at the White House. Bring in all the people who'd be running our national security apparatus if I'd had time to appoint them," Rachel added.

"Wynn, I need you to focus on finding Tommy."

10:03 am

The pilot briefly tried to argue that he'd been ordered to fly the plane to a secure air station in Louisiana. Rachel stared him down. "We're headed to the White House." The pilot stood back and saluted. "Yes, ma'am."

The day had already been brutal and seemed destined to get worse. This might be her last few minutes before the next wave broke. Rachel had thought about grabbing a Scotch, a double, on ice. She was in agony over the people shot down in the plane, over Tommy, fearing the worst, trying to tell herself he was all right. She asked instead for a yogurt smoothie.

10:05 am

Rachel was watching tv when the South Tower, the one that was hit second, collapsed with a deafening roar, each floor imploding into the one below. The world was stunned.

In the areas around the World Trade Center, people screamed in horror. Everyone ran for their lives. A mountain of dust and debris rolled down the canyons of the financial district, turning day into night, engulfing everything in its path. People ducked into any opening.

The North Tower, the one hit first, collapsed twenty-three minutes later.

An unknown number of people, estimated in the thousands, maybe tens of thousands, were still in the towers. This included hundreds of firefighters and police who had rushed into the Trade Center to try to evacuate workers and deal with the fires.

The tears flowed freely down Rachel's face. She prayed that Tommy was safe. She prayed for those who weren't.

10:17 am

A United flight from Newark to LA with 58 passengers and 6 crew aboard received the order to land as soon as possible, and to keep the cockpit door closed at all costs. The pilots turned the plane around, telling passengers they had developed minor mechanical difficulty and would be returning to the airport as a precaution. "Nothing to worry about. Sorry for the inconvenience."

10:25 am

Rachel's military command team was waiting on their phones. Secretary of State Darling has also wanted to join the call, undoubtedly planning to step in to manage the crisis. Sophie had known enough of Rachel's dislike for him to tell him that he'd have to come to the White House situation room if he wanted to participate. He was on his way.

"Thank you, gentlemen, for joining us. I'll be back at the White House shortly. Whatever our political differences, I trust that our need for national security will allow us to work together to deal with this problem. I don't want us to do something merely for the sake of making a response. Our goal is to isolate and punish those who are responsible, not escalate this into World War Three." Rachel said. "Gentlemen, are we clear about these ground rules?"

"Good." Rachel didn't give them long to respond. "Let's make sure that we are doing whatever is necessary to protect American lives. That starts with giving New York City whatever assistance is needed to rescue people. I want to make sure that every bulldozer, crane, emergency rescue unit, etc. is made available. If there is anything more that needs to be done, I want to hear about it. Sooner rather than later."

"So, what should our military response be?" asked National Security Adviser Walls. "We need to get moving."

"Whoever did this is clearly expecting us to respond with a vengeance. Don't they care, or are they hoping our response will lead to an escalation of the conflict?" Rachel asked. "If the latter, let's please avoid falling into their trap."

General Stuart Miles, Chairman of the Joint Chiefs of Staff, responded. "Madame President, we have no idea at this point if other terrorist attacks will be forthcoming in the near term. The openness of our society makes us very vulnerable. We have water supplies that can be targeted, nuclear power plants that can be hit. They may have biological weapons that can be deployed. I highly recommend that we immediately go to the highest national security alert, treat it as a declaration of war, shut down all the borders and mobilize the military."

"I agree about going to our highest security alert," Rachel responded, "but I want to avoid the term *war* at the moment. I don't want to cause unnecessary panic. Have you run any war-game scenarios that indicate what's next?"

"Well, ma'am, I hate to say this, but we never envisioned such a large-scale terrorist attack in the US, with such wanton disregard for human life," said Walls. "How can you imagine people being so sick? I don't know how many suicide attacks a terrorist group can launch at any one point in time without us getting more advanced warning. Normal terrorist style is a couple of hits to inflict the maximum media coverage, then go back underground until things cool off."

"We had no intelligence warnings about this?" Rachel asked. She knew she hadn't seen anything but she didn't fully trust the national security apparatus to keep her fully informed.

Winston Solomon, the CIA Director spoke up, carefully dodging the question. "Unfortunately, there's always someone threatening to blow us up."

Alexander Bullock, the Secretary of Defense and a Darling protégé, chimed in. "We have to hit bin Laden the moment we find him, and hit him hard. We have enough evidence that he's engaged in recent terrorist attacks against us, regardless of his role in today's attacks. I would also recommend that we launch immediate missile strikes against every terrorist training camp that we have identified before they all scramble away."

"If these terrorists were responsible for the attacks, wouldn't they have already gone into hiding rather than waiting around for us to hit them?" asked Sophie.

"Maybe, but they may not have known the exact date of the attack. They may be preparing to flee as we speak. But given their somewhat primitive conditions in these camps, they may not have heard yet," Bullock responded.

"When I get back to the White House, I want a full report on what defensive responses we've taken and what additional options there are. I also want your best guesses on what other attacks we should prepare for," Rachel said. She made a mental note to get Sophie to look at what prior warnings might have been received.

"If you can get positive information on the location of bin Laden or anyone else that we have proof was involved in prior terrorist attacks, you may take military action against them, following my approval. But I don't want to hear any debates about our evidence after the fact. You're to avoid harming civilians under all circumstances," added Rachel.

10:32 am

On the United flight to LA, three passengers stood up brandishing what looked like short knives. They claimed to have a bomb, and demanded that the pilots open the door or they'd begin killing people, starting with the flight attendants. The pilot announced over the intercom that two planes had already crashed into the World Trade Center, and a third had been shot down. Several male passengers exploded out of their seats, led by tall athletic types.

The fight lasted ten minutes. Five passengers and two hijackers were killed before the passengers overwhelmed them. A dozen more passengers were injured. The plane landed in Pittsburgh safely, where the passengers and crew were given a hero's welcome.

Billy O'Donnell was one of the men who'd led the struggle to overpower the terrorists.

. When informed that another hijacked plane had been shot down, O'Donnell nodded grimly. He told reporters that he supported the decision, trusting that the Air Force had done everything possible to alert the passengers to the need to take matters into their own hands.

"We heard what happened at the World Trade Center. We knew we were dead if we did nothing, and we knew that a lot of other people on the ground could be killed if the terrorists were able to carry out their plot. The Lord decided to spare us. We need to put an end to this insanity," O'Donnell remarked.

It became known later that day O'Donnell was the captain of a gay rugby team in San Francisco. Rachel vaguely remembered Anna introducing them once at some AIDS walkathon when they lived in the Bay Area. This became relevant the following day when one of the right-wing Christian TV hustlers, Jerry Falwell, said, "I really believe that the pagans and the abortionists and the feminists and the gays and the lesbians ... who are actively trying to make that an alternative lifestyle. All of them who have tried to secularize America. I point the finger in their face and say, you helped this happen."

****

2:03 pm

Wynn flew by military helicopter to New York City to see the damage first-hand and to look for Tommy. Chang had to block Rachel from getting on board. "You can fire me tomorrow if you wish, but under no circumstances are you leaving the White House at this point."

Wynn called Rachel shortly after 2 pm.

"Wynn, what's going on? Any word on Tommy?" Rachel asked, trying to keep the panic out of her voice.

"In most of the city, it's pretty calm. People trying to figure out what happened and how to get home," Wynn said. "But down by the Trade Center, it's total bedlam. Thousands of people wandering around in shock, standing in the middle of the street, crying and watching. It's like being in a city that was just bombed," Wynn said.

Rachel felt the muscles in her stomach tighten. "Wynn, what aren't you telling me? What do you know about Tommy?"

Wynn paused. "We don't know anything for certain. There are a thousand and one places he could be. We've been handing out his picture to the rescue workers and the Mayor's office is faxing it around to the hospitals."

Wynn took a deep breath, trying to soften the blow. "One of the fire marshals thinks he saw Tommy by the South Tower just before it collapsed. He tried to talk this fireman into letting him help carry a fire hose or anything else they needed into Tower Two, but was told no way. No one recollects seeing him after that. At this point, finding Tommy is like looking for a needle in a haystack. It'll be hours before things begin to sort out a bit."

"But if he's okay, why hasn't he called?" Rachel cried.

"The phone systems in lower Manhattan are a complete mess. I'm calling on a police line. He knows how to take care of himself. Don't give up hope."

"Damn it, Wynn. He would've figured out how to call by now," Rachel sobbed. "Put out an all-points bulletin or something. Anything."

"Rachel. Don't give up hope," Wynn said as reassuringly as he could. "It could be hours before he turns up, possibly days. The police and fire units have his picture, everyone is looking. But we have god knows how many people in the towers that we gotta focus on."

It appeared that most of the attacks were over, at least for the day. All civilian planes had landed shortly after noon. They'd found boxcutters on one of the planes that had been stopped before takeoff, and were now searching for another possible set of hijackers. Throughout the day the media reported rumors of additional attacks — such as a bomb at the State Department, an Amtrak train that had been derailed — all of which turned out to be false. Most people just watched tv in disbelief as the towers collapsed over and over and over again.

8:00 pm

Rachel delivered a short, somber speech from the Oval Office. She urged Americans to remain calm, to comfort one another, to avoid jumping to conclusions as to who was guilty.

"Today, America suffered a great tragedy. Enemies as yet unknown killed thousands of innocent people. America stands stronger than ever this evening. We have suffered great losses but our will to build a better world remains as resolute as ever. Terrorism will not win.

"The death toll in New York City is enormous. We will do whatever it takes to rescue those who are trapped at the World Trade Center. We will bring to justice those who are guilty of these unspeakable crimes. Our armed forces are on alert. We will take a day or two to examine our security measures at the airports before flights will be given clearance to resume. We ask for your cooperation and patience as we respond to this tragedy. I will be traveling to New York City myself tomorrow to offer my support and condolences."

She did not mention that Tommy was a potential victim.

Her face grew even grimmer.

"And now it is my sad duty to inform you of a truly unfortunate incident. Our Air Force was forced to shoot down a hijacked plane before it could be used to kill others. There were fifty-three passengers, as well as six crew members. Two individuals on the ground were killed when the plane crashed. I have no words to express the sorrow and regret for the loss of these lives.

"On behalf of the nation, I want to give truly heartfelt praise to those heroes who stepped forward to confront the terrorists on the United flight to Newark. Five of these courageous individuals were killed, several more were injured. We are interviewing the surviving hijacker to find out more about who is responsible for these horrible acts."

****

Rachel stayed in the Oval Office throughout the night, the White House a beehive of activity. She stared blankly at the television screen as she flicked from one channel to another, watching the jagged ruins smolder. Her grief and guilt were overwhelming, numbing. She agonized over the decision to shoot down the hijacked plane. *If the passengers in the Newark plane managed to overpower their hijackers, maybe we should have just given the others more time?* she thought over and over.

She stepped into the situation room every few hours to see if there was anything new. They were concentrating on tracking down the identity of the hijackers and determining what connections they had to foreign governments or terrorist organizations. They were also searching for the presumed hijackers who had left the boxcutters behind. More than four thousand FBI agents were being deployed, the largest investigation in its history. Doors were being knocked on, people were being slapped around, files were being combed.

Rachel talked several times to Wynn. Each call, each report of nothing new about Tommy became harder. It was too overwhelming. She told herself she had to focus on protecting the country, not on her personal grief. She got out some old photo albums of Tommy, called Pete and Emily, threw a few objects against the wall. She wanted to drink until she forgot, but didn't, needing to keep her mind clear. Sophie and other staff members took turns being with her through the night.

Eight

The Next Day

September 12

Rachel woke up on the couch in her office shortly before 6 am as the first morning rays sneaked in. She decided to take a shower to wake up. It was a long one, as she let the hot water wash away the tears.

The military was in hyperdrive, itching to slam someone hard, and soon.

Memorials to the victims sprang up everywhere in New York City, in front of apartments, in parks, in front of fire and police stations. Posters of missing relatives and friends appeared on lampposts and walls. Many began the painful trek from one hospital to another looking for the missing, though eerily, very few injured had been brought in for treatment. There was the growing realization that there would be no more survivors pulled from the Trade Center site.

The nation was in mourning, in shock, frightened. Americans gathered in churches, temples and mosques across the land to pay their respects and search for some solace. Television stations were still carrying nothing other than the attack, an around-the-clock wake. The media had concluded that bin Laden was the likely culprit and speculated when Rachel would order a retaliatory strike.

Hundreds of firefighters and police officers were missing and presumed dead. Overnight, tension between the police and many city residents disappeared. Across the country the Red Cross was overwhelmed with donations of blood and other assistance. Evacuation crews and teams descended upon the city from all over the country. The projected death toll continued to rise.

Over the objections of everyone but Wynn, Rachel left for New York that afternoon shortly after giving the order to lower the security alert to the second level.

Rachel insisted on a subdued visit — she didn't want to disrupt the rescue effort. She made a few somber remarks upon her arrival, but mainly wanted to be with people, with the families of victims, with rescue workers. She met with the mayor and governor, and repeated her offer for whatever assistance was needed. Her mind wandered to Tommy as the mayor gave her a briefing. The mayor halted when she failed to respond to one of his questions. She looked up to find everyone watching her curiously.

"I'm sorry. You're doing a great job, Mister Mayor. The people of New York are lucky to have someone as capable as you in this time of need." She paused. "Please continue. Perhaps we could visit the World Trade Center site soon. I would like to see my husband."

The mayor nodded. "Of course. I know that you must be worried about your son."

"Thank you. It's not just my son, it's all those people trapped there. It's so tragic. So many good people have died in the last few days, and for what? To make some type of statement?" Rachel asked, not expecting an answer.

Rachel made it to the Trade Center in late afternoon. It was a gorgeous fall day, except for the smoke that darkened the sky. And the dust. The dust was everywhere, covering twisted buildings and vehicles in a gray shroud. The rescuers were exhausted, ready to drop, but they worked at a feverish pitch, angrily waving off anyone who urged them to rest.

Rachel made sure that the EPA issued a health warning for the rescue workers and residents about the air quality. It was clear that this was a toxic plume, with all those chemicals, heavy metals and plastic in the two towers and building seven having been incinerated in the collapse and in the several enormous fires.

It was a war zone, skeleton buildings frozen in the midst of a ghastly waltz. It was hell. Rachel couldn't believe what she was seeing.

She declined to make any statement, instead handing out hot coffee and sandwiches to the workers. Many of them had heard by now that the president's son was missing. She thanked them for the work they were doing, spent a few minutes asking them about their own families and lives. A few related that they had friends, coworkers or brothers missing in the rubble, taking a moment to share a hug, offer words of encouragement to her. Several told her that she had done the right thing in shooting down the plane. One construction worker told her, "If anyone complains, just tell them to come visit me. Right here on this site."

One of the firefighters from a station house with 11 missing broke down sobbing as he described his friends to her. They clung to each other for a moment. That shot was broadcast worldwide repeatedly over the next few days.

She asked the relief workers with whom she spoke to call or write once the immediate crisis was over, to let her know how they were doing.

Before she left, Rachel and Wynn knelt in an out of the way spot and lit a candle. They stayed for ten minutes, praying and saying good-bye to her son, asking God and the souls of those recently departed for guidance. Hundreds had joined her by the time she got up to depart. They sang a chorus of "Amazing Grace." She thanked them all for their courage and leadership. "I promise to do absolutely everything I can to correct this injustice."

****

Wynn and Rachel grabbed a few minutes of privacy before Rachel flew back. He would stay to coordinate the search efforts for Tommy. Wynn held her tightly.

"Why me, Wynn?" Rachel pleaded to know. "I'm the best friend that the Arab world has had as president. I support the right of people to their own culture and religion. I oppose globalization. Why do they have to kill all those people, including my own son, when I'm the president? And force me to shoot down a plane with our own people on it? I'll carry a mental picture of those people dying, in my head, in my soul, to the grave."

Wynn held her tight as tears flowed freely. "It's not you Rachel, it's America they're attacking. And you know that it's not the Arab world, it's just a few twisted people. They had this attack planned long before you suddenly became president."

Rachel broke away. "These people are evil. They've killed thousands whose only crime was getting up and going to work in the morning. They've killed my own son, who wanted to change things as much as they do," she said.

Rachel straightened up, finding resolve. Hers was not a pretty face.

"It's my job to eliminate them. I know that violence just creates more violence, but I've got to put an end to these murderers first, and then figure out how to clean up the rest of the mess the world is in. All those people buried out there, thousands and thousands. These madmen are not going to stop. They'll just kill more and more people while I give sermons about peace and the rule of law. I can't have the blood of more innocent people on my hands because I was afraid to use force."

Wynn brushed a few strands of hair out of her face. "Rachel, you can't act from hate. Or fear. It's moments like this when you have to hold your values and beliefs most strongly, not walk away from them. You're not the guilty one. You have to figure out how to walk through the fires of hell and keep your soul intact. For whatever reason, you're the one who's been chosen to lead our nation at this moment. The earth goddess chose the right woman for the job." He gave her a smile, kissed her forehead, held her close.

Wynn was concerned about the woman, the mother, he saw in front of him. He trusted that this meltdown was because she was alone with him, that she'd pull herself together as soon as the door opened. He knew what she needed him to say. Someone had to give her permission.

"I'm sorry — it's unfair, it's cruel, but you have to let Tommy go, at least for the time being. Remember your love for him. If he's still alive — wherever he is — he feels that love, and he knows that you're doing the best you can to rescue him and the others. I'll stay here to make sure everything possible is done to find him. But Tommy would be the first to tell you to save the world. Those people in the plane that was shot down were already dead. You just had the courage to save others from being killed. Don't give those terrorists what they want, which is an all-out war, East vs. West — civil war in many of the Middle Eastern countries. Fill the hole in your heart with all the people on this planet who need you to love and care for them right now."

Wynn had her wrapped in a bear hug and felt her chest heaving, sobbing, against his. "You've got some horrible choices to make. More people are probably going to die. But you have to have the courage to say *no* to killing innocent people. Once you start sliding down the slippery slope of war, it's hard to stop," he whispered, kissing her.

Rachel began to pull herself together, straightening up, wiping the tears, giving a short, embarrassed laugh.

"Some speech," Rachel said. "Oh, Wynn, I wish there was a peaceful solution to all this. But they've already gone way over the line. Even the strongest advocates of nonviolence also believe in the right to defend oneself. If I fail to act, and they fly a plane into a nuclear power plant next, or set off bombs at a football stadium, or explode a nuclear weapon, then I will be responsible for killing thousands or even millions."

"No, Rachel you will not," Wynn said. "The terrorists will be responsible, not you. Launching a military strike will just kill more innocent people, make more terrorists. The way to peace is always much harder than the way to war, but the only way to peace is peace. To do that requires a woman of tremendous strength and courage and love.

You're that woman, Rachel. That's why I married you," giving her a long kiss.

****

September 13, 9:15 am

Anna called the Oval Office from Rainstein US Air Force Base in Germany. She'd talked her way onto an American military flight out of Nairobi, using her recent status as the president's personal envoy in the Nigerian crisis. She was now being denied permission to catch a military flight back to the US. Civilian flights were still banned.

"Hi, Rachel. I thought you might need some help, or at least someone to hug," said Anna.

"Anna," Rachel cried. "It's so good to hear your voice. Damn right — haul your butt back here. All hell is breaking loose. I really need a personal support team right now." Rachel tried her best to sound upbeat.

"Hold on a sec," Anna replied. She turned around to face the security personnel who were watching her. "Hey, the president wants to know who has the biggest ass that needs to get kicked? Volunteers line up right here. I'll give ya da phone as soon as I'm done." There were no immediate takers. It looked like they were planning to pull straws.

Anna got serious, lowered her voice. "Listen, I'm sorry, really sorry, about Tommy. I've been seeing reports on CNN. But don't give up hope. It's still early."

Rachel choked back a sob. "Oh Anna, I'm on an emotional roller coaster. One minute I'm the strongest person on the planet, the next I wanna just sit in a corner and cry — first about Tommy, then about all those people in the plane we shot down, and all those people buried at the World Trade Center. I've aged a lot in the last few days," Rachel told her.

"Rachel Moreno, you didn't shoot down that plane. I know you feel you did but you didn't. Everyone, and I mean everyone, realizes there was no choice," Anna argued.

"I was the last one who could have stopped those sixty-three people from being blown up and I didn't. And it was on my watch that the most horrific terrorist act on American soil occurred. Someone has to feel responsible for so many people losing their lives, and I do," Rachel countered.

"Hey Rachel, cheer up. I'll give you the best back rub that's ever taken place in the White House tonight," Anna promised.

****

September 13, 4:30 PM

Rachel was still torn about how she should respond to the attacks. Darling, Deutsche, and Baker each talked to her several times about the need for a strong, decisive military response. Darling had told her, "This is not the time to have a pacifist as president. Your job as commander in chief is to defend our country from attack."

Part of her agreed. She wanted to bring a sledgehammer down on those responsible for these attacks, for murdering her son. The situation room was feverishly analyzing several possible attack plans. They'd want her to give a green light pretty soon.

The peace activists she'd pulled together in the White House, many of them involved with the Greens, were working on a different scenario.

Rachel squeezed in an hour to meet with them. Wynn flew back from New York to attend. And Anna had arrived.

"All the polls show the desire for revenge is strong, and the public wants quick action," Rachel bluntly told them. She didn't want them thinking this was going to be easy. "We need a credible plan on how to bring those guilty of this horror to justice, and we need a plan to combat terrorism and improve security for the future. Merely saying that violence gets more violence isn't going to work for long, especially with Congress pushing in the opposite direction."

"Rachel," said Ray McDaniels, the Green congressmember from Seattle, "one thing that might help is to get some of the relatives of victims to join you in urging caution in our response. Several of them have issued statements that they don't want to see more innocent civilians killed in response to the deaths of their loved ones."

"That's a good idea. I want to make sure that the families of these victims have a voice," Rachel said. But she dreaded the idea of talking to the relatives of those who'd been shot down, though she'd asked Sophie to get her a list of the relatives to call personally. She'd been delaying this chore until Wynn could sit with her. Most appreciated her call; a few were angry, blaming her and the government for shooting down the plane.

"Rachel, you've gotta make people understand that American

foreign policy results in people hating America so much they're willing to launch suicide attacks against us. Our country has a long tradition of making deals with the devil to overthrow some government that we don't like, and then, surprise surprise, ten years later those same people are throwing bombs at us. Like bin Laden," stated Sandy Alvarez, the Green congressmember from New Mexico.

"Congress and the media are telling the American people that there was no way to predict this, but we all know that's a lie. Even the recent report by former senator Hart that was commissioned by Congress concluded that it was not a question of *if* a terrorist attack would occur on American soil but *when*," Alvarez added.

"I agree we need to educate Americans," said Rachel. "But we can't be seen blaming America for these terrorist attacks. People are very upset, and the Democrats, Republicans, corporations, media, military-industrial complex, you name it, are ready to pounce on any opening or mistake we give them." She then added, "Thousands of people have been murdered. The public needs a credible response."

Leslie Glick of the Peace and Justice Coalition asked, "Do you have a plan on how to proceed?"

"I've asked my husband, Wynn, to be my point person with you. Please develop concrete recommendations. Also, I need the Greens and the rest of you to help mobilize the peace community to provide an alternative to all the voices demanding war. But you have to respond to people's grief, be willing to accept their anger and fear as legitimate." Rachel, already late for a meeting in the situation room, turned the meeting over to Wynn.

"This isn't going to be easy," Wynn observed, "especially the way the media is promoting war. We need our best people, the ones with a lot of community respect, the faith leaders, on the talk shows. Make sure we start off by addressing people's grief."

"We need to work with the Green parties in Europe and elsewhere to develop a common strategy," added Glick. "Several of them are in coalition governments."

The German Greens were key to this effort. While the German Greens were the junior member of the governing coalition, Jüürgen Kelly of the Greens was Germany's Foreign Minister and the most popular politician in the country. Many American Greens felt that Kelly had betrayed the party's commitment to nonviolence by supporting the NATO bombing campaign during the war over Kosovo. Kelly countered that as junior member of the coalition, Green options were limited, but by agreeing to support military action to halt the alleged "genocide," his seat at the table had resulted in a much quicker ceasefire.

Wynn told them they needed to develop proposals on how the international community should confront terrorism.

"Neither Congress nor the American people are going to allow us much grace period in bringing the individuals responsible for September eleventh to justice. Most of them right now are expecting to see some humongous display of firepower that asserts our military superiority over the rest of the world."

Rosa Perez, a Peace Action activist from South Central LA, interjected: "The biggest terrorists have been the American government and our puppets. All those Central American dictators, the School of Assassins. The military juntas in Indonesia and Iran. The so-called freedom fighters in Afghanistan that Congress wants to give arms to, bigger than what we gave 'em 'gainst the Soviets. God, everywhere you look, Americans are brutalizing people, for money and power. Congress and the media act like some new line in warfare was crossed 'cause so many Americans were killed, but the US has killed a lot more civilians all over the globe. And let's not forget we're the ones who dropped the atomic bomb on Hiroshima."

Rosa, barely five feet tall, spoke with a passion that reminded Wynn of Anna. She was someone who readily felt the pain of others.

Rosa continued, "Rachel has to stop Congress from bombing Afghanistan. She has no choice. Rachel has to speak up for all those innocent civilians there that have been brutalized by their own leaders. Millions of Afghans — women, children, elders — are on the brink of starvation. The Afghani refugee camps in Pakistan have been the largest in the world for the last decade. We used the Afghans as pawns against the Soviet Union, and now we're about to starve and bomb them to death."

"The Greens have always stood against the use of violence, including military force, to solve problems. It's easy to be for nonviolence when no one is shooting at you. Rachel needs to stand firm on this," Glick added.

"Rachel can insist all she wants," Wynn responded, "but she doesn't control the Congress. There are enormous pressures on you when you're president. Power is a double-edged sword. It ends up trying to wield you while you wield it. It's our job to make it possible for Rachel to avoid war," he added.

****

September 14,- 1:45 am, White House personal quarters

Anna, Wynn and Rachel stayed up late, allegedly to help Rachel write a eulogy for an ecumenical service at the National Cathedral. Rachel was looking through some of her photo albums for pictures of Tommy. She put on some of his favorite CDs. The evening stretched on. Rachel did not want to find fresh nightmares in her sleep. They finished the speech about 1 am. Wynn got a beer for himself, some wine for Anna. Rachel was drinking Scotch.

Wynn and Anna argued over the historical implications of the attack on the WTC. Rachel was just numb.

"This is a clash between two freaking ruling elites, not a revolution of the weak and oppressed," Anna said. "Bin Laden lives off Saudi corruption. By attacking the US, he's just trying to get the locals to kick butt on the rulers in Saudi Arabia and Pakistan by forcing them to back the US in a god damn holy war. No one was even paying attention to this bastard until Clinton decided to lob some cruise missiles at 'im, making him a superstar. Even if we kick him down, the more awesome our response, the bigger this bad-ass becomes on the Arab street."

Wynn agreed with the need for caution. "While killing five thousand people is an enormous crime, these attacks were aimed at economic and political targets. Next time, particularly if Congress gets its way and drops plenty of bombs, killing civilians throughout the Middle East, the terrorists may decide to focus on killing the maximum number of Americans."

Rachel failed to respond to the discussion. Her body slumped, she puts her hands to her face. She suddenly felt amazingly tired and drained.

She looked up at her husband and friend, her voice breaking. "I'm amazed at how far Tommy can be from the center of my thoughts, but there is so much bearing down on me. Then he pops through, along with the faces of the passengers watching the missile blow them up.

"That's when the guilt hits. I try to convince myself I've got to let him go right now, that everything that can be done to find him is being done, that I have to focus on everything else before more people get killed," Rachel said, rocking back and forth on the couch, her hands pulling her knees tight.

"I feel I'm betraying him by sitting here while he's buried alive under the biggest building in the world. A building dropped on him and thousands of others because somebody had a beef with the government I'm in charge of," Rachel sobbed.

Wynn went over to embrace her. Anna joined them

****

September 14, 11 am, the Oval Office.

The meeting with the congressional leaders wasn't going well. It was clear that they had been conferring with the Joint Chiefs, since Rachel not only received the same proposals but the same words from both groups.

Senator Deutsche cited polling data showing that 80 percent of the public was strongly behind a quick military response. An equally high percentage supported increased police powers, including for surveillance and searches, even if it meant a curtailment in civil liberties.

Deutsche said, "The American people view this as another Pearl Harbor and demand a similar response."

"Pearl Harbor was a military attack by a foreign country seeking to expand its empire throughout the Pacific," Rachel reminded them. "This attacks appears to be by a terrorist organization, more analogous to the assassination of Archduke Ferdinand that touched off World War One. Besides killing millions, let's remember that the First World War led to the rise of a number of totalitarian regimes that oppressed their own people while striving to conquer others. And two decades later we fought the war all over again. That is a mistake I don't want to repeat."

Deutsche wasn't listening. Nor was Speaker Baker.

"Rachel, Congress, not the president, declares war. As Commander in Chief, the president usually takes the lead in such situations. But this ain't the normal situation," Baker remarked. "First, you've got Americans killed in our homeland. Two, only one outta ten Americans voted for ya. Not that I'm countin'. We Republicans may knock heads with Democrats on domestic stuff, but we generally agree when it comes to foreign policy, especially on matters of war. Congress ain't gonna sit on our hands while y'all lecture on pacifism as terrorists kill American people," Baker remarked.

Rachel got up from behind the desk, gave herself time to compose her response. If she couldn't figure out how to make peace with the Democrats and Republicans, what chance did she have with America's enemies? She looked out over the Rose Garden before turning back.

"Senator, Freddy — one of those people was my son. I was forced to order sixty-three people to be blown from the sky. There's a large part of me that would take great pleasure in pushing the button that would wipe whoever was responsible for this off the face of the world. But that wouldn't end it. There are terrorists all over the world. As much as we call it a war, it isn't. There's no government for us to beat up, destroy its army, make it surrender. We can't fight it with the old rules. It won't work."

Baker persisted. "Madame President, I know ya mean well, but the only thang these people respect is force. Force, and an iron will. They believe that America is too soft to spill our own blood to fight 'em. If we fail to attack 'em now, they'll just get stronger, bolder, more ruthless. They'll be heroes in the Islamic world, raise more money, more volunteers. They'll take over a few governments, then they'll launch bigger bombs till we run away and hide. Then they'll have won, and a lot of people who count on us, includin' a lotta women, will blame us for makin' their lives a living hell and for sacrificing 'em 'cause we didn't have the guts to stand up to 'em."

Rachel had a hard time focusing. It was like listening to a record that skipped over and over again.

"Gentlemen, I understand the urgency to do something to show we are in control and to prevent more Americans from being killed. But we need to be realistic about the limitations on the use of force in this situation. We're here to make the hard choices, the right choices, not the easy ones. Doing something now just to make us feel better isn't the answer," Rachel said.

Congressmember William Pierce of Texas, Chair of the Armed Services Committee, had little patience for these arguments. "Of course we gotta defend ourselves. Americans were killed on our soil. We know who's behind it. These terrorists believe they can push us around and that our respect for human life and the rule of law will prevent us from strikin' back. We gotta show 'em they've made a fatal miscalculation. Maybe drop a small nuclear warhead or two out in the Afghanistan desert — scare their backers so much that they'll send us their heads by Federal Express. I don't have a sense that any of the terrorists' supporters are involved in any soul searchin' at this point. If we don't bury them, they'll bury us," said Pierce, his face turning red.

Rachel did her best to exhibit steel in her response, hoping her heart wasn't pounding too loudly. She had always admired how Wynn seemed able to do this "command and dominate" thing so effortlessly, play this macho game.

"Let's be clear about one thing. You can forget about using nuclear weapons. We're not going to play a game of mutually assured destruction. Lots of countries, and probably several terrorists, also have nuclear weapons they can respond with." Rachel was almost shouting.

"And if we attack with conventional bombs and missiles and kill innocent civilians that have nothing to do with this, we'll just recruit more martyrs to their cause. They've shown they won't hesitate to kill American civilians. For all we know, they have hundreds of people already in the US, just itching for the call to kill themselves and a few thousand others."

"Whoever did this will be happy to raise the death toll to whatever level is needed to make us quit. Americans want revenge but that's going to get old pretty quickly if the other side keeps on striking back. You want us to fight a war against a collection of madmen spread out over dozens of countries, hidden away among innocent civilians who often no more support these terrorists than we do."

"And if we don't strike back, they'll just keep on striking at us. Either way the death toll is going to go up. Given that choice, we need to remove them as a military threat, rather than waiting for them to kill more Americans," Deutsche interjected. "Some of these terrorists have access to weapons of mass destruction."

Rachel didn't bother reigning her temper in. "I know you think I'm naïve to avoid a quick military strike, but you have your heads in the sand. Our military has spent trillions of dollars preparing us to fight World War Two all over again. What we have instead is a different type of war, with small groups of individuals operating clandestinely in many different countries, not attacking military targets but killing civilians in attacks designed to achieve maximum publicity and fear. Building billion-dollar stealth planes may help our defense contractors but it won't help us win the fight against terrorism."

"Sitting on our hands certainly won't win it," Pierce countered. "We've got the strongest military in the world for a reason. It's time to use it."

"If Congress is hell bent on declaring war, I can't stop you," Rachel said finally. "But you better figure out who you're going to declare war against, and how you expect to win. Bin Laden or whoever directed this attack expects us to strike back. Let's try to figure out a strategy that he doesn't expect."

The meeting broke up with little resolution other than the obligatory photo. Their clenched, grim smiles seemed appropriate for the nation's mood. The congressional leaders agreed to present her a clearly defined military response before making any declaration of war. They also agreed to her request to develop ways to prosecute the attack based on international law, and for suggestions on worldwide collective security measures that could be presented to the United Nations. Rachel agreed to come up with a detailed proposal on how to best seek a peaceful solution.

****

Saturday, September 14, Noon.

The Lord is my shepherd; I shall not want. He makes me to lie down in green pastures; He leads me beside the still waters. He restores my soul; He leads me in the paths of righteousness. Yea, though I walk through the valley of the shadow of death, I will fear no evil; For You are with me
— **Psalm 23:4**

A memorial service was held in the National Cathedral. Representatives from the country's many religious traditions spoke. All the living presidents attended.

Most comforting to Rachel was seeing Chandra Clinton, the young daughter of the former president. Chandra pulled her aside for a few words. To Rachel's surprise, she told her, "Tommy called me up a few weeks ago to talk about what it was like to be a president's child and to live in a fish bowl, asking for any advice I might have. What was very clear was how much he loved and respected you." Rachel gave her a big hug.

Each speaker tried to help the nation come to terms with its grief. Rachel allowed the tears to flow freely. She rested her head on Wynn's shoulder.

Then it was time for Rachel to speak.

"Just a few weeks ago we were here to lay President Harrington to rest. We are here today to cope with an even greater tragedy.

"Messages have been pouring in from all corners of the world. The American people are indeed grateful. I want to share some with you now. One of my favorites is from Rabbi Michael Lerner:

We should pray for the victims and their families. We should pray that American does not return to business as usual, but rather returns to a period of reflection … finding a way to turn the direction of our society at every level, a return to the notion that every human life is sacred, that 'the bottom line' should be the creation of a world of loving and caring, and that the best way to prevent these kinds of acts is not to turn ourselves into a police state, but to turn ourselves into a society in which social justice, love and compassion is so prevalent that violence becomes only a distant memory.

"This note was sent to me by Phyllis and Orlando Rodriguez, whose son Greg lost his life at the World Trade Center:

We see our hurt and anger reflected among everybody we meet. We fear that many want our country to head in the direction of violent revenge, with the prospect of sons, daughters, parents, friends in distant lands dying, suffering, and nursing further grievances against us. It is not the way to go. It will not avenge our son's death. Not in our son's name. Our son died a victim of an inhuman ideology. Our actions should not serve the same purpose. Let us grieve. Let us reflect and pray. Let us think about a rational response that brings real peace and justice to our world. But let us not as a nation add to the inhumanity of our times.

"Here is another note from Amber Amundson, who lost her husband, the father of her young children:

My husband would not want a violent response to avenge his death. We cannot solve violence with violence. Revenge is a self-perpetuating cycle. Gandhi said, 'An eye for an eye only makes the whole world blind.' I call on our national leaders to find the courage to respond to this incomprehensible tragedy by breaking the cycle of violence. I call on them to marshal this great nation's skills and resources to lead a worldwide dialogue on freedom from terror and hate. I call on them to focus our strength to work for justice and peace around the globe. I ask them to unleash our country's immense energy to create a world in which compassion and forgiveness are possible.

A sense of absolute quiet had descended over the cathedral. In a moment of stunning clarity, Rachel felt attuned with all the souls on the planet. She felt the soul of her son rising.

Rachel scanned the faces in the cathedral, connecting with each. Time became suspended, an eternal moment without boundaries. She felt the pain and power of those who stood in such a place before her to deliver such an address. She felt Harry Truman as he agreed to drop the first atomic bomb. She rode on the top of the first World Trade Center tower as it slowly descended into the ground, feeling each girder as it crumbled, one after another. She felt the sense of a terrible judgment rumbling across the heavens. She felt the primal forces of the planet crying out, the devil laughing, children crying, the death of her father, the oppressed of the world in rags on their knees praying for salvation, of missiles flying through the skies, of cities burning.

The souls of the recently departed loomed before her, an overpowering presence, urging her on, demanding justice. She was forced to take a step backward.

The clock ticked. Time resumed.

The faces in the audience still stared up at her.

"I pray today to many Gods, all Gods, asking for guidance in our time of anguish. I ask our Gods to give us understanding, so that we can see why so many innocent people had to be wrenched away from our embrace before their time. I ask our Gods to let our souls be at rest, for our grief and pain are great. Show us mercy, oh Lord, and show us the way to forgiveness, because that is such a hard path to find. Give the world justice, Lord, and may you shower your blessings upon your people and heal them and give them peace. We ask you this, oh Lord."

She lowered her eyes from the heavens to find the audience. Her voice went quiet and confessional.

"As a mother, Lord, I pray for the eternal life and salvation of my son, Tommy. He was a good person, struck down just as his adulthood was beginning. I know that there are many people out there who are mourning today for the loss of a son or daughter, a wife, a husband, a parent, a loved one, a person who was an integral part of our bond with humanity. That bond has not been broken, it has just been stretched to its limit." Rachel's voice quivered.

"Tommy had the soul, if not always the behavior, of a saint. He worshiped life in all its manifestations, from the smallest to the mightiest, from the butterfly to the majestic redwood, from the bottom of the seas to the skies above us. He was able to find the sacred in every living thing. He sought to live his life to the fullest. He died as he lived, extending a hand to others in trouble. As a young man, he still believed that all change was possible, that the perfect world could be achieved if only we could imagine it.

"The Lord has called us to a great moral challenge, to rid the world of evil. In accepting this challenge, let us remember that Jews, Muslims, and Christians have one thing in common. They all pray to Yahweh. If we all pray to God, the God of peace and love, we should be able to find a way to live and worship together. There is no way to peace, peace is the way.

"May God shower her blessings on us all. Amen."

****

September 18, 7 pm

The service at the cathedral had helped Rachel find her way.

She decided to make a televised national address on the one week anniversary of the attack. The demand for action was growing louder.

"I speak tonight with deep sorrow for the loss of so many lives exactly one week ago on September 11, 2001. I want to thank all the people, here at home and from around the world, who have reached out to offer what assistance and comfort they can. I especially want to express our gratitude and admiration for the heroic efforts of the firefighters, police officers and construction workers who risked their own lives to help others.

"While our country rightfully demands that those who are responsible for the killing of so many innocent individuals be brought to justice, our cries of grief should resist becoming a call for war. War is exactly what the terrorists want, a war between the West and Islam. Not only do they want to expel the US from the Middle East, but they seek the overthrow of existing governments in Islamic countries so they can impose their own brand of religious fundamentalism.

"As president, I believe that we must look at these horrific terrorist acts as a crime against humanity and prosecute them accordingly. These individuals are criminals and should be treated as such, just as we did with Timothy McVeigh after he blew up the federal building in Oklahoma City. We cannot allow the audacity of their crimes to provoke us into violating the rules of international law, which is exactly what they want.

"We cannot create more innocent victims, nor can we scapegoat people from a whole area of the world for the acts of a few individuals. America has always been a melting pot, a place where people from around the world can come to build better lives for themselves and for their children. We were wrong during World War Two to force law-abiding Americans of Japanese descent into camps. We must avoid making similar mistakes here. We were *not* attacked by Islam — we were attacked by a few individuals who care not how many innocent people are killed.

"Peace is always harder to achieve than war. A desire for peace does mean holding terrorists responsible for their crimes. But the overwhelming majority of the citizens of our planet want a world free from violence. They want a world that recognizes the sacredness of each human life, that seeks to ensure a decent standard of living for all, while protecting our environment, and tolerating and valuing the diversity of culture and religion.

"We need to be willing to work with other countries to create such a world, to strengthen the rule of international law, to promote true democracy, to create a global collective security that allows us and other countries to divert our military spending to meet human needs.

"War and terrorism, reprehensible as they are, occur within a political context. It is important for us as Americans to become more familiar with the issues that cause conflict with other countries. I ask you to have the courage to search for truth in this time of grief. This does not in any way condone the murders of so many innocent individuals. But if we are to build a world of peace and justice, we need to understand how other countries and cultures view the US.

"The truth will not always be pleasant. We need to ask why so many countries against whom we have waged war in recent decades, were at one time supported militarily and financially by the US. We need to examine why the people we wage war against are so often people of color.

"We must be willing to admit, and learn from, the mistakes of our past so we can avoid repeating them in the future. We need to recognize that other countries can share our goals of peace and justice but reflect different cultural values, religions, political institutions and lifestyles. We have entered a new millennium, where advances in communication and technology have created a global village, where in a few minutes we can connect with someone half way around the world. Our political institutions, our government, the way we make decisions, have not expanded or changed to deal with this new world that we have created. We need to understand that with the advent of the global village America can be safe only if all other countries also feel safe.

"We need more democracy in the US, not less. We must resist the call to curtail the civil liberties that the American people won during our own Revolution. We must not suppress free thought but call for informed and open political debate.

"There are some, perhaps many, who criticize me for not immediately launching missiles to destroy those who are guilty of such heinous crimes, and to punish those who have assisted them in such evil acts. But it is our moral obligation to punish only those who are responsible, not those who are themselves harmed and oppressed by these same individuals.

"We are at a crossroads. We can respond to this terrorist act by unleashing our military might to rain death upon people in the far-flung corners of the world, an attack that will most likely cause even more deaths in our own country and possibly lead to World War Three. Or we can say it is time to create a world that seeks to lift up and protect all human beings regardless of their nation, culture, gender, religion or color.

"It is also time to end our reliance upon fossil fuels. This dependency has been at the root of many of our disputes in the Middle East. We unfortunately failed to take action after the Gulf War to ensure our energy independence, to ensure that we would never have to send our sons and daughters to fight another war for oil.

"I have directed our Department of Energy to immediately divert all possible funds to support the expansion of our use of renewable energy sources, such as solar, wind, biomass and geothermal, and to promote energy conservation and energy efficiency. Not only will this greatly increase our national security, it will help reduce global warming and put more Americans to work. I have asked Congress to join me in the effort to support energy independence.

"I have also directed the Department of Defense to work with the Nuclear Regulatory Commission to implement a phaseout of nuclear power plants. They are, in effect, nuclear bombs scattered throughout our country that can be targeted by terrorists. We will begin with the immediate shutdown of nuclear plants located near major population centers.

"I believe that it is time for a world peace treaty. Such an international agreement can put an end to a century that has seen more human beings killed in war and conflict than at any other time in history. I will ask Congress and New York City to erect a World Peace Institute on the hallowed ashes of the World Trade Center, to create a permanent organization that will teach and guide us all in creating a more peaceful world. We have too many departments of defense and war in the world. It is time to create a Department of Peace. Ultimately its adoption and success depends upon you, the American citizens. Only you can make Congress listen. Only America has the power to move the political debate and struggle in the world to another level.

"I have been planning a People's Summit to coincide with the upcoming World Trade Organization meeting. I plan to move this to New York City to launch the peace treaty and World Peace Institute, and I invite all the other nations of the world to participate.

"I would like to end by reading the first two paragraphs of the peace treaty.

"We, the people of this planet, do hereby petition our governments and fellow citizens to negotiate and implement an International Peace Treaty. It is time to put a halt to the incessant and escalating use of violence and terrorism that has killed millions of our brothers and sisters in conflicts throughout the world. We seek to build a new world based on the rule of international law; the respect for and protection of the sacredness of each human life; and a commitment to preserve our cultural, social and ecological diversity from the threats posed by globalization.

"We call for the redirection of funds from armaments to human security and sustainable development; equal participation by marginalized groups, including women and indigenous people; and a commitment to collective global security that protects us all from the threat of violence. We support the empowerment of democratic international decision-making, including reorienting international financial institutions to serve human rather than corporate needs.

"I hope that God, in all her manifestations and beliefs, will bless America and all countries tonight, and show us the way to peace. Good night."

****

The reaction to the president's speech was decidedly mixed.

Her statements were well received by foreign governments, particularly those in Europe, with the notable exceptions of Britain and Israel. Her speech empowered the peace and justice movements throughout the world, leading to massive rallies in support.

The million-dollar American tv anchors weren't used to criticizing the country's leader during a time of war but they also weren't used to the commander in chief calling for peace. The talking head commentators, a mixture of former political leaders and defense contractors, were less restrained. The energy companies were, of course, furious.

The comments from conservative think tanks and radio talk show hosts were more pointed. "A horrible speech. She's blaming America for getting what we deserve, playing into the hands of the enemy." "She can't bring herself to shoot at these terrorists and the people helping them, but she didn't hesitate to shoot down a plane full of Americans." "She just surrendered. Next thing we know we'll have the UN Army patrolling our streets."

Some openly called for Congress to remove her. "I knew we were in trouble as soon as she kissed the ass of those terrorists over in Nigeria," said one caller to the White House. Another, from her home state of Colorado, said, "we've got to hit them back hard. I thought that draft dodger Bill Clinton with his Queen Hillary was bad enough, but at least he had the balls to shoot some missiles at bin Laden." A third opined, "This Moreno woman feels a need to prove she's a card-carrying feminist peacenik. I don't know anyone who voted for her, yet she gets to call herself president. Frankly, I think it's unconstitutional and it's time to throw her out where she belongs."

NINE

BAY AREA ACTIVISM

The Eighties

Rachel remained active with CAN after Wynn departed, even serving for a year as vice-chair of the Citywide Board.

Tommy entered America's free day care program, otherwise known as the public school system. Rachel tried to hold back tears as Tommy proudly marched into kindergarten on his first day, clutching his lunch box, telling Rachel "I'm not a baby anymore. I'm a student."

Tommy was a daredevil, ringleader of the local boys, the one that goaded them into doing mischief. He'd developed the art of acting confused when confronted, aided by an angelic smile to bail him out. "Tommy is a handful," Rachel confided to Maria one afternoon. "He gives me a hug one moment, makes me pull out my hair the next. He has a nose for getting in trouble."

Maria laughed. "Si, sounds like a boy."

Wynn kept in touch from Albany with long, rambling letters. She responded with hand drawn note cards. He also sent crazy gifts to Tommy, practical jokes, like whoopee cushions and noisemakers, which little boys love. Wynn called once a month or so, usually late on Saturday night, taking advantage of the time difference.

"I've gotten active in several environmental groups I met during the work on pesticides," Rachel told him. "We've started a campaign to cleanup a working-class neighborhood where several dozen homes had been built on top of an old toxic dump. I'm also working with Pete on the antinuclear campaign and at the food coop."

Rachel began to get paid for her activist work. She took a series of part-time community outreach jobs, such as signing up pregnant women for the Women, Infants and Children program.

Another job was as a door to-door canvasser for an environmental group. "Mighty impressive," Wynn told her. "Many activists describe canvassing as their hardest job ever. It's not like doorknocking for members, where you're trying to get them involved. All you focus on is the money. Most people can't handle the constant rejection."

"I have no problem with liberating funds for the cause from someone with a comfortable lifestyle," Rachel told him. "You have to figure out which households are likely to give and then zero in on them. Check the bumper stickers on their car, look at what type of garden they have. You've gotta learn how to turn the five-dollar contribution into twenty-five. Quota for the evening, five hours of doorknocking, is eighty dollars. I'm pulling in twice that most nights," Rachel told him. She was so good they allowed her to canvass on whatever days she wanted.

The Hostel for Wayward Youth didn't survive long after Wynn's departure.

"Have you heard about Steve?" Rachel asked Wynn. "One of Pete's friends had a slide show on the outdoor wall of the house last weekend, gorgeous shots from a recent trip to Hawaii — a tropical paradise, waterfalls and green everywhere. Steve got up the next morning and hitchhiked to LA, caught a hundred-dollar seat to Hawaii."

Steve lived in Hawaii for six months, living on the beach in a tent, or on the couch on someone's front porch, collecting food stamps — the state was quite happy to bring in more federal dollars. He made ends meet by doing odd jobs, renting snorkeling equipment to the tourists, painting condos, doing yard work.

His parents sent him money to fly home to New Jersey for the holidays. At a Grateful Dead show at Madison Square Garden, he met Roberta, an eighteen-year-old from Vermont seeing the Dead for the first time. It was love at first sight. They ended up buying an old school bus, which they fixed up into a camper and drove around to Dead shows for several years, surviving by selling Asian pancakes in the parking lot along with some jewelry that Roberta made.

After they had their first baby, delivered aboard the bus with the help of a midwife, they built an underground house in upstate New York. They got involved with an alternative school — Roberta became the kindergarten teacher and Steve the all-around handyman and school treasurer.

Pete hit the road a year after Wynn did. They threw a wild going-away party, the same night that their next-door neighbor — the president of Arizona State — threw a black-tie reception. They had a bonfire, blasted the Dead and consumed copious amounts of tequila and various other substances.

When the cop cars pulled up, Rachel went out to greet them and asked if they could get the party next door to "turn it down a little bit." Rachel and Pete ended up sharing a sleeping bag on the top of the roof, a fitting way to say good-bye to the Hostel for Wayward Youth.

Pete went back east to visit his family and dropped in on Wynn. He stayed in Jersey for a couple of years, trying to perfect his carburetor ideas. He did some carpentry work at a daycare center, and stayed on as a childcare worker. Pete was a pied piper among four-year-olds, loving to act goofy and clown around, always inventing a new game that involved a lot of noise and horseplay.

Pete eventually drifted back to the West Coast. He worked summers in Alaska on fishing and tourist boats, retreating to Seattle and San Francisco for the winter.

****

In Albany, Wynn organized with the Citizens Party while working with the off-campus students. He managed the mayoral campaign of Frank Michael Donahue in 1981. Donahue was best known for passing a state law to prevent utility companies from shutting off power to residents in winter months after an elderly couple froze to death.

Donahue's big issue was to create a municipal electric company in Albany. There were forty-six municipal systems in New York State, including one just five miles upriver in Green Island. Nationwide, the three thousand public systems charged rates 30 percent cheaper than the investor-owned utilities. Donahue, of course, was attacked for "being a single issue candidate advocating socialism."

The incumbent was Erastus Corning, mayor for 42 years, in what turned out to be his swan song. He died in office the following year. Albany had a legendary Democratic political machine, with an iron grip on the voters that exceeded even Chicago's. If they couldn't buy a vote for a fiver, there were plenty of votes in the graveyards that could be counted on.

That fall the Springboks, the national rugby team of South Africa, announced a twenty-game tour in the US. Protests immediately sprang up everywhere, forcing the cancellation of all the dates except Albany, where Corning gave them permission to play in the municipal stadium. The same Dutch trading company that settled South Africa had settled Albany in the late 1600s. Corning, a direct descendant of these settlers, defended scheduling the match as "a matter of free speech."

"South Africa enacted racial discrimination laws in 1948 that covered all aspects of life," Wynn said as he spoke at Albany State. "Apartheid allows the minority white population to dominate the economic and social system. It's about oppression, exploitation, humiliation, torture, murder. It is evil. The laws touch every aspect of social life, from white-only jobs to a ban on mixed marriages. Of the 27.5 million people living in South Africa, only 4.5 million were given the rights of citizens.

"After 1948, the legal discrimination steadily increased, as did police repression," Wynn told the students. "The result is that blacks are forced to live in rural wastelands, confined to the 13 percent most undesirable land. Whites get the other 87 percent, living a life of affluence and privilege. Blacks always have to carry a 35-page identification book, their badge of slavery. It has their fingerprints and other information, such as whether your boss or the government allows you to be on city streets after 9 PM."

Diane Urbina, an organizer with the Coalition Against Apartheid and Racism, also spoke. "Since 1960, the country has usually been in a state of national emergency. This means black South Africans can be thrown into jail for six months without any evidence. Thousands have died in custody, often after horrible torture. Many others who were tried were sentenced to death, or imprisoned for life, like Nelson Mandela.

"By the late seventies, world opinion had turned against the South African government. Most governments and individuals boycotted everything to do with South Africa, from weapons to music to sports. The US and Israel remain South Africa's major supporters," Urbina reported.

Wynn threw himself into helping to organize the protest. The Springboks' appearance in Albany drew intense media attention from the start. The spotlight grew brighter as every other community canceled. However, after helping to give the protest momentum, the media became critical. "The power elite is being threatened," Wynn told the other organizers. "The owners of the media have issued marching orders to marginalize the protest."

Albany became a police state, with a massive mobilization of force and surveillance. The cops acted like they were going to war, despite the call for a peaceful protest by the organizers.

The night before the march, Wynn and several other protest organizers were meeting in an apartment to go over last-minute details when the door suddenly crashed inward and heavily armed cops burst through. All were arrested on trumped-up drug and weapon charges. They were even denied a bail hearing until after the game was over.

The arrests made the protesters more determined. Several thousand — all ages and races —marched in a cold, biting downpour through the streets of Albany as police with guns lined the rooftops. Pete Seeger sang several songs as the crowd huddled together for warmth.

Wynn went back to organizing the mayoral race when he got out. Corning swept back into office, hailed for saving the city from the hordes of protesters who were up to no good. Wynn and the others were cleared of all charges after a year-long trial, and won damages against the police department for having an organized "red squad" that harassed and infiltrated local progressive groups.

****

In 1982, Wynn moved to DC to help coordinate the US campaign against apartheid, which included getting arrested several times at the South African embassy.

Wynn volunteered in 1984 for two presidential campaigns: those of Sonia Johnson ,of the Citizens Party, and Jesse Jackson in the Democratic primary.

Wynn remained active with the Citizens Party when he moved to DC, helping out in the national office. The CiP ran nearly one hundred congressional candidates nationwide that year. Unfortunately, most only pulled one percent of the vote.

The party was also weighed down by hundreds of thousands of dollars of debt left over from the Commoner campaign. The party had bet heavily that Commoner would pull more than five percent of the vote, qualifying Commoner and the party for significant public funding. It was a fatal mistake.

Johnson came to national attention when the Mormon Church excommunicated her over the Equal Rights Amendment. She was initially upset that the church elders were bringing politics — their opposition to the ERA — into the temple, which she viewed as sacrilegious. Once she read the proposed amendment, however, she went even further and became a strong supporter. "I can't believe that our church leaders are so upset over the idea that no one shall be discriminated against because of their gender."

Being excommunicated for challenging the male hierarchy of the Church of the Latter Day Saints radicalized Johnson. She almost upset Eleanor Smeal for the presidency of the National Organization for Women in 1984, with strong support from both the radical feminist and lesbian communities. She decided to use the national presidential race as a platform to promote feminism.

Wynn recruited Rachel to help with an appearance by Johnson at a women's conference at Arizona State University. Rachel supported Sonia since she was the first woman presidential candidate — though some argued that Victoria Chaflin Woodhull had been the first in 1872. At the time women didn't have the right to vote, let alone hold office.

Rachel found that many males in the CiP were put off by Johnson's radical feminism. "She's not a feminist. She doesn't believe in equality. She just wants to replace patriarchy with matriarchy," Jeff Dixon argued.

"All Sonia's saying is that we have to replace the values of the male culture with that of women's culture," Rachel responded. "Values like cooperation, compassion, listening, sharing."

"There are plenty of men who share those values," Dixon countered.

"That's true," said Rachel. "It's just that these values have traditionally been assigned to women in our culture. Some men have been able to break their conditioning and become feminists. Just as some women, like Margaret Thatcher in Britain, have become male. But Sonia's right that it's men who are responsible for wars and pollution and violence. Men are too much about competition, about who ends up with the most toys."

Johnson's strength was as a storyteller. She could take someone else's experience or idea that spoke truth to her, and retell it in a way that powerfully touched people. Rachel was moved to tears when Johnson spoke about her recent visit to Central America with a number of women leaders, including Congresswoman Bella Abzug and Jackie Jackson, the wife of Jesse.

"During our trip, we met with President Daniel Ortega, head of the Sandinista movement in Nicaragua that overthrew the corrupt and brutal military dictatorship sponsored by the US," Johnson reported. "Ortega recently announced an amnesty for the former military and contras who had engaged in a protracted and bloody civil war against the civilian population and political reformers. Ortega said, 'our country only has a future if we can break the cycle of violence. I know it's difficult to suddenly encounter someone on the street who has tortured you, but we have to learn how to forgive them and embrace them, asking them to join us in the effort to build a better life for our children and grandchildren."

Wynn stood with Johnson outside the White House gates when she called "upon all law-abiding citizens to make a citizen's arrest of Ronald

Reagan, a/k/a the president of the United States. Mr. Reagan has violated the Federal Neutrality Act by trying to overthrow the Sandinista government in Nicaragua, and for supporting the killing of civilians in El Salvador." Private citizens can arrest individuals who have committed a felony.

Wynn made up a "Wanted" poster using a picture from one of his western movies of Reagan holding a gun in his left hand. The Center for Constitutional Rights agreed to defend anyone who was "arrested" by the Secret Service for trying to apprehend Reagan. Unfortunately, Reagan was kept far away from the general public during the election, and yet another war criminal escaped prosecution.

Wynn also managed to squeeze in time to support the Democratic presidential primary campaign of Reverend Jesse Jackson, especially because of his effort to build a Rainbow Coalition outside of the Democratic Party. Jackson was one of the most prominent supporters of the antiapartheid movement. He had gone to South Africa in 1979 to urge disobedience protests against apartheid.

Jackson's candidacy tried to transform the electoral gains made by blacks in major cities — Los Angeles, Chicago and Philadelphia — into political power at the national level. Wynn had flown to Chicago the previous year for the last week of the successful mayoral campaign of African-American Congressman Harold Washington.

Though some felt he tried too hard to wrap himself in the mantle of slain civil rights leader Martin Luther King Jr., Jackson unleashed strong emotional forces both in the black community and among white liberal activists, forces that eventually transformed and transcended Jackson. The success of the Rainbow Coalition prompted Jackson to defy political convention and move his positions to the left rather than toward the center during the campaign. For instance, Jackson switched from supporting a slight increase in the military budget to advocating a 25 percent cut.

"So, Wynn, you're the one who got me involved with Sonia. What's this about ya backing Jackson?" Rachel asked.

"Hey, a guy's gotta keep busy. Working for one presidential candidate ain't enough," Wynn joked. "Seriously though, both are advancing progressive, independent politics. I gotta help Jackson after all he's done against apartheid. He's a powerful speaker, drawing huge crowds."

"I hear he's not so good on women's issues," replied Rachel. "Only became prochoice when he decided to run for president. And Sonia tells me that in 1981, while she was chained to a column for a week outside the Illinois State Legislature demanding that it ratify the ERA, Jackson was inside scheming with the black legislators to vote no in retaliation against the white leadership over something. Of course, it was women who got screwed, since we were three states short of enacting the ERA when they shot it down, with the deadline rapidly approaching."

"I dunno 'bout any ERA vote," Wynn responded, "but I'm sure he still needs to get better on women's issues. Listen, he's shown he's willing to change his positions, become more progressive. He's got lots of strong women supporting him. He's giving poor people and communities of color hope, creating the multiracial people's movement we have long dreamed about. He's far more progressive on issues than any of the other candidates with a shot, including on foreign policy. He has even mobilized support among rank and file union members."

"All I can say, Mr. Harris, is that women's rights better be part of your litmus test," Rachel concluded.

Despite Jackson's surprising success in the primaries, he was unable to win any major concessions at the Democratic national convention. Though his campaign enabled a woman, Geraldine Ferraro, to be nominated for vice-president, Jackson was let down at the convention by women's groups and Gary Hart, the second leading Democratic contender. Jackson was relegated to being a cheerleader for voter registration and get-out-the-vote efforts.

Wynn argued with Ronnie Shanklin, a deputy campaign manager for Jackson, that they needed to mount an independent campaign.

"The Democratic big wigs are only going to pay attention to our agenda if we're willing to walk away," Wynn argued. "Jackson should run as an independent. Maybe do a fusion ticket with Johnson and the Citizens Party."

"Wynn, we'd just get our butts kicked if Jesse ran as an independent," Shanklin responded. "Going down in flames might make some people feel good, but it won't win nuthin' for the people we represent. And we'd end up helping to reelect Raygun. We stay with the party, we'll get some things after the election. And we'll have a real chance to win four years from now."

"Come on, Ronnie, you know better than that," Wynn said dismissively. "The Democrats have always been happy to give us a place on the stage as long as they can count on our votes no matter what their policies are. They'll take us seriously when we start taking ourselves seriously. We need to show 'em we ain't gonna just settle for crumbs anymore."

"Get real," Ronnie said. "The election laws are stacked in favor of the two-party system. We've made history in mobilizing so much labor and progressive support for Jesse. We'll lose a lot of that if we bolt. Look, let's take the next four years to build our base. If Jesse doesn't win the nomination in '88, then maybe it'll be time to split the Rainbow Coalition off. Right now, just the threat gives us more power."

The 1984 elections prompted Wynn to take a sabbatical from electoral politics.

The Citizens Party collapsed due to the institutional roadblocks facing third parties, as well as the clashes between radical feminist supporters of Johnson and the more programmatic CiP supporters of Jackson. Ironically, the same weekend that the CiP held its last national meeting in Minneapolis, a founding, closed-door meeting of the national Green Party took place there as well.

The CiP had signed an agreement with the leaders of the German Greens and other ecological parties to form a worldwide federation of environmental parties. That relationship however wasn't sufficient for some Green followers, nor was the establishment of a green caucus within the CiP. Many of the initial American Greens came from the New Age movement and wanted a stronger spiritual orientation than the ecological political party approach of the CiP.

The final blow for Wynn was when he accepted a job working for a group set up by Frost to "educate" voters in six key states about the failures of the Reagan presidency, hoping this would lead to a Democratic win. Wynn quit the day after the first presidential debate, when Mondale, the Democratic nominee, announced that he supported military action against the Sandinistas.

"A typical brilliant move by the Democrats," Wynn told Frost. "They just alienated every peace activist in America while everyone who supports military action will still vote for Reagan. They're too stupid to avoid shooting themselves in the foot. I'm outta here. I should've known better."

****

It took five years of part-time schooling, but in 1984 Rachel received her nursing degree. Wynn surprised her by flying out for her graduation. They celebrated by taking a week's vacation together. Rachel, Wynn and

Tommy spent a few days in the red canyons of Sedona, dropped by to see how Arcosanti was progressing and watched a lighting storm at dusk over the Grand Canyon.

Rachel teasingly asked Wynn, "Are you ready to settle down yet?"

"Soon," he promised. "You find us the ramblin' old country house with a white picket fence with 'nough rooms for all our friends to crash in, and I'm there."

Before she graduated, Rachel worked at a series of healthcare clinics, both in Phoenix and on several Indian reservations up north. She enjoyed working on the Navajo reservation, liked the sense of community.

She had met some Navajos, the Din'e, in 1979 when a dam near Church Rock had burst, spilling waste from a uranium mine. The accident contaminated the river — the Navajo tribe's principal source of drinking water — with 360,000 liters of radioactive substances. While perhaps the most serious nuclear accident in American history, it received virtually no media coverage.

More than a thousand tons of radioactive sludge flowed downstream, contaminating Native American villages throughout Arizona and Nevada. The winds carried uranium sludge to nearby ranches and farms. Farm animals drank the contaminated river water and ate the grass. Young children played in the river.

Rachel told Wynn, "I've been working with the Center for Science on a health study of the local residents. In addition to the contamination from the burst dam, there are more than a thousand uranium mine sites on Navajo land. More than a third of the 110 communities within the reservation are affected by radioactivity. Many of the men die in their early thirties from radiation poisoning from working in the uranium mines."

"I've been offered a job at one of the Navajo health clinics, so Tommy and I are moving up there in a few weeks," she told him.

"Why?" asked Wynn. "Isn't that a little isolated? Do you think it's healthier for Tommy? I mean, you've been telling me about all this contamination."

"I just like the people," Rachel said. "It'll also give me an opportunity to help with some of the follow-up work on the uranium poisoning. Besides, I think it's good to expose Tommy to different cultures. There's also a shortage of medical people willing to work on the reservation."

"I dunno," he responded. "You're a great community activist,

Rachel. I'm sure the Navajo will appreciate your help, but it seems like you could have more of an impact in some place like Phoenix. Or come to DC. The nation's capital needs some shakin' up."

"Wynn," Rachel replied, "let's remember that kickin' butt isn't always number one on my to do list. This'll be just fine for Tommy and me."

Rachel and Tommy stayed for two years.

Tommy liked living on the reservation. All the mothers snuck Tommy little treats as their way of thanking Rachel. There were lots of interesting things to see. But Tommy however didn't always like being the cowboy when he played with his friends.

Rachel struck up a casual relationship with Willie Begay, a Navajo carpenter. Willie made her laugh and helped keep her warm on the cold winter nights. Willie taught Tommy about the outdoors — hiking, fishing and trapping. He introduced both Rachel and Tommy to Navajo traditions and spiritual teachings.

The Navajos' beliefs reflected Rachel's own sense of connection to the environment. Their religion grows from the land of their birth. "All living things – humans, plants, animals, mountains, Mother Earth — are tied together. Each being has a spirit that gives it a purpose. It's the duty of the Din'e to maintain balance, to ensure harmony with nature and the Creator," Willie told Rachel.

But the pay was meager. The social life outside of Willie was sparse, and the local school was severely underfunded. Rachel tried to do a couple of extra hours of home-schooling for Tommy each day, but she wanted a better situation. She was also increasingly concerned about the health risks. She had discovered that uranium waste had been used in the construction of the cheap housing that dominated the reservation.

In 1986, Pete invited Rachel to spend New Year's Eve in San Francisco where he was spending the winter. One of Pete's friends was the car mechanic for one of the drummers for the Dead and scored backstage passes for their annual New Year's Eve gig at the Fillmore. Wynn joined them for five days. Rachel fell in love with San Francisco.

Rachel decided to find a nursing job in the area, and moved there in the summer of 1987 after Tommy finished the fifth grade. She was able to move into the quasi-communal house that Pete knew about in a working-class/student neighborhood off Telegraph Avenue in Berkeley. They shared food and cooking responsibilities as well as rent; they also worked together on various neighborhood projects.

There were six bedrooms in the three-story house, with a good-sized backyard that had a large vegetable garden. They also had a plot in the local community garden. One of the housemates was a single mom with a son a few years younger than Tommy. Rachel was able to swap child care responsibilities, as well as have Tommy share a bedroom with the other boy. The household membership was relatively stable, without the party central flavor of the Hostel for Wayward Youth.

Rachel became known in the racially diverse neighborhood as Tommy's mom. The boy had grown up kicking a soccer ball with the neighborhood kids in South Phoenix and quickly fell in with the local soccer and skateboarding crowd.

Rachel became active with a variety of community groups, including the PTA at Tommy's school. Rachel served on the board of the food coop for several years, including helping the Food Not Bombs coalition, which handed out free sandwiches to the needy on Saturday afternoons in the coop parking lot. She joined a coop committee that was starting a local currency project, printing up Berkeley Bucks, patterned after a similar effort in Ithaca, NY.

"Ain't it against the law to print your own money?" people would ask Rachel skeptically.

"It's legal as long as you don't try to pass it off as American currency," Rachel explained. "Local currency is a form of barter and trade, while challenging the control of big business and the growing global economy."

"Well, how does it work?" they'd ask. "Can you just walk into any store?"

"The project helps recruit different businesses and services to join," Rachel replied. "Hairdressers, carpenters, therapists, musicians, bakeries, bookstores, you name it. We have a little booklet where all the participants are listed. Like the yellow pages for the underground economy. Someone who needs a couple of hours of carpentry to fix their back steps can pay for it with Berkeley Bucks. The carpenter can then spend the Bucks to get a bookkeeper to help with her tax returns. The bookkeeper can use her payment to pay someone else to provide childcare services. And so on."

Berkeley Bucks was particularly attractive to new businesses who had trouble fitting into the mainstream economy.

"One of the best things about Berkeley Bucks is that it keeps our money, the value of our labor, in our own community, 'cause you can't spend Berkeley Bucks on Wall Street. In the regular economy, big corporations are always extracting their profits from our community but often don't give anything back," Rachel said. "And since the Berkeley Buck is based on valuing each hour of work at the US equivalent of ten dollars, we also get to establish a higher minimum wage than what Congress or the State Legislature sets."

"I dunno," they'd say. "This sounds pretty radical. Are we the only ones doing it?"

"Nope, there are local currency projects starting all over the place," Rachel would reply. "Alternative currencies like Berkeley Bucks help save local jobs, because if they're based on local currency, you can't export those jobs overseas. The bankers and the big businesses and the politicians want to brainwash us into believing there's only one kind of money, only one way to value work, one way to manage the economy. We want to create an economy that values people, not corporate profits."

Rachel also began dropping into the local Women's Center, attending meetings of a support group for single moms. Tommy was old enough to increasingly challenge her authority. *No* had been a mainstay of his vocabulary since he began to talk. Now that he could better articulate his opposition, he saw little reason to comply with Rachel's demands. "Other kids hang out at the mall. Why can't I?" She was not looking forward to his teen years.

Questions about what happened at school were routinely answered with "Nuthin'." His grades were usually good, but he was clearly coasting along, doing the minimum needed to avoid getting in trouble with Rachel. As a teenager, sex was becoming an issue, not only for him but for her. She felt increasingly uncomfortable having a friend spend the night, having to answer Tommy's questions in the morning.

Rachel sat Tommy down for the occasional talk about the birds and bees, along with drugs. As a mother and nurse, she knew the importance of educating him about these issues, both for his own protection and that of others. She sent Tommy to a sex education class offered through the Women's Center. She had a number of discussions with him about the responsibilities and dangers of love and sex.

"Sex is beautiful if it's done with love. It's degrading if it's just done for your pleasure and not your partner's. It's foolhardy if done without adequate protection. That could kill you and your lover, starting with AIDS. You can also create a child that you're responsible for for the next 18 years, no matter what. If you fail to take care of any child you produce, I'll be the one hauling your ass in front of a judge. Remember that. If you ever hit a woman, I'll also be hauling your ass. Sex is about growing up, taking responsibility," Rachel told Tommy as he looked for an escape route.

Rachel had an ongoing relationship with Joel Davidson, a doctor she worked with at a local clinic. In addition to her own physical and emotional need for intimacy, she felt it was important for Tommy to have a role model, someone who could explain the fine art of throwing a curve ball or answering those "male" questions that Tommy didn't want to ask her. He liked spending time at Joel's, since he had a built-in pool out back with a hot tub and always had the latest in electronic games, such as Donkey Kong.

Tommy began to ask more about his father. Rachel hadn't told him much about Danny, other than he was a friend with whom things hadn't worked out. She didn't want to tell Tommy that his father had no interest in him. Her son became more persistent as he got older.

Rachel decided to contact Danny, which took a few phone calls. Danny was less than thrilled to hear from her. He had "settled down," was living in Orange County south of LA, still played in a band but had a day job teaching music in a junior high school. He was married with two children. "My wife doesn't know about Tommy. I've sort of put that part of my life behind me."

"Well, Tommy hasn't put you behind him. He's your son, your name is on the birth certificate, remember, and he wants to get to know you. I'm sorry that you haven't talked to your wife about him, but start thinking about how to break the news. And it's about time you start kicking in some child support, say at least a couple of hundred a month."

"So, is money what this phone call is about?" asked Danny.

"This call is about your son wanting to know his father," replied Rachel. "But sure, let's talk about money. Tommy is getting way too big for hand-me-downs, and new clothes cost a ton. I'm sure I can get more if I have to bring you into court, and believe me, I know people who enjoy nothing more than getting a recalcitrant father to cough up."

"So, whaddya want me to do?" he said resignedly.

"Show some interest. At least one face-to-face meeting with him. I'll leave it to you to set it up, but if you wait too long, he'll be knocking at your front door."

"Why are you calling after all this time?" Danny asked.

"I should've called you sooner, at least made you pay child support. But frankly, I thought it was better with you out of our lives. However, Tommy is getting older now, he has a mind of his own. He wants to meet his father. And I guess we're both old enough now to know that fathers have responsibilities that you just can't shrug off," Rachel said.

"Look, I'm not calling up to 'cause any problems, especially with your wife," she added. "It's just that Tommy wants to know his father. I kinda hoped you might be interested in him as well. It's not too late for the two of you."

Danny began to send two hundred dollars each month. Rachel could have insisted on more but let it slide. He also sent her a note. "I know I was a jerk. I'm sorry. Thanks for putting me in touch with my son."

Danny's relationship with Tommy ended up being better than she expected. There was certainly a lot of initial hostility. Tommy could deal with him not staying with Rachel but he had a lot of anger about him not trying to keep in contact.

Finally Danny said, "Tommy, you have to make a decision. There are lots of things I have done in my past that I'm not proud of. When you were born, I wasn't ready to have a child, or a wife. I walked away and pretended it was something that I wasn't involved with. I'm sorry. It wasn't the only thing in my life I messed up. But at some point most of us eventually grow up. I can't change the past. If you want a relationship in the future, we can work on that. It's your call."

Danny drove up every few months to see him, showed him a few things on the guitar. He caught one of his son's soccer games. Tommy especially liked finding out that he had a half-brother and sister, sending them funny gags and messages, and became close with them over time despite the age difference. Tommy had always wanted siblings. He bonded with them much more than with his father.

****

Rachel participated in several discussion groups at the Women's Center. She referred to it as her postgraduate work on activism and political theory.

One of the groups studied Ecofeminism. They started out by reading *Reclaim the Earth: Women Speak Out for Life on Earth*, then moved on to Vandana Shiva's *Staying Alive: Women, Ecology, and Development.*

In the 1970s, women's groups began to weave together with the peace and environmental movements. What emerged was ecofeminist action groups. The Unity Statement from the Women's Pentagon Action was an ecofeminist manifesto, identifying militarism as the force destroying the earth. It demanded an end to male violence in all its manifestations — war, poverty, battering, rape, reproductive control, racism, nuclear power and weapons, heterosexism."

"Ecofeminism regards the oppression of women and nature as interconnected," Rachel explained to one of her coworkers who asked about Shiva's book when she saw Rachel reading it during her lunch break. "Women have always been more aware of our relationship with nature, the earth goddess, than men. Men feel it's their god-given right to exploit both nature and women. Ecofeminists realize that to save Mother Earth we also have to stop the oppression of women, and vice versa."

The ecofeminist movement was Rachel's first exposure to the Green Party. Ecofeminists played a major role in the initial organizing of the Greens in the US.

"Ecofeminism is vital to green politics," the 1988 national platform read. "The forces which are responsible for the competition and patriarchal domination of women and other oppressed minorities are the same forces that are destroying the Earth. Ecofeminism involves close examination of cultural symptoms of alienation from the Earth; sexism, racism, classism, speciesism, militarism, and exploitation of resources are examples of such alienation."

The discussion group decided to get involved with the campaign to save the ancient redwood trees in Headwaters Forest in northern California. In 1990, environmentalists organized Redwood Summer, an outreach campaign combining education and action. More than 3,000 people participated in tree-sits, blockades and rallies.

Rachel convinced Tommy to spend a week during Redwood Summer on one of the tree platforms.

"Come on, Tommy," Rachel pleaded. "It'll be good for us to spend some time together in the wilderness. It'll be fun to commune with nature, listen to all the animals. We're not going to have too many opportunities to do this in the future. You'll be too old soon to want to hang out with your mom."

"Rachel, I've been too old to hang out with ya for years," Tommy replied. He was fourteen. Rachel wasn't thrilled with his new habit of calling her by her first name, but she had bigger problems with him to argue about. She won him over by promising to buy him tickets to an upcoming Pearl Jam concert.

It took almost two hours of hiking up a logging road to reach the site. They came in early on a Sunday morning to reduce the risk they would be spotted and arrested for trespassing. They passed several steep slopes that had been clearcut. A number of mudslides had taken place from the erosion.

Rachel had second thoughts when she stood at the base of an enormous, thousand year-old redwood tree, whose girth was wider than their living room. The plywood platform hung precariously almost two hundred feet above the forest floor. The organizers showed them how to pull themselves up to the platform by elaborately rigged pulleys and ropes. Rachel nearly had a panic attack when she was thirty feet off the ground, but suppressed it so as not to frighten her son. Tommy thought the climb was awesome.

Rachel had brought him several books to read, including Jack Kerouac's *On the Road*. Rachel came close to strangling him for his constant whining "that there's nothing to do, I'm bored, I wanna go home." Later, of course, Tommy told his friends that he had a great time.

"Whaddya expect, Tommy? That chainsaw-wielding loggers would be on ropes swiping at us as they swung by, and you'd shoot them down with your video gun? Learn to enjoy the solitude. Listen to the wind, listen to the trees whisper to one another, or read a book or count in your head, but whatever you do, stop driving me crazy with your whining," Rachel said in exasperation.

The view of the river valley from the platform was spectacular, only marred by the sight of the steam rising from Pacific Lumber's sawmill.

They spent one of the most terrifying nights of Rachel's life together.

Shortly after sunset, the wind began to pick up, followed by rain. It was eventually gusting up to fifty miles an hour. The huge trees began to swing, the platforms groaning.

"Hold on, Tommy," Rachel yelled. "Wrap some rope around your waist in case you get blown off. Damn. I hope the platform doesn't crack, she said as the two-by-fours groaned and buckled.

"Chill out, Rachel," Tommy said over the wind. "It's like riding a skateboard. Just go with the flow, don't fight it. Yee-hah," he yelled.

Rachel prayed harder than she'd prayed in years.

Then the lightning began, brilliant jagged streaks across the sky that Rachel thought would swallow them up, followed by thunderous claps that nearly broke their eardrums. Tommy clapped and howled after particularly spectacular discharges from the heavens.

When he stood up, stretching his arms wide to feel the full force of the storm, Rachel screamed and grabbed him around the waist, pulling him down. Tommy just laughed. "Okay, Mom," he said, giving her a hug. "Whatever. Here, let me tie the rope around the trunk and then around the both of us. Don't worry. We'll be fine."

"I was never so happy to see dawn in my life. It was like being reborn," Rachel told Wynn when she told him about that night.

NINE

UNDER SIEGE, POST 9/11

Late September 2001

Rachel's proposal for a government of national unity was receding rapidly in the rearview mirror. Her televised statement had polarized even further her fragile relationship with the congressional leadership.

The daily rhythm of life was slowly returning to a semblance of normalcy for most Americans, though the country remained on edge. Where would the next terrorist blow land? The public wanted strong leadership. Many still wanted revenge.

The foreign policy establishment in DC continued to press for steps toward war. Darling argued that Rachel was greatly underestimating the commitment of America's enemies to continue their terrorist attacks.

The Speaker of the House put forth a number of proposals to increase corporate welfare to help the economy recover from the shock of 9/11.

"Those terrorists hit the World Trade Center 'cause of its central role in our economy," Freddy Baker announced. "We've gotta prime the pump to prevent a recession. We need to help businesses recover, to protect our jobs — startin' with the airline industry, insurance companies and the Wall Street community, which got hurt the most. Our first step should be an emergency twenty-billion-dollar bailout of our domestic airlines. They lost billions when we forced 'em to ground their planes for two days."

Congressmember McDaniels was one of the few who spoke against the corporate handouts. "We can't blame September eleventh for all our problems. The stock market collapsed in 2000 largely because the house of cards known as the dot.com internet boom came tumbling down. It is outrageous that politicians and their campaign contributors are seeking to use this tragedy to get taxpayers to cover their losses."

Speaker Baker was undeterred. "We need some tax cuts to jump-start the recovery," he added. "This ain't the time for political posturing. We need to get money into the hands of the people who'll get our economy movin' again." He called for repeal of the alternate minimum tax for corporations, including refunding the tax for the last fifteen years. This would hand billions of dollars to a handful of the nation's wealthiest companies."

"Rather than bailing out a few corporate executives," McDaniels countered, "Congress needs to pay attention to the record lines at soup kitchens and shelters. It's not CEOs who are lining up there. The more than one hundred thousand jobs that have been lost in New York City since September eleventh have been in the low-wage sectors of tourism, transportation, retail and restaurants."

Rachel sided with McDaniels on the need to ensure that average workers, not just CEOs, were helped. She favored making it easier and quicker for families in New York to get help with medical and housing needs, and to qualify for unemployment. Controversially, she also urged Congress to do more for the many undocumented workers in New York's low-wage service industries.

Rachel quickly pushed through Congress the request by New York City and State for thirty billion dollars to help rebuild.

****

The Taliban dismissed out of hand the US request to turn over bin Laden. They disputed that they had control over bin Laden, or that they even knew where he was.

"We know nothing about the attack, though given America's unholy ways it does not come as a surprise," said Abdullah Haqqani, the Afghan Foreign Minister. "When you have some firm evidence that Afghanistan was involved, contact us. Don't think you can just make things up. We have long been falsely accused by Western imperial powers, usually as a pretext to invade us. We call upon our Muslim brothers in the world community to stand up and stop this from happening."

The evidence about who was responsible for 9/11 was difficult to come by.

While the FBI was "leaving no stone unturned in the search for answers or additional terrorists," neither they nor the CIA came up with much.

Charles Sampson, the FBI Director, told Rachel, "We haven't gotten any useful information about 9/11 out of Majed bin Muhammad, the hijacker we have in custody. Like most of the others, he was from Saudi Arabia. Says he's a follower of Sheik Omar Abdel Rahman."

Rahman was in prison for the 1993 bombing of the WTC, his second attempt, which killed six individuals and injured more than a thousand.

"It doesn't seem like Muhammad had any role in the planning," Sampson added. "He claims he didn't know any of the hijackers on the other planes, says he didn't even know they planned to fly the planes into buildings until shortly before he arrived at the airport. He assumed the hijack operation would demand the release of various prisoners, starting with Rahman," Sampson added.

Muhammad admitted he'd received training at an al-Qaida camp in Afghanistan several years ago but claimed that he had not been in direct contact with them since. He had no idea what role bin Laden had played, if any.

The FBI now believed that the hijackers had received their pilot training at commercial training schools in Florida and Arizona. Some of the instructors admitted that "it seemed a little strange that they were only interested in how to fly a plane, not how to do takeoffs or landings."

Individuals of Middle Eastern descent were complaining of increased scrutiny and harassment by the police and the general public as racial profiling became suddenly acceptable. Rachel had instructed the security agencies not to target people based on their national origin or immigration status.

The heads of the FBI and CIA argued with Rachel that her continued support for civil liberties was impeding their efforts to find coconspirators remaining in the US.

"The terrorists and their helpers have scattered to the winds, going deeper underground," said FBI Director Sampson. "Undoubtedly they have plenty of fake identity papers. The more time passes, the harder it'll be to find them. You got to cut us more slack. We need to do more wiretaps and searches. We have to be able to shake the tree harder, see what falls out. We've found a few people we believe are connected, but they're refusing to say a word. At least let me lock up any noncitizens we find, deny them any outside contact, even with lawyers and family members. Hold them in isolation for a few weeks. That'll get them talking," Sampson told her.

"At least let us send a few of the more promising suspects back to their home countries, which employ more aggressive interrogation techniques that we do," added CIA director Solomon.

The one request Rachel agreed to was more powers to follow the money trail. "She doesn't seem concerned about the Bill of Rights when it comes to banks and money laundering," Sampson told his staff.

Security measures were dramatically increased at public buildings and events throughout the country, even though Rachel doubted it would do much good against a planned terrorist attack. She did agree to nationalize the security workers at airports, making sure they'd get adequate training and a living wage.

Sampson had an ally in Senate Majority Leader Deutsche, who agreed to introduce the Patriot Act. "The act calls for an expansion of surveillance and police powers to investigate suspected terrorists. In the war on terrorism, we must be willing to give up a few of our individual rights for improved security. We need to unshackle our law enforcement personnel to enable them to protect us," Deutsche said.

The House Speaker echoed his sentiments. "We gotta have the tools to protect our country in this new era of cell phones and the internet," Baker said. "Our intelligence community is stuck in the seventies. We gotta take off the handcuffs we put on after Watergate."

The Patriot Act quickly passed, by a three to one margin, in each house. The margin would have been even higher except for Rachel's forceful opposition. Sophie told Rachel that those one hundred *no* votes were the base they would build from in Congress.

Rachel took her time to veto the act, and had her incoming attorney general write a detailed message about why the bill was unconstitutional. Groups like the ACLU used that veto message to write their lawsuit challenging the bill when Congress overrode the veto. Much to Congress's consternation, the Justice Department agreed to delay implementation until the courts ruled on it.

"The operative phrase in intelligence should be intelligence," Rachel said when she announced the veto. "Our problem hasn't been a lack of information. It has been our inability to correctly analyze the information, and to overcome the bureaucratic turf wars between the Defense Department, the CIA, the FBI and the Department of State. I have convened a task force of these agencies to figure out how to better process the information we already have, rather than curtailing the civil liberties that are the foundation of our democracy."

Sampson moved to the top of the list of Harrington's appointees she needed to replace.

****

Anna argued for Rachel to take quick military action against the Taliban rulers in Afghanistan. "The Taliban are one of the most oppressive governments against women in the world. They're lunatics. Ya gotta do somethin' anyway or Congress and the Pentagon will leave tank tracks on your back. Ain't a lot of options here. If you gotta use force, might as well do the world and women a favor and smoke the Taliban."

Anna arranged for Rachel to meet with a delegation from RAWA, the Revolutionary Association of the Women of Afghanistan. Rachel asked them for their view of the Taliban's background. It included the surprising news that the US had approved their rise to power.

"The government the Soviets left behind when they fled was good for women," said Laida Faryal. "But it only hung on for three years before the warlords — the mujahedeen — threw them out. The warlords had been armed by your country to fight the Russians. When the warlords got power, things got bad fast. The local warlords fought each other to see who could steal the most. The only law was who had the biggest guns," Faryal told Rachel.

"How did the Taliban take power from the warlords?" Rachel asked.

"The Taliban are rural people, Pushtun, the biggest ethnic group in our country. They follow a stricter form of Sunni Islam than the warlords. The Taliban started to become powerful in the fall of 1994. Islamic students came across the border from Pakistan to kick out the local warlords after a lot of abuses. They came after two village girls got gang-raped by one warlord's soldiers. The merchants supported the Taliban because they were fed up with paying high import fees to the warlords," Faryal said.

"The Taliban spread quickly. Many people just wanted order restored. In only two years, the Taliban bought off or beat all their enemies. But this couldn't happen unless Pakistan said it was okay, because they are the big power in the area. And Pakistan only says yes if the United States say okay, since US gives Pakistan their weapons."

"Why would the US support the Taliban?" Rachel asked. "I mean, even Clinton knew they were crazy, especially after they blew up the Buddha monuments."

"The Taliban fooled lots of people, not just your leaders. The rumor is that your government wanted order restored so they could build an oil pipeline from the Caspian Sea built through Afghanistan to Karachi. Otherwise, it go through Iraq, which America hates," Faryal said. "If the Taliban could stop the warlords from ransacking the countryside, the US didn't care how they did it."

Rachel scribbled a note to Sophie to check up on this.

"Tell the president how the Taliban brutalize women," Anna urged.

"The Taliban's official policy is that women are subhumans. We're fit only for household slavery and to produce babies," Faryal said. "They take away all our rights. We can't get medical care, go to school or even walk outside with any part of our body uncovered. Girls ten years old are sold as brides for a 100-kilogram sack of wheat flour. Women are beaten in public for the smallest violation, like laughing or showing an ankle. Many women get permanent injuries or even die from the beatings."

"Women are just spoils of war for the Taliban," Faryal added. "They do nothing if their soldiers rape women, even mass rape. Just another way to make war, like dogs lifting their legs to mark their territory."

"If we don't step in, it's only going to get worse for women there," Anna argued with Rachel. "Blow up the Taliban, liberate women, declare victory, and get yourself declared a war hero. Then you'll have the moral authority to pursue your real goals. If you oppose Congress on launching a military response, they'll do it anyway and your presidency will be in a shambles. You might even get impeached. What good will that accomplish?" Anna asked.

"Congress may declare war, but it's the president that decides when and if to send the troops," Rachel reminded her. "I'm not going to do the wrong thing just because Congress wants me to."

"But you could make the treatment of women a cornerstone of American foreign policy," Anna pleaded. "For once we've got the military hawks screaming about the need to liberate women. Who cares if they're just using it as a cover to invade another country? This is too good an opportunity to miss. Once you take out the Taliban for oppressing women, you can use the precedent to withhold military and political support to other countries that oppress women. We'll call it the Moreno Doctrine," Anna argued.

"Blowing up the Taliban might give us a certain satisfaction," countered Rachel, "but where is the evidence that they're responsible for September eleventh? And in the end, all we may accomplish is to push Afghanistan back into the chaos that resulted in the Taliban coming to power in the first place. We can't bomb them back to the Stone Age, they're already there. The warlords might even end up back in charge. The use of force often creates more problems than it solves," warned Rachel.

"I agree with Madame President," said Faryal. "If America invades our country, drops bomb on us, it will mainly be women, children and the elderly who suffer. More of our people will die. And you will just sharpen the dagger of the warlords once again. The Northern Alliance, the mujahedeen, will sweep down on us like hungry wolves. We need you to send in UN forces to make peace, not war. You need to remove the Taliban and give us democracy, so our people can find our own way."

****

Baker and Deutsche hastily decided to convene a joint congressional hearing in early October on how America should respond to the September eleventh attack. Rachel's televised address picked up a lot of support among voters. The peace movement was in full bloom, both at home and abroad. Peace vigils and rallies were held throughout the country daily. Major peace rallies were planned for New York, DC and San Francisco in a few weeks. Democrats from the more liberal and urban districts were under increasing pressure to support Rachel.

The congressional leaders wanted a forum to air their opposing views. They waited until the last moment to formally announce the hearing so Rachel wouldn't have time to respond.

The legislative leaders ignored a request by several of the relatives of victims to use the hearings to investigate who was responsible for the attacks and whether the national security forces had responded properly. "It's obvious who is responsible. And we can't give out too much information because it will just help the people we are trying to catch and jeopardize our security. We'll deal with those questions at a more appropriate moment."

The witness list for the hearing was stacked to build the case for war.

Deutsche was fixated on showing that Rachel was not up to the task of protecting the country. "Either she falls into line quickly or she takes an early retirement," he said at a strategy meeting of congressional Democratic leaders. "What does she know about national defense? The hearing will make clear that our only option is to attack Afghanistan as soon as possible. They are the ones who are providing support and sanctuary for bin Laden and the rest of the terrorist network. Cut off the head of the snake and the body will die."

The television cameras were packed into the hearing room, the cameramen and reporters jousting for elbow space. People hustled around looking important. Several network anchor stars deigned to make a quick appearance to tape a voiceover for the evening news. The esteemed members of the panel settled into their chairs. The Joint Chiefs of Staff, Secretary Darling and other members of the military establishment arranged themselves in front row seats, eagerly waiting their turn to tell Congress what needed to be done.

The simmering buzz in the room stopped abruptly. All eyes turned as President Moreno swept in, her security detail hurriedly tagging along. The room exploded into frenzied activity, camera lights flashing, reporters speaking into their headsets asking for direction, everyone talking at once. Rachel didn't stop to shake hands or exchange greetings.

She gave a curt nod to the various members of the Joint Chiefs of Staff and Defense Department officials, sitting there frozen. "Thank you gentlemen, you won't be needed. I'll handle this. Maybe you all can get back to protecting our citizens."

They didn't move.

Rachel leaned over and said quietly. "Maybe you didn't hear me but your commander in chief just gave you an order to move. Unless you're sitting there with a congressional subpoena in your back pocket, vamoose. You work for me, not them."

They moved, though not happily. Darling moved as far as the back of the room. She was free to fire him if she wanted.

Rachel sat down behind the microphones as Congressmembers scrambled to figure out what to do. "Senators, Representatives, I wish to thank you for the opportunity to explain to you and the nation what my administration is doing in response to September eleventh. Is there anything in particular that I could enlighten you about?"

Senator Harvey Branston (D-Missouri), the Chair of the Senate Foreign Relations Committee, exercised sufficient self-control to say, "May I suggest that it might be better if the president testified on a different day? This committee was not expecting you to participate. I am afraid that we already have a pretty tight schedule today."

Rachel leaned into the microphone and said, "Thank you, Senator, but today will be fine. I believe I just freed up most of your speakers' slots. If you need to know what my administration is planning to do, I am the one to ask."

After conferring with the other committee members, Branston made a long, circuitous welcoming statement, rebuke lightly sprinkled over with flowery language. "We wish to thank Madame President for gracing us with her presence, even if it was unexpected. It is always an honor to have the opportunity to hear first hand from our country's distinguished leader about the reasoning behind our government's actions, or lack there of, especially at a time when one might expect you to be otherwise engaged in trying to manage the defense of our country."

Finally, he asked her, "Do you really believe that bin Laden's collection of terrorists would put a halt to the killing of more Americans because you're holding peace summits and convening meetings of UN bureaucrats?"

"Thank you, Senator. I appreciate you getting to the point," Rachel responded. "If you're asking whether I think that the prior administrations and Congress should have taken more forceful action when you had evidence that such terrorists had killed Americans and others by blowing up our embassies, ships and military bases in the Middle East and Africa, well, of course I do. But I can't solve all of Congress's and the previous administration's mistakes in just one month."

Rachel ignored him as he stammered out a protest that her response was not to the question that he had asked. The television and radio networks were scrambling to go to live coverage. This was the high drama they lived for.

"I've been able to do some research in the last few weeks about the events leading up to the September eleventh attacks," said Rachel, "and I'm not happy about what I've uncovered. I look forward to more complete hearings on all of this. For instance, the CIA trained and funded terrorists like bin Laden as part of the Cold War with the Soviet Union, not only in Afghanistan, but Iraq, Iran, Chile, Honduras, Nicaragua, El Salvador, Guatemala, and so on. Do I think that was wrong? Yes, I do.

"Is it wrong to prop up corrupt governments that use their oil profits to fund fanatics that end up flying airplanes into the World Trade Center? Yes," Rachel said, pausing to take a drink of water.

"Am I aware that the prior administration had already drawn up plans to attack Afghanistan this fall as part of our ongoing use of military force to ensure our access to foreign oil and maintain the profits of multinational oil companies? Unfortunately, the answer is yes." Rachel continued. "Did our government have prior warning about such a terrorist attack from other governments? Yes, we did.

"Gentlemen, we need to learn from our mistakes rather than just keep repeating them. We keep going to war with leaders and countries we have previously supported. It is known as *blowback*. If we prop up despots who brutalize their neighbors as well as their own citizens, we shouldn't be surprised when someday they end up doing things we don't like. Like attack us," Rachel said angrily but in a firm, level voice.

The room was in an uproar. Branston banged his gavel for silence. He took off his glasses and jabbed them at Rachel while he talked.

"Madame President, we could spend our whole day debating the history of American foreign policy. However, the purpose of the hearing today is not to review our past but to figure out how we should respond to September eleventh. And I trust that you will not abuse your office to reveal classified military information, particularly information that could harm our men and women in the armed forces. Don't lecture me about security breaches! Perhaps we should take this into executive session," he said, looking around at the other committee members who were nodding their heads in agreement.

Deutsche and Baker were standing on the side of the room now, both frantically gesturing for Branston to cut this off. This wasn't what they were looking for.

Rachel had a few more points to make before she was finished.

"Mr. Chairman, with all due respect, the greatest threat to the lives of the men and women in our armed forces, and three hundred million American civilians, and the billions of humans on this planet is the effort to sweep our past history under the rug. Before we can move forward, we need to understand what brought us to this position in the first place. We need to be clear about the motives and agendas of the other countries and individuals that are part of this crisis. If you feel that you and your committee need to go hide from the American public behind closed doors, I guess I can't stop you, but I intend to tell the American people the truth," Rachel stated forcefully.

Committee members whispered feverishly among themselves, debating whether to halt this or let her hang herself. Rachel spoke to the cameras now.

"In my short time as president, I have discovered how the truth is often hidden from the American public, even from the president. Congress is telling the American people that we have to go to war with Afghanistan to punish those who attacked the World Trade Center. But this president has yet to see any firm evidence that the Afghan people were involved in the attack. Of the nineteen people we have confirmed were involved, fifteen were from Saudi Arabia, not from Afghanistan. The leader of the attack was from the Egyptian Jihad.

"The funding for this attack apparently originated from the ruling families of Saudi Arabia. Even bin Laden, the individual we are told was the evil mastermind behind this attack, is not only from Saudi Arabia, but from one of the richest and most influential families in that country. In fact, the bin Laden family has long had financial dealings through companies like the Carlyle Group with many of the key players in the American defense industry, including former president and ex-CIA Director George Bush. So why doesn't Congress want to bomb Saudi Arabia? The only answer I can think of is: oil and money."

The chairman decided it was time to cut her off. Rachel ignored him. He signaled for someone to cut off her microphone. None of the technicians was willing to do so.

"But I do assume that bin Laden," she continued, "or his terrorist network, played at least a supporting role in the attacks. There is certainly strong evidence of his involvement in prior attacks on American interests that killed hundreds of people. I would love to understand why Congress, the CIA, the Defense Department and the rest of you haven't arrested him previously? Why aren't you focusing on capturing him rather than bombing the Afghan people? Why didn't the Clinton administration take bin Laden when Sudan offered to turn him over a few years ago?

"I'm confused, Senator, about exactly what Congress is trying to accomplish. And until you can explain to me and to the American public what bombing Afghanistan has to do with bringing those who killed my son and thousands of others on September eleventh to justice, forgive me if I don't jump at the opportunity to bomb the poorest and most war-ravaged people in the world into deeper misery. This administration does *not* intend to kill more innocent people for the crimes of others," Rachel said icily.

"Thank you for the opportunity to speak today. I know my way out. In the future, when you need to hear what my administration is doing, call me first. Don't go around my back," said Rachel.

"Oh, one more thing," she said, coming back to the table, bending over to the microphone, her arm resting on the table. "If we're going to find the truth and hold the guilty accountable, we need to have some family members who have lost their loved ones asking the questions. They're the ones who will ensure that the truth comes out."

A path cleared for her as she marched out with the Secret Service in tow. She ignored all the questions thrown at her.

The committee quickly adjourned. Work on impeachment papers and other legal challenges moved into high gear.

****

Wynn, Sophie and Anna were waiting for Rachel when she got back to the White House. Sophie had given strict instructions to bring her directly to the Oval Office. Wynn went down to make sure it happened.

They closed the door behind Rachel. Sophie instructed the secretary to hold all calls.

Rachel poured herself a drink and threw herself on the far end on the couch, looking out the window, not at them. Her body was shaking.

Wynn sat down at the opposite end of the couch. He wanted to touch her, reassure her, but he refrained, feeling she might explode.

"Rachel, do you really think that was wise?" Wynn asked. "You seemed really on edge there, storming into their meeting without being invited. A lotta people are going to be wondering how well you're holding up. People need to see that you're in control of the situation, and they saw the opposite today. Why didn't you talk to us beforehand about this? Your credibility and stature are our principal assets in this struggle with Congress, and if we lose that, we're finished," Wynn explained.

"You really pushed the envelope today," Sophie added. "You didn't win any new friends in Congress. They might retaliate by charging you with revealing classified info. They're looking for an opportunity to take you down," Sophie added.

"Nonsense," Rachel said dismissively. "Most of the information I got initially from the peace movement. You don't think the CIA would tell the president the truth, do you? I just used my access to government files to confirm it was true. If the president can't speak the truth, who can?

"They're so infuriating," she continued, revved on nervous energy. "They act like something isn't a lie if they say it in public with a straight face. They don't give a damn about those three thousand people who were killed. It's all about power, their power, and greed."

Wynn moved closer to her, brushing his hand along her arm. "We're all on your side. But Americans are afraid right now. They don't want to feel that the president is at war with Congress rather than the terrorists."

Sophie played the role of presidential adviser.

"Boss, you make the decisions. We'll do whatever is needed to make it happen. But you need to be presidential, stay above the fray," Sophie warned.

Rachel put her face into her hands and rubbed her eyes. She sat back on the couch, draining her glass.

"I know, I know. It's just so frustrating," Rachel said. "These congressmen and generals keep on giving speeches about how they're going to save America after the horrors of 9/11, but *not one of them* ever stands up and apologizes for letting it happen. I mean, these guys forked over trillions of our tax dollars for decades to their favorite military contractors to build the mightiest arsenal the world has ever seen, just so a bunch of thugs with box cutters can hijack a couple of planes and kill several thousand Americans.

"Congress has absolutely no interest in actually determining who's responsible for September eleventh. They sure as heck don't want to put bin Laden on open trial where some difficult questions might have to be answered," Rachel lamented. "And they have the gall to argue that I'm the one being unreasonable."

Rachel was almost shouting now, stomping around the office. She grabbed a few pillows to throw on the floor. It looked like she wanted something that would make a loud crash.

She hoped this was at least going to be therapeutic, because she was in a lot of pain and it needed to come out.

The words spilled off her tongue, a waterfall crashing onto the rocks below.

"I feel like I'm in an insane asylum when I'm over at the Capitol, with the inmates holding all the keys. They want me to declare a war on terrorism, but they only want me to fight the bad terrorists, not the good terrorists. Of course, we usually trained the bad terrorists back when they were the good terrorists. There are only a few dozen countries that support the bad terrorists that we'd have to go to war with — that's not too many — though some of the good countries also allow bad terrorists to operate. So do we go to war with our allies or increase their foreign aid?" she asked.

Wynn tried to interject. Rachel bulldozed on.

"Nor does Congress seem concerned about any innocent foreign civilians that may be killed as 'collateral damage,' probably because they don't vote in our elections." Completely agitated, she was on a roll.

"And bin Laden's starring in his own home videos, urging us on, Come on America, start a war with Islam, help me overthrow all these corrupt regimes who defile the memory of Mohammed and oppress their own people. Please, start a war. Meanwhile, as far as our FBI and CIA can tell, there are already a couple of hundred terrorists running around our country, hanging out, just waiting to unleash some bioterror weapon that *our* military dreamed up that no one has bothered to tell me about yet. But the law enforcement agencies can't find these terrorists. So their solution is to lock up every Muslim in the country," Rachel finished, collapsing.

They held their peace, letting Rachel blow off steam, relieved that she at least still seemed relatively sane. They moved up to the private quarters. Wynn made some margaritas, ordered up some Mexican food.

After dinner, Anna turned to one of her favorite pastimes — discussing conspiracy theories.

"Boy, are there conspiracies everywhere here. US oil companies, Pakistani generals, Saudi Arabian princes, bin Laden's father getting paid to rebuild American airbases his son blows up. But you don't need to be a conspiracy buff to see that the ruling class is using these attacks as a pretext to rush through all their favorite little authoritarian and class warfare initiatives. So don't let them divert you from doing what needs to be done," Anna said.

"By the way, I assume someone has told you by now that the military has standing orders to shoot down planes flying off path in the DC area that fail to respond to orders from flight controllers, so there was no need to ask you for a confirmation," she added.

Sophie sat down on the couch next to Rachel, wrapping her arm around her, pulling her close.

"I know that September eleventh is all-consuming right now and that the last thing you wanted to be was a war president. We don't always get to choose our battles in life. But you have to remain calm in public. And Anna is right about the need to keep plugging away on the agenda we had before 9/11. We may never get another chance in our lifetime to do some of these things," Sophie said, gently stroking Rachel's hair.

Rachel asked them to have a "to-do list" drawn up. "I'm going to have to rely on you to focus on the domestic issues."

****

Rachel entered the room. It looked like a bunker — no windows, white, stark, concrete walls. It had seen better days. A single unshielded lightbulb hung from the ceiling, its chord hanging like a noose. A man sat in a chair beneath the light bulb. His beard and hair were unkempt, his clothes soiled, disheveled, chin slumped on his chest. He did not look well. His legs and arms were tied to the chair. He had a long white robe wrapped around him. It was torn and had blood on it.

He was bin Laden. Rachel entered the room. Bin Laden woke. He slowly turned his head to look at Rachel, an evil smile of satisfaction, a lust for blood and demonic power growing on his face as he recognized who she was. Rachel stood in front of him. She asked, "Why? Why did you kill all those people? Why did you kill my son?"

Bin Laden was now standing. His robe was now a blazing white. He began to laugh. A silent laugh. He had a turban on his head.

Rachel took a step backward. She raised her arm. She held a gun, a handgun, automatic, powerful. Bin Laden had an assault rifle in his hand, holding it high above his head, defiant.

She pulled the trigger.

Bin Laden's head exploded into a sun. The light suffused the room. When the light receded, the walls turned into windows looking out upon a meadow. The sky was blue. There was a bed in the corner. Someone lay there.

Rachel walked over. She shook the prone body. Once. Twice. A third time. The person rolled over.

It was Tommy.

Tommy smiled up at her. His hair was damp. He was beautiful.

"Hi, Mom. I'm glad you came. It's good to see you. I've missed you," he said, lazily pushing himself up on his elbows as he was prone to do.

"Tommy, I've been looking everywhere for you," Rachel cried in relief, sitting down on the side of the bed to touch him. "Where have you been?"

"I've been here. It's restful. Sleeping. I need to sleep." Tommy rolled over, turning his back to her.

Rachel shook him again. "Tommy, it's time to get up. It's time to go to school."

"Mom, it's okay. I'm not going anywhere. There's no school any more. It's okay if I sleep."

Rachel shook him even more desperately. "Tommy, wake up. It's time to get up."

He disappeared.

Wynn wrapped his arms around her. "Rachel, it's okay. You've been talking in your sleep again. I'm here. Everything is fine." He pulled her onto his chest, holding her tight, caressing her back, whispering that it was all right.

It wasn't.
She had lost Tommy again.

ELEVEN

ANNA BROWN

Throughout her stay in the Bay Area, Rachel was active with the Physicians for Universal Healthcare.

While she did most of her nursing work at an area hospital where the pay and hours were better, she always spent some time working at local health clinics. She was appalled that so many families lacked any healthcare coverage, often waiting until there was a medical emergency, especially for the parent, before seeking medical assistance.

The US, despite all its wealth, was the only industrial country that did not provide healthcare to all its citizens, with 36 million residents without coverage during the late 80s.

She met Anna Brown in the fall of 1989 when they spoke together on a panel on women's healthcare. Anna worked for Planned Parenthood. She asked Rachel whether abortion would be covered under universal healthcare. Rachel replied that since most countries did, the assumption was that a US national healthcare program would as well, but it would undoubtedly become a point of dispute.

Anna was in her late twenties, tall and thin, athletic, with intense deep blue eyes and short blond hair. She had an easy smile. Anna and Rachel rapidly struck up a friendship. Anna was a tireless organizer. She began to work with Rachel on the universal healthcare issue, coordinating letter writing and petition drives. Anna and Rachel often spent part of their weekends together, tabling or speaking.

Anna was active in the lesbian and gay rights movement. She wasn't a great fan of men. "Most men just see women as a possession, something to use for sex and housekeeping while they go out and do the so-called important things, like start wars, rape the environment and make money. Men are all about domination and competition. We'd all be a lot better off if women were in charge," Anna said.

Anna, like Rachel, had been a supporter of Sonia Johnson's presidential campaign, though she thought Sonia's involvement with the Citizens Party had been a mistake.

"The Citizens Party knew enough not to run a white male for a second time, but they didn't want a radical feminist either," Anna said, confirming Rachel's own experience. "The Citizens Party was still a patriarchy. They wanted a safe woman who would talk about the Equal

Rights Amendment and child care and cutting the military budget, not about overthrowing male domination. The male leaders felt threatened by the feminists who joined the party. They weren't interested in confronting their own sexism," Anna contended.

Anna added, "I don't hate all men, I just view them as the weaker sex. And I'm constantly disappointed that most of them are unable to realize even their limited potential."

Most of Anna's male friends were gay, often activists in the fight against AIDS and HIV. The Bay Area, with its large and open gay community, unfortunately was ground zero in the AIDS epidemic. Many gays had not learned about the dangers of AIDS and the need for safe sex until it was too late.

Rachel and Anna spoke at several city council and state legislative hearings in support of more funding for AIDS research and prevention, and helped organize several benefits. Rachel also helped provide nursing and hospice support to several of Anna's friends who eventually died of the disease.

Anna was involved with ACT UP — AIDS Coalition to Unleash Power. In response to government indifference to the rising toll, AIDS activists began to organize more militant demonstrations, combining civil disobedience and guerrilla theater.

Anna pulled Rachel and Tommy along to a demonstration she organized at the local offices of Burroughs Wellcome to protest the 10,000-dollar-a-year cost of AZT, the only federally approved drug for AIDS. Anna planted grave markers bearing the names of people who died from AIDS on the company's front lawn.

"They say we just like to make noise to get our faces on tv," Anna said. "They want us to sit on our hands and listen to them tell us they're doing all they can. Screw them. What they don't want to 'fess up to is all your friends wasting away waiting for these drug companies to discover something — or 'cause only the rich can afford to buy what they do put on the market. The taxpayers see gays and druggies and blacks, and they say, Who gives a damn? We don't like these people, it's their own fault anyway. If it was old white men who got this disease, they would have mobilized the armed forces and started a draft."

Anna was a one-person coalition. Going to meetings and protests was an essential part of her social life. Rachel asked her once, "Exactly how many groups do you work with?"

"Let's see," Anna said. "I'm active in fighting for more funding to build permanent housing for the homeless. I'm a member of

Democratic Socialists of America, though they mainly just talk. I'm a local board member of NOW. You'll be happy to hear that I've got them involved with the feminization of poverty, starting with the need to raise welfare mothers out of poverty. I work with various women's groups. Right now I'm circulating petitions against the forced genital mutilation of women that is common in way too many cultures, and I'm helping to organize Take Back the Night marches to make neighborhoods safe for women. I'm organizing a picket line next week to protest downtown business clubs that exclude women from their membership. On April fifteenth — tax day — we're leafleting at the post office for a cut in the military budget. You wanna hear next month's calendar?"

Rachel noticed that Anna was more likely to show up at an event if they were serving food. She didn't seem to have much time for cooking.

Anna and Rachel also shared a love of women's music, attending concerts together by performers such as Holly Near, Ferron, Meg Christian and the Indigo Girls. Anna was cohost of a weekly Women's Music Show on Sunday afternoon on the community radio station, interspersing activist news events with songs. She sometimes brought Rachel on to talk about the latest effort in the healthcare campaign, or just to help spin tunes. Anna and Rachel worked together to do a benefit concert for the Women's Center with Holly Near, who was also active in the antinuclear and environmental movements.

By the end of the first year of their friendship, it was becoming clear that Anna was interested in a more physical relationship. Other than an occasional kiss after a late-night event or a bottle of wine, she didn't press the point.

Anna and Rachel decided to spend the weekend together in Mendocino County north of San Francisco. They spent the day driving up the coast in Anna's convertible, visiting a vineyard where they had a little too much to drink, and took a hike that ended with them on a bluff overlooking the ocean to watch the sunset.

They stayed at a rustic inn in the forest that featured cabins along with a huge communal hot tub that was clothing optional. They jumped in after dinner, trying to work out the kinks in their muscles after the hike. Rachel had always admired Anna's firm body, and was a little self-conscious of her own love handles. There were already several other couples enjoying the hot mineral-water pool, also naked. They passed around a bottle of champagne. Someone passed around a joint. The water was hot and bubbly. It felt sinful.

Rachel and Anna walked back to the cabin holding hands, not bothering putting their robes back on, enjoying the hot summer air. Anna lit several candles, opened up a bottle of wine they'd bought at the vineyard, and asked Rachel if she would like a massage. Rachel had a sense of where this was headed, but she felt too good to ask.

Anna warmed up some body oil in a little metal container with a candle underneath it, and proceeded to give Rachel the best, longest and most luxurious back rub she could remember. Rachel was in heaven.

Eventually Anna gently turned her over, and began to kiss her breasts, slowly moving her tongue down to her soft belly as her knowing fingertips continued to massage her nipples. Rachel began to stroke Anna's hair. That encouraged Anna's tongue even lower. After Rachel came, she pulled Anna up on top of her and kissed her full on the lips, unsure of what to do next. Anna took her hand and guided her.

When Rachel woke the next morning, she and Anna were still tangled up in bed, with the sheets on the floor. She got up quietly and took a quick shower, sitting on the chair next to the bed waiting for Anna to wake. Anna eventually rolled over, gave Rachel a big smile and said, "Good morning."

"Good morning, Anna. How're you doing?" Rachel asked.

"I'm doing great. Last night was wonderful. How are yooou doing?" Anna drawled. "Why don't you climb back in here and help warm up this bed? It's a little chilly."

Rachel sat back down on the bed's edge. "Anna, I liked last night. I care a lot about you, and last night was really special for me."

"But?"

"But — I don't know how to say this — but I still like men."

Anna laughed. "Well, I didn't really think I was converting you to the team last evening. Maybe teaching you to be a switch hitter. And I'm not asking you to like going to bed with women. I'm only asking you to go to bed with me, even just occasionally. Love and sex is about two people, not about what other people expect us to be. If last night felt good, and it certainly felt good to me, then if the right moment comes along, let's take advantage of it. Your call. I'm willing to give it a try if you are, or we can just leave last night as something special."

"Well, last night wasn't totally unexpected, and I won't pretend that I didn't enjoy it. It was good it because it was you and it was a nice way to end a great day together. I'm still more attracted to men. But if you're willing to take it slow and accept it for what it is, that's fine with me."

Anna threw off the sheet and opened her arms. "Well, sweetie, how 'bout a little kiss then? And you can have a back rub whenever you want. I promise, I won't *always* use it as an excuse to seduce you." Anna gave her a big hug.

****

Wynn's work on the apartheid issue bore fruit.

On February 11, 1990, Nelson Mandela, at age seventy-one, walked out of prison after twenty-seven years to become the leader of his country.

As his supporters gave him a riotous welcome, he told the world, "I have cherished the idea of a democratic and free society in which all persons live together in harmony and with equal opportunities. It is an ideal which I hope to live for and to achieve. But if need be, it is an ideal for which I am prepared to die."

Wynn lit candles that evening in front of the framed posters he had on his apartment wall of Mandela and Stephen Biko. Biko, a South African black student leader, had been a major force behind the national uprising in 1976. He was arrested on August 27, 1977, while traveling to Port Elizabeth. After weeks of torture, with major head injuries, Biko died while being transported, naked, manacled and comatose, on a 700-mile trip over rough roads to Pretoria. Biko was one of thousands of political activists killed by the police.

Already a living legend, presumably more myth than reality, Mandela became the rare individual able to live up to his followers' hopes, showing an ability to forgive his oppressors and helping his country find a way to achieve a nonviolent transfer of power.

It took until May 1994 — four years after his release from prison — for Mandela to be sworn in as president of South Africa. Justice, including the ending of the economic oppression of the black majority, would come even more slowly.

When Mandela walked out of prison, it was a moment of joy for most people in the world. There was a sense that real change was possible. That sometimes the people won. It was a moment that both Rachel and Wynn drew upon when things appeared most bleak, when the cause of the people seemed doomed against corporate might.

The only comparable event in Wynn and Rachel's memories was the night three months earlier when the Berlin Wall fell, and the Soviet Union shattered as images of East Germans dancing atop the wall was broadcast live around the world.

If the Berlin Wall could fall, if Mandela could become president, then winning genuine democratic rule by the people from the rule of corporations seemed less impossible.

As South Africa haltingly made its transition toward justice and democracy, Wynn decided to move into the area of environmental justice, to resist companies that look to minority and low-income neighborhoods to store their toxic wastes and build their pollution machines.

Wynn took a job working for the National Toxics Coalition, based in DC, which had been started by Sophie Kretsky. She was a housewife who discovered that her family was living on top of an old toxic landfill, which did much to explain the health problems that her children were experiencing. The multinational that had created the dump had sold the land for a housing development. By the time she forced them to cough up, she had become a single parent and moved to DC both to escape the toxics and to launch a clearinghouse to assist other citizen activists with similar problems.

Kretsky sent Wynn out to California in the fall of 1990 for the last month of the Big Green campaign, a ballot initiative to regulate the use of toxic pesticides, reduce coastal pollution and mitigate global warming through the reduction of greenhouse gases and chlorofluorocarbon emissions. Big Green also proposed to create a new state agency to strengthen environmental protection.

The early prospects for Big Green looked good, getting an early push from the media hype accompanying the twentieth anniversary of Earth Day. That was followed by the Exxon Valdez accident in Alaska, which spilled hundreds of millions of gallons of oil in a pristine wilderness area. But with a month to go, the polls showed a dead heat.

Also on the ballot was a Forest First Initiative to save the redwoods.

"We always look good in these ballot initiatives at first," Wynn told Rachel, "because the public supports the environment. Plus all the grassroots work that there's been on various local environmental crises. And the news reporters assigned to the environmental beat tend to be sympathetic."

"Then in the last month," Wynn continued, "the industry just overwhelms us with negative ads in the paid media. The free media coverage turns more hostile because the media owners and publishers, a decreasing number of corporations, assert more control. They invariably support the corporate position, especially if they're pouring tons of money into buying ads. By the last week we're usually behind in the polls, we're being buried by paid ads and scare tactics, and the only chance we have is a strong volunteer effort to get out the vote, hitting the phone banks and going door to door."

Wynn spent considerable time traveling and training volunteers on how to identify supporters and get them to the polls. He tapped his national contacts to generate some last-minute funding for media buys. He was also responsible for outreach in minority communities, particularly low-income ones where issues of survival normally took precedence over environmental concerns.

Big Green was in trouble. A lot less of the basic organizing work, like phone banks and regional volunteers, had been done than he'd been told. Money was also a big problem. Wynn shifted to general campaign management, though there was the invariable tension with local organizers who resented a national group trying to direct the campaign.

His first move was to advise them, "Go hire whomever you can in your local area. Let them keep 50 percent of whatever they raise selling T-shirts, going door to door, holding house parties, etc. Remember, giving money empowers the donor, so the more people who give, the more we build support."

Wynn stayed with Rachel when he was in San Francisco, where most of the environmental groups had their state headquarters. She and Tommy had their own apartment now.

Rachel and Wynn were tentative with each for the first few days. She wasn't sure how she felt about Wynn just popping in and out of her life, looking to play it hot and heavy for a few weeks and then disappear again. Anna knew about Wynn, and Rachel sensed a certain level of jealousy, though she and Anna definitely were not a couple. Just special friends. She was also concerned about Tommy's reaction now that he was a teenager.

Wynn and Tommy got along great as usual. *Damn him. How does Wynn do that? That's no fair,* Rachel thought. She couldn't believe how Tommy would be yelling at her one moment over something trivial, like helping to do the laundry, and the next would be laughing on the floor as Wynn tried to beat him on the newest video game. Wynn also appreciated a teenage boy's sense of humor far more than she did.

For the first few nights Wynn had to sleep on the couch. Wynn was a little surprised but went with the flow. But when Wynn talked her into going out dancing on Saturday night, the fire quickly reignited. As he planned, they ended up in each other's arms that night.

When Tommy mentioned a few days later that it would be better if

Wynn could stay in Rachel's room so Tommy could play Mario Brothers in the morning without waking him up, the adults agreed. Wynn later denied that he'd bribed Tommy to make the suggestion.

The campaign for Big Green was headed for defeat. "The proponents miscalculated in how they put the initiative together," Wynn complained to Rachel. "By adopting the 'something for everyone' approach, they thought they'd create a bigger coalition. Instead, it's generated a broad-based coalition of corporate-funded groups to oppose it. Also, some of the proposals are way too specific, others too vague. It ends up confusing people."

Big Green went down big, getting only 36 percent of the vote. The Forest Initiative also failed, torpedoed by the timber industry's strategy of putting up a competing proposal to confuse the voters.

Shortly before the vote, Rachel invited Anna over to dinner to meet Wynn. More accurately, Anna arranged her own invitation, offering to do the cooking.

Dinner was late on a Saturday night two weekends before the election. When Rachel got home from work, Anna was already in the kitchen, cutting vegetables and drinking wine. Tommy was at a friend's house.

"I see that Mr. Harris has graduated from the couch to the bedroom. Tell me, what does that stud have that I don't?" Anna asked wickedly.

"A quiet demeanor. I'm going to take a shower," replied Rachel.

"A shower? Need someone to scrub your back? Or dry you off?" Anna helpfully suggested.

"No thanks," responded Rachel. "I think I can handle it. Why don't you put on some music?"

Anna put on *The Changer and the Changed* by Cris Williamson, one of the first "womyn" musicians. She carried her wine into the bathroom and sat on the toilet seat to talk to Rachel as she showered.

"Aren't you supposed to be cooking?" Rachel asked in exasperation.

"All done," Anna said cheerfully. "The rice is cooked, salad is made, vegetables are chopped. Just gotta throw 'em in the wok when we're ready to eat. I'd much rather wash you, er, I mean watch, no, I mean wash."

Rachel could sense that Anna was in fine form, planning to make the evening one to remember. She hoped that the theatrics wouldn't get out of hand. Politics and sex were two of Anna's favorite subjects and she had plenty of material this evening.

Rachel was still getting dressed when Wynn came in. Anna was in a mischievous mood. She wiped her hands on a towel, and walked through Wynn's offer of a handshake, embracing him in a big hug instead. "I've heard so much about you. What an honor to finally meet the legendary Wynn."

"People forget your faults when you're not around," Wynn laughed nervously. "But Anna, I'd have to say the same about you, given the stories Rachel has told me," Wynn parried. "Most recently, I recollect something about a campaign finance reform protest at a Republican fundraiser, and a male stripper."

"Republicans have no sense of humor. The waiters all enjoyed it," replied Anna.

It was an untidy dinner. Food and drink slopped on the table top several times. Anna was in a rush to get drunk and Wynn was trying to keep up with her — it was the male thing to do. Rachel was wondering if she should catch a movie.

Anna and Wynn had great fun comparing notes about what they liked in women, one in particular. Somehow the conversation had turned into a highlight reel of Rachel's embarrassing moments, primarily having to do with anything mechanical or reading a map.

"Ever hear 'bout the time when she had to drive to the Capitol in Sacramento, a little less than 90 miles east of here, and didn't realize she was heading in the wrong direction till she was almost in freaking LA?" asked Anna.

"No," laughed Wynn, "but I did hear 'bout the time she poured a quart of motor oil into the automatic transmission."

After using Rachel's discomfort to break the ice, Anna turned to the main sparring partner for the evening.

"So Wynn," Anna started coyly. "What's the greater oppression: gender, race, class or sexual orientation?"

Wynn ducked at first. "I'd probably say that a biracial, lesbian, poor woman who doesn't speak English and practices animal sacrifice as her religion would be the most oppressed. Of course, other species are even further down the food chain of oppression, but that wasn't part of your equation."

"Come on, Wynn, you can do better than that," Anna complained. "I want a serious answer."

"Rather than worrying about what the greatest source of oppression is, we gotta build the revolution among all of the oppressed. Power to the people," Wynn said, almost knocking over his glass. "I dunno. What do you think Rachel?"

Rachel was afraid of where Anna was headed and tried to change the conversation. She stood up and began to clear the dishes. "Anyone want dessert? Or coffee? Lots of black coffee?"

Anna ignored Rachel's effort. "Let's simplify it. Is a black man or a white woman more oppressed?"

"Is this one of those 'How pregnant is she?' questions?" Wynn responded. "Both are oppressed. I mean, John Lennon got it right. "Woman is the Nigger of the World." I'd believe that a rich white woman is usually less oppressed than a poor black man. But is a rich white woman less oppressed than a rich black man? That's a harder question,"

"Anna, is there a point you're trying to get at?" inquired Rachel, getting a little impatient. *If this is about me sleeping with Wynn rather than you, just come out and god-damn say it*, thought Rachel.

"The question is, What is the most fundamental oppression, and how should that impact upon our organizing priorities?" asked Anna, getting more serious. "Can you win real change without addressing the fundamental oppression?"

Rachel responded in her most patronizing tone. "I think we all understand if we just eliminate economic exploitation — capitalism, if you will — we won't be free. If we eliminate only white supremacy, we will not be free. If we end patriarchy and heterosexism, we will still not be free. If one person is oppressed, in chains, we are all oppressed. We all realize that justice for all is more than a slogan."

Anna pushed on. "Well, I could point out that women are half the world and that the subjugation of women extends throughout human history, way before things like class and race even existed. In almost every culture, women were the ones oppressed, which led to other oppressions."

"But let's take a different angle," Anna suggested. Wynn was the prey tonight, not Rachel. "Wynn, you've done community organizing with poor people, worked in the antiapartheid movement, and now the environment. I'd be interested in your long-term organizing analysis. Rachel tells me you want a revolution, not reform. How are we going to win?"

"Oh, you want the road map to revolution? That doesn't come free, you know," laughed Wynn.

"Name your price. Some more wine, perhaps?" Anna offered, filling hers.

"For the revolution to succeed, you need to mobilize the majority of people. Or at least you have to be perceived as the majority, since the reality is that it's always a small percentage of people who actually make decisions. I don't think that a minority, particularly in a country as powerful and large as the US, can create a revolution by themselves, no matter how much moral authority that minority may have," Wynn remarked.

"What about the civil rights movement?" Anna asked. "That was led by minorities, but it had a lot of impact. It led to integration — or at least the overthrow of Jim Crow, gave more rights to blacks — and strengthened the right to vote."

"We did a good job on civil rights but we couldn't move it from a moral issue to one of economic justice," Wynn observed.

Wynn had put on a Bob Marley and the Wailers album. He sang that he shot the sheriff but he didn't shoot the deputy.

Wynn continued. "The labor movement argues that workers are the logical group to lead the revolution, and while they may be right, I think their best opportunity peaked in the thirties. The unions and a lot of workers have lost a lotta their class consciousness. Dues and the pocketbook issues of their membership have become more important to the unions than class solidarity."

"So how come you're working on environmental issues?" Anna asked. "Most of the environmental groups I know have a very limited agenda. Especially the big ones, the ones with the staff and the big budgets. They usually avoid confronting the corporate interests that created the problem in the first place."

Wynn warmed up to his subject. "Since I think the American revolution will need to mobilize the middle class to be successful, the environment is a good starting point. Middle class families do worry about things like clean water and air. It's the ultimate issue — if you destroy the planet you destroy the human race. There's a large class and racial component, since the poor and people of color are the ones forced to live next to the toxic dump. It has a gender connection, since at the grassroots level it's often mothers who take the lead in protecting the kids."

"The grassroots environmental groups," Wynn added, "tend to be more radical than the national groups. They're worried about dealing with a local crisis, not about raising a lot of money for their organizational budget. The grassroots groups are anticorporate. It's crystal clear to them who's causing the problem."

"But a lot of working class people don't like environmental groups," argued Anna. "They think environmentalists are more concerned about saving the spotted owl than worrying about feeding poor kids or creating jobs. Most people are too caught up in the daily struggle of survival to worry about saving Mother Earth."

"You're jumping all over the map, Anna," Rachel pointed out. "Yes, we've got to do a better job of making connections between issues. Poor people need to understand why clean air is important to curing their kid's asthma. And economic justice activists need to understand that ending racism and sexism is critical to making sure people get paid a fair wage. All oppression is wrong and needs to be ended."

"We need to join the single-issue groups into a broader movement," Wynn added, "one that supports people power. If we could focus everyone's attention on the wealthy five percent that exploit the rest of us, then we would have a good chance of winning."

"That's why I like the groups like the Green Party that have a multiissue, multilevel, multistrategy approach," said Wynn. "Other times I think we need a charismatic leader like Jesse Jackson who so excites people that he can get the various groups to transcend their differences — get everyone headed in the same direction without fighting over the details.

"My mantra, however," he added, "is: any blow struck against the empire, as long as it's nonviolent, is a blow well struck. I don't know which blow will be the one that finally topples the empire. But I'll be glad to let you come dance at my revolution if I can come dance at yours."

"Why the nonviolence restriction on revolution?" asked Anna.

Here Rachel jumped in. "The end product of violence is always more violence. Even if you're ultimately successful in toppling your opponents through violence, the chances are that you'll end up so much like your opponents that it won't make much difference. And I know that some leftists want to have their own gun to fight the government when the final struggle comes. But if the revolution is fought with guns, the government will just blow us off the face of the earth. Even if we win, our task will be sheer survival of the human race."

"But how come so many of these environmental groups," said Anna, not ready to concede, "the big ones with the clout, in fact, all the big groups, end up being led by white heterosexual men, the root of so much of the problem?" asked Anna. "It's men who have led us to war, who've built the factories that pollute our communities, who've decided that raising children should be done for free by women. Shouldn't the groups that wanna change the world reflect the world they want to create?"

"Amen to that," Rachel and Wynn said in unison, raising their wine glasses.

Anna had too much to drink to navigate her way home. She suggested that Wynn and she play a round of poker to see who got to share Rachel's bed. Rachel threw a pillow at her and said, "You can have Tommy's bedroom."

"I'm afraid I'd have nightmares if I spent a night in a teenage boy's bedroom," Anna responded.

"Fine, I'll take Tommy's bed. I think the karma would be better anyway if I slept alone tonight. The two of you can figure out the rest of the sleeping arrangements any way you want," Rachel said.

"Hey, what did I do?" asked Wynn plaintively.

****

By 1992, the national movement for a single-payer healthcare system was in high gear.

"We support the adoption of a single-payer, universal healthcare program similar to that used in every other industrial country," said Rachel during one of her frequent speaking events. "With private health insurance, more than 30 cents out of every dollar goes to paperwork and profits, not to providing healthcare. A single-payer system works like Medicare, with one program paying all bills, while preserving freedom of choice as to your medical provider. By eliminating the bureaucracy and insurance company profits, hundreds of billions of dollars would be saved. These savings could be invested in providing healthcare to those presently uninsured," explained Rachel.

Bill Clinton raised the issue of universal healthcare during his successful campaign for presidency. His wife, Hillary, who headed up the effort to overhaul the national healthcare program, said that a single-payer system was "too socialistic for most Americans to support. Northerners might support it, because you're used to hearing about the system they have in Canada, but it would be dead on arrival in the South."

Opposition to universal healthcare remained strong in the Congress, their backbones stiffened by the tens of millions in campaign contributions from the healthcare and insurance industries.

Rachel and Anne flew to DC to participate in a civil disobedience protest at the Capitol office of Bob Dole, the Senate Majority Leader. While Anna had done civil disobedience many times before, this was the first time for Rachel.

Tommy asked Rachel why she was planning to get arrested. "You always tell me to stay out of trouble, and listen to the cops. Why don't you?"

"Well, I guess it's time for your adult speech about cops," Rachel laughed. "Tommy, universal healthcare is something I've worked on for many years. We need to make sure everyone who needs to see a doctor or get treatment is able to do so. We're so close to finally winning, but it's slipping away. The insurance companies and medical industry are throwing a ton of money into television ads, even more than was spent on the presidential candidates. I'm desperate. I feel it's time to throw the kitchen sink into the fight."

"So now your body is a kitchen sink," retorted Tommy. "How out of shape are you? I thought you were going to start jogging a few mornings a week."

"Very funny," said Rachel.

Rachel got a little nervous the night before the protest when the organizer doing the briefing said that there was no guarantee that they'd be immediately released, that they could end up dealing with the courts for a couple of days. Rachel was worried about how long she'd be away from Tommy.

Anna didn't share those concerns. She spoke up about the need for solidarity among those going to be arrested. "We need to stand together in solidarity. Some people here may not be able or don't want to give the police all the information they demand, like social security numbers. Or will refuse to post bail so as not to give in to the system. I think each of us needs to commit to staying in jail until everyone is released."

That idea didn't go over well with several of the demonstrators. "I came here to protest about healthcare, not about problems with the criminal justice system. I want to protest for single-payer and get out of here as soon as possible."

The protesters were diverse — grandparents and twenty-year-olds, a few union and religious leaders, organizers, medical care professionals. The plan was to break into several groups of ten or so, pretend to be tourists taking a tour of the Capitol, and appear in front of the Senate Majority Leader's office at an appointed time. One of the groups had rewritten several familiar songs to poke fun about the present state of healthcare.

"It's illegal to chant — even sing — in the Capitol. The police will give everyone a warning to depart. Those who stay will face arrest. People are free to back off when the cops begin to arrest people," one of their attorneys told them.

Rachel was unsure about getting arrested up until the moment the cops began to tie plastic handcuffs around people's wrists. Anna leaned over. "Still time to walk over to the other supporters and avoid arrest. No big deal." Rachel shook her head and didn't move.

A few tears began to fall down Rachel's cheek as she waited for her turn to be arrested. Anna leaned over and hugged her.

Rachel smiled and kissed her. "I'm sorry. I'm okay. I feel so silly. This wave of emotion just rolled over me. I guess it's one of those personal growth moments, where you feel like you stepped over to the other side. I don't know why it's affecting me so, but it does. A moment of personal liberation, I suppose."

"I'm proud of you, Rachel. Maybe I can get them to handcuff us together. Or we can run for it once they tie us up, and fall down in front of the tourists and beg for our lives," Anna said with a chuckle.

The arrest was the most boring part of it, though the first few hours were somewhat painful with her hands bound behind her back. The protesters were led downstairs into the bowels of the Capitol and seated in what looked like a briefing room. Rachel managed, as did several other protesters, to loosen the handcuffs and slip one of her hands out. She kept both hands clasped behind her so the police wouldn't find out.

It took eight hours for all the arrestees to be processed and released. Rachel found that being arrested with someone was a good way to strike up a conversation. The person next to her was a well-known leader of the Communication Workers of America. He promised to talk to the local out in the Bay Area about coming up with some more funding for their local healthcare organizing.

Their court date was set for the following week. They collectively groaned. "A lot of us are from around the country. What do you expect us to do?" The police officials said that if they failed to appear in court, their name would be logged into the DC computer for the following year but they would not send an arrest warrant to their local community. If they were stopped for any infraction in DC during that year, such as a traffic ticket, they'd be hauled away to jail. After one year they'd be deleted from the system.

"So, are you telling us we don't have to show up next week?" the protesters asked. "I'm just telling you the facts," the officer responded. "You can do with 'em what you want."

Wynn was waiting for them when they were released. The three of them went out to his favorite Mexican restaurant in the Adams Morgan neighborhood. He invited Rachel and Anna to stay at his apartment that evening. They declined, saying they wanted to stay at a hotel near the airport to make it easy to catch their flight early the next morning. "Whatever, just behave and keep out of trouble. DC can be a dangerous city," Wynn said with a wink.

Rachel and Anna shared a bed that evening.

****

In 1993, President Clinton used the passage of the North America Free Trade Agreement with Canada and Mexico to get his presidency off life support, overcoming the widespread perception of weakness and incompetence. To secure the votes of various Congressmen, Clinton made numerous deals unrelated to NAFTA.

NAFTA was the start of an alphabet soup of trade agreements pushed by multinational corporations and the leaders of both major American political parties.

Wynn spent six months helping to coordinate the unsuccessful national campaign to stop NAFTA. Environmental groups were among the biggest opponents.

"NAFTA will create hundreds of thousands of jobs in the US, while helping to lift wages and living conditions in Mexico," said Seymour Henderson, the US chief negotiator. "NAFTA will also allow American companies to become more competitive in the international markets, taking advantage of the cheaper labor in Mexico. NAFTA will lower prices for consumers, while ending the unwise practice of using tariffs and other devices to protect inefficient businesses."

"NAFTA will weaken environmental protection, labor rights, and food and safety standards," countered Wynn in his talks to local groups. "It will also speed up the demise of family farms. Wages in the US will be lowered and union drives busted by companies threatening to move production to Mexico. NAFTA weakens our laws by giving companies the right to sue for damages if they feel our consumer and environmental rules cut into their profits. The only good thing about NAFTA is that it's bringing together union, environmentalists and community groups to oppose corporate globalization."

The Clinton administration responded, "We've negotiated side agreements to deal with the various labor and environmental concerns that have been raised. NAFTA will open up the Mexican market to US companies. If Congress rejects this agreement, Japan will be knocking on Mexico's door the next day to sign their own deal."

NAFTA demonstrated how many of the big national environmental groups based in DC were owned by the Democratic Party.

To help Clinton pass NAFTA, groups such as Environmental Defense Fund, Natural Resources Defense Council and National Wildlife Federation, formed the Environmental Coalition for NAFTA. The coalition, according to Justin Brooke, leader of NRDC, "broke the back of the environmental opposition to NAFTA. After we established our position, Clinton only had labor to fight. We did him a big favor."

While the National Toxics Coalition begged to differ, Clinton used the support of the inside players of the environmental movement to provide political cover.

Clinton repaid the favor to the big national environmental groups by giving them "access," such as coming over to the White House to have breakfast with the vice-president. "I can't tell you how wonderful it is," said Brian Foxworth, the Audubon Society's chief lobbyist, "to walk down the hall in the White House or a government agency and be greeted by your first name." But getting friendly with the White House staff and drinking orange juice out of silver cups did little for the environment.

Wynn included a note to Rachel in his end-of-year holiday card. "What is surprising is not that some of the environmental groups sold out, but how little it took to buy them off. Season's greetings."

TWELVE

OPPOSING TERRORISM

The tragedy of September 11 had diverted Rachel from the selection of a vice-president. With the nation poised on the cusp of war, the need to clarify the line of succession was especially critical. She needed someone who supported her efforts to lead the country toward peace, while serving as a bridge to Congress.

Rachel selected John Mumfi, a civil rights activist who was serving his third term in Congress from Harlem. Mumfi had been one of the first major African-American leaders who had joined with the Greens to protest the harassment of black voters in Florida. He was influential with black and progressive members of Congress. An ordained minister, he had broad support among religious groups. His stature in New York politics would also help.

Mumfi was a vocal critic of the racist nature of America's wars and had urged a cautious response to September 11. "We don't need any more blood of our black brothers and sisters spilled once again on foreign soil fighting Muslims in order to protect American oil companies. We want justice, not war," he said at the major peace rally in DC a few weeks after 9/11.

Though allied with the Greens, Mumfi wasn't ready to bolt his party. "I'm disgusted by the slowness of the Democratic Party in responding to the racism in the Florida election. I'm also fed up with the lack of progress on issues affecting people of color, especially the high rates of poverty and crime that still plague many inner city communities."

"Rachel, I still believe that the Democratic Party is the most realistic alternative we have in the short term to promote a progressive agenda," Mumfi told her. "But I agree that the Democrats take the votes of minorities and poor people for granted, and don't do enough for us when they do have power. They don't fight hard enough for a living wage, or to rebuild inner city neighborhoods, to lift kids out of poverty. They won't crack down on the guns that kill so many of our youth. And this war on drugs stuff. I mean, it's my people they're stuffing into these prisons."

"If the Greens become a more viable option for those whose needs have been ignored, that will make the Democratic leaders pay more attention to our agenda," Mumfi said. "I'd be honored to serve as your vice-president."

While the Democratic leadership and their campaign contributors were not thrilled with Mumfi's selection, viewing him as too independent, they publicly praised the choice, fearful of alienating black voters if they failed to embrace him. Deutsche viewed Mumfi as more pragmatic than Rachel — he understood how the game in the Beltway is played, and was willing to do a little wheeling and dealing if needed.

The Republicans felt that Mumfi would help the Greens weaken the Democrats' stranglehold of black voters while doing little to shore up Rachel's political standing with centrist or conservative voters.

Rachel's concept of a unity government appeared dead. The Democrats and Republicans both took a step back after September 11, waiting to see how the dust settled. The candidates put forth by the two major parties for various Cabinet positions were re-evaluating whether they wanted to be part of an administration headed for a major fight with Congress over the issue of war.

****

Rachel met with the Senate Majority Leader and the Speaker of the House a few days before her appearance in the United Nations to discuss her proposals to bring bin Laden to trial, to create an International Tribunal on Terrorism and to push for an International Peace Treaty.

They dispensed with the usual pleasantries.

"I don't know what you were hoping to accomplish with your stunt at our hearing," began Senator Deutsche, "but you didn't win any points with Congress and I doubt with the public either. Frankly, I am shocked that you could act in such a way while proposing a unity government. You can't throw a tantrum every time we tell you that you're wrong," the Majority Leader said.

"Senator Deutsche, I perhaps was a little too forceful in highlighting for Congress some of the problems that I saw, and in hindsight, I should have called your office to alert you to my appearance. But you should have contacted me to discuss how my administration would like to participate before announcing such a hearing. Communication is a two-way street," Rachel pointed out.

"Tensions are running high, and I'll do my best in the future to avoid such public confrontations, as I trust you will. But I felt the need that day to speak the truth," Rachel said, trying to sound conciliatory. "At least it helped cleanse my soul a bit. Truth is always the first casualty in war. However, now I'm ready for some tripartisanship," Rachel said, with a smile that was not quite as welcoming as she wanted.

The congressional leaders wanted to invade Afghanistan immediately, remove the Taliban from power and destroy bin Laden and the al-Qaida network. Rachel argued for her proposal to have the UN indict bin Laden and create a police force to apprehend him. Deutsche and Baker thought it was a waste of time.

"I'm more than willing to fight terrorists," Rachel told them. "What I won't do is harm any more innocent civilians. Declaring war against Afghanistan, with no evidence that their government has taken action against us, violates a whole set of international agreements that our country is party to. Let's not forget our own role in allowing Afghanistan to fall apart to the point where terrorists could operate so openly. And let's remember that countries like the Soviet Union and Britain thought they had conquered Afghanistan only to lose a guerrilla war in the mountains.

"Goddamn it," Rachel sputtered in frustration, "we're supposed to be the moral leaders of the world, as well as the most powerful country in history! We preach to the Israelis and Palestinians, the Irish, to India and Pakistan, Russia, and everyone else about the need to break the cycle of violence. Yet when we're the ones hit by a terrorist act, not only do you want to strike back with overwhelming force, you want to attack a whole country."

"The UN is a debating society," argued Deutsche, smoothing his tie. He was always immaculately groomed, with a neatly folded handkerchief protruding from the breast pocket of his suit. "The only way they could ever take out bin Laden is if he died of old age waiting for them to act. While most Mideast leaders would be happy to have us eliminate him and his terrorist buddies, they just don't want to be seen authorizing it. And even on the off-chance that they do capture him, it'll be years before we they bring him to trial. Meanwhile, the al-Qaida network will still have the resources to launch terrorist attacks against us."

"Senator, I promise you that I will not rest until whoever is responsible for September eleventh is brought to justice," replied Rachel, still wearing a black mourning dress. "Let's start by bringing bin Laden to trial. But we need a long-term solution here — not just a fireworks display, but one that gets rid of terrorism. If you want to propose how to reform the UN, if you want to propose a different international forum, I'm all ears. But I think it's essential that we work with the rest of the world to solve this problem," she argued.

Rachel now made her best effort to reach some understanding with the two leaders.

"Jonathan, Freddy, I want you to think about your grandchildren for a moment, and your grandchildren's grandchildren. Why type of planet will they inherit from you? Will it be a world where terrorism is an aberration, an abomination, or a nightly fixture on the evening news? Bin Laden is just the latest boogeyman. There are plenty of madmen who'll be willing to fill his shoes once we take him out. If we start bombing, then the answer in the future is to make sure you buy more bombs or more dangerous weapons than the other guy. That's a losing proposition," she pointed out.

"I do think 'bout my grandkids, Rachel," said Baker. "I don't want 'em livin' in a country that cowers when it gets attacked. I teach 'em to stand up for themselves. It's my job to stand up for 'em."

"America's not going to be top dog forever," Rachel responded. "We're not always going to get our way just by flexing our muscles. For once, we have some real moral authority to demand justice, and the type of justice we insist upon will do a lot to determine what *justice* will mean in the future. We have the opportunity to create the international institutions and laws that give vision to the type of world we want to leave for our children.

"We need to show that we have a real commitment to improving the quality of life for people in third world countries, not that we just want to open up their countries so our corporations can get rich off of them," Rachel observed.

"I want to give the UN the opportunity to do the right thing," she added. "I'll insist on a tight timetable, and if they're unwilling to move, then I'm willing to send in US troops unilaterally. But we need to be willing to listen to what answers they come up with."

Baker urged Rachel to be more realistic about the challenges they were facing.

"You're right, Rachel, bombin' Afghanistan won't end terrorism," Baker said. "We gotta take out any safe havens for these bastards. We gotta go after Iraq, Yemen, Syria, North Korea. Take out these sonuvabitches who support terrorists. And in places where there ain't no central government, we gotta go in ourselves and wipe 'em out, exterminate their foul nests."

"Rachel, while you preach about tolerating diversity," Deutsche added, "you don't seem to grasp however how diverse the world actually is. You act like these countries and leaders we have disputes with are just like you and me, only with different clothing and a different language, that if we sit down together we can talk our problems through."

"These countries have radically different views on the role of religion in government," Deutsche continued, "on the rights of women, religious diversity and personal liberty, than we do in America. Some of them are also fighting religious, ethnic or tribal disputes that go back hundreds or thousands of years. That is not something that you or anyone else is going to resolve in a matter of months or even years."

"We don't really have much choice," Rachel responded. "The changes in technology, weapons, communications and travel have changed the world forever. I keep seeing the two of you on the Sunday talk programs arguing that the 'war on terrorism' is a different type of war, yet you seem to want to fight it using the same old rules and tactics. We can't just smash some opponent because the opponent isn't a country with clearly defined armies or borders.

"This war is about people who feel marginalized and oppressed, and are striking back, trying to sow fear — and create media spectacles, not win battles. This war will only be won by creating a sense of justice, and by providing a realistic forum for their grievances to be resolved."

They ended up agreeing to disagree for the time being. "Madame President," Baker told her, "we're gonna send American troops to Afghanistan to take out bin Laden and the al-Qaida network. That you can bank on. We'll give you some time to work the UN. But not much. And your ideas 'bout international peace and justice, well, they're nice slogans, but it ain't gonna work. Nor will taxpayers be willin' to pony up to help some people who got dirty hands in gettin' Americans killed."

"The bottom line," Deutsche warned her, "is you have to deliver bin Laden quickly and you have to show that the UN is committed to confronting terrorism."

****

The UN Special Session on Terrorism adopted the US resolution establishing an International Tribunal on Terrorism with authority to indict, arrest and try those responsible for the September 11 attack. An international police force was created to assist the tribunal. Several prominent Muslim and African leaders agreed to serve on the tribunal. The resolution also called upon member countries to take steps to seize the funds used to finance terrorist activities.

Many countries praised Rachel's willingness to comply with international law in her response to September 11, including abiding by UN provisions on the use of force, and for her efforts to persuade Congress to ratify the International Criminal Court. Rachel's proposal to outlaw the killing of civilians in disputes, however, faced a rockier road.

While UN delegates were quick to condemn the September 11 attack as a crime against humanity, blanket condemnations of "terrorism" were less forthcoming, as was agreement on who was a terrorist. Many countries took pains not to be seen as condemning the Palestinians for their efforts to resist the military occupation of their homeland, while seeking to include Israel in the definition of terrorist.

Several African countries defended the need for the oppressed to fight legitimate wars of liberation. The Cuban delegates, while expressing sadness for the recent deaths, cited "the many poor peasants in Latin America who had been murdered by forces supported by the military and outside governments," a clear reference to the US.

Many of the poorer countries spoke enthusiastically about the proposal for an International Peace Treaty. "It's gratifying to hear that the US is aware of the true challenges facing us. We need to work together cooperatively to raise the living standards for all peoples, while respecting the importance of preserving our local autonomy or culture." The wealthier countries asked for more details, wanting to hear the price tag.

At a reception the opening night of the UN Special Session, a couple of delegates from Non Governmental Organizations pulled Wynn aside to discuss terrorism. They were blunter than the government representatives.

"It's fine for you in the West to talk about nonviolence," said one delegate from the Congo. "You have a court system with real judges, and TV stations that will show people getting cracked over the head by the government. But in places like Africa, the Middle East or South America, you protest, no matter how nonviolent it is, you get thrown in jail or get discarded along the side of the road with various parts of your body missing. A lot of these governments took power by brute force and they have no aversion to doing whatever is necessary to stay in power, especially when their own fate won't be too pretty if they get kicked out."

Another NGO representative from Ethiopia said, "Don't people who are being tortured, raped and murdered have a moral right to do what is needed to overthrow their oppressor? What do you do when your best leaders, your young people, are all publicly eliminated or simply disappear? Some of these dictators actually enjoy boiling their enemies in oil, or slowly chopping them into little pieces to feed to the animals. Do you really believe kneeling in the street in protest is going to make these monsters behave?" he laughed.

"Nonviolence may have worked for Gandhi in India but that was the exception, what with the British liking to pretend they were civilized. The leaders in my country don't worry about such pretenses," echoed the Congo representative.

Wynn responded. "It's not just about what's moral, it's also about what's going to be effective. Any time you use violence you're admitting defeat, and the use of violence changes you. How many freedom fighters who resorted to violence ended up looking an awful lot like the dictators they replaced? Can you name me one violent grassroots revolution that produced the type of society you'd want?"

They both mentioned South Africa.

"Maybe, but Mandela seems a pretty unique individual. Not many leaders are going to be willing to come out of prison after nearly 30 years and embrace their opponents. And it was the worldwide boycotts and corporate pressure that convinced the whites to transfer power, not the guerrillas' use of force."

The NGO representatives were unconvinced. "What about the Israeli-Palestinian situation?" said the Ethiopian. "Israel grabbed power and territory through terrorists like Begin. They then forced the Palestinians to live under the daily humiliation of military occupation for decades in deplorable conditions, hundreds of thousands in refugee camps, ignoring resolution after resolution in the United Nations. Israel used whatever force they thought necessary, bulldozing homes, killing people, supporting local militias that carried out vendettas against the Palestinians. If the Palestinians hadn't eventually retaliated with their own killings, do you think that Israel and the United States would ever have agreed to sit down at the negotiating table?" he argued.

Wynn snorted. "All that violence has not won the Palestinians' cause. They would have been better off, once world opinion swung in their direction, if they'd employed nonviolent protest tactics. It's a classic situation where a significant portion of each side believes the other side is the embodiment of evil and is willing to fight to the death to avoid anything that resembles surrendering. We've already sacrificed at least two generations of Palestinians to the conflict."

****

The Taliban sent their foreign minister to the UN to speak at the Special Session on Terrorism. They lacked a permanent representative since the UN, along with almost all of the world governments, failed to recognize them as the leaders of their country.

After a long introduction detailing his country's grievances against the world for the long suffering they had endured at the hand of one imperial power after another, "sacrificed to the intrigues of far more powerful countries," Abdullah Haqqani, dressed in a long white robe and black turban, put forth the Taliban's proposal.

"The people of Afghanistan believe in justice and the rule of law. It is integral to our belief in Allah, in the one true God that we all share," Haqqani explained.

His voice defiant, he noted, "Justice and the rule of law have been denied to us throughout our history. We, far more than most countries, understand the pain of seeing innocent people killed, of the rich and the powerful abusing the poor. We share in the sadness for the recent deaths of so many people, and we share in the goal of ending the killing of innocent civilians, whether they be rich financiers or poor peasants. We ask that those who preach for the tolerance of diversity actually practice such tolerance.

"Our leader has consulted with tribal elders," Haqqani continued, "and Afghanistan is now prepared to participate in a trial to determine the guilt or innocence of those who are accused of being responsible for September eleventh. We have only a few conditions that we attach. All that hear them will undoubtedly agree they are fair and just.

"One, the tribunal that is established must respect and comply with Islamic law, the law of our people. We do not say that other legal traditions and judges may not be involved, but it is essential that Islamic law be given its rightful place, and that prominent Islamic judges sit on the tribunal."

"Second," he went on, "this tribunal must be willing to seek the truth about September eleventh, not just listen to the stories of the American government and their allies. We in Afghanistan want to ensure that the whole story about September eleventh be told, that no one be spared from the shining light of truth. It must also be willing to investigate how American and other western countries have harmed our country and many others. It is likely that those who attacked the US have long-standing grievances that have not been heard, and these must be listened to and investigated as well."

"Third, we want the United Nations to apply an even and just hand to all terrorism. Our brothers and sisters in Palestine are subject to terrorism every day by the United States and Israel, and yet they are denied justice. Our brothers and sisters have been slain in Indonesia. Poor people are killed by western imperialists in every corner of the globe. The United Nations must address the terrorism of the rich and powerful."

"As a sign of our good faith, if you agree to all these three very just and fair stipulations, we are prepared to turn bin Laden over tomorrow to a group of Islamic judges. We will leave it up to them to determine whether or not the United Nations is conducting a lawful trial," Haqqani concluded.

The Afghan proposal generated immediate opposition from many quarters. Most of the UN delegates dismissed it as posturing. Congress and the foreign policy establishment certainly did not want to put their own deeds on trial as part of the prosecution of the September 11 events, nor did other countries want the UN to interfere with how they "managed internal dissent."

The UN overwhelmingly passed the US-sponsored resolutions, with only a handful of countries abstaining.

"Move quickly while you have support across the board," Sophie urged Rachel. "Get the UN to issue an arrest warrant for bin Laden as soon as possible. Let the trial worry about sorting out the evidence."

The International Tribunal on Terrorism was convened by the UN in two weeks. In took just another two weeks for a preliminary presentation of evidence about bin Laden and al-Qaida. While most of the evidence focused on his role in other terrorist attacks, the tribunal concluded in early November that there was sufficient evidence for the issuance of an arrest warrant for bin Laden.

The UN set a deadline of November 20 for Afghanistan to turn over bin Laden and other key leaders of his network. "Otherwise, the UN will airlift troops into Afghanistan to arrest Osama bin Laden. Any effort to interfere with this arrest will be considered an act of war and met with corresponding force," the UN Secretary-General informed the Taliban leadership. A dozen nations committed significant troops to the police force, and nearly forty committed some type of resource.

Afghanistan failed to meet the deadline, arguing that the UN had not sufficiently complied with the conditions the Afghans had requested for the tribunal. "We believe that progress has been made, however. If we continue to negotiate, we are confident a mutually satisfactory resolution can be found," Haqqani said.

The Taliban continued to make proposals until the UN troops were airborne to Kabul. The Taliban then agreed to a "firm deadline to turn bin Laden over within a week if the airplanes turn back. There are just some logistics we have to work out." The planes kept coming.

The remnants of the Northern Alliance, the loose network of northern warlords — the original mujahedeen — had managed to hold onto local power in the rural areas of the North after their lawless reign led to the Taliban's emergence. The Northern Alliance launched attacks on several northern cities shortly after the UN planes took off.

The UN planes came under fire as they approached Kabul airport. The UN launched a dozen missiles in response at military sites around Kabul. Suddenly, the shelling stopped. The Taliban government announced they were granting permission to the UN troops to land, and that the attack had been a mistake, launched by troops not under the control of the government.

The Taliban foreign minister went to the airport to greet the troops and to protest the violation of our sovereignty. Haqqani also accused the UN of "arming the Northern Alliance to attack us in violation of the UN Charter. This is an invasion by the UN under the direction of the Western imperialists."

The UN police force was led by General Tomas Johansen, head of the Norwegian Military Police, with its distinctive red beret. He wore a black brassard with MP in bold red letters on his right arm. He'd previously commanded UN police forces in Somalia, Lebanon and the Balkans. Johansen denied any UN involvement with the Northern Alliance.

"We're here to arrest bin Laden, not to attack your government. However, any attacks by your government or anyone else will be met by force. We plan to depart as soon as the arrest is made. We urge the Afghanistan government to turn him over to us so we can avoid unnecessary bloodshed. We will guarantee his safety and a fair trial, with representation of his choice. As for any internal strife, that is not something we will get involved with unless any of the combatants interfere with our mission," Johansen told the Taliban.

The UN diplomatic representatives went with Foreign Minister Haqqani for high-level talks, including a meeting with Mullah Mohammed Omar, the Taliban leader. Meanwhile, the UN troops began an immediate deployment to find bin Laden.

In the several weeks it took to locate the elusive Saudi, the Northern Alliance took one city after another in northern Afghanistan. Bin Laden released a videotape announcing his intention to turn himself over to Islamic Judges in southern Afghanistan to spare the Afghani people.

In early December the UN troops surrounded bin Laden and his bodyguards in a small village in southern Afghanistan. Local residents were given 24 hours to depart. After 48 hours of trying to convince bin Laden that resisting arrest was futile, the UN attacked the compound. Eventually they sent in several missiles to take out the fiercest resistance.

On the fourth day, the United Nation troops breached the wall of the large house where bin Laden was holed up. When they entered the room at the center of the house where bin Laden was believed to be, a massive explosion leveled much of the building. There were dozens of fatalities, with many more injured.

Bin Laden's body was never found. All the evidence, including forensic, pointed to him having been killed in the explosion. Local residents told the UN soldiers that they had heard that bin Laden had a special chair built for himself in which he would sit for the final assault. If he were removed from the chair, it would automatically trigger a massive explosion.

The UN agreed to requests by all sides for a cease-fire. An international peacekeeping force was sent to maintain the peace, though sporadic fighting continued throughout the more remote areas.

Much of northern and central Afghanistan came under the control of the Northern Alliance. The Taliban were able to maintain power in the south. Kabul, the capital, was nominally still under Taliban control, though it was the UN peacekeeping force that maintained order, enabling the various factions to meet there to negotiate the future of the country.

The UN mandate included inspecting alleged terrorist bases. They were all long deserted by the time the UN arrived. Any further military or police action against al-Qaida would have to await the proceedings of the tribunal.

Rachel asked Vice-President Mumfi to be the US representative in the UN-sponsored peace talks to help put the war-ravaged country back together. "Just make sure that not only does their constitution give rights to women, but that it gets enforced," Rachel told him. "And make sure the peacekeeping force protects women."

Rachel got Congress to increase its humanitarian aid package to help

Afghan citizens survive the coming brutal winter. Reconstruction would be a slow and expensive process.

****

Bin Laden's death was greeted with jubilation in America. Even her more vociferous critics had to acknowledge the success of Rachel's approach. Her standing skyrocketed in the polls, putting Congress on the defensive. Sophie used the honeymoon to push their Cabinet appointments through the confirmation process.

Rachel used the afterglow from the events in Afghanistan to pressure the Senate to finally ratify the International Criminal Court.

"The UN has been discussing an International Criminal Court to prosecute crimes such as genocide for more than half a century," Rachel said on her regular Saturday radio broadcast. "The court is the missing link in our international legal system. Without an International Criminal Court to prosecute individuals, acts of genocide and other human rights violations often go unpunished. As the Judgment of the Nuremberg Tribunal stated, 'Crimes against international law are committed by men, not by abstract entities, and only by punishing individuals who commit such crimes can the provisions of international law be enforced.'

"Congress says we must do more to confront terrorism, and I agree. Here is a system that most of Europe and the rest of the world have already agreed is an essential part of this fight. One hundred and sixty states participated in the 1998 UN conference to develop the proposal. Fifty-five nations have ratified it. Five more countries must sign on before it becomes law. I look forward to quick action by Congress. Their delay is seriously harming the effort to stop terrorism," Rachel said.

Some of the most powerful and reactionary members of Congress, starting with Alabama Senator Jack Hands, had led the charge against ratification. Hands argued, "Having an International Criminal Court would impede the US use of military power. The court could be used by our enemies — those who disagree with our commitment to democracy — to prosecute our soldiers in unpopular conflicts. We would also expose Americans to criminal prosecution for past disputes. We should only agree if the US is given a permanent veto over any prosecution."

Hands argued that US officials could be prosecuted for past acts, such as the support for the contra war in Nicaragua or the various US-led coups such as in Chile.

"Nonsense," replied Rachel, when asked by the media about Hands' remarks after she delivered a speech calling for increased action to confront global warming. "Let's not forget the US played a large role in drafting the proposal for the court, so our interests have been protected from the start. The court is prohibited from prosecuting actions that took place before it was created. The US is also protected since the court can't act if the country in question has a judicial system capable of handling the prosecution, which we clearly do."

Polls taken shortly after Rachel's radio address found that more than 75 percent of Americans supported the creation of the court. Many Senators voiced their concerns but agreed to support it as a show of international solidarity. When the upper house finally ratified the establishment of the International Criminal Court, it became one of the first major victories of Rachel's administration.

****

December 23, 2001

Air Force One took off for the three-and-a-half-hour flight to Phoenix. Rachel was going to hand out toys to kids at a low-income community center. They included children whose parents had been deployed as part of the police force in Afghanistan. It was also an opportunity for her to say hello to some old friends before heading up to Seattle to spend Christmas. It would be the first time they'd been home since Rachel had become president. She could certainly use a few days of rest.

She spent the first hour and a half of the flight returning her essential phone calls and reviewing the proposed list of convicted individuals to grant clemency to during the holidays. Most of the cases involved women who had been victims of domestic violence and had finally lashed out against their abuser or individuals charged with nonviolent drug offenses.

The most controversial was Native American activist Leonard Peltier, imprisoned for more than twenty years for the 1975 shootout at Wounded Knee reservation that had ended up with two FBI agents dead. In the preceding two years, more than 60 Native Americans affiliated with the American Indian Movement had been murdered at Wounded Knee during the ongoing protests over Treaty violations and the continuing repression of Native Americans.

Many progressives both in the US and worldwide felt that Peltier

had been made a scapegoat. Even the FBI admitted that no one knows
who fired the fatal shots that killed the agents. Peltier had participated in
a wide variety of charitable and humanitarian causes while in prison..

Sophie had included a warning that "FBI agents have threatened to
picket the White House if you release Peltier." Rachel angrily scribbled
in the margin, "I guess they have a lot of time on their hands since they
can't seem to find any of the 9/11 terrorists." Rachel approved the
clemency request.

As happened with every city she visited these days, a folder had
been prepared that laid out any connections with the September 11
tragedy, including names of victims' relatives. Rachel picked up the
packet to leaf through while she ate lunch. She noticed that one of the
presumed hijackers still at large had spent several weeks in Phoenix.

A half-hour later she called Sophie back at the White House.

"Hi, Sophie. I seem to recollect a message pad that was found in a
hijacker's apartment in Florida that had a phone number or something
written on it. Can someone track it down? Thanks."

Sophie called back twenty minutes later. "I think what you're
referring to is SWA 1375. The notes say the FBI ran through a bunch of
possibilities as to what it might be, such as a phone number, but they
never came up with anything."

Rachel bit her lip, an old habit when trying to access her memory
cells. "When Wynn and I first met in Phoenix, we were involved in
fighting pesticide spraying. One of the companies that did crop dusting
was South West Aviation. Have someone check to see if they still exist."

Sophie called as they were passing over the Texas Panhandle. "The
company is still around, though barely. They've gone through some hard
times, went through bankruptcy a couple of years ago. They've still got
about a dozen planes. The FBI ran a routine check on them after
September eleventh as they did with all crop dusters. They didn't find
anything unusual, but they're on their way over to pay them another
visit."

Rachel told Sophie to have the FAA check to see if it was a plane
number or something related.

Twenty minutes later, an agitated Sophie called back. "It looks like
you might be right. They do own a plane that has the same first four
numbers, though SWA isn't part of the registration, which is why they
didn't pick it up. They're having a little difficulty finding the plane. The
owner claims a pilot has been leasing it on a month-to-month basis,
using it for some spraying contracts he has with local farmers. Sounds

like the owner didn't ask too many questions. Paid him in advance for three months' use. The FBI speculates that he might be using it for drug smuggling over the Mexican border. They're trying to track the plane down."

Wynn, on the other side of the cabin calling friends in Seattle about their visit, was paying attention now.

The captain of Air Force One came on to the intercom about fifteen minutes later. "Madame President, the air controller in Phoenix has patched through someone who claims to have a large quantity of anthrax in his plane. If Air Force One diverts from our flight path, or another plane comes in his direction, he will immediately release the anthrax over Phoenix."

Her Secret Service agents had rushed in as the captain made his announcement. Rachel wondered whom they thought they would be protecting her from on Air Force One. Probably just wanted to be ready to jam her into the escape pod if necessary. And they knew they would need a full team to do it.

They were less than forty miles from Phoenix. Normal arrival time would be less than fifteen minutes. The pilot had already begun his approach, cutting the plane's speed to a little over 200 mph, down from its cruising speed of about 650 mph.

Several people were now talking to her at once. Rachel put Sophie on the speaker phone and told everyone else to be quiet.

"Sophie, what are our people saying?" asked Rachel. "How realistic is his threat?"

"We're trying to get hold of our experts on this, but if he has what he says he has, he could kill a lot of people if he has the opportunity to disperse it."

"Madame President," said Chang, head of her security detail, "I advise you to abort the flight and head to LA immediately. This is far too dangerous a situation. I doubt he has the capability to track Air Force One this far out from Phoenix."

"They're trying to maximize publicity," Wynn interjected. "They want to make sure you're there when he starts spraying. They could've sprayed at any time."

"More likely he wants to crash into Air Force One to try to kill Rachel. If they could spray anthrax, they wouldn't need anything else to get publicity," Chang pointed out.

"The media has been playing up the danger from crop dusters, but the reports I've read indicate they're not an effective way to distribute poison gas," Sophie stated. "To effectively spray a chemical or biological toxin, you have to create a very fine mist of particles less than five microns, small enough to be absorbed by the victim's lung. A crop duster sprays much larger, heavier particles, and anthrax tends to clump together. Also, though anthrax is very hardy, most biological agents can't stand exposure to sunlight, so spraying it wouldn't work."

"Thanks for that science lesson," said Rachel.

"But who knows what modifications they may have made to the crop duster?" Chang interjected. "If they figure out how to distribute even a small amount of anthrax, we're still talking about the potential deaths of dozens if not hundreds of people, plus a lot of panic."

"They'd have to spread it over a large area to cause a lot of harm," argued Sophie. "If we decided to shoot them down, they would have less than a minute to disperse it, maybe only twenty seconds or so," argued Sophie.

The pilot broke in. "Madame President, he's now demanding that our escort jets turn around immediately or he'll begin to spray. We have less than ten minutes before we land in Phoenix."

"Tell him we will comply," Rachel said.

"Madame President, I don't think that—" Chang protested.

"I didn't say to tell the pilots to break off," Rachel interrupted her. "This buys us a few minutes. Anyone have any ideas what would happen if we blew the plane up with a missile? Would it destroy any biological weapon they're carrying, or would it be dispersed? Sophie?"

"We're still working to get some experts on the phone, but a lot of people have left for the holidays," explained Sophie.

"Shit," said Rachel. "We need to resolve this. Now. We're out of time."

Everyone began speaking at once.

"I doubt that a crop duster would be used to try to take out Air Force One. This plane is a whole lot faster than any crop duster," said Wynn.

"Not at our landing speed," said Chang, "and a small plane is a whole lot easier to maneuver. The advantage in this situation is theirs if they want to ram us."

"Maybe they have a bomb in the plane and just want to get close enough to us to detonate it," said Wynn. "Or maybe they have a hand-held missile launcher."

"We've got to make a decision," said Rachel, "not think of more complications. If they wanted to ram us, or shoot a missile, wouldn't they have just kept quiet and waited for us to start landing?"

"They wouldn't have been allowed in the air—" replied Chang.

Chang stopped in midsentence as Air Force One suddenly banked hard to the right and then accelerated. Off to the left they saw one of the jet fighters speed off toward Phoenix.

"Captain, what the hell is going on?" Rachel asked.

"Sorry, Madame President. I probably should've given you all warning to buckle in. I received instructions to immediately divert to Los Angeles."

"On whose orders, Captain?"

He paused a few seconds. The Captain sounded nervous. "I received orders from the White House." He paused again. "I was told that they were your orders."

"Well, they weren't. Resume your course," instructed Rachel.

"What the hell is going on? Sophie, what do you know about this?" asked Rachel.

There was no response.

"Damn, we seem to have lost the connection. Someone get Sophie back on the phone."

There was an explosion up ahead. The jet fighter had shot down the crop duster, obliterated it in a fireball.

Sophie was back on the line.

"What happened? Do we know who gave these orders?" demanded Rachel.

"Why, Madame President, you did. I wrote them down on my notepad. You said 'Shoot. We need to resolve this.' Once you gave that order, I wanted to make sure that Air Force One was out of the way."

Rachel's face was turning red. She made everyone else leave the office, even Wynn.

"Sophie, you know that is not what I said. You deliberately disobeyed me," Rachel snapped.

"Rachel, I didn't disobey you," Sophie replied. "You said it was time to make a decision. A decision was made. If you want it to be your decision, it is. If you want it to be mine, that's okay. I know you don't believe it, but your life is critical to this country at this point. I know that you still have nightmares about the hijacked airliner being blown up. I heard two things. We need to do something, and something that sounded like shoot. That was enough for me. It was time to act. It seemed pretty clear that the only real option was to take them out, and we did. That is why you made me chief of staff."

"I didn't make you chief of staff to go off on your own and make decisions like this," Rachel said, sounding more resigned than angry.

"Actually, that *is* why you hired me, even if you didn't realize it. So fire me if you're dissatisfied. Your life was in danger. That is not the best time for you to make such decisions. We were safe back in the White House. We had more information at our disposal. I used my best judgment. Merry Christmas."

Sophie softened her tone. "The information we had indicated that it was unlikely that there was a credible threat to launch a biological or chemical attack with a crop duster. If I didn't do something and you were killed, I wouldn't be able to live with myself. If I made the wrong decision, I'll take the blame."

Rachel sighed. "Sophie, you know it's not a matter of blame. I appreciate that you want to protect me, but I've got to protect all Americans. I don't think the life of one president is worth the lives of tens or hundreds, maybe thousands, of other people. And if I can't accept the responsibility to make such decisions, then I shouldn't be president. Are you telling me that you question my ability to handle this office?"

Sophie protested. "Come on, that's not what I'm saying. You know there's no one I respect more to do the right thing. But you also have gotta trust the people you hire to make decisions too. You said we couldn't wait any longer. I'm sorry."

The decision turned out to be the right one. The terrorists had been working on a biological agent but hadn't solved the problem of how to disperse it. When they heard that Rachel was coming to Phoenix, they decided to act, assuming it was only a matter of time before American agents tracked them down.

They'd loaded the crop duster with a chemical agent, though they had little hope it would do much. The pilot had hit the spray button when he saw the missile streaking toward him, and had tried to fling a container of the material out the window. Neither was effective before the plane was blown up.

The pilot had flown his two colleagues across the Mexican border the previous evening, skimming low over the hills. They were now making their way back to the Middle East.

The government investigation concluded that there was no public health risk from what the terrorist had released. There were of course cries of a government cover-up.

The official report stated that Rachel said, "Shoot."

To the disbelief of her critics, the incident further established her credentials as a decisive military leader and swung public opinion behind her even more.

THIRTEEN

PETE AND EMILY'S WEDDING

1994

The reused envelope in the mailbox was of course from Pete, saving the environment as always.

Inside was a handmade lithograph with mountains, birds and clouds — a wedding invitation.

On this day, June 21, 1994
Near the lake in the mountains
in the home we have built together
Emily Frist and Peter Reeves
Invite You to Join Us
In a Ceremony Acknowledging our Life Long Commitment
And the Arrival of our daughter Amelia Sojourner Frist

Well good for them, Rachel thought. *It's about time.*

She had long thought Pete was headed for permanent bachelorhood. "He's an acquired taste," she'd told Anna, "one of those types who you always thought would make a great mate for someone that could appreciate all his special qualities. But you could never quite figure out which one of your friends would fit him."

****

Pete spent the winter of 1986 camped out in a friend's backyard in Seattle in a yurt during his annual sojourn from Alaska. He'd even rigged up a wood stove inside the framed Mongolian tent.

Pete told Rachel, "I met Emily when she was workin' as a waitress and part-time cook in a worker-owned café and performance space in Olympia. She was takin' classes at Evergreen College. I loped in one day and ordered the working stiff's lunch special. I told her 'I sure qualify as a stiff.' She laughed. Five hours later I had an apron on and was takin' orders for dinner." A few weeks later he was sleeping on her living room couch, shortly after that in her bed. He never made it back to Alaska.

Pete had found his soul mate. They volunteered at the coop

together, went for wilderness canoe trips and hikes, and went contra dancing. Emily willingly joined in on most of Pete's wild-eyed ideas. She, however, had a head for detail and planning.

She helped Pete realize his dream of building a solar-powered, energy-efficient house off the grid. Emily handled the money. She made Pete write down each step that had to be taken, what materials they needed, a timeline and a budget.

"We got a bargain on twenty acres of land," Pete told Rachel, "a few miles down an old loggin' road, a real bone crusher with big rocks and a lotta ruts. Too far from the nearest power line to hook up. We're smack dab in the middle of the wilderness. Our property runs up against a state forest — lots of animals and birds, lots of birds. Unfortunately, the state allows loggers on their land. But most of 'em are learnin' to keep their distance. They get too close, somehow their equipment ends up breakin' down. My buds from Earth First! are only too happy to help out."

"We decided to build an old-fashioned post-and-beam house," Emily added. "We thought about a straw bale house, with the straw for both structure and insulation. But we decided instead to mill lumber from our land. Pete's been driving around town on garbage nights, picking up discarded windows, cabinets, doors, sinks. He also goes up to houses being renovated, asks if they got anything they want to get rid of. They're often happy to give him things to save the time and cost of throwing it into a landfill. He managed to get the beams for almost half of the house from an old barn being torn down."

Rachel had known that Emily was the right woman for Pete when she remarked that the only complaint she had about the house was that it had too many straight lines and right angles.

"It's passive solar. We got a ton of glass on the south wall. Use a wood stove as backup, got one with a glass door, the cleanest you can buy. For our septic, we're using something I saw at New Alchemy Institute on Cape Cod. We've got a bunch of large tanks in a greenhouse, what we call our ark. One tank grows fish to take out some of the wastes, the other grows vegetables," Pete told Rachel. "It'll work a whole lot better once we get the water figured out," he admitted. "Kinda labor intensive at the moment."

They spent less than 30,000 dollars on the house. "More than half the cost was for the photovoltaic units for electricity," Pete told visitors. "But we'll never have to fork over a dime to the utility company again. The sun is free." Pete also climbed the tallest tree near the house and attached a small windmill they use on sailboats to generate electricity.

They started living at the house a few months after they began construction, shifting their living space around as the house grew. Each new step — each new wall going up, roof being shingled, wood stove being installed, door being hung — gave them the joy of accomplishment.

Celebrations were frequent. Physical labor in the isolated woods heightened their carnal feelings. Emily and Pete loved lying on their backs after sex, watching the moon rise and the stars twinkle, reading poetry by candlelight, trying to identify the animals they heard, strumming a guitar, talking about their love and dreams, practicing their wolf howls and bird calls, listening to the tunes of Paul Winter on an amazing wraparound outdoor sound system that Pete installed into various hollowed-out tree trunks.

Their biggest challenge was drinking water. They couldn't get a well-digger up the hill, so for the first year they hauled water in. The second year they ran a hose a quarter mile from a little pond that filled up each spring. The hose ran into a 500-gallon storage tank. They eventually built a system for collecting the water from the roof.

Emily had been the primary breadwinner while Pete focused on getting the house built. Emily supplemented her work at the café by growing organic flowers and vegetables. They also had chickens for eggs, selling them at the café and the local farmers' markets. Pete would do a week of construction for pay, then work on the house for a couple of weeks till they were out of money again.

Once the house was livable, Emily worked with Pete on his automobile ideas. She helped develop a budget for the supplies and machine work She took a few business classes at Evergreen, and got one of her classes to develop a plan for Pete's ideas as their class project. She also convinced Pete to take some classes on engineering and mechanics.

One day, Emily told Pete, "I've found a machine shop that'll turn out 75 of your carburetor modification kits for 2,000 dollars. We can get a ten-page booklet printed on how to install it for a buck apiece, another 7 dollars per for copies of the 30-minute instruction video. If we sell the kit for 100 dollars, we'll make a profit of around 60, minus a little money for marketing. We can discount it to 85 dollars for bulk orders."

They spent six months peddling it at every flea market, community festival, auto shop and street corner they could find. They ran ads in self-help and car magazines. They placed a second order for 500 after the first two months, getting the cost for the kit down to 25 dollars. They got a few write-ups in alternative and automobile self-help publications.

"We're gettin' a couple dozen orders a day now — by phone, mail, people somehow finding their way to our house," Pete told Rachel when she called to wish them a happy New Year. "Emily recently grabbed a lease with an option to buy on an old warehouse. She's plannin' to hire people to help with production, marketing and distribution, payin' them primarily out of profit sharing. Seems risky to me but she crunched the numbers."

Getting the warehouse allowed Pete and Emily to move to the second stage of their business plan. The first product had been targeted to motorheads — people used to working on their own cars. The second product was a complete replacement carburetor, something even someone with limited mechanical knowledge could install. Or you could pay a mechanic to pop it in, making back your investment in a few months. Business boomed.

Over the years, each time Pete came up with a new solution to improve carburetor efficiency, he found that an automobile company had already bought up the inventor's patent, squelching its use. Pete knew that the car companies would take legal action to try to stop him. But now he had enough money to pay lawyers to fight back.

Pete felt that his ultimate success depended on the court of public opinion. Otherwise, judges would gleefully rule in favor of the car companies and their high-priced lawyers. Judges needed the political parties to get elected; political parties needed corporate campaign contributions. The corporations expected the parties and judges to back them up when it was needed.

Fortunately, Pete and Emily launched the carburetor replacement kits shortly after the 1991 Gulf War. With America having gone to war to ensure its control over Mideast oil, the two entrepreneurs were able to wrap the American flag around their product. They held a press conference on the steps of the Capitol in Olympia, with Pete's biodiesel fleet of delivery trucks as a backdrop. Local peace activists lined the steps behind them.

"It's our patriotic duty to make America energy independent. We need our government to take leadership in reducing dependence upon foreign oil by promoting mass transit, building more bike paths, promoting carpooling and halting sprawl. But a small step that everyone can take today is changing their carburetor to get double the miles per gallon," Pete said.

When one of the reporters asked if this wasn't just a publicity stunt to make them more money, Emily's response surprised them. "We're going to allow any other company to copy our product design, free of charge, as long as they agree to cap their profit margin. The design specifications are already posted on our web page. Feel free to print them in your papers. We're also going to allow any peace, environmental, community or veteran's group to market them, and they can keep twenty dollars for each one they sell. And they don't have to pay us anything up front, just when they sell them."

"We also plan to take the profits we raise to launch Green America," Pete added, "a nonprofit corporation to help develop and promote green technology, including clean, renewable energy rather than fossil fuels. We're starting with production of wind and solar power systems," Pete added.

Emily organized a rally outside the US senator's office in Seattle urging the federal government to liberate all the patents automobile companies were sitting on to prevent higher fuel efficiency. While the lawsuits came fast and furious, it was a public relations disaster for the automobile industry, with congressional hearings being convened within a few months. The companies quickly negotiated a settlement that allowed Green America and other companies to continue production.

Pete and Emily diversified their first company to market an increasing number of environmentally friendly consumer products with their own 50-page catalogue. Their profit-sharing approach and environment-first mentality had creative business people beating a path to their door. They transformed their company into a worker-owned business, and created a division to help set up worker cooperatives to develop and launch new products. Within a few years they had more than 100 people working at Green America and the affiliated coops.

Green America also branched into sustainable agriculture issues. They organized a series of green festivals and farmers' markets throughout the Pacific Northwest, providing outlets for farmers as well as the multitude of Green America product lines, which now also included crafts. They had a Community Supported Agriculture farm at the Green America headquarters. Consumers bought a ten-dollar-a-week share to buy organically grown vegetables. They were organizing a farmers' cooperative to market various organic goods, vegetables, dairy, honey, anything you could grow.

Green America organized an alternative currency project, Olympia Dollars, which incorporated agriculture products, in addition to the traditional green services and products.

Emily and Pete used some of their increased income to buy an old religious camp on the other side of the ridge from them. It had a lake with several dozen cabins and two large buildings. Most of it was used for the headquarters for Green America, the rest for a nature preserve and conference center where they made plans on how to green the American economy. They also built their new house on the site, utilizing state of the art sustainable technology: solar, windmills, green septic systems, composting toilets and greywater systems.

Now Emily and Pete were getting married.

****

Rachel looked forward to seeing Wynn at the June wedding. Their relationship had grown more serious since his stay in San Francisco for the Big Green campaign. They were seeing each other once a month, a bicoastal relationship. Wynn looked for opportunities to come to San Francisco for environmental meetings. Rachel occasionally went to DC to lobby on healthcare. They also took an annual two-week vacation together.

Tommy was graduating from high school in a few weeks, an accomplishment she doubted a few years ago. The high school years had been bumpy, though her friends told her it was just par for the course. She had so prided herself on being different, at being far more open and attentive with her son than her mother had been with her. She assumed they'd avoid the typical teenage turmoil. She was wrong.

It seemed like they argued over everything — his failure to help around the house, the disaster he called his bedroom, the loudness of his music, the weirdness of some of his friends.

They had a huge argument when she discovered he was having sex with the latest girlfriend in his bedroom. He had become sexually active his sophomore year.

"Rachel, get over it. I'm having sex. Period. You taught me that sex is wonderful, and now you're acting like every other uptight parent. There's nothing you can do about it. The only issue is whether we can do it here where it's safe, like normal human beings. Doin' it in my own room makes it easier to use birth control, take protection against AIDS like you're always lecturin'."

"These girls are too young," replied Rachel. "Some aren't even at the legal age of consent. You don't love them, you're just playing with them. You get a steady girlfriend, a mature girlfriend who doesn't let you

use her as a doormat, we can talk about what you can do in the
apartment, but you have a different girl every other month," she added.
"And what are you going to do if one of them gets pregnant?"

"Why do you feel the need to diss my friends?" Tommy angrily
retorted. "I respect my female friends even if you don't. They have their
own minds, ya know. Just 'cause they make a decision you don't agree
with, like thinkin' your son is somethin' special, doesn't mean they're
stupid."

Tommy had also discovered pot. He was suspended from school
for a week when he and some friends were caught sharing a joint
between classes. Rachel had lectured him about the health and
emotional dangers involved with all forms of substance abuse, about the
dangers of an addictive personality and about some of the drug abuse
cases she'd seen as a nurse.

"Rachel, you know as well as I do that marijuana isn't addictive.
What is it, do parents turn into a government zombie when their kids
start to grow up?"

"All drugs are a vice, Tommy. It may feel good but there's often a
long term price And you may laugh, but marijuana does lead to harder,
more dangerous drugs. You're too young for any of this. Your body is
still growing, you're still developing mentally and emotionally," she
argued.

"Oh come on, who do you think you're foolin'? It's outlawed
because the government doesn't want us to have a good time. And
'cause the oil companies wanted to stop hemp from being competition.
Smoking a jay just relaxes me, makes me feel good. It makes me *think*
better. It's great when you listen to music, gives you new perspective.
And I know that you and your friends used to smoke, probably still do
when I'm not around," Tommy argued.

Damn her past. She wondered what stories his father had told him.
"I don't want to find you in a morgue someday because you or one of
your friends did something stupid while you were high, like driving a
car. And where are you getting the money to pay for this?" she
demanded.

He moved out of the house shortly after turning sixteen when she
refused to let him miss two days of school to attend a Phish concert in
LA. He went anyway.

Tommy spent several months moving around from friend to friend,
until their parents reached the limit of their patience, usually hastened by
the guitar that he constantly played.

Fortunately, a few of his friends had their heads on straight and pushed him to reconcile with Rachel.

Melissa, a freshman in college, told him, "You and your mom are having the breakdown everyone goes through. You've gotta work things out. Okay, she has to accept you as an adult, which means giving up the power to tell you what to do. But you have to be willing to act like an adult, without the need for someone to always be nagging you," she said. "And Tommy, Rachel understands the score a whole lot better than most. Good luck."

He stopped by once a week to have breakfast, do his laundry — which Rachel refused to assist with — and let her know he was still alive. He left as soon as an argument broke out, telling her, "Just leave the laundry on the doorstep when it's finished. I'll pick it up later."

They negotiated an uneasy truce after two months. She wasn't happy with the terms, but she wanted him under her roof. No drugs in the house. If he was going to sleep with someone in their house, Rachel was to meet the girl first. "I'm not going to contribute to a statutory rape situation. And her parents will need to know what she's doing, otherwise we're all going to have a little talk," Rachel informed Tommy. "Honesty is our policy here. We do things out in the open."

Whenever Tommy complained, Rachel said, "You agreed to the rules. A signed copy is posted next to the fridge. You turn eighteen, we can discuss new ones. And if you break the rules, they'll become more restrictive quickly and permanently. You play games, you're out of here. I'll call child support services for you if you want," with her best no-nonsense scowl.

"You're crazy," Tommy argued. "You're so unfair. You have sex with people you aren't married to. You seem to be okay for the experience. You started having sex at an earlier age then I did. I'll stop doing it when you stop doing it."

"You're the child here," Rachel responded. "If you want to do adult acts, you have to act like an adult when you do them. I'm not proud of the mistakes I made when I was a teenager. There's no need for you to make the same ones. There's too much pain involved. I'm just sorry my mother didn't do more to keep me out of trouble," she added, beginning to cry.

"Cheater," he said as he stormed out. He never could handle her crying.

When Tommy was 17, she asked Wynn if he would take him for the summer, see if a male authority figure would help. "I'm afraid I'm losing him, Wynn. He runs to trouble wherever he can find it and jumps in head first. He thinks he's indestructible, god's gift to the world. Whatever I do doesn't work. I know it's a lot to ask, but he's always looked up to you. If nothing else, perhaps you can figure out a way to get him through his final year of high school."

"What about his dad?" Wynn asked.

"Tommy doesn't respect him enough to listen to him," Rachel replied.

That summer worked wonders. Wynn got Tommy an internship with the Toxic Coalition. Wynn told Tommy, "I'm not your parent and I won't be a spy for your mom. I'll treat you like an adult but I expect you to act like one. Our work is important, so don't screw it up. If you can't live by the rules, I'll put you on the next plane home. That applies to stuff at work and in your personal life. Keep out of trouble — except of course when we tell you otherwise for work."

Though Tommy found much of his work as an intern boring, with too much data entry, mailings and phone banking — hardly a protest a week — he enjoyed hanging out with several of Wynn's musician friends. They taught him some new tricks on the guitar. He also got to attend concerts for free in the DC area, helping to table for the Toxic Coalition.

Tommy seemed like a new person to Rachel when he returned home. He'd shifted into earnest young anarchist mode. Though he continued to party, he concentrated enough on his studies to get good grades for the first time in years. He relished challenging the politics of his teachers whenever possible. He did surprisingly well on his SATs for college. Rachel shook her head in amazement, asking Wynn, "How did'ja work this magic?"

"Come on grandma, you were a youngster once," Wynn replied. "He's no longer your little boy. He'll be okay, he's just redefining his boundaries with you. I'm not his parent, he doesn't need to fight with me."

Tommy would be starting college in the fall. While Rachel had often prayed for this day, now she was sure she wouldn't survive the separation. She argued the merits of the various local academic possibilities, from community colleges to the University of California at Berkeley.

Her separation anxieties had increased a few weeks previously when Anna had casually announced, "I'm moving to Guatemala to help local women organize their own cooperatives. I'm going to help them make a living wage by cutting out the capitalist middlemen."

Anna had been working for an international women's group based in San Francisco the last two years. Throughout the developing world, women and young girls are often forced to work long hours in sweatshops under abysmal working conditions for minimal pay, often just dollars a day, for American and other multinational corporations.

"For how long?" Rachel asked. "Is this a short-term gig, or are we talking about something permanent, like, It's been nice knowing ya?"

"Who knows?" Anna had said breezily. "A couple of years at least. I wanna roll up my sleeves and go work with these women directly. Of course, if it curtails my sex life too much, I'll have to reconsider. A gay lifestyle ain't exactly in vogue down there, but I know how to live underground when I need to. Find me a nice houseboy to provide cover."

****

The Goddess smiled favorably upon Pete and Emily's wedding. The temperature was in the low eighties, with low humidity — sunny, a rarity, with billowy white clouds. Their ceremony was performed by a local peace activist who'd been a priest before he got married. Flowers were everywhere, the perennial gardens bursting, with a heart-shaped arch of roses over the hand-made altar. A flutist played to greet the guests.

Emily had made her own ankle-length gown, the white fabric adorned with beads. Pete wore a white shirt with dress pants, a Grateful Dead tie, a colorful vest, black top hat and sneakers. It looked like he had actually run a brush through his hair that morning.

Pete and Emily wrote their own ceremony. Rachel cried throughout. Friends read favorite passages about the meaning of love, commitment and life from various spiritual, Native American and women writers.

Rachel sang a song, "Forever Young" by Bob Dylan, accompanied by Tommy on the guitar.

May you always do for others
And let others do for you ...
May you grow up to be true
May you always know the truth.

Emily and Pete exchanged vows to "Support, challenge and inspire one another, to raise our infant daughter together to recognize the sacredness of life and our collective responsibility to build a better world for future generations."

Pete read a passage from Chief Seattle.

Teach your children what we have taught our children — that the earth is our mother. Whatever befalls the earth, befalls the sons of the earth. The earth does not belong to man; man belongs to the earth. This we know. All things are connected like the blood which unites one family, the river that brings the mountain to the ocean. Whatever befalls the earth befalls the sons of the earth. Man did not weave the web of life; he is merely a strand in it. Whatever he does to the web, he does to himself.

Pete and Emily joined hands and cradled their daughter. "We stand today before our family and friends to exchange our life vows. Our marriage acknowledges the sacredness of the love and respect we have for each other, and for our child, for our friends, family and neighbors. We pledge to support each other throughout life's long journey, no matter where our path may take us."

They held their daughter up to the heavens. "We ask the goddess of the sun and the moon, the goddess of the wind and rivers and mountains, to bless the soul of our child, Amelia Sojourner Frist-Reeves, to keep her safe, to guide her and us as we grow together. We ask you, Gaia, to show us, and all the beings of this wonderful planet you have created, the way to find harmony, peace and laughter."

Emily said, "Thank you for joining us for this important step in our lives. We hope you'll stay with us to enjoy some food and company." Pete added, "Let the party begin!"

They selected Imagine by John Lennon as their wedding song.

Imagine no possessions ...
No need for greed or hunger ...
Imagine all the people
Sharing all the world.

The reception, featuring vegetarian food, was under a large tent overlooking the lake. A bluegrass band played. That evening they had a contra dance. The multitiered carrot wedding cake had shocking pink frosting.

At the food table, Pete pulled Rachel aside. Rachel gave him another of her endless supply of hugs.

"Congratulations, Pete," Rachel gushed. "The ceremony was wonderful. Emily was just radiant. And Amelia is so cute. How is fatherhood going? Have you learned to live with sleep deprivation yet?"

"Fortunately, sleep was never my number-one priority. Emily has it worse, because she's the only one who can breastfeed. But it's wonderful. I look down at Amelia and wonder how I managed to bring something so beautiful into the world. Every time I look at her I discover something new and wonderful about her," Pete remarked.

"So, Rachel, how're you doing?" Pete asked, pulling her over to some wooden Adirondack chairs. "You and Wynn seemed rather chummy during the ceremony."

"I was the one doing most of the squeezing," Rachel laughed, "and crying. Wynn seemed embarrassed by all my sobbing. Wynn and I manage to see each other once a month. I'm doing fine except for dreading when Tommy goes off to college in the fall. Assuming I can convince him to continue his education."

"Rachel, I wanna talk to you about a new program Green America is starting," Pete told her. "I've been negotiating with the state to run a pilot program to train and hire welfare participants to work at Green America. I'm hopin' we can entice you to move here to run it. It'd be great for Amelia to have her auntie Rachel hangin' around."

As part of Clinton's effort to "end welfare as we know it," the federal government was providing wage subsidies to private companies to hire welfare participants.

"These subsidies are just another handout to the low-wage corporate economy," Pete said. "Companies like Wal-Mart and Sears are always happy to hire anyone who's willing to work long hours for low wages. Now Clinton's givin' 'em a tax subsidy to do it. But I figure Green America could use the funds to help low-income folks start new green businesses that don't require a lot of upfront capital. Sure, we can train some welfare participants to work in other parts of Green America, but we do that anyway. I want to create some new models."

"What types of businesses do you have in mind?" Rachel asked.

"Things like house cleanin' using only nontoxic cleaners, or doing lawn care without usin' pesticides," Pete replied. "It'll be good for the environment and good jobs for welfare participants. They'll be able to make a decent salary. We can help them start their own business, help them become an independent contractor after their first year, give them a loan to buy their own equipment. We'll make support services available to them at a reasonable cost, like bookkeeping, payroll, insurance. They can purchase healthcare through us," said Pete.

"Sounds fine, but why me?" asked Rachel. "I'm a nurse, not a businessperson. And if you want to get involved in welfare reform, wouldn't it be better to lobby against Clinton's proposals?"

"Good point," responded Pete. "Part of your job would be to lobby at the State House and in Congress about what reform really should look like. You did a great job on the healthcare issue, despite the Clintons blowin' it in the end. You could bring to the Capitol some of our employees who would be able to speak from first-hand experience."

"So how come you're so big on welfare reform all of a sudden?" asked Rachel.

"Oh, Emily's been pushin' me," he replied. "She's really riled up about it. Says it's just another example of a bunch of old white farts tryin' to tell women how they should behave. Let's blame poor women for creatin' poverty. And it's pretty racist. Sure, kickin' welfare moms has always been a favorite pastime of politicians and other right wing loonies, but it's gotten totally out of control ever since David Dukes, Mr. KKK, almost became governor of Louisiana by usin' welfare as a code word for race. Even Democrats feel free to dump on the poor. Mario Cuomo, the great liberal hope, has started fingerprintin' food stamp applicants in New York.

"We need someone like you to help get it off the ground," Pete told her, trying to close the sale. "You're good with people, and you've been on welfare so you know the system. You've been a single mom, you understand how to juggle things when you've got a job. We need someone willin' to go the extra mile to help them be successful."

"What about creating a childcare center on site? Childcare is always the biggest problem," Rachel suggested. "That and transportation."

"That's the spirit," said Pete. "Green America already has our own daycare center. We're havin' a bit of a baby boom."

"It would great to see you more often," he added. "And maybe we can convince Tommy to go to Evergreen. He'd love it, and you could see him whenever you want. I don't need an answer right away, but will you at least think about it?"

"We shouldn't be talking business on your wedding day. The other guests are beginning to glare at me for monopolizing you," Rachel said.

"By the way, in case you don't know it," Pete said in parting,

"Wynn's crazy 'bout you."

****

Rachel caught Wynn's eye as he was regaling a group of fellow activists with tales of his latest action. He excused himself and came over to Rachel.

"Hi. How you doing? Wanna take a walk around the lake?" Wynn asked.

"Thought you'd never ask. But if you have something else in mind, Mr. Harris, let's go somewhere else. Don't expect me to be rolling around in my good dress," Rachel said, giving him a quick kiss. Wynn pulled her in closer, making it a long one.

"Rachel, trust me, if I have you rolling around, you won't be wearing your dress," Wynn replied with a lecherous smile.

Wynn grabbed a couple of cold beers. They walked along the lake, holding hands as they caught up since their last visit. They stopped to kiss a few times.

"Pete has offered me a position," Rachel told him, "starting a green jobs program for women on welfare. Sounds interesting."

Rachel stopped and turned to face Wynn, holding both his hands. "I've also been thinking a lot about you, Wynn. I've written you out of my life a half-dozen times. I've tried to come to grips with the fact that there's always one more dragon for you to slay," she told him. "But I want more than you falling into my life for a weekend every month. It's just too hard on me when you walk out the door, and I have to start counting the days till I see you again."

Rachel started crying again. "I'm sorry," she laughed through the tears. "Weddings are always an emotional roller coaster for me."

"I've been thinking a lot about *you*," said Wynn, somehow producing a handkerchief. "I can't tell you how many times I've kicked myself for leaving you and Tommy in Arizona. I've been busting my butt organizing for two decades, and all I have to show for it is Ronald Reagan, Bill Clinton, global warming and one war after another. Part of me tells me not to give up, but it all seems pretty senseless when the price I have to pay is giving up people like you that I love."

"Why can't you have both?" Rachel pleaded.

They sat on a log along the path.

"Rachel, I love you," Wynn said. "It's time we did something about it. I've been offered an organizer job with Greenpeace in DC coordinating their global warming campaign. But they have an office in Seattle. I'll tell them if they want me, I need to be based here. If not, I'll just find something else. Or we could stay in the San Francisco area if you want," said Wynn.

"Could we try to find a house with a white picket fence and room for my garden?" Rachel asked as she began to kiss his neck.

"Sure, as long as we stick a hot tub back there," said Wynn, as he began to carefully remove her dress.

****

They moved into Pete and Emily's old house. It was sort of a honeymoon, living in the woods by themselves, taking long hikes, working in the huge perennial garden that Emily had established, making new friends and finding new favorite places.

Living in their old house required a certain pioneer spirit, starting with being handy with a chain saw, that neither Wynn nor Rachel were looking for at this point in their lives. Even in good weather, the two-mile dirt road to the house was barely passable. Visitors were few and far between, and once you were home, you tended to stay put. Rachel and Wynn were used to spending much of their evenings attending meetings and events or catching a late meal out.

They finally informed Pete and Emily after six months, "We've decided to buy a house in Seattle. It's will be easier for Wynn to get to work, and besides, if we really want to work with welfare participants, we need to be closer to where most of them live."

Emily laughed at their discomfort. "You guys are acting like moving out is a personal rejection of us. Relax. So what if it's a 50-minute drive when Amelia needs her goodnight kiss? Hey, it's great that you guys are becoming homeowners and joining the great American middle class. Does this mean that you need someone to start planning your wedding reception?" Emily was anxious to help out with *that* party. Besides, the clock was ticking if they were going to have babies.

"Hold your horses, sister," Rachel. "We've found a house with room out back for a large garden. It has a great redwood hot tub heated by a wood stove. It's at the end of a dead-end street, with some woods behind it. We can catch a bus at the corner to get to work."

Tommy moved into Emily and Pete's house a few months later. He'd spent the year attending City College at San Francisco, a two-year school, having a grand old time. He even attended class occasionally.

Pete sold Tommy on the merits of attending nearby Evergreen State College, one of the most progressive in the country. The grunge music scene in Seattle, home of national acts like Pearl Jam, Nirvana and Soundgarden, was also an attraction. Being closer to mom was even somewhat of an attraction.

What closed the deal was when Pete told Tommy that if he worked summers and 15 hours a week during the rest of the year for Green America, Pete would cover his school costs.

Tommy quickly turned the house into the Hostel for Wayward Youth II. Wynn laughed when Pete told him, "I laid down the law after last weekend. People in *downtown* Olympia claimed they could hear the music. I went over to check it out. Christ, there were cars, tents, teepees, bikes, motorcycles, people, nudity, drugs, *litter*, you name it, everywhere you looked. I mean, everywhere. It was a freakin' Woodstock Festival West Coast. And worst of all, they weren't even composting or recycling. I got *that* straightened out quick enough."

Green America had opened a distribution center for its various products in Seattle, since it had better access for national and international transport. They had an office near Puget Sound where they were establishing a community-based sustainable fishing cooperative, along with renting out kayaks and other boats for recreational and educational use. They were also starting a sailboat manufacturing and repair business.

It made sense to establish a second job training and green business office there, since Seattle had a much larger welfare population than Olympia. Rachel also opened a second Green America childcare center there.

An office in Seattle provided a much larger market for green cleaning and sustainable landscaping services. Green America also decided to launch several new green oriented businesses, including the recycling of old computers and servicing cloth diapers.

Seattle was a center of the mushrooming computer industry. With the speed and power of computers doubling every 18 months, the marketing mavens had taken planned obsolescence to a new level, with millions of computers filled with toxic materials being discarded every year.

Emily negotiated with several of the area foundations established by the computer industry to fund a pilot recycling program. Green America also proposed legislation to require a deposit — say 50 dollars — on each computer to ensure they were brought to a recycling center rather than thrown out.

Emily discovered there were only a handful of diaper services washing cloth diapers, as the market had shifted to plastic. She thought this would be a good pilot program for microenterprise development, a low-capital small business with potential for growth.

"Plastic disposable diapers, full of human excrement, are a growing percentage of landfills, adding five million tons of untreated waste and a total of two billion tons of urine, feces, plastic and paper to landfills annually," Emily told the board of directors of Green America. "The untreated waste in the landfills contaminates groundwater. It takes 80,000 pounds of plastic and more than 200,000 trees a year to manufacture the disposable diapers.

"While some manufacturers claim their plastic diapers are biodegradable, this only works if they're exposed to the air and sun — which rarely happens since they're buried in a landfill. Even then it would not be quick. Once buried, as virtually all of them are, decomposition takes several hundred years, with some of the plastic never decomposing. We have to stop short-circuiting nature."

"Cloth diapers sound great," said Tom Wilson, a board member and proud father of two, including a six-month old, "but disposables are much more convenient, especially with today's lifestyles. Besides, don't low-income households have to use disposables because they're cheaper?"

"Part of our marketing plan would be to highlight the benefits of cloth diapers," Emily explained. "Cloth is better for the baby. It's softer on the skin, breathes better and is naturally absorbent, all of which adds up to less diaper rash. The new Velcro covers for cloth diapers make them about as easy to use as disposables, and just as watertight. And cloth is actually cheaper," Emily added.

****

Working with welfare participants was a rewarding but exhausting challenge for Rachel. They were certainly motivated, as welfare was a dehumanizing program, with inadequate benefits. Not only did everyone want to be off it as soon as possible, but they were desperate to stay off. Green America was their opportunity for a better situation for themselves and their children, and they held onto it for dear life. But being on welfare meant that crises were the norm, making the transition to stability difficult.

The welfare participants were treated like any other Green America employee. The company avoided segregating them into their own little niche. If Green America established a special program for them, such as a social worker support system, other employees could use it as well.
Each new worker at Green America completed a comprehensive education and skills assessment to see how they matched up with any existing job openings and to identify potential barriers to employment.

"Relax," Rachel told new employees worried about losing their job if they flunked. "You're hired. All doors out of here lead up. This is about figuring out how to make you as productive and employable as possible. We're going to give you the job skills needed to be successful."

"We're also going to ask you about what career opportunities you're interested in, both within the company and without," Rachel told them. "We're here to empower you. My job's to work with you to develop a training program to meet your individual development goals and needs. This can include high school equivalency, English as a Second Language, or more advanced training programs at the Adult Learning Center or community college. All employees are eligible for subsidized college tuition, up to two classes per semester. We also have within Green America skills and management training programs you can participate in."

Green America had a policy of paying a living wage to all workers — including those at entry level. In addition, annual salary of the highest paid worker was no more than four times that of the lowest paid worker, though profit sharing affected that a bit.

There had always been two distinct populations in welfare. Most women used welfare as a transitional program, staying on it for a year or two; they were employable but needed help getting on their feet when their significant other departed, leaving them with the children. The other group, smaller but significant, were those who faced significant barriers to employment, such as lack of education or job skills. They tended be on welfare for many years.

Most of the welfare participants in Green America were in the first group, guaranteeing a higher success rate, which kept the welfare department happy and the subsidies and support services flowing. Their job and educational skills were comparable to other low-wage workers.

The participants without prior work experience or with limited education were the most challenging. Rachel initially limited that target group to five participants per quarter. She established a special transitional program for them, combining work with on-the-job training and education, as well as providing training on "soft job skills," such as answering a phone and how to interact with coworkers, supervisors and customers.

"It doesn't help to throw someone in over their head when she doesn't know how to swim," Rachel told Emily when she asked why the program didn't take everyone who wanted a job. "We need to be realistic about the barriers these women face. We don't have enough resources to solve all their problems. You also got to be mindful of employee morale. Staff are willing to help train people but they weren't hired as social workers. It can lead to resentment when they're forced to spend their time solving other employee's personal problems," she added.

"I also notice that you always refer to them as welfare participants rather than recipients," Emily remarked. "Why is that?"

"Calling someone a welfare recipient implies they're receiving a handout," Rachel said. "These women are doing a job, namely raising children. It's just that since this is a job primarily being done by women, our society tends not to give it a monetary value. Conservatives stress the importance of moms staying home to raise children, but not only do they want women to do it for free, now they want poor women to have to do additional work in order to receive welfare benefits."

All newly hired workers without significant job experience were placed in a mentor program, where a coworker not in their direct line of supervision would help show them the ropes and answer questions, support them in their career development.

Rachel taught a workshop on how to deal with emergencies. "When you have a crisis, you have to call your supervisor to let them know you won't be in," Rachel told them. "Plan ahead. Your child will get sick or some other problem will come up with your childcare arrangement. You need to develop your backup plans before the emergency occurs. Who has some suggestions?"

Real crises did occur, particularly in the first few months after someone joined Green America. While these problems were usually similar to what most people experienced — a car that broke down, no heat in the house, being late with the rent — poor people on welfare have far fewer options to resolve them. More difficult problems included custody fights or having a child placed in a foster home, as well as incidents of domestic violence and substance abuse.

Not everyone succeeded. A few had to be let go.

It broke Rachel's heart when people begged for their job. Many times it was not only their lifeline, but their sense of self-worth.

"Angela, we've bent over backwards. We've kept on giving you chances. It's not fair to your coworkers and it's not helpful to you. You need to spend time focusing on resolving your problems — we can't do it any longer at work," Rachel told her.

Rachel would work with them to develop a plan to get their life back in order. "If you successfully complete this, which won't be easy, we'll give you one last chance. But that is a big *if.* And if you do get one last chance, there'll be very firm benchmarks. You've lost your margin for error," Rachel said. "I hope you make it, but it is up to you."

Most however made the transition without any more problems than any other new employee. Many thrived at Green America. Several successfully started their own small businesses. And some of the employees Rachel was most proud of were ones who initially presented the greatest challenges.

****

At the national level, welfare reform went from bad to worse. The Republicans took control of Congress after the 1994 midterm elections, and Newt Gingrich triumphantly became the Speaker of the House. Gingrich announced that he and his fellow conservatives had been swept into power to implement his Contract with America — something most voters hadn't heard about until after the elections.

Gingrich wanted to limit welfare to two years and deny benefits to any child born to a parent receiving welfare. He would eliminate benefits for immigrants. Rachel referred to it as "The Contract *on* America, an attack on poor people and the environment. The Newt seems to hate children. He wants to take poor kids away from their mothers, especially teenage moms, and throw them into orphanages. Even Oliver Twist would've been scared of this Grinch."

"The Contract on America is about making the rich even richer," Rachel would explain to groups she talked to, trying to get them to oppose Gingrich's agenda. "America now has the greatest income disparity in the world, having recently surpassed Britain. The wealthiest 1 percent of American households — those with a net worth of at least 2.3 million dollars each — own nearly 40 percent of the nation's wealth."

The Democrats looked at the high poll numbers for welfare "reform" and rolled over. They rushed to the right, showing, "We're not out of touch with joe six-pack." Even many progressives felt uncomfortable defending welfare. "Welfare is not a solution. Why should we fight for something that's broken?" they argued.

"Because welfare is poor children and their moms," Rachel chided. "If you want to make welfare better, step right up to the plate. Speak out for job creation, a higher minimum wage, more education and training, and childcare. But let's not throw the baby out with the bath water. Politicians aren't looking for real answers, they want sound bites. They want to appear tough with the poor. They have their stereotypes firmly in place and they don't want the facts to get in the way."

"But why should we pay for things like healthcare and housing for poor people when a lot of others work hard but can't get any help from the government?" they responded.

"Two wrongs don't make a right," she said in frustration. *You numbskulls.* "Of course we should do more for working people. But that's no excuse to cut the meager benefits we give to people on welfare. In other industrial democracies, all children, not just the poor, are provided financial support from the government through a 'children's allowance.' There's no mystery why the US has twice the rate of childhood poverty than any other industrial country. It's shameful that one in five of our children grows up in poverty."

As Bill Clinton and Newt Gingrich played a game of one-upmanship, with poor children and women as their poker chips, Rachel tried to rally women's groups, unions, minority organizations and communities of faith to oppose the repeal of welfare — to put some backbone into Clinton and the Democrats party.

Rachel spoke out against the proposal for five year time limits. "I'm all for a full employment economy, where everyone is guaranteed a living wage job. But I don't see how you put everyone to work merely by imposing a time limit on helping the poorest of the poor. This is just blaming the poor for being poor. We're saying that poverty isn't caused by a lack of decent jobs, or a lack of education or training, but merely because people are lazy or abusing drugs and alcohol."

"When times are tough and a lot of people are out of work," Rachel noted, "the government makes it easier to get welfare to prevent large-scale social unrest. When the economy is good and employers have a hard time filling the jobs at the bottom, the government tightens up the welfare rules. We're now in the 'economy is good, get tough on welfare' mode."

Rachel and several of the former welfare participants who worked for Green America spoke at a congressional hearing held in Seattle.

Rachel and the other women were forced to wait four hours before they got to testify. Most of the congressional representatives and media had long since departed.

Green America's first speaker was Terri Sutter, a mom with two children. She went on welfare for eighteen months when her husband suddenly left her and failed to pay any child support.

"The hearing today isn't really about welfare, because otherwise we would be talking about the really big welfare programs, like corporate subsidies for agriculture, like paying McDonald's to advertise Chicken McNuggets in France or paying defense contractors huge sums build weapons we've no need for. But politicians only want to reform the small ADC program. You know, Aid to Dependent Children, not Aid to Dependent Corporations," Terri remarked. The other welfare participants clapped wildly. Several of the panel members tried to stifle yawns.

The chairman interrupted her. "This is a hearing on the Aid to Dependent Children program. If you have something you would like to say about that, please do so. Otherwise, we can call the next speaker. It's getting late and it's been a long day." To the audience he said, "And please, no more outbursts, or you'll be escorted out."

"You want poor women to do 20 hours a week of make-work," Terri continued, "in exchange for welfare benefits so meager she can't buy clothes for her children and has to go to her local food pantry to feed her family. But you don't want to talk about making corporate executives do any work for the billions of corporate welfare they receive. After all, this is America."

"In America, Ms. Sutter, we reward hard work," the chairman interjected. "This is your last warning to stay on topic. Are you saying that you oppose making welfare more focused on work, on moving people into jobs that will allow them to support their families?"

"I'm happy to work. I've worked all my life. But workfare isn't going to help me at all. I need a real job, one with a decent paycheck that gives me and my kids a better life," Terri said. "You gotta be more realistic about the barriers poor women face. You need to raise the minimum wage to a living wage, so work lifts us out of poverty, not deeper in debt. We need childcare and healthcare. And you gotta deal with transportation, 'cause decent paying jobs aren't in poor neighborhoods."

"And don't fool yourselves that a job is the solution for everyone.

Some people are disabled, some have to take care of others, and some people just have some real serious problems. You need to make sure there's a strong safety net for those people. And for children," she concluded, sliding the microphone over to Rachel.

Rachel told the panel about Green America's experiences in hiring welfare participants. "We find welfare participants to be highly motivated. We need to provide them with a real job with a paycheck. Something that provides them with real job experience, while also allowing them to obtain the other skills they need. Green America has found that if you pay people a living wage and make available the tools they need to succeed, they will succeed."

"But it's not an overnight success story where you just wave a magic wand. It requires time and patience and caring. If you simply impose time limits on welfare and don't invest in support services, it's not going to work and you're going to hurt a lot of poor people and children. We will be glad to answer any questions you have at this point," concluded Rachel.

"Thank you," said the chairman. "We are running late at this point. Next, please. And could you keep your remarks brief?"

After the hearing, she did an interview with Karen Edwards, a NPR reporter.

"Conservatives argue that individuals are to blame if they're poor, while liberals argue that being poor is primarily due to the failures of the system," Edwards said. "Who's right?"

"It's some of both," Rachel acknowledged. "Unfortunately, those who blame the poor tend only to talk about punishment, about tough love, not about the tools needed to help people. What types of employment opportunities do they expect for someone who can't read or write and has two young children to rear? It's a recipe for failure."

"The debate about what causes poverty certainly isn't unique to the US. But we're more extreme in blaming the poor for their plight. Politicians let the rich and powerful win, while scapegoating the poor. They rob the poor of their dignity, while promoting a dog-eat-dog approach to the economy. Meanwhile the middle class works harder and harder for a lower standard of living, spurred on by the frightening prospect that you'll smash on the bottom, and have to go on welfare if you miss a paycheck or two," Rachel added.

One of Rachel's few victories was to convince Washington State to increase the Earned Income Disregard, so that welfare participants could keep more of their earnings once they found a job. Rachel argued,

"Welfare participants who work are the highest taxed workers, because for every dollar of earnings they lose a dollar of benefits. And they have to pay income, sales tax, property tax and social security tax on top of that."

The legislature eventually allowed them to keep 40 cents out of every dollar they earned until their income rose above the poverty level.

On August 22, 1996, President Clinton, who'd campaigned four years earlier on a promise to do more for children than any president in American history, signed the bill repealing welfare. The main antipoverty program for children that had existed since the great depression was no more. When he signed the law, with a grinning Newt Gingrich next to him, Clinton had a twenty-point lead in his reelection campaign against Sen. Bob Dole. Standing up for poor children and their moms wasn't worth risking a few percentage points.

FOURTEEN

SALVAGE RIDER

President Clinton infuriated Rachel — and many other environmentalists — when he signed the salvage timber rider in 1995. Clinton argued that the rider was needed to improve forest health by allowing the logging of timber damaged by fire or bugs. He said it was a short-term measure to help save the timber industry and tens of thousands of jobs in the northwest, while giving the federal government time to complete its work on a long-term forest management plan, which had begun back in 1993.

Environmentalists contended it was a backroom deal Clinton cut with senators from the northwest in exchange for winning support for his Americorp jobs program for students.

The rider allowed several billion board feet of lumber to be harvested from federal forests over the next sixteen months. Decisions like this prompted longtime environmental leader David Brower to say that Clinton and Gore had done more damage to the environment in four years than Reagan and Bush managed to inflict in twelve.

The Salvage Rider removed many environmental protections in national forests, allowing the removal of dead or damaged trees — or which the lumber company thought looked that way.

"It puts 100 million acres of trees at risk," Seth Hinman, a local Earth First! activist with a big, bushy beard, complained to Rachel. "Clinton just gutted a bunch of court orders protecting a lot of old growth forests. They're going to cut down 600-year-old trees, without any appeal process. It's going to a freaking free-for-all. There'll be wholesale clearcutting, roads everywhere, and a huge loss of watershed and animal habitat. He sold us out."

Four hundred acres of old growth trees in the Olympic National Forest was impacted. Rachel watched giant 250-year-old hemlocks being clear-cut by a mill whose yard was already stacked high with unsold second-growth logs. Even many old time forestry workers voiced their opposition.

"Our community is dead without lumbering. But we don't need to harvest old growth forests,' said Bill Vickers, a neighbor of Pete and Emily and a twenty-year veteran of the logging industry. "For one thing, they serve as firebreaks. They're also building miles of roads through the forests without any buffers to protect the salmon and trout streams. The local sport fishing industry is hanging on by a thread, and the federal bureaucrats are sitting with their thumbs up their butts allowing this to take place."

Working for Green America had brought Rachel back in touch with some folks in Earth First! whom she'd met fighting to protect the redwoods in California.

Earth Firsters were deep ecologists, believing that man's exploitation of nature was the fundamental oppression to resolve. "Humans don't have a moral right to dominate and exploit other species," Hinman told Rachel. "Wilderness is important in its own right, not as something for humans to play in on the weekend. All species have a right to exist for their own sake. Man has to learn how to live in balance with nature's needs, instead of always trying to sledgehammer nature to meet the wants of humans."

Partly inspired by Edward Abbey's *The Monkey Wrench Gang*, Earth First! favored direct action. "Rather than wasting time on lobbying or litigation, we prefer to go out and mess up the bulldozers and other equipment they use to chew up the earth," Hinman added. "You wanna save a tree, don't ask some bureaucrat to sign a piece a paper, just hammer some big spikes into it that'll wreck their chain saws. Or climb up it so they have to kill you if they want to kill the tree."

Earth First!'s no-compromise approach challenged many of the existing ground rules of the environmental debate. Earth Firsters viewed many of the larger, traditional environmental groups as negotiating over how quickly the earth would be ravaged. "Requiring companies to obtain a permit to discharge wastes into the environment is still giving them a permit to pollute," said Hinman.

Earth First! of course had its detractors, even among its own members. Several of its prominent members have walked away over its disorganization. "It's become militant vegan feminist witches for wilderness. People talk about tree-spiking and bombing, not ecosystems," said Earth First! co-founder Howie Wolke in explaining why he quit the organization.

Emily disagreed with Pete and Rachel over the effectiveness of Earth First. "They raise some good points, but their tactics and destruction of property turn a lot of average people against the environmental movement. Sometimes they seem more interested in publicity than results. And spiking trees can seriously injure a logger. Sure, groups like the Sierra Club sometimes wimp out, but throwing a court order in front of these lumber companies has saved far more trees than anything Earth First! has done," Emily said.

"I don't always agree with Earth's First!'s tactics," Rachel admitted, "but I respect their honesty and willingness to lay their bodies on the line. I've certainly shared their frustration of waiting for lawmakers and judges to take action to protect the environment, help the poor or make healthcare a right. Earth Firsters also know how to have a good time. They utilize humor as part of their actions — the theater of the absurd. And they throw great parties afterward."

Many people felt that Rachel pushed the envelope too far. It was nice to occasionally work with some activists that were beyond the envelope.

Some contended that Earth First! had been set up by the Sierra Club and Wilderness Society to make themselves look more reasonable in the environmental debate. Rachel responded, "So what? We need *someone* to expand the envelope."

As David Brower told Audubon magazine: "The Sierra Club made the Nature Conservancy look reasonable. I founded Friends of the Earth to make the Sierra Club look reasonable. Then I founded Earth Island Institute to make Friends of the Earth look reasonable. Earth First! now makes us look reasonable. We're still waiting for someone else to come along and make Earth First! look reasonable."

Rachel and Wynn participated in a series of protests to save the old growth trees in the Olympic National Forest.

Both were arrested when they chained themselves to an access road gate leading to a logging site. They set up a table of coffee and donuts for the loggers, welcoming them when they showed up for work shortly before 6 am. This slowed the loggers down for a few hours until they found another road into the woods.

Another time, Wynn and several of his friends climbed up one of the trees that had been marked for cutting, saving it for several days. The protesters gave media interviews and did radio talk shows on cell phones as the chain saws buzzed below them.

One protest that brought a smile even to the police involved pouring concrete into a couch in the middle of logging road. A coffee table, lamp and tv set completed the decor. Three activists chained themselves to the couch. The blockade worked for two days. Finally the Forest Rangers stepped in and cut all the clothing off the protesters, intending to starve and freeze them out since it was the middle of February. It worked.

Rachel wrote to Anna about a protest she and Wynn worked on. "We drove up to the house of this logging company CEO when he went out of town. Wynn and Pete unloaded dozens of old tree stumps on this circular driveway leading up to his mansion, creating an instant clear-cut forest. We hung several banners sixty feet up between the trees lining the driveway. The visuals were great.

"We set up a lemonade stand at the end of the driveway and offered free tours of the 'lost forest' to anyone driving by. The police eventually showed up but since they couldn't contact the owner, they couldn't force us to leave. All they could come up with was to shut down the roads leading into the neighborhood, which I'm sure generated even more irate phone calls from neighbors to the CEO. Three of the television stations carried the protest live on the six o'clock news. We left the stumps and banners behind for the owner, who didn't return home for more than a week," Rachel added.

Over a thousand people were arrested in the protests in the Olympic National Forest, though all the cases were eventually thrown out. More than 14,000 acres of prime old-growth forest were cut down in Clinton's 16-month chopping spree, primarily in Washington and Oregon.

****

Barry Frost agreed to be the Green Party presidential candidate in 1996 after a nationwide grassroots campaign to convince him to run.

Wynn, who knew Frost from his days with PIRG, called him to urge him to run. "Barry, we need a progressive third party in the US to raise issues the two major parties ignore. It's the only way to keep the Democrats honest. Otherwise, they take progressives for granted and move to the right to compete for votes with the Republicans. You'd give the Greens instant credibility. If you run, I'll help coordinate the West Coast for you."

"I agree with you about the need for a third party," Frost said, "but I'm not the type of guy you'd want running for President. I've never run for office before. Glad-handing voters is not my style. Besides, I have too much else on my plate."

"Running for office would be a great way to get your agenda before the public," Wynn countered. "Besides, I know you're frustrated by how little progress we've seen from Congress in the last two decades on public interest issues. Clinton's going to win anyway. This'll push him back in our direction. It'll let him know that a least some progressives won't stand for his constant pandering to corporations."

"I'll think about it, Wynn, but if I run, I'll do it my way," Frost said. "I'm not going to crawl to special interests seeking funding. And I'm going to run on the issues I want to, particularly corporate power and grassroots democracy. The Greens are a national party with lots of other candidates. If they got other issues they want to deal with — social issues like abortion or gay rights — they'll have to get others to raise them."

Many Greens were disappointed when Frost campaigned the way he said he would. Not only did he avoid fundraising, he decided to spend less than $5,000 on his campaign, avoiding the need to file financial disclosure forms with the Federal Election Commission. Frost worried that such disclosures would be used by his political and corporate enemies to attack the many public interest groups he'd established and continued to support. It was a decision that many Greens and progressives viewed as a major mistake.

Frost's campaign put the Green Party on the national map, though he only got on the ballot in half the states, pulling only one percent. Frost's thirty years of activism had built a broad base of support around the country that his campaign and the Greens were able to tap into. But the lack of funds severely hampered his campaign. It also meant that Frost couldn't coordinate with Green Party members, since otherwise their fundraising would count toward the 5,000-dollar threshold.

After the campaign, the FEC denied the Greens the legal status of a national political party, ruling that since Frost had not filed with them, the Greens hadn't run a presidential candidate.

Rachel wrote several speeches and policy statements for Frost on welfare and healthcare. Pete was also a big supporter of Frost. He had a framed autographed poster on his wall with a quote from Frost from two decades before, saying, "We will have solar power in this country as soon as the utility companies figure out a way to put a meter on the sun."

The Green presidential campaign brought to a head the ongoing feuds within the Greens, nominally between the "realos" and the "fundis" — the movement activists versus political candidates and realists. Rachel was unsympathetic to Wynn's complaints over the bickering. "It's just typical of leftist groups dominated by men. Let me guess. The disputes are primarily about personality conflicts, personal power and arguments over past incidents."

The Greens / Green Party of the United States of America had emerged in 1991 as the principal national green group, as the original Green Committees of Correspondence joined with the Left Greens. LG had a strong base of anarchists and social ecologists. Social ecologists believe that the exploitation of the planet grew from the same mentality that results in the oppression of women, people of color and the poor. Thus the Green Party needed to work on a broad range of social and economic justice issues as well as ecology.

While GPUSA expressly stated that running candidates for elected office was a priority, some Greens wanted a party primarily focused on elections. The exchange on the national green e-mail list serves was lively though dominated by a handful of individuals.

"GPUSA talks about elections, but seldom runs candidates except at the local level. Even then it's more about waving the flag than doing the nuts and bolts electoral organizing needed to win. Since anarchists oppose the existence of the state, they find it a contradiction to run for offices like governor or president," argued Jack Singleton of Texas, a founder of the Green Politics Network. "GPUSA is mainly interested in protesting, not challenging the two major parties at the ballot box. They should be the activist wing of the party, while we create the electoral wing."

GPUSA partisans countered that they ran plenty of candidates. "We just believe in practicing electoral politics at the retail level. We focus on races where we can talk to voters one on one, educate them about Green values. We believe that elections should grow out of our work on community issues. The big races are about raising lots of money and running marketing campaigns. There's little connection with real people," said Marcia Hammond of Missouri.

Singleton, a realo, fired back, saying "We have to realize the limitations of the existing system. We need to use our influence to win improvements on small but important issues, helping us become more powerful in the future. We gotta be strategic in picking our battles. There are plenty of activist groups that protest in the streets. The Greens need to be in the Capitol negotiating for solutions. That means we have to make it a priority to win elections."

"This debate between the realos — for realistic, and fundis, for fundamentalist — wasn't invented by the Greens," Wynn replied when asked by newcomers about the divisions. "All political movements have to balance the need for ideological purity against making the compromises needed to expand your base and actually win. Do you

work for the best reform package you can get the other side to agree to,
or do you hold out for revolutionary principles even if it means defeat?"

"The fundis argue that people are being bought off for minor
reforms, too interested in being an insider, a player. They argue that the
party has to stick to its principles no matter what, to make the case for
the true solutions," Wynn explained.

"What's unusual about the Greens is that the debate is never
resolved, it just keeps going on," Wynde said. *It drives me crazy*, he
thought.

Singleton and Greens involved with the Green Politics Network
took the lead in recruiting Frost to run. Some GPUSA members resisted
Frost's candidacy, feeling it was premature to run a presidential
candidate. They also felt that Frost didn't adequately address the breadth
of the Green platform. Immediately after the election, GPN convened
an Association of State Green Parties over loud protests from GPUSA.
While activism still remained a foundation of ASGP, the state parties
made it clear they wanted to run strong electoral campaigns, including
ones at the national level.

****

Following the presidential campaign, Rachel became the coordinator of
Green America's growing government relations program, lobbying
government at all levels to support green initiatives. She tried to
convince lawmakers to include funding for green businesses in their
economic development incentive packages. She pushed legislation that
required packaging to be made of reusable, returnable or recyclable
materials; phasing out pesticides; providing tax credits and low-interest
loans for renewable energy; increasing gas mileage requirements for cars;
and increasing the minimum wage and welfare grants.

Rachel took advantage of Green America's college tuition plan to
take two classes a semester toward a Master's Degree in political science
and administration. She wanted to better understand the mechanics of
government and political campaigns. She also wanted an opportunity to
study some theories of social change and community organizing.

Rachel was struck by the changing demographics she saw at
protests. She and Wynn were no longer doing traditional Alinsky-style
community organizing. They were now involved with general activism
and community mobilization.

"Too many of our meetings and protests are dominated by people with graying hair, receding hairlines, and growing paunches around the middle" she complained to Wynn. *Hey, I work out,* Wynn thought, patting his stomach. "We need to work harder on linking up with young people. And we're not mobilizing working-class communities," Rachel added.

"Young people have always been attracted to protest movements, but their leadership and ranks had been much smaller during the early '80s and '90s, with the notable exception of some of the more militant groups, like Earth First!," she wrote in a class paper on social change movements in the last quarter-century.

"However, there seems to be an upsurge of activism in the mid-90s among students. The campaign to make colleges to stop buying sweatshirts and other clothing from companies that forced their workers to endure sweatshop conditions — low pay, long hours, unsafe working conditions — had swept across campuses. The AFL-CIO, under the new leadership of John Sweeney, has invested in hiring and training college students to help with organizing during the summer. They put these lessons into practice once they returned to their college campuses."

****

Wynn became the lead Greenpeace organizer in the Northwest protecting ocean fish.

"Commercial fishing provides food for hundreds of millions of people," Wynn told Greenpeace members during his power point presentation. "Fishing is now a mining operation spanning the globe. Fish populations worldwide are being rapidly depleted, as gigantic floating factories work around the clock. Key species in the complex web of marine life are being hunted to extinction. Catches are falling, leading to ever-larger fleets that chase around the world looking for fish. Many national governments provide massive subsidies to these unsustainable fishing practices to maintain the jobs."

"Commercial fishing factories also kill tens of millions of unwanted fish and other marine animals," Wynn said. He switched to the next frame. "Coastal and marine habitats that provide essential breeding grounds for fish have been depleted by development, as well as by fishing practices such as bottom trawling that harm marine habitats like the ocean floor and coral reefs. As the most commercially valuable fish stocks become depleted, the factories move further down the food chain, targeting smaller species of fish."

"Okay, they should change their fishing practices to cause less damage. But don't we need the fish as food?" asked an audience member. "And people have been fishermen from the dawn of civilization. It's understandable that countries want to protect these jobs."

"They should promote small-scale, community-based fisheries that employ sustainable fishing practices. The community fisheries generate the same amount of fish as the fishing factories but with much less waste. The local businesses also employ twenty times more people," Wynn added.

"The only US fishing grounds still large enough to support a domestic factory fleet is the Alaska pollock fishery of the Eastern Bering Sea, Aleutian Islands and Gulf of Alaska," Wynn continued, "comprising one-third of all fish caught in the US. Alaskan pollock is a vital component of the marine ecosystem, serving as major prey for other fish and seabirds. It's rapidly being overfished to the point of depletion."

Many of the American corporate fishing factories operate out of Seattle, catching pollock for fish fillets at McDonald's. One of Wynn's favorite actions was when he coordinated a dozen Greenpeace activists to hang from the Aurora bridge with mountain climbing gear. The fishing fleet had to pass under the bridge to head to open waters. When one of the trawlers tried to depart, the Greenpeace protesters rappelled several hundred feet down to hang in front of the boat, preventing it from moving forward.

Rachel stood on the bridge and gave Wynn a big kiss before he went over the side. "Please try to come back in one piece. And if the ship doesn't stop, promise me you'll pull yourself up," she said.

It took the Seattle police nearly half a day to commandeer enough tugboats to enable them to cut the protesters down so that the trawlers could depart.

****

After attending a workshop on genetic engineering one evening at the food coop, Rachel pounced on Wynn when he got home, demanding to know what Greenpeace was doing about it. Wynn laughed and asked, "Do you ever look at the newsletters I bring home, or do you just use 'em to start the wood stove? We've got a whole national campaign on it."

They both had so many balls in the air that it wasn't unusual for either of them to be unaware of the details of what the other was working on.

Rachel retorted, "It's your job to educate the public about these issues. If you're not educating me, you're messing up." Wynn pulled her into his lap. "Let me whisper sweet nothings into your ear about genetic engineering," he said coyly.

"Cut it out, wise guy," Rachel said, pushing him away. "Did you know that almost two-thirds of all processed foods in the US contain genetically engineered materials? Genetically modified organisms are freaking bein' released without anyone knowing what their impact is on the environment, wildlife and our health. It's madness, capitalism run amok. USDA doesn't require any health or safety tests before GE crops are marketed. Christ, they leave it to the companies to decide whether it's safe or not. They don't *even* have to label it. We're having a goddamn going-out-of-business sale on biodiversity, with humans as guinea pigs. America is ground zero in the biggest field test in history, with more GE crops than the rest of the world combined."

Genetic engineering takes genes from one species and inserts them into another, hoping to transfer a desired trait — like resistance to the cold, or to particular insects or pesticides. Traditional breeding, in contrast, works only within one species, isolating and highlighting a specific genetic trait over many generations from within the species' gene pool — genetic diversity is created from within nature's limits. Strawberries and flounders in nature can't crossbreed, but with genetic engineering, genes from flounders have been inserted into strawberries to try to make them more resistant to frost.

Mainstream media stories to the contrary, most genetically engineered changes to food have nothing to do with nutrition and often fail to fulfill its promise on increased yield. Some are designed to make the product nicer to look at, easier to sell. Most were designed to allow chemical companies to sell pesticides that kill everything but the genetically engineered plant. Or the plant has been genetically engineered to emit its own pesticide to kill insects.

"The genes in these Frankenstein foods can combine in unexpected ways," Rachel added, continuing to rant despite Wynn's rather indifferent response. He had heard all of this before. "The companies pretend they know what they're doing but they mostly don't have a clue. They're just mad scientists experimenting. They claim to know how one gene from a particular species will work in another, but that's bull. It's mainly guesswork at this point. I mean, the freakin' mapping of the human genie, genome — whatever — showed that genes don't act like the Nobel Prize winner predicted. And the guys working on genetic engineering haven't won any Nobel Prize.

"They're still trying to figure out how to isolate and transfer specific genes," Rachel added. "They could end up creating superweeds that are even more resistant to pesticides than before, or create new species that push out the old ones. Genetically engineered salmon have already escaped from their ocean pens and are displacing natural salmon because they have been engineered to eat and grow faster, giving them a competitive advantage," Rachel told Wynn.

"Did ya know the pollen of genetically modified corn kills monarch butterfly larvae? And a few years ago, Hi-Bred International was days away from introducing a soybean with a Brazil nut gene when independent tests found it caused a reaction in people with nut allergies. It could have killed people," Rachel exclaimed. About two percent of adults and eight percent of children suffer from food allergies.

"Fascinating," Wynn said, finally managing to get a word in. "Wouldn't you like to retire to our bedroom to discuss the birds and the bees in more intimate detail?"

Rachel continued to ignore Wynn's entreaties. "Why are we allowing a handful of multinational chemical companies to do this?" she demanded to know. "So they can make more profit?"

"Of course—" Wynn tried to interject.

"I mean, they're buying up Mother Nature's seeds of life," Rachel plowed ahead, "so they can just make something else to be bought and sold, play the game of supply and demand. It's biopiracy. They go into third world countries and ask the natives about plants they use for healing. Then they go out and patent them to make a fortune."

"Did ya hear that USDA put out a rule to classify genetically engineered foods as *organic*? That's an outrage. We've gotta do something." Rachel was pounding her fist on the kitchen table. She barely noticed the cup of tea Wynn had set down in front of her. *Maybe I should rub her shoulders?* he thought.

"I think we should reconsider all these night meetings you go to," Wynn said. "I mean, a man comes home after a hard day's work down at the seaport, and instead of finding a hot meal on the table, he's confronted by a hysterical housewife ranting about some new conspiracy between the government and Big Business to poison our food supply."

"Very funny, Wynn. And speaking of a wife, if that's a proposal, you're going to have to do a whole better," Rachel added.

"I probably shouldn't tell you this," he said, "but some people believe that the advances in nanotechnology — making very small, independent machines — combined with genetic engineering, artificial intelligence and computers will make it possible within the next 30 years that humans could be displaced at the top of the pecking order. Some silicon-based human-life form will be created that's more powerful, more intelligent and longer lasting than Homo sapiens."

"Now, the person talking about this on NPR," Wynn said, worried by the look on Rachel's face, "didn't think it was necessarily a bad idea. He just thought that humans should discuss it before it happened. He's also worried that hundreds of thousands of individuals would have the technological ability to create this new species. Any one of 'em could decide unilaterally to do it. At least with nuclear weapons, only a handful of countries had the ability to pull that off."

Rachel sat there with a stunned look on her face, trying to absorb this new information.

"You sure you don't want to come to bed?" Wynn asked plaintively.

****

In the spring of 1999, Tommy graduated from Evergreen State College. Evergreen was a center of student activism. Tommy helped push for death row inmate Mumia Abu-Jamal to deliver a thirteen minute taped commencement speech. The Governor of Washington, who'd also been scheduled to speak, withdrew in protest. Area state and federal officials tripped over themselves in denouncing Mumia's participation.

The theme for the graduation was "Lives lived deliberately." Mumia talked about people like Malcolm X, John Brown, Black Panther leader Huey P. Newton and Ramona Africa. "These people dared to dissent, dared to speak out, dared to reject the status quo by becoming rebels against it," Mumia told the students. "They lived lives of deliberate will, of willed resistance to a system that's killing us. Learn from them. This system's greatest fear has been that folks like you, young people, people who have begun to critically examine the world around them, people who have yet to have a spark of life snuffed out, will do just that: learn from those lives, be inspired, and then live lives of opposition to the deadening status quo."

Mumia had been a longtime leader of the Black Panthers and radio commentator in Philadelphia, which was notorious for the racism of its police department. As he was driving a cab on a December night in 1981 to pay his bills, Mumia pulled over when he came upon a confrontation between the police and his brother. When he woke up in the hospital, Mumia had been shot and a police officer was killed. His brother was missing.

Many individuals and groups, such as the European Union, Amnesty International and the ACLU came to believe that Mumia had been denied a fair trial, and he became America's most famous political prisoner, and a major icon in the struggle against the death penalty.

Rachel beamed with pride as Tommy received his diploma. "You raised him well," said Wynn. "Without your guidance, I doubt we'd have the state police standing in protest at his graduation. I'm so proud of the both of you." Rachel gave him an elbow in the ribs.

Pete and Emily offered Tommy a full-time position with Green America. He declined, instead taking a job with a computer company designing video games. He told Rachel, "You and Wynn always talk 'bout how your job is more than your work, it's your life. I thought I'd take it a step further, make my job my play time as well."

FIFTEEN

THE BATTLE IN SEATTLE

In the fall of 1999, Wynn and Rachel helped organize the "mother of all protests" in Seattle at the international meeting of the World Trade Organization.

"The Battle in Seattle" was a turning point for the movement against corporate globalization. It highlighted the reemergence of young people as a critical organizing base for progressive social change. Young people and the anti-corporate globalization activists would form the core of Frost's and the Green Party's support in the upcoming presidential election, since Seattle highlighted how firmly wedded the Democratic Party was to the corporate agenda.

Created in 1994 as the new incarnation of the General Agreement on Tariffs and Trade, the WTO was part of the alphabet soup of new international trade groups, such as NAFTA, that were creating a world government of, for and by multinational corporations. The agenda for the WTO meeting included the Global Free Logging Agreement, the Multilateral Agreement on Investments (MAI) and trade-related intellectual property rights.

"The WTO gives corporations the power to use secret administrative tribunals to weaken or overturn labor, environmental or human rights laws that impede their ability to maximize their profits," Frost said at the initial organizing meeting for the protest. "National sovereignty is now secondary to the needs of corporations. These artificial creations, hardly more than a century old, have broken free of the chains of governmental control and are roaming the world looking for opportunities to exploit the environment and local residents."

While his demeanor seem far removed from the street action protests that came to characterize the Seattle protest, Frost and various groups he had founded were a major driving force behind movement against corporate globalization.

Wynn worked on the Seattle demonstrations almost fulltime for six months for one of the global trade groups started by Frost. Wynn had lost his job, along with 400 other regional organizers, when Greenpeace USA closed their US organizing offices. In exchange for several international Greenpeace groups helping to retire their multimillion-dollar debt, the US chapter agreed to focus on lobbying Congress.

Both Wynn and Rachel worked closely with the Seattle Greens in organizing for the demonstrations.

The WTO united protesters across the political spectrum in the need to protest, though individual groups disagreed over what issues to focus on and tactics to employ. Seattle was critical to creating a green-blue alliance between labor and environmentalists. Trade unions, environmentalists, consumers, teachers, farmers, women organizations, religious groups, students and anarchists all planned events.

"It's critical that we wake up the world to the runaway train of globalization corporate-style," Wynn told a local NPR reporter. "Most Americans had no idea that the WTO even existed, let alone how much power they had over the economy."

Some groups preferred traditional rallies with speakers. The AFL-CIO was seeking a seat at the table to negotiate on international trade and distanced itself from the more aggressive actions planned for downtown.

The more militant groups, including the Greens, Earth First! and Direct Action Network, wanted to shut the WTO down, both in Seattle and permanently. They organized small independent groups to take creative direct action, including civil disobedience. The WTO and local officials were unprepared for the magnitude and intensity of the protest about to unfurl.

The WTO protest also demonstrated how critical the Internet had become to organizing, its speed and access allowing groups from around the world to easily network together and share information at virtually no cost. The Seattle99 website served as the virtual clearinghouse for the protest.

One of the organizers Wynn worked closely with was Ray McDaniels, a local union leader. A lifelong community activist, Ray was president of the local teachers' union. He featured authors such as Howard Zinn, Rachel Carson, Noam Chomsky and Malcolm X in his high school history class. He also built community playgrounds and gardens, served a few years on the school board and, with his wife, carted their two children around to soccer and T-ball games.

The AFL-CIO were planning a massive legal rally to protest the export of jobs and the race to the bottom. "The corporations want to impose third-world working conditions everywhere," McDaniels said. "The politicians they buy with their campaign contributions tell us that free trade will lift up workers everywhere. The reality is that corporations will merely shift as many jobs as possible to countries where there are no minimum wage laws, no right to unionize, no right to safety in the workplace and no need to worry about where they throw their toxic waste. They'll use the threat of job relocation to demand more and more concessions from US workers," said McDaniels.

"Clinton is looking to the Seattle to cap his administration by producing one last Free Trade victory," McDaniels continued. "A WTO agreement in Seattle would help ensure that corporate donations continued to flow freely to the Democrats in the upcoming national elections. Don't forget that Clinton saved his Presidency — floundering after the mishandling of gays in the military and national healthcare — by pushing NAFTA through Congress, aligning himself with the Republicans and the business community against many of the Democrats' traditional allies."

Clinton tried to seduce the unions and big environmental groups by arguing, "The new global economy is a reality, so rather than opposing it we need to shape it. Of course, we have to ensure that environmental standards and workers' rights are part of every future trade agreement."

But most national union leaders realized they had been burned too often by Clinton's smooth talking. "American CEOs are now paid 420 times more than line workers. Median hourly wages are down 10 percent in the past 25 years," McDaniels reminded them.

The WTO proponents argued that it would help consumers and labor, while promoting peace. "Getting rid of protectionist trade barriers means lower prices for everyone," said a WTO spokesperson. "The WTO helps promotes peace by helping trade to flow smoothly, while providing countries a fair way to deal with trade disputes. Increased trade will help promote economic development, which will lead to job growth and higher incomes."

"Clinton thinks he can convince developing nations that they can strengthen environmental standards and improve conditions for workers while maintaining their low-cost competitive advantage," Frost pointed out. "Fortunately, the developing countries see this as just the latest subterfuge to keep the US and other western allies in the dominant economic position. The question is whether he can bribe enough of them to get them to go along."

It was the grassroots environmental groups and student activists that brought the edge, the militancy, to the WTO protests. The Rainforest Action Network and Ruckus Society organized the Global This! Action Camp, bringing more than 150 activists together to plan how to shut down the WTO meetings. The entire Moreno clan along with many local Green activists attended the camp an organic farm north of Seattle.

The Direct Action Network was organizing affinity groups of fifteen to twenty individuals. They would act independently to blockade the streets near the meeting site when Clinton delivered his welcoming speech, hoping to keep delegates from entering. Groups like the San Francisco-based Art and Revolution Street Theater Troupe were constructing giant puppets and banners to give the protests a carnival-like atmosphere.

Wynn got permission to use some of Green America's resources, such as their computer staff, to help establish an Independent Media Center. Rachel agreed to be Green America's liaison for the project.

"The American media is increasingly owned by a few large corporations. We need to develop alternative mechanisms to ensure sure the information about the protests gets out to the larger world," Wynn explained to Emily.

"We're setting up a media clearinghouse, using web and satellite links, to provide up-to-the-minute reports, photos, audio and video footage. We wanna leave an independent media center up and running when the protests are over. We're also going to take the web technology we develop and give it to activists worldwide to set up their own IMCs."

The IMC uplinked video segments every day to distribute nationwide to public access cable channels. Rachel was one of many who took a video camera to the protests, bringing the tape back to the IMC at the end of each day. The center also produced its own newspaper, distributed throughout Seattle and to other cities via the internet. The IMC also produced hundreds of audio segments, and established a 24-hour micro and internet radio station.

Rachel and Tommy helped paint the banner that kicked off the WTO protests. On Monday morning, two volunteers climbed down a six-story building to unfurl a 500-square-foot banner that read "Sweatshops: Free Trade or Corporate Slavery." Meanwhile, several Rainforest Action Network activists unfurled a huge banner from a building crane in downtown Seattle highlighting the undemocratic nature of the WTO.

Later that day, Rachel attended a protest at a downtown McDonald's organized by José Bovée, a French sheep farmer who earlier that summer had demolished a McDonald' under construction in his community to protest the globalization of food and agriculture. One of the demands of the Seattle protest was a halt to the genetic engineering of the food supply.

"The chemical salesmen worldwide are trying to peddle their 'miracle seeds' to farmers rich and poor. Desperate farmers saddled with debt and declining crop prices are their best customers. They sell to those most disconnected to the land, those who look at farming as just another assembly line factory to be exploited. They want to reduce food and land to just more commodities to exploit," said one protester.

One of the biggest arguments touted by the genetic engineering salesmen was the need to feed the poor of the world. The spokesperson for Noventis contended, "The affluent environmental elite in the US and Europe are indifferent to the plight of the billions who were threatened with malnutrition and hunger."

Yet it was often the poor farmers who were most opposed, because they could see that it was just another attempt by the rich to take control of their lives, to force them to buy seeds and chemicals from the rich rather than using the seed collecting and agriculture methods developed by the people over millennia.

"They just wanna become our new landlords, our new masters. They're not concerned about our empty stomachs, they're concerned about their fat wallets. They just want us to work for them, growing food at wages that keep us permanently in debt, servant to the rich, taking away our independence and our ability to live off the land in harmony with our mother planet. They'll force us to grow food that they can sell to North American consumers to pay off our so-called debts, not food to feed hungry people, our people," said Henri Boyer, a spokesperson for Haitian subsistence farmers.

****

Anna flew in from South America for the last two weeks before the WTO protests. She was helping coordinate a Fair Trade campaign for her women's economic development group.

"Our Fair Trade program is about economic justice," she told a Seattle radio interviewer, "a sustainable model of how we should do international trade. We sell goods and foods in the US and Canada at a good price, while giving third world workers a decent income. We work with indigenous peoples and women in Asia, Africa, Latin America and the Caribbean. We practice Fair Trade, not Free Trade."

Anna spoke at downtown church on Monday night about Jubilee 2000, a campaign her group supported to cancel third world debt.

"Jubilee is the Old Testament concept that every fifty years all debts should be forgiven and that the fields should lay fallow to give the earth an opportunity to rest and renew itself. Jubilee 2000 is urging President Clinton, Congress and international lenders and governments to forgive the debt of third world nations, allowing them to build a better life for their citizens. Debt repayment is foreign aid in reverse. For every dollar sent in aid to the poorest countries, a dollar-thirty flows back to lenders for debt service. Hundreds of millions of people around the world are living in poverty because of third world debt and its consequences," Anna told the crowd.

"Of the 32 countries classified as severely indebted low-income countries, 25 are in sub-Saharan Africa. Africa spends four times as much on debt repayment as on healthcare. For instance, while 15 billion dollars is needed annually to fight HIV/AIDS in Africa, Africa pays 13.5 billion in debt service every year," she pointed out.

During the question and answer session, some church members expressed skepticism about the Jubilee proposal.

"I certainly support giving people a fair price for their crafts, and sure, we should be a little more generous in how they pay off their loans," said one older gentleman. "But we've got plenty of problems right here at home that need money. And aren't we just rewarding bad behavior, like corruption and poor government, when we forgive such massive loans? Why should America always have to pay for other people's mistakes?"

"A lot of the corruption starts with American companies," replied Anna. "They lobby a country's leader to build an enormous project, but the only ones that benefit are the companies that build it and the politicians they bribe. And American and other international banks get rich from loaning them money."

"Well, how did the debt get so big?" he asked. "Why did the financial community keep on lending them money when it was clear they wouldn't get it back?"

"It's like buying a lot of stuff on a credit card. Pretty soon you owe so much that all you can afford to pay is the monthly interest. The balance never gets any smaller," Anna replied.

"Most economists trace the third world debt crisis back to the late 60s. The US was spending more money than it earned, so it decided to print up more dollars," she explained. "Over the next few years, when the dollar fell in value, the oil-producing countries jacked up their prices. They made huge sums of money, and deposited it in Western banks, which caused interest rates to decline, creating an international financial crisis.

"The international banks then gave huge loans to developing countries, often below the rate of inflation, to continue development and to pay for the rising cost of oil. Most of the funds, however, were spent on large centralized projects favored by the international lenders. A few got rich but most residents saw little benefit.

"At the same time, third world countries, encouraged by the West to grow cash crops, suddenly saw declining prices for their raw materials, like copper, coffee, tea, cotton, cocoa. Too many countries were producing the same crops, so prices fell. Then interest rates began to rise, pushed up further by an increase in US interest rates. Meanwhile, oil prices rose again. The debtors had to borrow more money just to pay off the interest.

"In 1982, Mexico told its creditors it couldn't repay its debts," Anna said. "The IMF and World Bank stepped in with new loans but under strict conditions. The third world debtors had to cut spending on public services, cut imports and increase exports to Western countries. This pattern has been repeated over and over again for decades, forcing a decline in living standards in many countries to pay off the debt.

"More than 50 countries in the world have debts that'll never be paid back," Anna continued. "The debt burden of the poorest countries is more than 90 percent of their income. Every year resources are diverted from health, education and sanitation for debt service. The harm caused by debt is often as devastating as war, because it decimates the budgets for schools, clinics and hospitals. The UN has stated that 21 million children's lives could be saved if the money used for debt service was put into health and education."

"The debt of these third world countries is much more the responsibility of the West and the wealthy than it is of the poor. We have sucked enough blood out of those who often do not know where their next meal will come from. Let's use the dawn of a new millennium as an opportunity to build a world that raises all people up," Anna concluded.

The rich will figure out how to get it back from them fast enough anyway Anna muttered under her breath.

After the service, several hundred of the participants marched through the streets of Seattle in the cold rain. They hoped to form a human chain of linked arms around the hotel where the WTO delegates were having their opening reception, but the police pushed them away.

Rachel and Anna ended up holding arms with hundreds of other protesters in a back alley blocked by a fence, singing "We Shall Overcome."

****

On Tuesday, the day of the largest planned protests, a police riot broke out.

The mainstream media reported that "black-clad anarchists are breaking store windows and violently confronting police, who have shown remarkable restraint in responding to the hooligans." With the Independent Media Center and hundreds of individuals distributing first-hand reports over the internet, many Americans found out that the reality was quite different.

The affinity groups organized by the Direct Action Network tried to blockade thirteen entrances to the convention center. Tommy joined an affinity group organized by the Food Not Bombs anarchist collective he worked with. "Whose streets?" someone shouted. "Our streets!" was the reply. "Whose democracy?" "Our democracy!"

Young people, college students, were everywhere. One intersection was blockaded by 200 "sea turtles." They looked like a tribe of teenage mutant ninja turtles trying to swim across the street.

Protesters sat in the streets, their arms locked together inside steel pipes. Other protesters sat on top of 20-foot tripods. Official looking protesters in hard hats studiously draped "do no cross" tape on the street poles surrounding the Convention Center. Many of the protesters from a legal march organized by national environmental groups, including Anna and Wynn, soon joined the blockade.

The affinity groups had a clear objective and their members were committed, disciplined and well trained. The police were not. The WTO delegates were furious. Official and unofficial protests were ringing in the ears of the US representatives. The president, governor and mayor were all deeply embarrassed. The police were ordered to get things under control. They accomplished the opposite.

Meanwhile, tens of thousands of labor activists gathered at the Seattle Memorial Stadium at 10 am. The national labor leaders hurried to catch up with their grassroots members who were clearly out in front of them in opposition to the WTO. The biggest cheers came when the President of the ILWU announced that the unions had closed all the ports on the West Coast in solidarity with the protest.

During the march downtown to the convention center, the labor leaders tried to keep their distance from the direct action protesters, employing ribbons to separate the marchers from the other protesters. But many labor activists joined in the peaceful street actions rather than following the labor march back to the staging area.

The police tried to open up access to the convention center, one intersection at a time. The protesters peacefully but resolutely resisted. Shortly after the labor march headed away, loud booming was heard, followed by clouds of tear gas that quickly enveloped downtown Seattle. A few demonstrators threw the tear gas canisters back at the police.

The police offensive continued to escalate, especially after a few black-clad anarchists smashed windows of sweatshops outlets such as The Gap and Old Navy, as well as Seattle's homegrown symbol of corporate globalization, Starbucks. Many of the other protesters were aghast, saying this violated their agreement to be peaceful, and urged them to stop. A number of the protesters accused the anarchists of being police informers and provocateurs. The police used this an excuse to hose people with pepper spray and beat and arrest protesters who had nothing to do with the vandalism.

Rachel was stunned. She kept her camera rolling, taking her role as reporter seriously. The IMC had made up official-looking press credentials, one of which hung from Rachel's neck. She went up to interview several of the police officers. "Why are you doing this? These protesters have just been sitting here. Why are you tear gassing them?"

The officers pushed her roughly away, trying to knock the camera out of her hands. "Get out of here," they shouted at her, "or you'll be next."

One posting on the IMC website that evening reported on the sounds of history.

It's the sound of hundreds of protesters sitting in front of an entrance to the Seattle convention center, chanting "The whole world is watching," as gas-masked riot police advance on them. It's the sound of a pounding techno beat pouring out of a sound van as a rave takes place on a blockaded side street. It's the ringing of gongs carried by Korean fisherman in traditional dress, dancing in front of an armored police vehicle, as their gongs ring out. It's the thunderous cheer that rises up from tear gas-weary protesters surrounded by police as thousands of teamsters and longshoremen show up to join them on the barricades. It's 10 Radical Cheerleaders in red and white, bouncing on top of a concrete and iron-pipe platform placed in the middle of an intersection and u-locked to the necks of 20 Earth Firstlers.

The police managed to clear the street intersections around the convention center by late afternoon, though protesters, media and bystanders were everywhere. The mayor held a news conference to announce that the First Amendment had been suspended. "A state of emergency has been declared. We've established a no-protest zone around the convention center. A curfew will be in effect for 50 square blocks of downtown."

"Don't Americans have a right to peacefully demonstrate?" shouted out a reporter from Indy Media who had managed to sneak into the news conference.

"My job is to provide for the safety of our citizens and our international guests," the mayor replied. "There will be plenty of spaces available for those who want to peacefully demonstrate. But we've already seen a lot of violence and unlawful behavior near the WTO meeting sites, and we have to make sure no one gets hurt. The governor has agreed to send in the National Guard to help maintain order."

As darkness descended, the police unleashed a new wave of tear gas assaults, chasing many of the protesters into Capitol Hill. Local residents poured out of their homes, appalled at this police invasion in their neighborhood, as tear gas and concussion grenades exploded everywhere. The police assault continued throughout the night.

Rachel managed to make her way back to the IMC to turn over her videotape. Her frantic efforts to find Wynn were unsuccessful. There was no answer at home, and none of their friends had heard from him. Tommy at least had left a message, saying, "I'm okay. I can run faster than the cops."

Rachel spent most of the night at the IMC, helping to edit and upload video and stories to their website while continuing to call around looking for information about Wynn. She went home about 3 am to see if there was a message from Wynn or Anne.

That morning, Rachel attended a rally organized by farmers protesting agribusiness, hoping Wynn would be there. Barry Frost spoke, condemning Monsanto and its efforts to genetically manipulate the world's seed stock.

One of Wynn coworkers came over and said, "We hear the police just grabbed Wynn while he was doing a radio interview with an Australian reporter. They called him one of the professional troublemakers responsible for the whole mess." Someone else told her, "I saw Anna dragged away by the police from one of the street blockades closest to the site. They maced her pretty badly. She wasn't too happy, and she was letting them know it."

Rachel spent the rest of the day helping to get Wynn and Anna out of jail.

The WTO summit collapsed on Friday night, led by a rebellion of the developing countries. The delegates failed to agree on even whether to discuss workers' rights and the environment in trade negotiations. The delegates sulked to the airport without even issuing their normal final statement declaring the whole thing a success.

Clinton was furious at everyone but himself. He was mad at his allies in Europe and Japan for digging their heels in about ongoing disputes at agriculture and steel, and at the local police for failing to control the protests. The developing nations were equally angry with Washington for once again trying to use its enormous economic power to benefit the multinational companies at the expense of weaker nations.

"The Battle in Seattle was a watershed moment in the struggle against corporate-dominated globalization," Frost said in one of his many post-protest interviews. "For the first time many Americans heard about the secretive international business groups forced on them by Clinton and the corporations. They are trying to create a new world government without any input or democratic control from 99 percent of the world's inhabitants, including average Americans. Fortunately, many concerned citizens came to Seattle and held our own version of the Boston Tea Party. We're not ready to let them steal our democracy."

****

Pete and Emily threw a dinner for Anna the weekend after the WTO protests. She was flying out the next morning to a Fair Trade conference in South Africa. For once, Tommy tagged along with Rachel and Wynn. He'd hit some of the livelier post-protest parties in Seattle after he grabbed a bite to eat with the old folks.

Pete made several of his favorite Tex-Mex dishes, with homemade organic salsa laced with as hot a jalapeno pepper as he could grow. Rachel made a tossed spinach salad. Wynn and Anna had brought dessert and a couple of bottles of wine. Tommy brought a six-pack of home-brewed beer, drawing a disapproving stare from Rachel who felt he was drinking too much.

The dinner conversation quickly turned to politics. After reviewing the week's protests and hearing all the details about Anna and Wynn's arrests and planned lawsuits, Emily posed a question to Wynn. "I don't understand all this time and energy you spend with the Green Party, especially with elections. You wear yourself out for six months, and for what? For the big offices, like governor or president, all you get a small percentage of the votes. Okay, I know the Greens have won dozens of local races across the country, but come on, there's something like a half-million elected positions. Why not just focus on building something like Green America?"

Rachel jumped in before Wynn could respond. "The Democrats don't share the Green's vision of the type of world we want. Oh sure, they pay lip service to putting people ahead of corporate profits. But they never do. And they're clueless about what sustainable development is, that we can't use up the earth's resources faster than nature can replenish them." Rachel helped herself to seconds.

"Boss Tweed used to say, let the people vote for the candidate of their choice, as long as I get to choose the candidates," Pete added. "That's the service the Democratic and Republican parties perform for corporate America."

"Every few years we have a referendum on the future of our country," Wynn told Emily, drinking some of Tommy's oatmeal stout beer. "Now granted, that referendum right now is stacked against the people at the moment — we gotta reclaim our democracy — but the ballot box is a lot better than armed revolution. Elections give us an opportunity to speak to the whole vision we want to promote. If progressives fail to participate in that process, we just surrender our future to the corporations and the wealthy."

"Wouldn't it be easier and more effective just to take over the Democratic Party?" Emily asked.

"People have been trying to reform the Democrats for more than a century without success," Wynn responded. "Liberals underestimate how entrenched money and corporations are in the Democratic Party. The party ends up changing you far more than you change it. Reformers have to make so many compromises to get ahead in the party, by the time they have the power to actually do something, they've forgotten what they're trying to change."

"One of the advantages of a third party," Pete interjected, "as opposed to trying to reform the Dems from inside, is that ya can't co-opt the party by just buyin' off one person. If the third party has an agenda that the voters like, either the other parties have to steal their issues or the third party begins to win more and more votes. Hopefully it eventually picks up enough support that it wins in a three-way race."

"Name me a third party that's been successful in America," Emily challenged.

"The Republicans," Pete replied. "It won the White House with Lincoln just eight years after it formed. There were a lotta people in the country who wanted to end slavery, but the two major parties, the Democrats and I believe the Whigs, were both proslavery. So the antislavery vote went to the Republicans."

"Even if you don't win," Wynn added, "third parties have raised lots of issues that the two main parties end up adopting. Much of the New Deal enacted by FDR came from the Socialist Party platform, things like the minimum wage, social security, unemployment insurance and child labor laws. It was third parties that first championed the right of women to vote."

Anna interjected, "Yeah, but all those issues were won because there was a grassroots movement agitating for change. Lincoln sure as heck wasn't a leader of the abolitionist movement. He may have been sympathetic to their cause, but it was the tens of thousands of average people fighting for freedom that made the difference. And it was the socialists and commies in the 20s and 30s that pushed things like the minimum wage and unemployment benefits. Their power didn't come from the ballot box but from organizing on the factory floors and in the community. Unfortunately, while the Greens are okay as part of the general activist scene, they're doing squat in terms of real community organizing."

Anna added, pouring more wine for everyone, "The Greens need to come to grips with the reality that even if you win an election, even a big one, the corporations will still be in control. The politicians are just the front men. Their job is to keep the masses under control while the rich loot and plunder. And with this new global economy, if you win in the US, they'll just shift ownership and production to whatever country offers the highest bid."

Tommy jumped in. "I agree with Anna. The Greens are fighting the wrong battle. They want to become the new leaders of the state, but they fail to recognize that the state itself is the problem. The wealthy use the state to concentrate their power and exercise their will, whether it's capitalists or communists or greens. The ruling elite created the state to do the dirty work for them.

"As states have amassed more power," Tommy added, "the ruling class has increased its ability to exploit workers, rape the environment and kill more people — both their own and the citizens of other states that they have economic disputes with. The worst mass murderers and terrorists have been state leaders."

"We need to focus on decentralizing power and decision-making, empower every individual to have a real say in what happens in her workplace and community and school. Smash the state!" Tommy shouted, shaking his fist and spraying beer over the table.

Everybody was talking at once now. Rachel asserted parental prerogative. "Tommy, you weren't one of those anarchists who smashed windows this week? That wasn't very helpful. Those were the images that the corporate media broadcast to the rest of the world. It made us look violent and turned off a lot of people who otherwise would have agreed with our message. And it was contrary to the nonviolent approach that the organizers had agreed to."

Tommy opened up another beer, leaning back in his chair with a smirk on his face. "What are you guys, the Gestapo? Talk about guilt by association. You'd make a good police detective mom, extracting information to fit your preconceptions," he laughed. "To the best of my recollection, I was not involved in breaking any windows. I'm more of the type who wheat-pastes posters on the windows."

"But isn't it a little hypocritical," Tommy added, "for people over thirty to get riled up about a few broken windows when these corporations are clearcutting old growth trees? Be real. Corporate America is polluting our water and lungs, oppressing workers, paying military dictators to kill their own people and using whatever force they need to keep power. And who decided that a few self-anointed protest leaders — who claim they want democracy — can announce rules for everyone who wants to take down against the WTO? I wasn't at *that* meeting.

"And let's not forget that the police began shooting tear gas and rubber bullets at people hours before anyone broke a window. You argue that people have been trying to reform the Democratic Party for a couple centuries. Well, it seems like y'all been protestin' corporate power for just about as long, with your lobbying, rallies, lawsuits and third party efforts, and you know what? The corporations have won. It's time to reconsider your tactics."

Wynn snuck in a few words before Rachel could respond. "Those who use the tactics of their oppressors to justify their own actions have taken the first step toward becoming what they claim to be fighting against. Gandhi and King showed the importance of maintaining the high moral ground, that nonviolent direct action, not passivity, can expose the corruption of the oppressor and force change."

Everyone but Tommy gave Wynn a round of applause.

Emily tried to steer the conversation back to her initial point. "No one has said anything about my suggestion that we'd be better off spending our time creating our own economy, a green economy, you know, the '60s idea about building a new society within the shell of the old. For most people, their first priority is providing a decent life for their own family," she observed. "They distrust all politicians and reformers of whatever color and persuasion. Including anarchists. They don't believe in any of the promises. They want to focus on what they can control.

"If we can show them a way to put food on the table while protecting the environment, they're all for it. And rather than waiting around for crumbs from the government or corporate elite or whatever you want to call the ruling class, you're moving ahead to build the type of world you believe in," Emily added.

Pete said, "I agree with much of what Emily's been sayin', but she hasn't mentioned the big problem — we don't have fair economic competition. The wealthy control most of the resources and they use the government to make sure it continues that way. They pass laws to keep new ideas from challengin' them."

Rachel had the last word. "Well, this has been a lively conversation as usual, but us old-timers need to be getting home. Tommy, we'll talk more tomorrow. This is why I call myself a political schizophrenic. All of your approaches make sense, but all have the odds heavily stacked against them. Since none are likely to succeed, I believe in trying all of 'em at the same time, in the hope that one will be successful. I assume if any of us win, I can dance at the victory party. Good night everyone."

SIXTEEN

GREEN PARTY CONVENTION 2000

Greens view elections as a necessity, and work toward a system of shared, rotated power. We seek the best person to stand for office and eschew the "winner take all" model of egocentric leaderism. We do not seek to take power, but to end it as it is. We run for office to offer true alternatives to the entire status quo. We base our actions on ideals and ethics and the needs of our constituents. The work matters, not the candidate.

Though the Green Party had existed in the US since the early 80s, Frost's 1996 presidential campaign was the first time that most Americans had heard about the Greens. Unfortunately, his one percent vote total showed that most Americans still had not heard about them. Frost was gearing up for another run in 2000.

The Green Party was an international movement, existing in more than eighty countries and in the state or national parliament of several dozen. The Greens were always a minority party, garnering between five to ten percent of the vote in major elections. However, since all of the word's democracies outside of the US, Canada, England and France used a proportional representation system that allocated seats based on vote totals, the Greens were able to win seats in the national parliaments in Europe and a few South American countries. Greens had managed to secure several cabinet positions as part of coalition governments in Europe.

"The Greens see ourselves as the antiparty. Electoral politics is just one among many strategies. When the Greens started in West Germany, their real base was in popular protest and mass movements. Marches and civil disobedience were the hallmarks of their early years," Wynn would say.

Despite little media attention, the Greens had grown slowly but steadily since it first sprouted in the US. Wynn had emerged as one of the lead Green organizers in Seattle. He spoke at colleges, union halls and community centers about Green philosophy. "The Greens are centered in ecology, on the need to save the planet because there's no replacement. Our other core values are grassroots democracy, nonviolence, and social and economic justice."

The Greens' commitment to grassroots democracy started within its own organization, with a passion for individual responsibility and decentralization rather than leaders at the top. It was a party of free thinkers. If there were five Greens in a room, there were an equal number of perspectives about what it meant to be a Green.

Frost's 1996 race hadn't ended the debate within the Greens about the balance between high- profile national and state-level elections, and the need to run local candidates for town and city offices, school boards and water commissioners.

The debate over elections versus activism also continued. Some felt, "It's time for the Greens to get serious about elections, to focus more on running candidates that are able to attract a significant vote, to win." Others were concerned that "Green politicians want to take control, weakening our positions on issues to be more attractive to voters."

"We need to ensure that our roots are planted deep, that our growth and survival are not dependent on any one person or event. Think globally, act locally," Wynn often said at state Green meetings. "The presidential election is what educates most people about the green agenda, helps recruit new volunteers. Local elections and organizing are where we begin to make a difference."

In addition to local victories in nonpartisan races, the Greens had managed to elect one Green to the California State Assembly. A handful of communities had a majority of elected Greens.

Clinton's track record over eight years had alienated many progressives from the Democratic Party. Frost and the Greens entered the 2000 election with a much larger base than four years before.

"Clinton's efforts to make the Democrats more business-friendly on issues such as Free Trade, welfare and corporate handouts has further eroded the small differences between the two major parties," Frost said in announcing his candidacy.

"The growing movement against corporate globalization, highlighted by the Seattle protests against the WTO, show that many Americans want a different path than that offered by the two major parties. Polls also show that a majority of Americans want a third party."

Frost promised Wynn and other green organizers that the 2000 presidential campaign would be different. "I'm going to hire staff and we'll work closely with Greens at the national and local levels. I've set a goal of raising five million dollars, including federal primary matching funds. We want to get on the ballot in all 50 states, rather than the two dozen we made last time." While he still felt it made sense for him to speak out on the issues he knew best, Frost acknowledged the need to incorporate more of the Green Party platform into his campaign.

In the 2000 election, it was Frost's turn to complain about the lack of fundraising and coordination by the Green Party. Many Greens had an aversion to asking for money. Quite a few opposed the idea of paid organizers, arguing that the Greens should rely on volunteers. "Once you hire someone, power begins to flow in their direction. You start creating divisions between paid staff and everyone else."

"Working for social change is an honorable profession," Wynn said in supporting the hiring of staff. "If you don't allow people to make a living doing it, you end up with the group dominated either by people who are personally wealthy or who have a lifestyle that doesn't require much money."

Many Greens also spent too much time arguing with one another over e-mail rather than going doorknocking to recruit new supporters. "Greens suffer from the problem of fixating on the five percent of the issues where there is some disagreement, rather than mobilizing around the ninety-five percent we all agree on," Wynn lamented to Rachel.

During the winter of 1999, Frost tried to talk Wynn into moving back to DC to help coordinate the national campaign. Wynn didn't even bother broaching this with Rachel. He did agree, however, to help coordinate Frost's effort in the West, particularly ballot petitioning. Rachel agreed to serve as one of the presidential electors on the Green ticket in the State of Washington, and to help mobilize her contacts in the environmental, women's and healthcare movements.

The Green presidential 2000 primary was little more than a pro forma exercise, a tad disappointing for a political party that preached grassroots democracy. Primaries made some Greens uneasy, as if allowing the party members to choose among competing candidates reflected a lack of party discipline and coordination.

Besides Frost, three other candidates sought the Green Party nomination, wanting to highlight issues they thought the public and Greens should pay more attention to.

The challenger who campaigned the hardest was Dr. Joseph Lewis, an award-winning author, activist and professor. Lewis argued, "The Greens need to sharpen their analysis of class issues, starting with the inherent faults of a capitalist system dedicated to making a few people wealthy, at the expense of the environment among other things."

Lewis withdrew after the California primary, citing the unwillingness of many Green leaders to give him equal time with Frost at campaign forums. "The Greens want pep rallies, not public debates," he told

Wynn.

The challenger who got the most media attention was Jello Biafra, the former lead singer of the punk rock group the Dead Kennedys. Now a spoken word performer, he energized the young, radical base of the party.

In states where the Greens didn't have official ballot status, it needed to collect anywhere from a few hundred to tens of thousands of signatures to get the Green presidential ticket on the fall ballot. Petitioning was the major focus of the Frost campaign during the spring and summer, hiring organizers across the country to help local Greens collect signatures. For the first time the Greens got on the ballot in every state.

The Green nominating convention was held in Denver in early August. With the end of the primary, the public matching funds for the Frost campaign also ended.

To qualify for matching funds during a primary, a candidate has to raise 5,000 dollars in each of twenty states. The maximum individual contribution was 1,000 dollars and only the first 250 from any one individual counted toward the 5,000 threshold. Once a candidate qualified, the federal government would match individual contributions up to 250 dollars during the primary. This was the only public campaign financing that would be available to Frost.

"How come the Democrats and Republicans get eighty million dollars for the general election and convention and we get nothing?" Rachel asked Wynn.

"It's democracy, American-style," Wynn responded. "For a party to qualify for public funding for the fall, its presidential candidate must have received at least 5 percent of the vote in the last election. But not only do the two major parties get all these public funds, there is this big loophole that allows them to raise additional funds for party and independent expenditures, so the corporate bidding continues unabated. That subverts the whole point of public funding, which was to reduce the influence of special interests in the presidential election."

****

The selection of a vice-presidential running mate was the main decision facing the convention. Frost had wanted his 1996 running mate to run again but she declined, citing the need to spend more time with her family.

"We should run the candidate with the highest name recognition, even if they're more moderate than most Greens, to generate media coverage, funding and resources," said the realo faction. The fundis wanted to run "a Green Party activist, even if they're unknown to the general public, to ensure the Green message and organization are highlighted."

A few wanted to run a symbolic candidate, such as death row prisoner and activist Mumia Abu-Jamal or Native American activist Leonard Peltier. "What better way to show our opposition to the death penalty than running someone on death row who's been denied a fair trial due to racism?" they asked. "How about by running someone who can actually talk to voters?" was a frequent response.

Some proposed that the Greens field a team of "regional vice-president" candidates, having different VP candidates in various parts of the country to assist with public appearances. This would be legal since voters don't directly elect the president and vice-president — voters elect members of the Electoral College, who then elect the president.

As one of the few Greens known nationally for her work on healthcare and welfare reform, Rachel was asked to deliver a twenty-minute speech at the convention. Her name was also being floated as a vice-presidential candidate for the Northwest if the Greens adopted a regional approach. Rachel was ambivalent about running, but figured she could handle three months of making speeches in California, Oregon and Washington.

Rachel spent most of Friday, the first day of the convention, attending the various workshops and meetings. Since her speech would be midafternoon on Saturday, she decided to sleep in. Wynn got up early to do some politicking. Rachel spent a half hour pacing up and down in front of the mirror, rehearsing her speech, reminding herself to talk slower.

Wynn came back to the room shortly before eleven.

"Well, hello Ms. Vice-President. Don't you look beautiful? You without a doubt will be the sexiest vice-president in American history," Wynn said appreciatively.

"Be quiet," Rachel replied. "You're the one who got me into this. And I am not the vice-presidential candidate. I just agreed to be part of your rainbow of speakers to make it more interesting for the media. Just another speech, nothing more."

"Well, have fun with it. Fire them up. Just think about giving all those CEOs checking us out on C-SPAN a heart attack. Though your dress is giving me a heart attack. You know, I have always wanted to make love to the vice-president, or at least to the vice-presidential nominee, and if you're telling me that I won't have the opportunity after today, I better seize the opportunity while I can."

Wynn had draped his arms around Rachel's neck as she had practiced talking to the mirror, and slowly began to kiss her neck and ears. Rachel gently slapped his hand and told him to stop it. He didn't.

****

The Greens were running about an hour late. The floor manager made hand signals to the present speaker to wrap it up.

Pete introduced her. "I've known Rachel Moreno for two decades. I've seen her speak up for poor Mexican-Americans being sprayed with pesticides. I've seen her fight utility companies. I have seen her sitting in majestic redwood trees as the loggers fired up their chain saws. I've seen her on the front lines of the fight for universal healthcare, for real welfare reform, for renewable energy and for economic justice. She helped organize the WTO protests in Seattle. I give you Rachel Moreno, the next vice-president of the United States."

Rachel gave Pete a quick kiss on the cheek, and lowered the microphone to her level. The delegates continued to wander in and out of the room.

"What we're doing today is vital to the future of our planet. I want to salute you for caring about Mother Earth and for all you do to make our world a better place.

"I'm a Green because I believe that the people, not corporations, should rule. I believe in justice for all, not riches for a few. I'm a Green because I believe we should have the right to control what goes into our bodies. That our food should be free of pesticides. That we should be able to breathe clean air. That we should be able to drink water that hasn't been contaminated by toxins.

"The Democratic and Republican presidential candidates tell us that we live in the greatest country in the history of the planet, and if we just vote for them, the next four years will be even better. And it will be. For the rich, who will get even richer as the reward for their campaign contributions. The rest of us will work more hours and get deeper in debt and have less to say about what happens to our children and our communities. And we will continue to export our McDonald's and Pepsi and MTV and the next Britney Spears to the far corners of the planet.

"America is the richest country in the world. We are the dominant military and economic power in the world, yet one in every five of our children lives in poverty. We live in a country where we pay farmers not to grow food while tens of millions of Americans go hungry each night. We are losing family farmers every day, yet most of the government's agriculture subsidies go to the corporate-owned food factories.

"Now, I know that I'm not telling the Greens anything new, but maybe some of you listening on CSPAN may be hearing this for the first time. Don't take my word for it, find out for yourself. Find out why the US has the greatest income disparity of any industrialized democracy in the world. Find out why the US is the only industrialized country without a universal healthcare program or one of only two such countries without childcare for all. Find out why Wall Street knows that the best investment they can make is a campaign contribution, as politicians return the favor with sweetheart contracts and tax loopholes.

"The Democrats and Republicans — the Republocrats — have put a For Sale sign on Mother Earth. There is nothing sacred that the political parties and their corporate masters won't carve up, chew up, and spit out if the price is right. They treat human beings as just another commodity to exploit.

"The rest of the planet's living things don't even count, of course. We're in the midst of the sixth great wave of species extinction since life started on this planet billions of years ago. Unlike the first five great die-offs, human beings caused this one. And it's getting worse.

"I could stand here for hours and tell you about everything that is wrong. About how the corporations rule the world, how billions of human beings on this planet are denied basic rights to food, to clean water, to an education, to housing, to be free from violence and the threat of war or murder. I could talk about how we oppress women and people of color and third world countries and workers of all colors and stripes and nationalities.

"I want instead to talk about how the Green Party and Barry Frost want to build a different world, a better world.

"We need a peace budget, not a military budget. We need a human budget, not a corporate budget. We need to make decisions based on ensuring that we leave a better world to our children's children's children, rather than on maximizing short-term profits for a few powerful corporations. We need to ensure that all have enough so that all of us can thrive, can reach our full potential.

"If we want to, *truly* want to, we can make sure that everyone has enough to eat. All too often, crime, violence and war are born not so much out of greed or evil but out of desperation of watching your families starve and die while a few grow fat.

"Building a better world is not going to be easy. To realize America's potential, we have to reclaim democracy. The corporations — and the politicians they buy — do not want to give up their power and privileges and mansions. But it's time for us to say: enough is enough.

"I am a single mother who had to struggle to bring up my son. I got help from the welfare system when I needed it most. Welfare put food on my table. It allowed me to go to school to become a nurse, so I could provide for my son while helping to take care of others. I want to make sure that all Americans get the opportunity to succeed.

"Vote for Barry Frost. Vote Green."

The audience applauded at all the right moments, and gave Rachel a standing ovation when she finished. The floor manager smiled at her since she went only two minutes over her allotted time.

****

Wynn stood at the back waiting till she finished. When she reached the end of the aisle, he gave her a big hug. "Hey, you were great. Nice job," he said. "Do you have a few minutes? Barry would like to talk to you."

Rachel had met Frost a few times, most recently at the WTO protests, but didn't have a close relationship with him like Wynn did. Frost was in his late sixties, though he had the energy of a much younger man. He was reserved, with occasional glimpses of a wry sense of humor.

Frost was on the phone as they came in. Everyone else left the room except his campaign manager, Elizabeth Appleton, a young public interest attorney who had run the West Coast office of one his public interest groups.

"Rachel, great speech. You certainly know how to work a crowd, and the TV cameras like you," Barry remarked. "I'd be curious about what advice you would offer my campaign."

Rachel hesitated. "Wynn is much more of the campaign strategist than I am, and he knows a whole lot more about what you're already doing. I'd only be able to offer general ideas."

Frost leaned back in his chair. "Go ahead. I won't hold anything against you. Just give me your general impressions. It's helpful to hear from people who have a little distance from the situation."

"It depends on what you want to accomplish," Rachel replied. "If you want to maximize your vote, I'd go after constituencies that feel alienated from both parties, look for issues where the two major parties have the same position. One target is poor people, especially people of color and women. Neither party is going to address the fact that two million Americans are in jail, primarily people of color. I'd go after the war on drugs, it makes no sense. I would go after people who are worried about their economic future, who see Wall Street booming but yet can't keep their heads above water. I'd go into states where one of the candidates is a clear winner, because that frees people to vote for you."

Rachel was getting warmed up now. "I would of course play to your strengths, the anticorporate, antiglobalization movements. They understand Clinton and the Democrats have sold them out. You're never going to get the media coverage or money you need or deserve, so you have to mobilize your base to do the outreach for you. The Greens need to spend a whole lot more time focusing on getting their voters out on election day. That's one thing the major parties do much better than we do."

"Any ideas about how to beat the media blockade?" asked Elizabeth. She had on a no-nonsense business suit, with her blond hair tightly pulled back into a bun.

"I think you need a more aggressive media strategy than Barry had last time," Rachel said. "You need someone whose job is to get you into that day's new cycle for the presidential race. If a news story pops up, you have to respond immediately, even if it's something you don't know intimately. Trust your instincts, or find people who you trust. If the news story is whether or not to send a little Cuban boy home to be with his dad, speak out on it."

Elizabeth nodded as Rachel spoke. She'd been making the same arguments with Frost.

"Offer a positive vision for the future. People don't vote for the negative," she added.

Frost laughed. "Well, that certainly was comprehensive," he noted. They talked for a while about some of her specific suggestions.

"Rachel, I always tell the Greens that an election is a collective effort," Frost said in summation. "I'm just one voice among many, albeit the loudest one, in promoting the Green Party. I prefer doing what I do best, and let others do what they do best. I think you have better instincts as a candidate than I do. A lot of people have talked to me about you in the last few weeks, starting with Pete and Wynn. When I've run your name by other people, I've gotten overwhelmingly positive feedback.

"Rachel, I'd like you to run with me for vice-president. Nationally, not regionally. You bring several strengths to the ticket that I don't have, particularly on women's issues and with community groups. Plus you're on the West Coast, where much of the Green base is concentrated."

Rachel didn't know how to respond. "Well, Barry, I'm flattered, I truly am, but isn't there someone who's more qualified? Someone who's been more active with the Greens or has a bigger name? No one knows me. And I haven't run for office before. I don't think I'd be very good at it."

"Rachel, it would be nice to have someone with instant name recognition," Frost answered. "But usually those folks aren't willing to put themselves on the line, especially for an uphill cause. But you've been putting yourself on the line all your life. And more people know you than you realize, especially among the activists we need to mobilize to work on this campaign.

"People will also respect you for being a nurse and for being a single mom who raised a family. You've also got Wynn, which is a big plus in my book. Hopefully with you running he'll spend more time thinking of crazy things for you to do rather than me," Frost chuckled.

"Voters don't pay attention to academics who've been locked up in an ivory tower. They like people who've been out doing real things, helping real people. This campaign is also going to be hard pressed to raise money. With you on board, Pete is convinced we can get some considerable support from his network of young, progressive business people who support the type of things Green America has been doing, who want to build a green, clean economy, with windmills rather than oil rigs," Frost added.

Wynn broke in. "Rachel, it'll be a lotta work, but it'll be fun too. All those speeches you've been practicing on me, now you can deliver them to a national audience. You're always telling me you're tired of politicians from both major parties attacking welfare participants for being parasites and lazy. Well, here's a platform to fight back. You were willing to consider being one of the regional candidates, so this isn't a whole lot different. I'd give you the speech about how the country needs you, 'cept you'd probably throw one of your shoes at me. But it's true. We need to wake people up, and you're a great person to do that.

Besides, it's only three months till November. It'll be over before ya know it."

Rachel fixed Wynn with one of her famous stares. "So, Mr. Harris, exactly when did you know this deal was on the table?"

"Rachel, this came together really fast," Frost said. "I asked Wynn to let me talk to you myself, so blame me, not him. Rachel, I don't want to pressure you, but the nomination takes place tomorrow. The VP slot is yours if you want it. If you want some time to think about it, I can wait a couple of hours."

Rachel continued to stare at Wynn, then turned back to Frost. "So Wynn does what I tell him to do, that's part of the deal?"

"I agree to that," Frost said with a laugh. "Absolutely. Whether you can enforce it, that's another story."

****

Rachel knew that a vice-presidential campaign, even for a third party, would be time consuming and intense. She just couldn't believe how time consuming. Election campaigns have a surreal sense of time; it seemed that every second counted. Every task, every event, every person always seemed to want more of her time. Having a few minutes to herself became an incredible luxury.

For the first few weeks, she felt like she had no control. She demanded a time out. She got Wynn, Elizabeth and Frost on the line together. "This isn't working. It's too chaotic. We need some ground rules, starting with you, Wynn. If you want to talk about the campaign every moment we're together, then move out and I'll see you after election day. I need to establish some free times during the day when I can talk to friends, to Tommy, get some exercise, no campaign phone calls.

"Second," Rachel continued, "I need a campaign manager or assistant other than Wynn to manage traffic control. Someone who's going to stay in a fixed place who I can get a hold of when I need to, like explaining to me why I'm suddenly going to Eugene rather than Sacramento. I also need to blow off steam at someone occasionally and it's not healthy for that to be your significant other. And since everything in this campaign seems to be crisis, we need to start distinguishing between the routine crisis and the real crisis. Folks, this isn't life and death here. Well, okay, it is, but let's pretend it's not, since no matter how hard we work, we won't be moving into the White

House. I'd like to have at least a few of you still be my friends after election day. Remember, my contract said this was going to be fun."

"Where does it say that?" Elizabeth interjected. "That certainly didn't cross my desk."

Rachel's campaign seemed to find its pace after her outburst. Once they realized that they couldn't accomplish the impossible every day and settled for the improbable, everyone loosened up a bit — except for Wynn. Rachel resorted for her old standby to relax Wynn — sex.

****

The radio station was owned by one of those media companies that operate six radio stations simultaneously, both FM and AM, offering programmed progressive rock, top 40, country & western, and news-talk. There was a row of small booths in the back where the DJs operated. Most of the office space was devoted to the sales force. The present and future of corporate media ownership.

"This is WKVX, San Diego, the voice of Southern California. I'm David Sinclair and with me is Rachel Moreno, the vice-presidential candidate of the Green Party. She's running with longtime consumer advocate Barry Frost. Ms. Moreno is a nurse and public policy coordinator for Green America. She is a longtime advocate for universal healthcare. Rachel, could you give our listening audience a brief overview of the Green Party and why you're running? Are the Greens a new party?"

"Thank you, Dave. The Greens have been active in the US for sixteen years, and are committed to ecology, social and economic justice, grassroots democracy and nonviolence. Unlike the Democrats or Republicans, Greens advocate the concept of sustainable development. We can't continue to use up our planet's resources faster than the earth can replenish them," Rachel explained.

"This means we need to move from an energy program based on fossil fuels and nuclear power to one based on energy conservation, efficiency and renewable energy sources, like solar, wind, biomass. It means moving away from a centralized agriculture system dominated by corporate farms that heavily rely on pesticides, chemical fertilizers, and heavily subsidized energy and water use to one that is localized, organic and sustainable.

"We need to stop the sprawl that paves over our farmlands and open space, and forces us to spend hours each day driving cars that poison our air. We need to invest in rebuilding, or greening, our cities to make them more livable places." Rachel was learning how to squeeze as much as she could into the few minutes of airtime she got.

"So the Greens are an environmental party? Are you one of the groups that want to save the spotted owl or the darter snail, regardless of the cost or the number of jobs involved?" Dave asked.

"The argument that we have to choose between the environment and jobs is a false one," Rachel remarked. "We have to choose both. The Greens believe every American should have a right to a living wage job, that those who work hard and contribute to the well-being of their community should be able to provide a decent life for their families. We support the right to universal healthcare and childcare, decent housing and a good education, including college.

"To do this," Rachel pointed out, "we have to change our economy from one that maximizes the profits of the few to one focused on improving the quality of life for all. That won't happen until we reclaim our democracy. We can't elect our government based on which candidate is able to raise the most amount of money from wealthy individuals and large corporations. We need campaign finance reform, including public campaign financing to end the system of legalized bribery we call campaign contributions.

"America may have been the modern birthplace of democracy but we're fooling ourselves if we believe that we're the leading example of democracy in the world today. Over the last two centuries, the rest of the world has improved upon our system. For instance, most democracies now use proportional representation, where you elect your government based on the percentage of the vote each party gets. This creates legislative bodies or city councils that reflect the diversity of viewpoints among the voters.

"We're one of the few countries left that uses the old winner-takes-all system, which, combined with our system of campaign contributions, results in a political system dominated by two centrist parties that offer voters sound bites, while gerrymandering voting districts at the state and local levels and offering their services to the highest bidder."

"Interesting, to say the least," Dave remarked, looking for a commercial he could play early. "Rachel, with all due respect, you sound quite leftist. You attack the corporations at every chance, you want free this and free that, all paid for by our tax dollars I presume. Are you and the Greens socialists?"

"Dave, throughout my life I've found that when opponents don't know how to respond to your arguments, they call you a socialist. When I lived in a poor Mexican-American neighborhood in Arizona and we stood up to say that we didn't want to be sprayed with pesticides that made us sick, we were called socialists. When I fought to make healthcare a right, I was called a socialist," Rachel said.

"If what you're asking is I whether I support a Soviet-style bureaucracy that mismanages the economy to reward political cronies, pays no attention to the environment, and denies basic democratic and human rights to its citizens, then no, I'm not a socialist.

"Of course the main difference between the US and the old Soviet Union is that American politicians allow CEOs to mismanage the economy rather than doing it directly. The US has crony capitalism, with the powerful using their control of the political and economic system to help their supporters amass great wealth," Rachel explained.

"The Greens oppose allowing a few to profit from the labors of the many, while companies are free to pollute the environment. The Greens want a political and economic system that seeks to help every American, that gives everyone an opportunity to realize their potential, that lends a helping hand to those less fortunate or unable to take care of themselves, and which safeguards Mother Earth," Rachel concluded. She took a sip of water. Wynn gave her a thumbs up. This was fun.

The switchboard was lighting up. Dave decided to give this a few more minutes. Anything for ratings. Controversy attracts listeners.

"Let's go to the phone lines. Our first caller is Ralph, from Escondido. Ralph, how are you today?" Dave asked.

"I'm fine, thank you," Ralph responded. "Dave, I want to thank you for having Ms. Moreno on. I agree with a lot of what she has to say. But I'm concerned that she and Mr. Frost will just end up getting the Republicans elected. The Democrats certainly have their problems, but they're much closer to the Greens on many of the issues than the Republicans. Ms. Moreno, won't you just be a spoiler? Why don't you get out of the race and support the Democrats, maybe in exchange for them agreeing to support your healthcare proposals?"

"I'd like to thank Ralph for agreeing with the Green agenda," Rachel responded. "I just hope he has the courage to vote for his beliefs rather than his fears. There are a couple of points I'd like to make about the spoiler argument. One, there's ultimately little difference between the Democrats and Republicans. Both are certainly closer to each other than they are to the Greens.

"Second, we don't vote for a president, we vote for something called the Electoral College, who then elects the president. In most places, such as California, it's clear ahead of time which candidate is going to win the state. So your vote for president doesn't really count, since the winner in your state get gets all the Electoral College delegates whether they win by 1 vote or 1 million. We know the Democratic presidential candidate is going to easily win California. So people like Ralph are free to vote for whom they want for president without worrying about being a spoiler."

Ralph took offense to the suggestion that there was no difference between the parties. "What about abortion, the environment, labor, the Supreme Court?" he sputtered in disbelief.

"You left out women and the poor, the other issues people usually cite as differences," Rachel pointed out. "What we see is that the actions taken by Democrats when they are in office are much more similar to the Republican positions than their campaign rhetoric would lead you to believe.

"While we could argue each issue for the rest of the day, both major parties agree that corporations should be given free reign to manage the economy to maximize their profits. Both parties believe that economic growth, as defined by the corporations, is essential to our future prosperity, and that American foreign policy should focus on promoting our economic needs — which the two parties believe are the same as the needs of the multinational corporations. And both parties are financed by the same corporate interests. The Republicans may get more money from the religious right and the Democrats more from the unions, but the corporations give to both."

Rachel was hitting her stride. Dave was looking to cut the interview short, as the station manager was peering into the booth with a big frown.

The next caller agreed with Ralph. "You're understating the differences between the two parties. I mean, it's the Republicans in Congress who always blocks the Democrats from raising the minimum wage," Alexis from Mission Bay argued. "And the Democrats support things like affordable housing and child care that the Republicans don't care about."

"Sure, there are some differences between the two parties when it comes to how to implement this agenda and what type of safety net or protections the rest of us should have while the wealthy get even wealthier. But under Bill Clinton, those differences have gotten even smaller. Clinton felt free to harm the environment to pay back all his corporate campaign contributors. It was Clinton who campaigned to end welfare as we knew it," she added.

"The Supreme Court is the Democrats' favorite bogeyman. They scare liberals by arguing that a Republican victory would result in Roe v. Wade being overturned. Well, look at Clinton's record on Supreme Court nominations. The most recent liberal member came from Bush, not Clinton. The Democrats tend to nominate candidates they think Republicans conservatives like Strom Thurmond and Orrin Hatch won't kill. Republicans nominate people they believe in. History has also shown that, once on the Supreme Court, justices often move in different directions than initially predicted," Rachel stated.

"Both parties feel free to ignore the interests of the poor, of children, the environment and of labor, because they assume that these groups will always vote for the Democrat no matter what happens. The Greens believe it's better to vote for what you want, so that eventually you might get it. If you vote for the lesser of two evils, you guarantee that evil wins," Rachel noted.

Dave was signaling it was time to wrap up.

"Just a last point on the Electoral College. A lot of people dismiss it as a technicality. Some day an election will be decided by the Electoral College, and people will wake up to what it is and they won't be happy. For instance, if the Greens were ever to win more votes than the other two parties, but less than a majority, the Democrats and Republicans would gang up in the Electoral College and elect someone else. A legal coup d'etat."

"Thank you, Ms. Moreno," Dave said in relief.

"Thank you, Dave. Vote Green and free yourself. Help overgrow the government."

****

The Green Party's campaign was not one of private jets ferrying around staff and media contingents. Though the media ignored largely ignored the Green campaign, Frost was turning out large crowds across the country, mobilizing a broad spectrum of activists, from young antiglobalization activists to senior citizens. Rachel, with less name recognition, initially was speaking to events of less than a hundred.

The first few weeks of campaign appearances were often lonely for Rachel. It got better once Wynn began to travel with her after they hired an assistant.

Wynn worked with local Green organizers to get larger audiences for Rachel. "We need five or six things for Rachel to do to justify the time and expense of getting her to your town. Look for preexisting audiences, such as schools, senior citizen lunches and conferences. Act like the Greens are important when you ask to speak," Wynn implored them.

"Sound excited. Get us into some black churches. Bring Rachel to places where the Greens don't normally go. If a group has an issue they're fighting for — cleaning up a toxic site, stopping a new Wal-Mart, establishing a civilian police review board — Rachel will be happy to hold a news conference or walk a picket line with them."

Pete convinced his old friend Ronnie Faith to bring Rachel out on stage on her concert tour. Ronnie had long used her shows to promote her favorite political causes, particularly the environment. Two years ago she had supported Sarah London, the redwood forest activist, in her successful run for Congress. Now Rachel was getting at least a few minutes to give a short speech to anywhere from 5,000 to 15,000 people. Ronnie would give her a rousing introduction. "We need to stand up for the environment. I want you to meet a great fighter for mother earth!"

Wynn worked on organizing some of the Seattle-based grunge bands to support Frost and Rachel, as well as organizing Rappers for the Greens to help in communities of color. Like all musicians, rappers spoke from the reality of their life experience, and for many of them, that included poverty and oppression. Several well-known music groups responded to the Greens' anticorporate message. This helped give the party a lot of credibility in minority communities and among young voters.

Frost got musicians, like the lead singer from Pearl Jam, to perform at "super rallies" in a dozen key cities. These events each pulled in more than 10,000 participants, who paid a piece to pay for the cost of renting the hall. The campaign then passed the hat to raise more funds. Tommy, who'd been doing a lot of speaking at college campuses and with local Green groups, was all too happy to volunteer to help with the super rallies, assisting backstage with logistics, hanging out with the celebrities.

Tommy even managed to convince them to allow him to introduce his mom, telling the crowd, "I've known Rachel all my life." Rachel accused him of playing fast and loose with the facts. "You make it sound like you grew up in a John Steinback novel."

Rachel's big media break came at a small music festival outside of

Santa Fe shortly after Labor Day. She'd just finished a speech to several hundred people when there was an announcement for a doctor to come to the first aid tent. A woman had gone into labor a month early and was too far along to get her to a hospital in time.

Rachel calmed everyone down, starting with the mother. "Relax, I've helped deliver hundreds of babies. Everything looks normal. Focus on your breathing and I'll tell you when to push." It was the woman's third child. The delivery went fine — a healthy eight-pound girl.

A photographer snapped a picture of Rachel, the parents and the infant just before they climbed into an ambulance. It was picked up by one of the wire services and appeared in newspapers across the country, "VP Candidate Delivers Baby."

The late-night talk show hosts used it for a couple of jokes. "It's not enough anymore to kiss the babies on the campaign trail, now you have to deliver them." Both Letterman and Leno invited her to appear on their shows, followed by Oprah, where she did an hour about midwifery, birthing and problems with healthcare.

Rachel's sudden surge in media exposure got her into the televised vice-presidential debate.

The major parties had excluded Frost from the first two presidential debates. Several thousand Green supporters had protested outside the first debate. When Frost showed up with a ticket at the second debate, saying, "I just want to listen from the audience," he was threatened with arrest.

The heavy-handed tactics employed to exclude him, combined with the dreary performance by the two major party candidates, led to several of the late night pundits to declare Frost the winner.

The late night talk show hosts took up Rachel's cause to get into the debate. David Letterman had Rachel come back on his show to read a top ten list of why she should be included in the upcoming VP debate, starting with, "I promise not to mention the lock box." The lock box was the favorite line in the first two debates of Harrington, the Democratic presidential candidate, in explaining that he would not touch surplus Medicare Trust funds to "pay for pork barrel spending or tax cuts." The lock box had become a staple of the *Saturday Night* tv comedy skits.

Her debate opponents made the mistake of patronizing her, viewing her inclusion as a novelty act due to her role in delivering a baby.

She coolly asked, "Do you find my participation humorous because I'm a woman, or because I have a political message that is not dictated by campaign contributions and polling? The two major parties seem to have no problem sending our sons and daughters to die on foreign soil in the name of democracy, but the thought of democracy breaking out in our own country scares you to death. Your exclusion of Frost and Buchanan from the presidential debates is shameful. Tell me, were the two of you asleep during civics lessons in school?"

When her Democratic opponent responded, "Madame, I can assure you that my political positions are not dictated by campaign contributions," Rachel icily responded, "I'd like to see some proof of that. Let me read you a list of the ten largest corporate contributors to the Democratic Party in recent years, along with an example of tax breaks or government contracts each received worth far more than they contributed. We'd all love to hear your explanation as to what prompted each of these corporations to finance your party. I have a Republican list as well."

Having put her two opponents on the defensive, Rachel ignored them during the second half and talked directly to the American public. "As a mother, I know how difficult it is to raise children today. Too many of our children are denied the opportunity to achieve their full potential. I ask my opponents tonight to put politics aside for once and join me in pledging to make a better world for our children, to pledge that no child goes to bed hungry, that every child will have a decent roof over their head, and that no child will be denied quality healthcare or a quality education."

Many of the news reports afterwards described her as the debate winner. Some asked, "Why isn't Ms. Moreno running for president, since she has delivered the best performance in the debates of any of the candidates?"

****

Since Frost initially felt uncomfortable addressing racism, Rachel became the point person on the issue.

"The Greens need to diversify our base," Wynn argued with Frost. "If we want to mobilize people of color, you've got to speak out on race issues. And it's not just overt racism like police brutality. We have to confront the reality that blacks are still discriminated against in everything from the economy to housing to education."

Frost was concerned that the more he spoke on issues that appealed to particular constituencies — racism, gay rights, abortion, or the Israel-

Palestine conflict — the more his central message of challenging corporate power would get diluted.

"I don't want to just wave around the normal list of leftist causes. The left already know they should vote for the Greens. I believe these other issues could be resolved if the average person was the one making the decisions rather than corporate and wealthy interests. That is the issue I want to focus on. Besides, the organized African-American and Hispanic groups are entrenched in the Democratic party," argued Frost.

Wynn responded, "African-Americans know that the ruling class systematically oppresses and exploits them. They're already headed in our direction. They just need to hear the Greens speaking out about their issues. Even more important, they need to see the Greens working in their communities, not just looking for votes at election time. Sure, the Democrats buy off some of the leaders, but that's true of the leadership in any community. If the Greens help win more funds for affordable housing, after-school programs, childcare and jobs in inner cities, we'll pick up some of their votes."

Both Rachel and Frost agreed to schedule more campaign events in black and Hispanic neighborhoods. Frost focused on environmental justice issues, the fact that factories that pour out toxic wastes into the air or water are far more likely to be located in poor, minority neighborhoods. He extended his arguments for increased democracy to include community control over the police.

Rachel's spoke out against police brutality. She met with the mother of Amadou Diallo, the hard-working immigrant from Guinea who was killed in the Bronx by four police officers. They pumped 41 shots into him as he reached for his wallet while standing in the entrance to his apartment building.

Rachel also spoke out against racial profiling where mostly young black males are targeted on the ground that they fit the profile of those likely to commit certain crimes such as drug offenses. She often led crowds in chanting, "No Justice No Peace."

"All Americans have the right to feel secure in our homes and neighborhood," Rachel told reporters. "We understand that police have a hard job. But we need them to work with the community, not against it. The police need to look more like the communities they're supposed to be protecting. All too often people are arrested and even killed not because of what they did but because of the color of their skin.

"True criminal justice reform," she went on, "means confronting and changing the social, political and economic systems that result in such a high rate of incarceration among the poor and individuals of color. We need to invest in job creation and education, not in building more jails. It costs the taxpayers far more money to put someone in prison than it does to provide them with a quality college education.

"America has built a Gulag in its midst — an immense and growing prison-industrial complex to warehouse inner city youth discarded by the modern economy. A whole generation of young men is being thrown away because our society can't come up with a decent paying job for them," she added.

Rachel pointed out that more than three quarters of all inmates lack a high school diploma. Nationally, one third of all black men between the ages of 18 and 29 are in the criminal justice system.

Frost spoke out strongly against the war on drugs, joining with the Republican governor of New Mexico in calling for the "legalization of marijuana and for more funding for drug treatment and prevention rather than prisons." He noted that people of color were overwhelmingly the ones put in jail for drug offenses, even though most drug sellers and users were white.

He also spoke out against the growing privatization of the criminal justice system. "Prisons are just another way for corporate America to fleece the taxpayers."

Their opponents accused the Greens of coddling criminals. "People are in prison because they've done something wrong. The Greens blame the victims rather the criminals," said Prescott, the Republican nominee. "Our country's crime rate has dropped because we're locking up more career criminals for longer periods. I support federal legislation for mandatory long-term sentences for anyone with three criminal convictions."

The parties clashed most sharply over the death penalty. The Greens supported its abolition. Both the Democrats and Republicans wanted to expand it.

The death penalty was one of the media's questions during the vice-presidential debate.

"The death penalty undermines our deeply held belief in the sanctity of life," Rachel argued. "The death penalty is immoral. The death penalty *fails* to discourage murder and violence. The death penalty targets poor people and people of color. Almost all of the world's democracies banned the death penalty long ago. Centuries of capital punishment show that it is nothing more than legalized murder. The death penalty has been used to silence unpopular political, religious and racial minorities. The death penalty has executed far too many innocent people."

"The death penalty is about justice," said Senator Richard Pendingrass, the Democratic nominee from Illinois. "It's reserved only for the most heinous crimes. Victims and their loved ones have a right to punish those who have committed unspeakable crimes against them. Criminals also need to know that they will pay the ultimate penalty for certain acts."

"But it's been shown for years that the death penalty is *not* a deterrent to violent crime," Rachel responded. "An FBI study shows that states without the death penalty have *lower* murder rates. Texas is the leading user of the death penalty. From 1982, when it reinstituted the death penalty, to 1991, the Texas crime rate rose by 24 percent and the violent crime rate by 46 percent. In comparison, the national crime rate rose by only five percent during the same period."

Rachel argued that the administration of the death penalty was flawed, with innocent people being sentenced to death and people of color disproportionately given the death penalty.

"Since 1976, more than 80 people nationwide have been released from prison after being sentenced to death," Rachel noted. "Between 1900 and 1992, there were 416 documented cases of innocent persons convicted and given a death sentence; in 23 cases, the person was executed."

"We should definitely improve the administration of the death penalty," conceded Pendingrass, "but that doesn't mean we should stop using it. If we fail to stand up to murderers, and people end up being killed because we've taken away the deterrence of the death penalty, then we're responsible for the loss of innocent lives. And the American people have made it very clear that they support the death penalty."

Congressman Wilbert Lancaster of Virginia, the Republican nominee, added, "God supports support the death penalty: 'Whoever sheds the blood of man, by man shall his blood be shed: Genesis 9:6."

"Let me ask you, Ms. Moreno. If a family member of yours, say your son, was tortured and murdered, or if you had a daughter who was raped and killed, wouldn't you then want to see the death penalty. Be honest, now. What would your feelings be then?" Lancaster argued.

"Mr. Lancaster, who do you think I am, Michael Dukakis? Of course I would be furious. I'd want to hurt really badly whoever was guilty. But does my anger make it right? I mean, I'm angry right now because you used my love for my child for a cheap political stunt. I don't like to ever hear someone threaten a child."

That's not what I ... Lancaster tried to say.

Rachel kept on talking. It was her two minutes. "Would it be right if I went over there and slapped you? No, it wouldn't. It's always better to try to resolve differences through civil discussion rather than resorting to violence. That's why the death penalty is wrong. It sanctions the use of violence as punishment?"

"But don't people who kill and rape innocent people deserve punishment," Lancaster interjected.

"Punishment yes, accountability yes. But *how* we punish people says more about who we are as a society than anything else. That's why the Constitution outlawed cruel and unusual punishment. It's time to outlaw killing people for their crimes. We have to recognize that the death penalty has always been racist in this country. And some of us still believe in that old-fashioned concept of rehabilitation.

"Nationwide," she concluded, "African-Americans are 43 percent of the prisoners on death row, though they are only 12 percent of the US population. A person accused of killing a White person is 4.3 times more likely to receive the death sentence than an individual accused of killing a Black person."

"Ms. Moreno, you are just a liberal," Lancaster responded when she finished.

"Well, at least there's one thing we agree upon," she replied.

****

The last super rally filled Madison Square Garden two weeks before election day.

Wynn and Rachel flew in the night before. Wynn convinced Rachel to take a few hours for themselves. "I want to show you a sunset from the top of the Empire State Building. It was one of my favorite places to visit when I was growing up in Brooklyn."

The view of New York was breathtaking. The Empire State Building was no longer the tallest in the city — that honor belonging to the World Trade Center — but it still offered a 360-degree panorama of the New York skyline, looking out over the Hudson River, Central Park and the Brooklyn Bridge.

Wynn stopped at a florist on the ground floor to buy a dozen long-stemmed red roses for Rachel. "It's not every night you speak to a sold-out Madison Square Garden. I want something to mark the occasion."

"Well thank you, Wynn. You know, you can get me flowers anytime. It's even more romantic when there isn't a special occasion." She gave him a kiss.

The observation deck was crowded. Rachel pulled her coat tightly around her to ward off the cool October air. The lights of the city sparkled as the sun set. Several people recognized Rachel from her appearances on late night tv and wished her luck. Wynn maneuvered her over to the quietest corner.

Wynn pulled Rachel close and gave her a long kiss and hug. Suddenly he dropped to one knee and held her hand, taking out a small jewelry box. Rachel put her hand to her heart and almost dropped the flowers.

"Rachel, you've been the special person in my life since the moment I first saw you," Wynn told her. "There's no one who I love and respect more. Spending these last two months together listening to you talk about your hopes and dreams has reminded me how much I love you. I want to spend the rest of my life with you. I know that I should've asked you a longtime ago, but will you marry me?"

The crowd was watching. Several people turned on their video cameras.

"Mr. Harris, you've certainly taken your time," Rachel sputtered. "And if there weren't so many people watching, I'd probably ask you a few questions about what suddenly made you come to your senses. And there's a few changes in your behavior that I'd like to discuss. I love you very much. I would have said yes years ago, so yes, I will marry you." He slid the diamond ring on her finger.

Wynn and Rachel embraced as the crowd applauded.

SEVENTEEN

ELECTORAL COLLEGE

Rachel spent the final week of the 2000 campaign flying to rallies in San Francisco, LA, Portland, Eugene, San Diego, Phoenix, Santa Fe and Denver.

Rachel spent the last three days campaigning in Washington State. It was time to allow the volunteers to focus on the get-out-the-vote efforts, phone banking to mobilize their supporters. There was some discussion about doing a joint election night party with Frost in DC, but since it was unlikely that the national news would cover it, she and Wynn decided to stay home for the final push.

Washington was going to be their strongest state, with an outside chance that the presidential ticket could win in a tight three-way race. The protests in Seattle against the WTO had mobilized the progressive movement to join forces with the Green Party.

Ray McDaniels, the union leader and Green Party candidate for Congress in the Seattle area, was posting a ten point lead. Many progressives were also supporting a liberal woman Democratic candidate for US Senate. There was significant cooperation among the grassroots organizers of the three campaigns, much to the chagrin of state and national Democratic leaders.

In Washington, many of the local unions broke with the national AFL-CIO to support the Greens, providing much-needed volunteers and phone banks. Organizers for environmental and women's groups had also defied the national leadership and were mobilizing their membership for Frost and Rachel.

The national race was a toss-up between the two major party candidates. Frost had been hovering around five percent in the polls, but was moving up with the increased attention he was receiving in the closing weeks as the race tightened. Frost was helped by the widespread dissatisfaction with the two major party candidates.

Harrington, the Democratic candidate, had finally begun to pay attention to the Greens in the last two weeks. His attacks only energized Frost. "Harrington has spent his entire life in the board rooms of the privileged. He's paid for by the same corporations that finance the Republicans. When corporate America walks in the door, the only disagreement between Tweedledee and Tweedledum is over who gets to

The Unauthorized Biography of the first Green Party President   304

kiss their feet first."

Rachel and Wynn argued with Frost to spend his last few days in states like NY where the race wasn't close. "Barry, we have to focus on getting the 5 percent of the national vote the Greens need to qualify for public funding," Wynn told him. "That's our victory on election night. It's goin' to be tough. Support for third parties historically goes down in the last few days because we can't compete with our opponents' free and paid media coverage, and the lesser of two evils argument gets stronger. And in a lot of states, it's hard to find us on the ballot."

"But the media won't pay attention to me if I'm in New York, since the race isn't competitive there," Frost argued. "The media's going to be following Prescott and Harrington in the toss-up states. That's where we need to be if we want media. And media coverage in those states will reach far more voters than a couple of my speeches in safe states."

"You might get some extra media by going to the toss-up states," Wynn conceded, "but you're not going to pick up many votes there. If the media wants to give you twenty seconds on the national news, they can pick up footage from wherever you're campaigning.

"In places like New York, where Harrington is winning by 20 points, people feel much more free to vote for you," Wynn argued. "You can even argue in those states that a vote for Harrington is a wasted vote, since he ends up with the same number of electoral votes. However, a vote for you and Rachel counts towards the 5 percent nationally the Green Party needs to become a major party."

"And the people who come hear you are the ones who'll go out over the next few days and urge people to vote for us," Rachel reminded him.

Of the 50 separate state elections for the Electoral College, there were only a handful where the election was up for grabs, including Washington. The Democrats and Republicans crisscrossed the country in their private jets in the closing days, concentrating all their media buys there.

The Democrats had somehow managed to misplay a sound economy and an inept opponent into a cliffhanger. Clinton, his popularity still high despite his repeated personal scandals, had been locked up in DC. Harrington didn't want Clinton's sexual escapades rehashed by the press whenever he made a campaign appearance.

Frost belittled Benjamin Prescott III, the Republican nominee, as a "corporation disguised as a person. His only qualifications for office was that his uncle had been president and he's willing to take money to pitch any product a corporation wants to foist on the American people. There's never been a less qualified presidential candidate."

Tommy took responsibility to organize the election night celebration in Seattle. He promised to make it a night to remember, lining up several bands to perform. "While the Greens may not be able to win the White House, we can throw the best party. It's time to rock," he said.

Rachel crossed out a few of the bands, and reminded Tommy that this wasn't a rock concert — the decibel level would have to be manageable. "Don't worry, mom. We won't crank it up until after you go home."

****

Rachel and Wynn voted shortly before 9 am. They'd catch the tail end of the morning news shows out West while hoping for one last appearance on the noon newscasts back East.

A crowd of supporters greeted Rachel, handing her several bouquets of flowers. "For once, I get to vote for someone I believe in. Thanks for speaking up for all of us. You spoke to my own experience. I want to thank you for your courage. God bless you."

Rachel thanked them for their support and work, gave a lot of hugs, autographed a few campaign posters and began to cry. Rachel had been on an emotional roller coaster the last few days. She was proud of the effort that Frost and she had made, of the vision that the Greens had laid out. "I know we're going to lose," she told Emily. "But every once in a while I indulge in a moment of fantasy, imagining the wild celebration if the Greens were to win."

Rachel spent election day calling voters in McDaniels' district. The campaign had a list of likely supporters gathered through months of doorknocking and phone banking. It was time to remind them to vote and make sure they had a ride to the polls. Dozens of volunteers began calling voters shortly after 9 am, starting with the senior citizens who tended to vote early. Date of birth was one of the pieces of information included on voter lists.

Several voters were stunned to hear Rachel's on the other end of the line. A few hung up, saying, "I hate getting theses prerecorded messages." Rachel and Wynn focused on calling the voters listed as undecided. Rachel also did interviews on radio stations throughout the state, making last-minute appeals.

Rachel felt liberated, giddy. The election was almost over. Her political instincts sharpened by months of campaigning, she showed no mercy to the talk show hosts who tried to debate her. Wynn kept motioning to her to tone down her comments. She turned away from him. The volunteers in the campaign office loved it, repeatedly breaking out in applause.

The election night party was in a performance art space in downtown Seattle. A room had been set aside upstairs for Rachel, Wynn, Ray and the other campaign organizers to track the election results. McDaniels was headed for a big win in his Congressional district and had been accepting congratulatory phone calls since shortly after the polls closed.

A stage was set up at one end for the bands. The place was already packed with mainly young supporters shortly after the polls closed. The election returns had been coming in for several hours from the East Coast. "It looks like we'll easily break the 5 percent threshold," Wynn told her. "We might even hit double digits."

Most of the crowd wanted to focus on partying after a long campaign, celebrating McDaniel's victory. Rachel went up to him and flung herself into his arms, giving him a big hug and kiss that nearly bowled him over. "Congratulations Ray. You ran a helluva campaign. You're going to make a great congressman. Go to DC and give 'em hell."

"Thanks, Rachel," Ray replied, trying to regain his breath. "It's too bad you and Barry won't be there in the White House. I wouldn't have won without you guys. Heck, you might even carry the state. It's unbelievable how much support you have out there. You made the Greens real to people, put us on the map."

"That's kind of you to say, Ray," giving him another hug. "But I'm really glad it's you and not me going to DC. I'm not cut out for all the wheeling and dealing, the compromises, that go with holding office. Even though I knew we weren't going to win, there were still times when I held back in what I said. You start to get nervous about how the media will twist your words. I'll be glad to go back to being a private citizen."

"Well, don't think you're going to get off that easy. I hope you and Wynn will consider working for me, either on my local staff or in DC. And there's going to be a lot of demand for you to speak around the country. The Greens are going to need your help," Ray grinned.

"The only thing I'm doing for the next few weeks is preparing our

garden for winter, and reading Barbara Kingsolver's new book in front
of the wood stove. And getting some exercise. I've been eating way too
much junk food. Plus there's a ton of people I have to send thank you
notes to. And if anyone wants me to speak anytime soon, there better be
warm weather and a sandy beach nearby," she said, moving over to hug
to one of the local district coordinators.

****

Election night didn't turn out to be the final curtain Rachel expected.

Harrington took an early lead due to the Democrat's strength in the
East and the rust belt. He even initially appeared to have pulled an upset
in Florida, where Prescott's brother was governor, but now the
networks moved the state back into the "too-close-to-call" column.
Prescott closed the gap as the southern and mountain states came in.

The media was suddenly giving the public a civics lesson on the
Electoral College. The Founding Fathers had created this group of
prosperous men to protect themselves against "mob rule." They also
hadn't imagined a "national" political party, assuming that voters would
always vote for regional interests.

While Harrington had a lead of half a million in the popular vote,
no one had locked up the 270 electoral votes needed to be declared
president. One of the critical states was Washington, where the Green
presidential ticket unexpectedly held a slight lead over Prescott, with
Harrington third.

Once it was clear that the Greens were going to get 5 percent of the
national vote, Rachel stopped watching the results. She was enjoying
herself on the dance floor when Wynn came up to her shortly before
midnight. "Mind if I cut in?" he asked.

"Wynn, you've got to loosen up," Rachel said as they walked off the
floor. Her eyes were aglow. "Come on, you've always preached to me
about the need to celebrate with the members after a tough campaign,"
she said, as she steered them to the cash bar in the corner, pausing to
hug several friends along the way. "Black Russian, please — Wynn, want
a beer or 7 and 7? It's time to party."

"Actually, it's time to listen up."

"Par-teee," she laughed.

"Rachel, I think we got a hung election — and the Greens might be
the kingmakers. If you and Barry carry Washington. Prescott needs
Florida to get his 270 electoral votes. If Harrington wins Florida, no one

has 270. They'd need some electoral votes from us to win, or it goes to Congress to decide, where it looks like Prescott wins," Wynn explained.

"Florida is a complete mess. They used something called a butterfly ballot in Palm Beach, very confusing, with the candidates' names on different pages. The news reports are saying lots of Jewish senior citizens who support Harrington were duped into voting for Buchanan," Wynn told her.

"We're also getting reports from the Florida Greens that black voters were harassed all over the state. Many blacks were prevented from voting on the ground they were convicted felons, even though many of them had *no* prior record. They put up roadblocks in front of polling places in some black neighborhoods. Our own little apartheid system.

"It looks like there may need to be a recount. You should consider going out there to help lead the protests, do some media interviews. It looks like that's where the action's gonna be for the new few days."

"Oh Wynn, I'm tired of doing these 12-second sound bites," Rachel whined. "Frost should do it anyway. If any reporter wants to talk to me, which I doubt, we can do it over the phone. I'm sure it will all be cleared up by tomorrow. I just want to go to bed for a couple of days, not fly across the country. How reliable are these reports? Can't we wait a couple of days to see how things shake out? Besides, it's Harrington's problem, not ours. We lost." It was time for this election to be over.

"Okay, we don't need to fly to Florida tonight," Wynn conceded, barely able to make himself heard over the music. "But we should put out a statement calling for an outside investigation about the voting, especially the civil rights violations. And we need to make sure the Greens in Florida stay on top of this, starting with contacting the African-American leadership. It's the Green's job to fight for the right of people to vote.

"And I'm really serious — you and Barry need to start talking about the Electoral College. You need to start thinking about what we'd want in exchange for helping to elect someone president," stated Wynn.

"I will Wynn, I promise. I'll get on it the first thing when I wake up. Write us a memo tonight if you want. But come on, nothing's going to happen tonight," said Rachel, as she pulled Wynn to her and gave him a kiss "Remember, you promised to marry me, or have you forgotten already? Let's pretend it's our honeymoon or something. Can't you find someone else to write the world's greatest political statement tonight and dance with me instead? And isn't the campaign staff supposed to fall into bed together on election night? Act wild? Isn't that part of the tradition? We'll get back to the grindstone tomorrow morning, noon at the latest, I promise."

****

America woke up the next morning with a constitutional crisis. And much of the media were labeling the Greens as spoilers.

Wynn convinced Frost and Rachel that they should be front and center in Florida as the fiasco was getting sorted out. "Harrington and the Democrats have royally messed up their campaign every step of the way. Why would we possibly trust them to get a vote recount done properly?" Wynn argued. Rachel agreed to fly out to Florida.

Frost dispatched the remaining campaign staff to Florida. Frost left it to Rachel to do most of the public appearances. "Rachel, you're much better with street level protests than I am. Use your judgment, say whatever you want, make trouble, and have fun. You and Wynn direct the staff."

Frost did make time for the Sunday morning tv talk shows. Appleton, his campaign manager, began initial talks with the Harrington and Prescott campaigns about the Greens giving them their electoral votes. The two major parties initially resisted the overtures as premature. Appleton told them, "You do whatever you have to do. But don't come crying to me if we reach an agreement with the other camp." By the end of the week, both were begging for a meeting.

Over the next few days, Rachel seemed to be in the middle of a news conference every few hours, calling for the UN, European Union, Jimmy Carter and Nelson Mandela to be brought in to oversee the election recount. She convinced the Greens in the European Union to send over official observers.

Rachel thoroughly enjoyed pointing out how badly the state of Florida had messed up the voting process. "Maybe Castro can send over some people to help count the votes. Or Haiti. It's clear as heck, however, that Jeb Prescott and his buddies can't count correctly."

Frost and Rachel had won more than 200,000 votes in Florida, far outstripping the one-thousand-vote difference between Harrington and Prescott. This stark fact led to repeated questions from the media about how Rachel felt being a spoiler. Rachel developed a stock response, accompanied by a large grin: "You can't spoil something that's already rotten. Besides, there are many ways Florida spoiled this race. Like the butterfly ballot and preventing blacks from voting. Like hanging chads where the election machines can't determine who was voted for. As Greens, we know that votes are routinely stolen. The only unusual thing about this election is simply that the rest of the country now knows it as well."

By Thursday, the Greens began mobilizing community support around the slogan "Save Democracy." The Republicans began mobilizing to block the recount on Sunday by sending in their top political operatives, both their high priced "elder statesmen" lawyers in their thousand dollar suits, and of course their dirty tricks specialists.

"We don't understand what the problem is," said Theodore Hayes, a former US Secretary of State. "The votes have been counted and Prescott had the most. In America, you don't try to overturn elections just because you lost by a few votes. You accept defeat graciously and move on. That's what makes us a democracy." The state Republicans hurried to complete the paperwork certifying the results.

They were almost finished when the Democrats, after a week, decided to launch a field operation to support a recount.

The Greens held several large rallies calling for a fair recount. Rachel and Wynn got a big kick out of getting all the senior citizens together in their wheelchairs and walkers to protest the theft of the election.

"Who made up this ballot? I would never have voted for a fascist like Buchanan," screamed Mrs. Horowitz. The Jewish voters of Palm Beach County were incensed when they found out their district had "voted" overwhelmingly for Buchanan. Even Buchanan himself acknowledged with a chuckle that it was an unlikely result.

Wynn led the effort to document the abuses against African-American voters. A phone bank operation was set up to contact voters in minority districts about their experiences. Canvassers were sent out to collect statements from black voters at local stores, community centers, barbershops, union halls and churches. Wynn organized a series of public hearings in minority districts to collect testimony. Congressman Mumfi of New York agreed to come down to serve on the panel.

The closer the Greens and others looked at the exclusion of black voters, the clearer it became that the Republicans had deliberately violated election law.

Through their control of the Florida State government, the Republicans created a list of half a million individuals, primarily of color, who had allegedly been convicted of felonies in other states. Though many states restore a person's right to vote once they've served their sentence, Florida excludes them from voting for life. Governor Prescott and the Secretary of State, his alleged mistress, decided to ignore existing court orders against Florida using such lists from states that automatically restored voting rights to former felons.

Prescott also intentionally ignored various cross-checking techniques that could have reduced errors, while also taking steps to increase the number of blacks who'd be caught up in his sweep.

Hundreds of thousands of individuals who had voted for years and had never had any major problems with the criminal justice system were disenfranchised. African-Americans were far more likely to vote for the Democrats than the Republicans.

Harrington displayed the same indecisiveness and missteps that had allowed the Republicans to pull even in the election. The Democrats wanted to concentrate the recount in three of the counties with the heaviest Democratic enrollment, particularly where the "butterfly" ballot had been used. Initially the Democrats discouraged any street protests or grassroots mobilizing. They were forced to play catch-up with the Greens as the community protests swelled both in Florida and nationwide.

Once the Democrats decided to swing in behind the Greens, the political momentum shifted. By that time, it was also clear that the Greens would back Harrington in the electoral college.

In a Tallahassee press conference, the CBS reporter asked, "How do you reconcile the Green's contention that there is no difference between the Republicans and Democrats with your efforts to help Harrington win in Florida and nationally?"

"What we care about is democracy," explained Rachel. "Our goal is not to win Florida for Harrington, but rather to ensure that the will of the people is upheld, that every vote is counted. We know that both major parties routinely block people from voting. Hopefully, this fiasco will lead to reforms to stop these practices in future elections. We also want to make sure that Florida election officials are held accountable for their efforts to disenfranchise minority and poor voters."

"But," shouted a young man holding an MSNBC mike, "isn't the upshot that you're helping Harrington win. Have you made a deal with him?"

"As for using our electoral votes to help elect Harrington, that is how our constitutional system works. Politics is about power and how you negotiate with those who have power to get what you want. We think it's great that the Greens and our supporters won some power in this election. The Greens are now the third largest party in the country. If the media wants to claim that we cost the Democrats the election, we're happy to accept credit or blame, depending on your viewpoint, because it means we have the power to decide who gets elected president."

Now the BBC White House correspondent weighed in. "And how will you use that power? Can you tell us what you're demanding of the Democrats as the price of your support?"

"We want to use that power to restore democracy in our country, to stop the selling of government to the highest bidder. And we want to use that power to negotiate for reforms like universal healthcare, environmental protection, global warming, campaign finance reform and other ways to improve the quality of life for the average American. That's why we ran in the first place," stated Rachel.

"But Harrington and the Democrats want to use the courts to get a recount. Isn't it time to stop the demonstrations and let the legal system do what it is supposed to do?" demanded the CNN reporter.

"The courts routinely fail the people when it comes to elections. Where were the courts when black voters were being turned away from the polls? Even when voters started showing up in courthouses on election day to complain, the judges failed to act. The judiciary is the most political of the three branches of government. They get to say that the law is whatever they say it is. Judges owes their jobs to the party bosses and they usually do what their bosses want in political cases. Only the politically naïve would trust the Supreme Court to be fair and uphold democracy in such a partisan political case," Rachel claimed.

"Well, that's what Harrington is arguing," they countered.

"That proves my point about who would trust the Supreme Court," she quipped. "Anything else?"

The protests in Florida and across the country reached a crescendo the second weekend after the election. Both sides mobilized their supporters. The Green-Democratic protest was far larger, gathering nearly 50,000 individuals at the Florida State Capitol, attracting students, blacks, unions, gays, seniors and the antiglobalization forces. Trains, buses and even airplanes brought in protesters from DC, Atlanta, NY and California.

The international observers released a damning report comparing Florida to the worst of third world countries. Various groups including the NAACP, AFL-CIO, and NOW threatened a boycott of Florida's tourist industry and agriculture products. Civil rights groups demanded a thorough investigation into the intimidation and exclusion of black voters. The Clinton Justice Department finally swung into action. Editorials across the country began to support the demand for a fair and comprehensive recount, and for an investigation into possible civil right violations.

The Republicans caved in a few days later, agreeing in court to an outside group of jurists and attorneys to oversee a full recount of the state. Two weeks later Harrington was declared the victor.

Rachel and Wynn decided to hold a large victory party two days after the recount had been agreed to. The campaign would be closing up shop. Frost called to say he was flying down for the event. Rachel put him on the speaker phone so Wynn could hear.

"Rachel, you and Wynn did a great job. Without you, the Republicans would have tied this up in court until it was too late," said Frost.

"I've been talking to Harrington about what we want in exchange for our electoral votes. I told him we want to name the vice-president. He doesn't like his running mate all that much anyway — one of those shotgun marriages meant to balance the ticket," Frost explained.

"Well congratulations, Barry, you'll make a great vice-president," said Rachel.

"Actually, one of the few things Harrington and I agree on is that I'd make a lousy vice-president," Frost laughed. "I'm not famous for knowing when to keep my mouth shut, and I'm getting too old."

"So who are you thinking of?" asked Wynn.

"Well, actually, we agreed that *you,* Rachel, would make a much better vice-president. He probably thinks you're more controllable. Just shows he doesn't know you. Harrington also feels the party leaders will be less likely to grumble over your selection rather than mine — not that they're going to be happy, but they need our votes to win."

Rachel was speechless. "I don't know what to say. I've never given this any thought. When does Harrington need to know?"

"He said you could have a few days, maybe a week. Nothing is going to happen publicly until after the recount is finished. But he needs time to run it by the Democratic Party leadership first," Frost said.

"And if you do decide to accept the position," he added, "I'd suggest that the two of you consider tying the knot before it gets announced. Unless you don't mind turning your wedding into a media circus."

EIGHTEEN

THE PEOPLE'S SUMMIT

2002

Rachel and Sophie's New Year's resolution was to end the crisis style of management that had engulfed the White House during the first six months of Rachel's term, even while they continued to deal with the aftermath of September 11.

They now had their staff in place in the White House and many appointees in the federal government. They were busy working on Rachel's first budget proposals, moving forward with the energy and healthcare initiatives, and implementing the Blueprint for America. They were reorganizing the national defense team.

Most of their Cabinet was confirmed. The few "unity nominees" from the two parties that had stuck with her after the uproar with Congress over 9/11 were the ones willing to put the needs of the country ahead of partisan concerns.

Rachel's standing in the polls was sky high. Congress shied away from direct confrontation with her.

"It will be impossible to meet the soaring expectations people have for you Rachel," Frost warned her. "Have Sophie place a few stories with friendly reporters that put a more realistic spin on the challenges ahead. Corporate America still has most of the power, starting with Congress. Your standing in the polls will only take you so far. And the polls will come down."

As part of the healing process following 9/11, Rachel had brought Americans together in Citizen Assemblies in November and December of 2001 to establish priorities for her upcoming budget. Tens of thousands of Americans participated in these Citizen Assemblies, meeting at local schools, community centers, churches, temples and mosques to talk about their hopes for themselves and their families. Attendees included longtime citizen activists as well as many residents who usually avoided getting involved with government as a waste of time. Rachel gave them hope and inspiration.

"The combination of the stock market collapse and the impact of September eleventh has put the economy into a recession, with a resulting drop in federal revenues. I want your input into how your tax dollars should to be invested to get the economy moving and improve services," said Rachel in her videotaped message welcoming people to the Assemblies. Participants were also invited to address nonbudget issues.

The Assemblies broke into small groups on key topics such as education, healthcare, defense, environment, social services, agriculture, taxes, jobs and foreign aid. After brainstorming proposals, the groups came back together to establish priorities for their communities. Each participant was also asked to fill out an individual questionnaire about budget and other policy issues.

The Assemblies selected volunteers to represent them at follow-up gatherings at the regional, state and national levels to refine the proposals into a comprehensive agenda.

A number of Congressmembers dismissed the Citizen Assemblies. "It's a publicity stunt, nothing more than window dressing. You can't expect the average citizen to understand the complexities of the federal budget."

Congress soon discovered that Rachel and the Assembly participants were dead serious about changing the budget-making process. Local participants began meeting with their Congress members on a regular basis. They also set up websites to help monitor the progress of their proposals.

****

Rachel used the opening ceremonies for the People's Summit in March 2002 to formally launch the Peace Institute.

The ceremony was held at the World Trade Center site. "This is sacred ground," Rachel intoned. "We must never forget the sacrifices made here. We must turn away from the hatred and prejudice that led to such massive destruction and create a new beginning, a new sense of hope. The Peace Institute will be our beacon," she declared.

Rachel announced that Congressional leaders had agreed to provide 300 million dollars as an initial endowment for the Peace Institute. Congressional leaders had initially balked at committing any substantial funds. Baker argued, "It'll just be more patronage for international bureaucrats. We'll be fundin' the anti-American cheerleaders." They reluctantly coughed up some funding when Rachel's appeal to the public and other countries rapidly generated several hundred million dollars.

The various relief funds that had been set up to assist the families of those killed on September 11 had raised almost a million dollars per victim. Rachel donated Tommy's share to the Peace Institute. Other relatives of the victims presented a check for nearly 50 million dollars at the ceremony.

"I have asked many Nobel Peace Prize winners to serve on the board of the Institute, particularly those who were selected not as public officials but for their lifelong dedication to peace. Among those who have agreed to serve are Amnesty International, Doctors Without Boarders, Bishop Desmond Tutu of South Africa, Elie Wiesel, Tenzin Gyatso (the 14th Dalai Lama), Rigoberta Menchu Tum of Guatemala, Aung San Suu Kyi of Burma, Nelson Mandela, Jody Williams of the Land Mines campaign, and Joséé Ramos-Horta of East Timor," Rachel stated.

"The September eleventh victims' groups will name additional representatives, as will groups representing the victims of the Holocaust, the genocides in Turkey, Cambodia, Rwanda, Tibet and Bosnia, the victims of apartheid and colonialism in Africa, the death squad victims throughout Central and South America, the survivors of indigenous peoples on all continents and women's groups. The People's Summit will also choose some Governing Board representatives," she added.

Rachel urged the People's Summit to develop a democratic alternative to the corporate agenda for globalization. "The challenge of the People's Summit is to draft a blueprint for a sustainable global economic system, one that enables local residents to decide how to use their local resources to meet their needs rather than being forced to allow outside economic forces to transform their communities into yet more consumer markets for global economic interests," she said in her opening remarks.

Richard Newhouse, the Director of the WTO, issued a statement defending the Free Trade agenda. "Trade barriers that countries erect to protect local businesses and reward political favorites result in market inefficiencies, producing inferior products at higher prices. The WTO is creating a level playing field. While this may cause some short-term pain, everyone will benefit in the long run with higher wages, lower prices and better products. And once everyone is part of the same economic system, there will no be reason for war."

The critics of the WTO were unconvinced. "The role of the WTO is to accelerate corporate globalization, concentrating wealth and decision making power in the hands of the few while increasing poverty for the majority of the world's peoples, especially in third world countries," said Congressmember McDaniels. "The WTO promotes unsustainable patterns of production and consumption, contributes to the collapse of national economies and fosters environmental and social degradation."

The recent collapse of the Argentine government and economy, largely due to the policies of the IMF, gave the People's Summit increased leverage to demand reforms. Before its sudden and drastic decline, Argentina had long been cited as the principal example of a country that had prospered under the IMF's policies to address global debt.

Delegates to the People's Summit came from all corners of the globe, from the Living Democracy Movement in India, the Social Forum groups in Brazil, the Sustainable Chile Movement, the Zapata movement in Mexico, from South Africa, the worldwide Green Party movement, Third World Network, World March of Women, Spanish Network for a Solidarity Economy, Environmental Rights Action in Nigeria, Association for the Taxation of Financial Transactions in Aid of Citizens (ATTAC) from France, the U'wa People of Colombia, Buddhists from Thailand, Cuba, labor unions, teachers, fishermen and more. Ayesha Anyanwu attended with the Ogoni delegation from Nigeria.

Many came to bear witness to how their lives and culture were threatened by globalization.

"The villages of our ancestors have been flooded to build a new dam to power faraway cities. Now landless peasants are forced to migrate there, ending up living in slums."

"For the first time, our society has experienced hunger as sustainable agriculture practices developed over generations have been cast aside. Our national leaders make us grow cash crops to export at deflated prices to pay off debt to the international banks."

They spoke in a dazzling array of languages about rain forests being incinerated to make grassland to fatten cattle for North American hamburgers, only to become barren dust in a few years. They spoke of 14 million children dying annually from hunger and disease, of 100 million children living or working on the streets, and of 300 thousand children fighting as soldiers during the last decade.

Haiti's president Jean-Bertrand Aristide spoke on behalf of the poor people of his country:

On a planet with half the population — 3 billion people — living on less than two dollars a day, the statistics that

> describe the accumulation of wealth in the world are mind-boggling. Behind this crisis of dollars there is a human crisis: among the poor, immeasurable human suffering; among the powerful, the policy makers, a poverty of spirit which has made a religion of the market and its invisible hand. A crisis of imagination so profound that the only measure of value is profit, the only measure of human progress is economic growth.

In her opening remarks, Rachel challenged the five thousand People's Summit delegates to dream big, to imagine that another world is possible.

"The first step to securing fundamental change is to articulate what those changes should be," Rachel said to the cheering delegates. "Over the last two centuries, the people of many countries, including my own, have been able to throw off their kings, winning the right for individuals to choose their own leaders.

"But we must be constantly vigilant about the rich and powerful. They've manipulated our laws and courts to make corporations our new rulers. But if we can replace kings — if Nelson Mandela can walk out of prison — then we can make corporations serve us rather than rule us. Today brings us one step closer to creating a world that fulfills the promise of democracy, justice and liberty."

She read the opening paragraphs of the Peace Treaty to the delegates. "We seek to build a new world based on the rule of international law, based on respect for and protection of the sacredness of each human life, and based on a commitment to preserve our cultural, social and ecological diversity from the threats posed by globalization."

Rachel concluded her welcoming speech by proposing radical changes in the composition of military forces. "We'll never have peace as long as individual states and countries have the right to maintain their own military forces and weapons of mass destruction. In the short term, countries need to agree to reorient their military strategy to defensive rather than offensive capabilities, to ensure the safety of their citizens rather than the ability to dominate others.

"In the longer term, we need to move to a system where military forces, particularly those of an offensive nature, are under international control. We need to put an end to the arms race, to build down rather than build up. As a first step, I will ask the US Congress to unilaterally halt the militarization of space."

The People's Summit was a chaotic affair, a whirlwind of debate, of impromptu late-night meetings, of boring speeches lasting too longer followed by young people breaking out in song and drum circles, threatening to fall apart at every moment only to find new energy and direction from unexpected sources. Rachel and Wynn were everywhere, trying to keep the various committees on track, putting out fires and urging them to focus on points of agreement rather than disagreement.

The delegates produced a long list of exciting proposals that they formally submitted to a special session of the UN. (See Appendix A) The proposals strengthened protection of local economies, the environment and human rights. Strict controls on corporate behavior were proposed. The challenge would be to convince the various national and international bodies to adopt them.

****

Corporate America swarmed over Capitol Hill after the summit, throwing a fit. "Moreno's proposals are a declaration of war against American business. It's great that she wants to give all these handouts to third world countries, but who's going to give handouts to the American people when the domestic economy falls apart?" they angrily asked.

The congressional leaders sought to placate them. "The president loves to give speeches, fire up her troops. Gettin' Congress to agree with her is a completely different kettle of fish," Baker reminded them.

If anything, corporate America was even more upset with Rachel actions on the home front.

On Frost's recommendation, Rachel selected Doris Stewart as Attorney General, the first African-American to hold the position. Stewart was the former director of one of Frost's public interest groups working on corporate responsibility issues. She'd been professor of corporate law at Georgetown Law School for the last three years.

When Rachel interviewed Stewart, she told her, "I want someone who'll relish putting CEOs on the FBI's most wanted list. White-collar criminals steal far more money and kill more people than street criminals. I want to focus our prosecutions on the biggest criminals."

Stewart's prosecution of corporate crime was as successful as Frost had predicted. While Americans may have instinctively known that a lot of big companies were crooks, it was still an eye-opener to see the details documented.

Stewart's first major corporate criminal prosecution involved RunEnergy Inc. In the recent election, RE had ferried around Prescott, the Republican presidential nominee, in their corporate jet. RE had used energy deregulation to transform itself into one of the ten largest companies in America and a major player in the international energy market. Its collapse was even more startling and explosive than its growth.

In announcing the indictment of seven RE officials, Stewart reported, "Company officials and outside auditors fraudulently manipulated the company's financial statements. They hoodwinked ever more investors to supply the capital to keep them afloat while they hyped themselves to Wall Street. RE used hefty campaign contributions to get elected officials to deregulate energy, creating new markets where more people could gamble their life savings away to support the lifestyle of the top RE executives."

Rachel added, "RE's victims are littered across the globe. They start with California residents who were ripped off by massive price hikes and blackouts. It includes residents of foreign countries, such as India, where RE sucked out billions of dollars in failed projects. RE even fleeced their own workers, forcing them to invest their pensions in RE and then prohibiting them from withdrawing their life savings as the stock price plummeted to pennies. Top managers, of course, were free to cash in their golden parachutes, while both employees and average middle-class Americans investors lost everything."

Several congressmembers, state legislators and regulatory officials were indicted by the Justice Department for their legislative and regulatory actions in support of RE in exchange for campaign contributions, political favors and jobs for friends and relatives.

The congressional leaders tried to distance themselves from the indicted businessmen. "I meet with CEOs and business lobbyists all the time," said Senator Deutsche. "We're always looking for ways that Congress can help create more jobs for the country. My colleagues and I are certainly disappointed to hear that some of these corporate executives may have broken the law. They, of course, are entitled to a presumption of innocence until the courts have determined otherwise. However, since it's the Justice Department's job, not ours, to investigate such possible wrongdoing, we hope in the future that the Attorney General will keep us apprised of any potential problems."

"It's a witch-hunt," Baker told his Republican colleagues behind closed doors. "Heck, these government regulations are so convoluted

that I don't understand half of 'em. I mean, whadda they expect ya to
do? Ya got your high-priced lawyers tellin' you its okay. If ya look hard
'nough, there's always some rule ya messed up on. Ya don't get ahead in
the real world unless ya willin' to take risks."

The indictments kept coming. "Today we have indicted the CEO of
Fowler Laboratories for Medicare reimbursement fraud," Stewart
announced. "Among several fraudulent schemes, the company marketed
its drug for prostate cancer by giving free samples to doctors and then
encouraging them to bill Medicare for the samples."

The AG sued Tasty Treats, one of the world's largest food
companies. "More than two dozen individuals were killed and hundreds
seriously injured from contaminated hot dogs. The company stopped
performing tests for bacteria after they were finding too many bad
results."

Tobacco officials were sued for their worldwide killing of four
million people annually from cigarettes. In the US alone, they kill more
than one thousand people daily. Several large insurance companies were
indicted for ripping off investors for hundreds of millions of dollars in
fraudulent investment schemes and policy practices. Stewart went after
multinational banks and corporations for their role in laundering money
from the drug trade.

Rachel used the indictments to submit a series of corporate reform
proposals to Congress.

"A small but important start is to ensure that if a company wants to
do business with the government, that it complies with all
environmental, civil rights and labor laws. This includes compliance with
requirements for living wages, affirmative action, sexual orientation,
community responsibility, lending practices and consumer protection.
We also need to return the banking industry to its initial mission of
building local communities, starting with limiting federal deposit
insurance only to banks that invest their money locally," Rachel said.

Rachel also unveiled a long list of proposed legislative and
regulatory changes that didn't need congressional approval. Rachel was
quickly mastering the art of developing creative ways to use her powers
to do what she wanted to do, though industry responded with a tidal
wave of lawsuits.

Frost led the fight for increased controls on the auditing profession.
"Any discussion of auditing rules normally puts most Americans to
sleep," Frost stated, "unless of course it's the IRS at their door. But it's
the job of auditors to ensure that the companies don't hide money or

their financial health from investors or the government."

Arthur Andersen, the best known of the big five auditing firms, allowed RE to exclude huge amounts of business transactions from its financial statements so it could grossly overstate its profitability and financial soundness. When the RE scandal hit, Arthur Andersen began shredding key documents.

Frost pointed out that similar problems with auditors had occurred two decades earlier during the savings and loan scandal. "Accounting firms failed to report problems that led to the collapse of hundreds of firms. Congress forced taxpayers to pay a half trillion dollars to bail out the industry. The bulls were rampaging through the china shop and the accountants somehow missed them? With the S & L scandal, not only did Congress fail to ensure independent audits in the future, they outrageously gave banks, insurance companies and securities firms the ability to join into even larger financial conglomerates. Congress and thieves have no shame."

Frost helped Rachel draft legislation to increase federal oversight of accounting firms, and to prohibit auditing firms from being involved in management consulting. The idea was to avoid conflict of interest, when the profits of the auditors were influenced by how well the companies they were auditing did financially.

Rachel had the Federal Trade Commission go after the big drug companies for their efforts to illegally extend the length of their patents, to oppose the use of generic drugs and price fixing.

Stewart revitalized the antitrust division of the Justice Department, seeking to halt the never-ending corporate mergers, as bigger companies sought to gobble up as many companies as they could. "The trust-busters were right a century ago when they broke up Rockefeller's oil monopoly. Lack of competition was bad then and it's still bad for consumers today," Stewart told Rachel. "In 1999 alone, one-fifth of the country's largest 50 companies disappeared due to mergers."

The first target of the antitrust division was the communication industry. "A free media is essential to democracy," Rachel said in her weekly radio address. "We have to reverse the increasing concentration of corporate ownership of the media, particularly of the public airwaves. A few dozen billionaires and their companies have almost complete control of the American media. We need to ensure a diversity of viewpoints."

Stewart stopped the proposed merger between Time-Warner cable and America Online dead in its tracks. "The internet is the last hope of giving average citizens an alternative to the media marketplace dominated by a few corporate giants. This merger would've been a fatal blow."

Their biggest antitrust initiative was going after the oil companies, suing them for environmental damages and price fixing. They had fought Rachel's agenda for clean energy with every resource they had.

Suzanne Michel of Public Citizen told Rachel how "five oil companies — Exxon-Mobil, Chevron-Texaco, BP Amoco-Arco, Phillips-Tosco and Marathon — now control three-fifths of the retail market, two-fifths of domestic production, and half of the domestic refining. They produce more oil than Saudi Arabia, Kuwait and Yemen combined. This concentration has produced record prices and profit, which they've used to finance their lobbying efforts to open up the Alaska wilderness to more oil drilling, to oppose improved gas efficiency for cars and trucks and to block the Kyoto protocol to reduce global warming."

****

Rachel persuaded Anna Brown to stay on as her public policy adviser on women's issues.

"I know you want to go back to your job working with women in third world countries," Rachel told Anna one evening, "but there are lots of issues in the US that need your help. Childcare, pay, reproductive rights and harassment in the workplace, to name a few. But most of all, *I* need you Anna. Wynn is great — invaluable — but I need a strong woman to lean on," she pleaded.

Anna could hardly say no, though she did point out, "You're the one who insisted on marrying a man."

One of Anna's first assignments was to coordinate the campaign for the Fair Pay Act to end pay discrimination against women. The Act would prohibit employers from paying lower wages to women than they pay men for equal work.

The press conference to announce Anna's appointment was a riotous celebration among women activists. Vivian Hunt of AFSCME explained, "Full-time women workers earn 73 percent of what full-time working men earn. Women and people of color are still largely segregated into a few low-paying occupations. More than half of all women workers hold sales, clerical and service jobs. The more an occupation is dominated by women or people of color, the less it pays.

The wage gap, about 4,000 dollars annually, results in lower Social Security benefits for women, a major factor in the high poverty rate among older women."

The House Speaker led the countercharge. "It's just a myth that women git paid less than men. Sex has nuthin' to do with it," Baker told reporters. "Men just have more education and experience — and they don't take time off to have babies. And if women did accept less than men for doing the same job, a lotta companies would be glad to fire all the men and hire women. This is just a back door way to get government to set wages."

"How come Republicans are all for family values and a woman staying home to rear a child," Anna responded, "except when it's time to open up their wallets? Two-thirds of women with children are working, not staying home to raise the kids. The solution isn't to lower the pay of men, it's to raise the pay of women."

Anna told Rachel, "If we want this to pass, we're going to have to get new people in Congress. The business community has this one locked down tight."

Anna also assisted NOW's campaign to stop sexual harassment and other workplace abuses. The campaign included support for affirmative action for women, and increased support for what the administration was calling Family Friendly work policies, such as flex time, job sharing, on-site childcare and provision of benefits to domestic partners, including same sex-couples

One of Rachel's early successes in Congress was passage of the Local Law Enforcement Enhancement Act. LLEEA eliminated the requirement that victims of hate crimes be engaged in a federally protected activity. The law also extended protection to include sexual orientation, gender and disability.

"All too often, individuals are attacked because of their sexual orientation or gender. Hate crimes instill fear in all members of the targeted group, impacting where they work, live and travel. With so few states having comprehensive hate-crime laws, it's essential that the federal government provide protection to some of our most vulnerable citizens," stated Rachel.

Rachel reintroduced the Equal Rights Amendment to the Constitution. "It was a travesty that this common sense proposal failed the first time. It's long overdue to erase this stain on our legislative history." She also pushed the Senate to "finally ratify the UN Convention on the Elimination of All Forms of Discrimination Against

Women. The treaty was adopted by the UN more than two decades ago, and is the only comprehensive international treaty guaranteeing women's human rights and the prevention of discrimination against women. It's a disgrace that our country has taken so long to ratify it."

****

By the summer of 2002, the politicians had unsheathed their knives again.

Americans either loved or hated Rachel. There was little middle ground. "She's an uppity woman, personifying everything that's wrong with the country," was a common lament among men. "She's a socialist, or worse, a tree hugger who doesn't understand the real world. She's all about empowering women, blacks, the poor and immigrants who don't pay taxes. She's in cahoots with America's enemies, wanting to makes us weak, wanting to emasculate American males."

Many of the attacks on Rachel, particularly on the internet, were vulgar and obscene. Sexual harassment was often the first line of attack by men who felt threatened by strong women. Pornographic depictions of Rachel were everywhere. Many were also racist due to Wynn and their mixed-race marriage.

On the other hand, Rachel's confident, warn and caring manner rallied many Americans behind her. They wanted a strong but sympathetic leader to respond to the tragedy and threat of September 11. She struck the correct balance between toughness and empathy.

But those close to her saw the toll that 9/11 and the presidency was taking on her. Sophia and Anna organized a support group of women friends and advisers to help her heal, give her strength and to help her refocus. Her kitchen cabinet.

Her opponents called them her "witches' coven" or the "bitch brigade."

They were a mixture of longtime friends and some others whose work as activists or writers Rachel admired. Every few weeks they had a late night gathering. Wynn was told to make himself scarce. There was no set agenda, just an opportunity to talk. While they sometimes provided advice about a specific issue, more often they focused on the broad vision that Rachel needed to lead the country. They sought to strengthen the spiritual as well as the political side of Rachel.

"The first step is for you to heal yourself, to rediscover your center," said her old friend Starr Fire at the first gathering. "You need to draw upon your strength, our strength, the strength of all those who love you. You need to feel the collective power of all those who are counting on you to succeed."

"Have the moxie to make the presidency what you want it to be, rather than being shaped by the limitations of others," added Sandy Alvarez, the congressmember from New Mexico. "Understand the parameters of this office and figure out how to change them. Always remember that your real power for change flows from the people. Mobilize them, empower them."

"Kick back once in a while," said Anna. "Make sure you take care of yourself."

Wynn also did his best to support Rachel. Any couple's first year of marriage could be difficult. Wynn and Rachel's first year was a particularly challenging one. There were not many tranquil Sunday mornings lazing in bed and reading the paper between bouts of raunchy sex. In fact, the frequency of their lovemaking was at an all-time low.

In a major role reversal, Wynn became the diehard romantic. He arranged for candlelit dinners in their quarters, bubble baths, roses on the pillow. Rachel would often find a little note or poem from Wynn. He arranged for old friends to join them for dinner, a movie screening or a concert at the White House. "Live from the White House" became a staple on NPR and public television. Ronnie Faith was the most frequent performer, virtually become the White House house band.

As they grieved over the loss of Tommy, Rachel and Wynn considered having a child.

They had never felt the need to produce a child to "bless" their union. When they felt the need for additional parenting in recent years, there was always Pete and Emily's growing brood to occupy them.

"I don't feel a need to contribute to the world's overpopulation," Wynn had said. "Plus our hectic schedules of 'saving the world' is not exactly conducive to making time to properly raise a child."

They were also concerned about Rachel's age. While many women successfully bore children in their early forties, the risk increased. They worried about the stress of Rachel carrying a child while president, and of raising a child in the fish bowl of the White House.

"My head says that our time for being parents is over, and this is just my reaction to Tommy's death," Rachel admitted over dinner one evening. "But there's a deep burning inside of me that needs something to quench it."

Rachel developed an extreme case of baby hunger. She'd invariably stop if she saw someone in a crowd with a baby, hoping to steal a few minutes of cuddling. Her advance aides became used to announcing her entrance by saying, "Only three more babies to go."

"Wynn, if we have a child, we're not going to have someone else raise it," Rachel told him. "And realistically, over the next few years that means the burden's going to fall on you more often than not. Are you ready for such a commitment?"

"I'm a little nervous," Wynn conceded. "But I loved Tommy — I *love* Tommy still — and any child of yours would be something special. I know how much pain you're feeling and I'd do anything to make it go away." He paused. "If you want a child, I'm all for it. I'm sure I can master the art of diaper changing. Besides, I hear raisin' a child keeps you young. With all the creaks in my joints, it'd be great to have some youth pills."

Now it was Rachel's turn to be pensive. Finally she sighed. "I don't think we're at the right place to have a child," Rachel concluded, tears rolling down her cheeks. "Maybe once we're out of the White House."

****

The investigation into September 11 was a tortuous, emotional affair. Congress used their usual arguments to impede any investigation, seeking to avoid any embarrassing revelations. "We know what happened — bin Laden and his cohorts blew up the World Trade Center and killed 3,000 people. And you killed bin Laden. So what's left? An investigation will just expose our intelligence operations to our enemies."

"Bin Laden's death doesn't answer all the questions about September eleventh. If it's just myself and the victim's families calling witnesses, that'll be just fine," Rachel told Senator Deutsche. "In fact, the more I hear from Congress, the better off I think we'd be if you didn't participate. As president and commander in chief, I have sufficient authority to compel government employees to cooperate. We're going to find out who planned this operation, who paid for it, and why our government failed to prevent it."

The victims' families wanted to know why more wasn't done once the FAA became aware of the hijackings more than half an hour *before* the first plane hit the first tower. The FAA had standing orders to notify the Port Authority of NY & NJ of any hijackings ever since terrorists vowed to "take the towers down" after a 1993 bombing failed to do so.

One of the committee's first conclusions was that "the intelligence, aviation and security communities are unable to provide a reasonable explanation as to why normal procedures were not followed that day to intercept and shoot down, if necessary, the hijacked planes."

The investigation continued to broaden, as each new discovery led to new dark corners where more loose threads waited to be pulled. The investigation shook the military and political establishment.

House Speaker Baker complained, "It's just Monday morning quarterbacking. If some mistakes were made, let's fix 'em. President Moreno's just lookin' for an excuse to clean house, remove defense officials who butt heads with her. She's jeopardizin' the nation's security."

"At best, the intelligence community was negligent in protecting America," the committee said in its initial report. "At worst, the lives of Americans were consciously sacrificed to generate the pretext for armed intervention to advance the interests of certain members of the military-industrial-intelligence complex who wish to establish America as a global empire."

Before 2000, for instance, during the Clinton administration, German intelligence had informed the CIA of the first name of the terrorist who took over the controls of United Airlines flight 175, which flew into the south tower. They even gave the CIA his telephone number in the United Arab Emirates.

"The Harrington administration," the committee found, "was aware of a possible terrorist attack against a target in the US several months before September 11. Warnings were received from the presidents of Russia and Egypt, the Mossad intelligence service in Israel and even from members of the FBI. And Russia warned us that bin Laden would shortly launch a spectacular terrorist attacked against US facilities or interests designed to inflict mass casualties."

The warnings had not been passed on to Rachel when she took office. The intelligence agencies claimed that "they just got lost in the paperwork."

There was considerable evidence, though not conclusive, that the September 11 attack was a response to a warning issued to the Taliban and bin Laden by the Harrington administration in July of 2001 that a war was likely if they didn't agree to the construction of a trans-Afghan oil and natural gas pipeline crossing their country and ending in Karachi, Pakistan.

"The negligence of the Armed Forces," the report continued, "to respond to the hijackings, both before 9/11 and on the morning of, borders on criminality, with standard procedures not followed. At times our national defense system could not have performed more poorly if they were intentionally trying to do so."

Rachel ensured that charges and other disciplinary actions were pursued against responsible individuals. Numerous careers were ended. So many defense officials jumped to the private sector that Sophie told Rachel "We'll have to increase the military's funding next year for parachutes." Several companies were barred from future contracts with the American government.

The final report was comparable in scope to the Pentagon Papers, documenting the twisted turns of American government policy and business dealings that contributed to September 11. It explained the concept of blowback to the American people.

"The United States government since the end of World War Two has repeatedly supported and assisted individuals who have ruthlessly attacked and overthrown governments and leaders that were at odds with what were perceived as US political and economic interests. We have sanctioned and promoted the use of torture, oppression and mass killings by such individuals. Once in power, such individuals have routinely turned against the US government and international law, often leading to armed intervention by our country."

Rachel saw even worse material that was not released due to national security concerns. The report brought a stabbing chill as she read it, keeping her awake many a night.

"It just blows me away how prior administrations thought nothing of sacrificing the principles of democracy and justice in the pursuit of the almighty dollar," Wynn told Rachel. "I mean, I was cynical before but even I didn't believe it was this bad. Bribery and corruption was just a way of life for these guys, both the government and CEOs. If this doesn't make Americans understand why so many people view our country as the epicenter of evil, we should pack our bags and head for the border."

"Just look at this," Wynn almost screamed. "Key members of the defense services were prayin' for someone to attack us so they'd have an excuse to go in and grab control of oil supplies in Iraq and elsewhere. They'd been planning to invade Afghanistan for years. Listen to this: 'Following the attack on the US warship Cole, bin Laden had been selected by the Clinton administration as the most frightening icon on which to build public support for the invasion of Afghanistan.'"

But no one had expected an attack as deadly as 9/11.

The report, however, was far from a fatal blow to the foreign policy establishment. They found enough scapegoats and compliant media outlets to allow them to survive and regroup. A lie told often enough and loudly enough eventually becomes the truth for many people.

Their resolve to get rid of Rachel increased exponentially.

****

Both the American and UN tribunals concluded, "The September 11 attacks were not initiated by bin Laden, though the al-Qaida network had previously provided training to some of the hijackers. Bin Laden was informed about the attack before it occurred and helped raise funds for it. Most of the funding, however, came from oil interests in Saudi Arabia who knew that part of their payments to Arab charities routinely were diverted to organizations that supported terrorism."

Rachel told congressional leaders, "I plan to sever all diplomatic and military relations with Saudi Arabia unless they immediately halt their support of terrorism and cooperate in holding accountable those individuals responsible for 9/11 and other terrorist acts. Nor am I willing to continue to assist them in preventing democratic and human rights reforms from being instituted in their country."

"Saudi Arabia is one of America's staunchest allies," Darling complained to Rachel. "You need to be more mindful of the domestic problems the Saudi rulers are facing. The alternative would be a fundamentalist Islamic regime that views the US as its enemy. It wouldn't hesitate to use oil as a weapon, including using their oil reserves to finance increased attacks on Israel. Such a government would also be far more oppressive to women and political dissidents."

Congressional leaders echoed Darling's comments.

"Saudi Arabia is perhaps the most corrupt government in the world," Rachel responded to reporters. "The billions it receives from their oil are used to buy off all competing interests while the ruling elite enjoys their opulent lifestyle. Why does Congress want to help Saudi Arabia avoid answering questions about 9/11? Congress needs to stop propping up governments that violate basic human rights."

Congressional support for Saudi Arabia eroded as the public debate intensified. It didn't seem likely that the Saudi Arabian rulers would survive the UN investigation and the withdrawal of American support. At home, it faced attacks not only from religious conservatives but from a growing middle class that had seen a substantial drop in income over the last decade while the ruling families continued to plunder the nation's wealth. The Saudi leaders had already announced plans to create a more representative parliament as they scrambled to hold on to power. Their wealth was safely deposited in bank accounts scattered throughout the world in case they needed to flee.

As Darling's influence within the administration lessened, he went more public with his concerns, almost daring Rachel to fire him. After one of his appearances before a congressional committee in April, Rachel insisted that he come to the White House to explain his actions.

Darling was patronizing to the end. "You're jeopardizing America's security interests by playing touchy-feely with war. The use of force in resolving disputes between countries has happened throughout history. You can't rule unless you're willing to use force when all else fails," he lectured.

Rachel cut the meeting short, having little interest in revisiting old arguments. "Mr. Secretary, I think we both realize it's time for you to move on. I appreciate that you can't support something you don't believe in. If you want to be commander in chief, I wish you luck in the Democratic primaries."

In announcing Darling's resignation, Rachel thanked him for his long service to the country.

NINETEEN

2002 MIDTERM ELECTIONS

The UN Earth Summit was held on the summer solstice in 2002, the tenth anniversary of the first such summit in Brazil.

The gathering was an opportunity to expand the People's Summit challenge to corporate globalization, starting with rejecting the WTO's assertion that it had the sole power to determine ecological issues if they impinged upon Free Trade. The other big point of contention was access to water.

Wynn was coordinating the US positions for the Earth Summit. He gave Rachel a final briefing during the flight to South Africa.

"The WTO insists that it alone has the power to resolve conflicts in international agreements on trade and environment, a position which has a lot of support in Congress. For instance, the WTO wants to rule that it is illegal to use trade sanctions to enforce environmental agreements such as the Kyoto Protocol on global warming. The WTO also wants to control the terms for export-based farming, a/k/a cash crops, forestry, mining, and fishing. Basically, they want to be able to gut any rules restricting the plundering of natural resources."

"Since the last Earth Summit, economic globalization has accelerated tremendously," Rachel said in her opening remarks in Johannesburg. "Unfortunately, that hasn't been accompanied by a corresponding increase in environmental protection. Instead, global warming continues to worsen, we continue to lose our rain forests at a frightening speed, the ozone layer continues to deteriorate and our fish stocks are depleted. I'm ashamed to admit that the US has been the main culprit impeding progress. We need to adopt sustainable agriculture and forestry practices, curtail the production of toxic materials, protect the biodiversity of our seas and land, and develop mechanisms for effective environmental enforcement"

The Senate had for years balked at ratifying the Biological Diversity agreement. The US pharmaceutical industry feared that it would block biopiracy. Instead of stealing natural remedies and drugs from developing countries, the companies would have to share the benefits of these genetic resources.

Rachel used the Earth Summit to announce her new proposals on global warming. She knew they would receive a far chillier reception back home from Congress and American polluters.

"We have to take drastic action now, hopefully before it is too late," Rachel warned. "A recent Pentagon report identified global warming as a greater threat to our national security than terrorism. The report warns of sharp drops and rises in average temperatures around the world, massive famines, threats to coastal cities, and wars — possibly nuclear exchanges — over resources in coming decades. We need to not only ratify the Kyoto agreement but move beyond, imposing stringent caps on greenhouse gas emissions. We need to heavily tax carbon emissions, and use the revenues to fund the development of renewable energy sources in all countries."

Rachel however opposed the idea put forth by some environmental and business groups to create tradable carbon credits that could be bought and sold like any other commodity. "Why allow business to play an economic shell game with carbon?. We need severe, specific reduction requirements."

The staffs of Baker and Deutsche raced each other to see who could be the first to denounce Rachel's proposals. "The president wants to put a restrictor plate on the engine of America's economy," bellowed Baker to reporters. "She's just goin' to shift jobs overseas, create more of those sweatshops she doesn't like."

"Carbon taxes are regressive," Deutsche added, "they hit hardest on the poor because they spend more of their income on energy. Radical actions like the president is proposing will shock the economy, put us into a recession. We need a more reasonable phase-in period."

Many developing countries were also reluctant to restrict carbon emissions. "Too many of our citizens are forced to live in poverty. Pollution unfortunately is a byproduct of industrialization. We need the opportunity to catch up with North America and Europe. Otherwise, we will always be trapped with a second-class economy and lower living standards," said the president of one central African country.

"Global warming is killing us all," Rachel responded. "We all have to reduce our greenhouse emissions. The solution is for the wealthy countries to make significant financial contributions to help your country develop a sustainable economy that avoids pollution while focusing on raising everyone's quality of life." She admitted however that it was going to be a struggle to convince Congress to tax corporate polluters to raise the needed funds.

The Summit adopted her proposals on global warming. Getting approval from Congress was going to be an uphill struggle.

In most of the world, the biggest headlines from the Summit were over water.

"More than one billion human beings lack access to safe drinking water, while half the world's population — three billion — lack adequate sanitation," Wynn had briefed Rachel. "The lack of safe drinking water is the major cause of illness in the world. More than five million people, primarily children, die each year as a result. As many as half of all the people in the developing world are suffering from one of the six main diseases involving contaminated water supplies and sanitation.

"Water privatization has already led to major upheavals in several South American countries," Wynn added. "The IMF and several multinational corporations have been pushing to turn water into just another commodity, pressuring governments everywhere to privatize water resources."

Water is also essential for food production and other economic activities. Less than one percent of the earth's total water is fresh water available for use.

"The water crisis is worsening," Rachel told the delegates in her opening remarks. "The use of water globally is doubling every twenty years, twice as fast as population growth. If the present trends continue, by 2025 the demand for fresh water will be fifty percent greater than what we have available. The demand for water has led to an explosion in the construction of large, environmentally destructive dams. These dams often displace indigenous families and farms, as well as devastating the local ecosystem."

More than 250 rivers are shared by two or more countries, leading to increasing conflict as both pollution and the demand for water increases. Disputes over water have been as much a part of the strife in the Middle East as oil.

Pablo Reyes of the International Forum on Globalization spoke about how water privatization invariably hurts the poor. "Water flows uphill to money. Many poor families without access to public water pay twelve times more for water than those using municipal systems. The expense of purifying their water, even boiling it, is a major cost for many poor households. Some households in India pay as much as 35 percent of their income for water. At the same time, water-intensive industries, such as agriculture and high-tech, reap huge public subsidies."

Rachel agreed to meet at the Summit with Jack Houston, the CEO of Wechtan, a multinational company heavily involved in acquiring water monopolies. Pete knew him since Wechtan bought some water purification systems from Green America. He told Rachel that Houston was a straight shooter — "at least as straight as you're going to find among the major players in the water business."

"Rachel, I know you think we're all crooks," Houston told her, "but exploitation of water started long before we came along. Sure, we want to make money, but we also want to build a good water supply system that's going to last. Right now, the poor pay through the nose. Our systems bring down the cost and pretty soon we'll be piping into homes even in the poorest barrios."

"Jack, I appreciate your efforts to improve a bad situation," Rachel replied. "But we shouldn't turn water into just another resource to profit from. We've got too many companies speculating in water who are more concerned about the profit margin than anything else."

"That's not my company though," Houston responded. "We reduce contamination, starting with human and industrial wastes, and we put an end to the corruption. You may think our profit margins are high but it's reasonable in light of all the good we do."

"But corruption hasn't ended," Rachel noted. "Payoffs are still going to politicians and their friends under privatization. Or they get to cheaply buy up land where water's suddenly flowing six months later."

"I didn't say ending corruption was easy. Water's often the easiest way for the local politicians to line their pockets," he noted. "Much of the local opposition to our projects is just someone looking for their cut of the pie. But the national governments don't want to keep pouring resources into this endless money pit while not getting anything in return. They need the private sector, companies like Wechtan, to make it happen."

"Natural resources belong to the planet," Rachel replied. "And as you acknowledge, there's still corruption under privatization. We need community control and ownership, and to ensure that environmental standards are the first priority."

The Summit adopted a declaration affirming that water was a human right and a world resource, not owned by any individual, company or country. Rachel worked with the UN throughout her presidency to make it a worldwide responsibility to ensure that every human being had access to a minimum amount of safe water every day and to protect existing water supplies. The upfront costs were enormous, but it put people to work, especially in many third world countries — a worldwide public works project. Some historians contend that it was the most unifying event in the planet's history, the first real sense of a unified global effort and commitment.

****

The Democrats and Republicans were in an uproar as the country headed into the midterm congressional elections. Their campaign contributors were apoplectic, demanding they rein Rachel in. Corporate media spokespeople, such as Bob Moore of General Power, accused Rachel of "starting a class war and of trying to destroy American business."

Rachel responded, "I'm merely trying to put an end to decades of class warfare. It's unfortunate that some businesspeople feel the need to defend a few bad apples."

The rank and file membership of the two parties joined in the upheaval. The Democrats were feeling the most heat, with half of their base either leaving to join the Greens or demanding that the Democrats embrace Rachel's agenda. A significant portion of the rest felt the Democrats were already too much in bed with the Greens and were considering jumping to the Republicans.

The Republicans for their part were undergoing a conservative revival, with the religious right proclaiming that Satan had taken over the White House.

The Greens witnessed a major upsurge in their membership rolls. Women in particular were attracted to Rachel and the Greens.

Anna asked Wynn, "How much money do we need to raise to elect a Green majority in Congress? With Rachel's standing in the polls, if we turn this into a referendum on her, the Greens should be able to take control."

Wynn laughed. Electoral politics had never been a major passion for her.

"Anna, you seem to think we have democracy in the US. Wake up. Congressional districts are so heavily gerrymandered to favor one particular party that you usually know which party will win regardless of the candidates. In addition, incumbents are almost invariably reelected to Congress due to their huge campaign war chests. To top it off, in almost half the states, the Greens aren't even an official party, making it much harder for us to even get on the ballot.

"And you may remember," Wynn added, "that the Republicans almost managed to steal the last election. This may come as a shock, but there ain't been much improvement since then. We still have the same old voting machines that don't work so well, especially in poor communities. We've made some progress on preferential voting and proportional representation but the vast majority of elections are still winner take all — vote for the lesser of two evils."

To improve the odds, the Greens helped collect signatures in fifteen states and dozens of municipalities to put various electoral reform initiatives on the November ballot. Clean Money, Clean Elections was a system of public campaign financing where candidates qualified for public funding by collecting a minimum number of five-dollar contributions. Most of these initiatives passed in November. The Greens were less successful with referendums on proportional representation and preferential voting, or IRV, though several did win.

The Greens also invested heavily in voter registration drives. "Many of our supporters don't vote because they believe the system is rigged. Who wouldn't feel that when the only choices are the Democrats and Republicans? We got to convince people it's time to cast a vote and recapture Congress from special interests," Wynn said to the national Green coordinating committee.

Despite Rachel's push for public campaign financing for congressional elections, Congress enacted only a few measures to reduce the use of "soft" money television campaign ads to support or defeat particular candidates.

The corporations were happy to use their tv ads to attack Rachel instead of individual congressional candidates. "President Moreno wants to raise your taxes to support all the freeloaders on welfare and in third world countries," said one ad. Another depicted "the long unemployment lines that would result from all the companies going out of business due to all the new environmental rules and from foreigners flocking to America to take your jobs."

Another ad featured the tag line, "You could turn on a light switch and nothing would happen — because of her energy policies." They showed families gathered at the cemetery, "Remembering the love ones they lost while waiting for the government bureaucracy to get them into surgery." There was an updated version of the nuclear bomb ad used against Goldwater, highlighting the threat from terrorists left unchecked by Rachel.

Some progress was made in expanding access to the airwaves by congressional candidates. "The airwaves are public property but are leased to private, for-profit companies for free. This is one of the great giveaways of public resources. At a minimum, tv and radio stations should be required to provide candidates with free air time," Rachel told the Federal Communication Commission.

Rachel arm-twisted the FCC into requiring each congressional candidate to get at least one hour of free airtime per station, including up to 30 one-minute commercials. Political parties were also allocated one hour on each local station to divide among their candidates for state and local offices and to promote the party.

Despite the long odds, the Green Party threw itself into the challenge of building a true opposition party. One key strategy was to unite progressive groups in an electoral coalition, such as inviting peace activists to run on their line. The Green Parties in other countries were often the electoral umbrella for a broad array of movements, bringing together farmers, peace activists, women, trade unionists, gay and civil rights advocates, students and environmentalists.

While Rachel's popularity made far more groups interested in joining, negotiations over how much "clout and resources" each group would have was difficult.

"Their members — to the extent they have any — are already joining the Greens. A lot of these groups are little more than their letterheads," Wynn remarked, "a DC-based direct mail fundraising operation. We're open to making them feel part of the team effort. But the longer they wait, they less important the leaders become."

"The Greens' idea of a coalition," some groups complained, "is that they get to make all the decisions and we can stand behind them in the photo op to announce it."

National liberal organizations, such as the Sierra Club, Peace Action, NOW and NARAL, experienced infighting over whom to support in the congressional elections. The national leadership had long been invested in supporting the Democratic Party. But much of their grassroots membership were now Green supporters.

The national Democratic leaders were constantly arm-twisting the leadership of these groups with a combination of threats and promises. "The Greens have little more than Rachel. They have no realistic chance of winning a decisive number of congressional seats. And a lot of their proposals are just slogans. The devil is in the details, something the Greens tend to ignore. It's great that Rachel has stirred up grassroots interest in a lot of issues that have always been a core part of our agenda. But the Democrats are the only ones with a realistic shot of delivering what you want. Vote for the Greens and you'll turn Congress over to the Republicans."

Sandy Alvarez, Ray McDaniels and Wynn worked to strengthen the Green Party's national campaign operations. They organized a series of regional forums to mobilize community activists. The conferences briefed potential candidates on green issues and provided training on the mechanics of running an election, including fundraising, media, message development and get out the vote efforts.

The party greatly expanded its national office following the 2000 election, with more than ten staff members and dozens of college interns. The office helped coordinate grassroots activism in support of Rachel's various initiatives. It created a national media strategy to ensure that Green voices were heard, learning how to utilize the newest innovations in communication technology. A national Green satellite channel was created to profile Green activists and issues. The Greens moved to the cutting edge in using the internet.

Rachel was dispatched to a stream of fundraising events in the summer and fall, and tens of millions of direct mail fundraising letters were sent. Regional organizers were hired and voter registration drives launched.

During the first two years of Rachel's presidency, the Greens fielded nearly five thousand candidates for local offices, a tenfold increase over the prior two years.

Some Greens of course argued, "It's premature to make a major push in the 2002 congressional elections. Rachel's elevation to the presidency was a fluke. We need to concentrate on developing support at the community level before investing heavily in a congressional strategy requiring a massive amount of funds."

Wynn responded, "We need to do both. We can win local elections, 'cause the role of money is reduced. But right now the presidency is where we have the most power, and we need more members in Congress to support Rachel's administration. And we need the practice for Rachel's reelection effort two years from now."

The Greens were attracting an eclectic mixture of folks. To many new members, the Greens were merely the party that Rachel belonged to. They felt the party's role was to rally support for her. They were startled to discover that some Greens disagreed with some of Rachel's policies — "she doesn't attack capitalism forcefully enough" — and felt she wasn't sufficiently aggressive in implementing the entire Green Party platform.

Some new members felt the party needed to rewrite its platform now that its membership was larger. "There are all these positions that I hadn't heard about before. When do we get to vote on them?" some new members asked at local meetings. Both new and older members argued, "We need to moderate some of our positions in order to attract more support."

Veteran Greens such as Elizabeth Geyser, one of the five national cochairs, explained, "We're not the anyone-but-the-Democrat-and-Republican coalition. We're not interested in pulling together a political coalition based on whatever maximizes our vote. Sure, we're willing to discuss particular issues and consider new solutions, but if you don't agree with our core principles of ecology, justice, nonviolence and democracy, please form your own party or join another one that you do agree with."

The Greens also had to deal with opportunists who sought to use Rachel's popularity to advance their own careers.

Vice-President Mumfi pressured Rachel to support progressive Democrats in targeted districts.

"I understand you have to help the Greens build their base. But we need to pick up some votes in Congress if we want to get our agenda enacted. The Greens are still marginal in many districts. In the Democratic primary, you should help progressives defeat incumbents who have voted against our agenda. And if the Greens can't field a credible candidate in the general election, we need to help supportive candidates who have a shot at winning," Mumfi argued.

Mumfi's request posed a dilemma for Rachel. "John, I'm the de facto leader of the Green Party. There will be a lot of bruised feelings if I start supporting Democrats, especially if there's a Green in the race. Maybe on some of them we can work below the radar screen. I hear what you're saying, but we need the Greens to sign off."

****

Elections are won or lost in the three weeks before election day, when most voters begin to pay attention. Rachel and Wynn sprinted around the country attending rallies for the Green congressional and state candidates.

Twenty Greens were elected to the House, mainly in progressive districts that had conservative Democratic incumbents. Nearly forty incumbent congressmembers were defeated, primarily those who were most opposed to Rachel in moderate districts. A sizeable number of

Democrats who campaigned as supporters of Rachel won.

The Democrats and Greens were increasingly dividing the votes in many districts. In states without preferential voting, the Republicans won many elections with less than a majority. This enabled Baker to hold on to his Speaker position in the House, though he now only had a razor-thin majority in that body.

In many ways the midterm elections were a major victory for Rachel and the Greens, showing significant progress in broadening the party's base. Yet most of the mainstream media declared it a defeat, since the Greens finished a distant third in the number of seats won.

TWENTY

THE GREENING OF AMERICA

Being out on the campaign trail during the midterm elections reenergized Rachel, reminding her of the myriad of issues that were important to her and average Americans before 9/11.

The end of any national election cycle was also the beginning of the next one. Democratic and Republican contenders began the jockeying to replace Rachel.

As they worked on the 2003 budget proposals, Rachel told her inner circle, "Let's complete what we can in the next two years. Don't count on a second term. I don't want any regrets about missed opportunities. Let's put the pedal to the metal."

"But," Sophie cautioned, "let's not get too many irons in the fire. We don't want to get overextended and lose focus."

"Don't worry," Rachel replied. "We'll pick a few big issues to push in the media and to fight with Congress over. We're going to have some fun. But let's fly beneath the radar and win everything we can at the retail level. Accelerate executive orders and administrative regulations."

Sophie instructed the staff, "Look for ways to support community initiatives that don't need congressional approval. If a federal agency is giving out grants for energy research, let's make sure it goes to solar, not nukes. Nickel-and-dime it if you have to. Twenty-five thousand here, two-hundred thousand there, you're talking about real money to a nonprofit trying to build a community center, clean up a river or start a community jobs program. Go find the money."

Building on the Blueprint for America and the work of the Citizen Assemblies, Rachel proposed major increases in the 2003-04 federal budget for childcare, housing, education, mass transit and environmental protection.

"Increased government spending is needed to stimulate our economy," she told the country. "I'm proposing increased funding for green economic development to create millions of new sustainable jobs that pay a living wage. I want to target the funding to small businesses, microenterprise development and worker ownership."

"Why do liberals always think the solution is to throw more money at a problem?" asked House Speaker Baker. "They always wanna make government bigger."

"Why do so-called conservatives always think it's a bad idea to give money to the poor and working people," responded Rachel, "but a great idea to give money to the rich? What's so hard about understanding that the way to expand childcare is to give more money to childcare? How come conservatives think the only way to create jobs is to hand out more welfare to the Fortune 500, with no strings attached?

"Most big businesses are only concerned about profits," she added. "If they can increase profits by cutting the workforce, they do it without a second thought. Yet politicians keep throwing money at them. Could the difference be that CEOs make campaign contributions while kids and small businesses don't?"

"I propose diverting existing government funding for fossil fuels and nuclear power to clean, renewable energy," Rachel said. "Twenty-five percent of our nation's electricity should come from renewable sources by the end of the decade."

The budget included a series of proposals to make the tax system fairer. "We can reduce taxes on low and middle-income taxpayers and small businesses if we close various corporate tax loopholes that enable huge corporations to evade taxes on the income they earn. We should also slightly raise the personal income tax rate on households making more than $150,000," Rachel said.

She also proposed a major hike in revenue-sharing with state and local governments. "The federal government has far more taxing powers than local governments, which are often restricted to using regressive taxes, such as the property and sales taxes. By sharing more of our tax base, we'll make the overall tax system fairer," Rachel said, drawing hearty applause from governors, mayors and local officials.

"To pay for these initiatives, I'm proposing modest cuts in military spending — 20 percent in the first year, and 35 percent by the end of the five-year cycle. We're long overdue for a peace dividend. Our military spending unfortunately wasn't cut after either World War Two or the end of the Cold War. We can't keep diverting funds from our communities to finance a war economy. We have to put people back to work and take care of our schools and children."

Some Green Party members were dismayed that Rachel didn't push for at least a 50 percent cut. "She's wimping out," growled David Smythe. "It's time to just say no to pork barrel handouts for defense contractors. Let 'em go organize a bake sale if they wanna buy more missiles."

But as she expected, even Rachel's more modest proposals drew howls of outrage from the military lobby in Congress. "The president's proposals compromise our defense needs. Ya'd think she'd get it that ya gotta beef up military spendin' when 3,000 Americans get killed," Baker said on the Sunday morning talk shows.

"I know that our most affluent and privileged Americans are willing to do their patriotic duty and bear their fair share of the sacrifices we need in this time of peril," Rachel responded.

Rachel made several proposals to strengthen Social Security. With many baby boomers beginning to retire in the next few decades, there will be a lower ratio of workers paying into the system by the middle of the next decade.

"First, it is important to realize that the Social Security system is solvent, and will remain so as long we avoid raiding the present surplus to pay for other programs — or adopting some of the radical proposals being put forth by Wall Street. It's true that after 2016, the amount of revenues coming into Social Security will be less than the benefits going out. But we can avoid the need to cut Social Security benefits or other government spending at that time by using the existing Social Security surplus now to pay down our government debt. The reduced interest payments will be more than enough to cover the shortfall," Rachel noted.

"We should also avoid the misconception that Social Security is a pension plan. It's a government benefit program — welfare for the elderly — to help lift our senior citizens out of poverty. In effect, present workers pay to ensure a decent standard of living for elderly ones who have retired," she noted.

"But we should address the regressive nature of the Social Security tax," Rachel added. "Since the 7.65 percent levy on wages applies only to the first 78,000 dollars of earnings, low and middle income workers pay a much higher percentage of their income in Social Security taxes. I'm proposing that we cut the tax rate in half, but eliminate the ceiling so that all wages are taxed."

"Nonsense," Baker responded. "Social Security has nothin' to do with welfare. The president's using a lot of mumbo jumbo to hide that she wants a big tax hike. What we oughtta do is give Americans the right to invest it like they see fit, whether it's in the stock market or bonds or whatever. People should have the right to control their retirement funds. Liberals think people aren't bright 'nough to make their own decisions."

Rachel used the pomp and pageantry of the State of the Union address to Congress to renew her push for a universal, single-payer healthcare system. More than a year had passed since she'd made her initial proposal — it was time to turn up the heat.

She invited people who had been ill-served by the country's present medical system to attend, calling upon them to stand up to put a human face on the need for reform.

"We can't allow more people to lose loved ones due to a lack of medical coverage. We have the ability to create the best medical system in the world. But it's not just a matter of human rights, of human dignity. It's also essential to the effort to keep our economy strong and growing. We can't afford to keep on spending 14 percent of our Gross National Product on healthcare. This puts American businesses at a competitive disadvantage with foreign competitors who spend far less on their healthcare costs, yet get better healthcare. We need to take decisive action to control runaway healthcare costs, particularly for long-term care for senior citizens and for prescription drugs."

The budget battle was contentious and lasted many months. The pro-Rachel forces in Congress were backed up by strong grassroots activism, starting with the Citizen Assembly. She eventually won a sizeable increase in funding for her domestic initiatives.

After months of rallies by peace and community activists around the country, Congress reluctantly agreed to a ten percent cut in military spending. It also approved raising the ceiling on the Social Security tax by forty thousand dollars, with a small reduction in the overall tax rate. Universal healthcare moved closer to becoming a reality.

"These Citizen Assemblies are a royal pain in the butt," many congressmembers complained to each other. "A lot of 'em act like they're the ones who were elected."

****

The Attorney General continued to rein in white-collar crime while expanding her efforts to curb corporate power.

"We need to end the fiction that corporations are people, that they're entitled to the same legal rights as individuals but not the responsibilities," Stewart told Rachel. "This right was bestowed on corporations a century ago by a clerk of the US Supreme Court, who slipped the pronouncement into the official notes summarizing a court decision. The Court itself hadn't even addressed the issue."

Stewart fought in court to downsize corporations and their powers. "Corporations were granted the right to exist to perform a specific, narrow service, such as building a road or canal. They were never supposed to become a many-tentacled octopus extending its power and influence everywhere. They're supposed to be our servants, not our masters," she argued.

Stewart brought several cases seeking to revoke charters of corporations that routinely violated the law. "If a company is a persistent lawbreaker, its right to operate should be terminated, and its assets sold to others," she argued in court.

Judith Miller, a longtime scholar on foreign affairs who had been active with the International Committee of the Greens, had been recruited by Rachel to replace Darling as Secretary of State. Miller had been Associate Director of the Peace Institute. For years she had worked for making the protection of human rights an integral part of the foreign policy agenda.

Miller and Stewart worked with Amnesty International and others to hold American companies accountable for their human rights violations in other countries, from Russia and Mexico to Ecuador, Indonesia and Cameroon.

Many of the worst culprits were oil companies. such as ExxonMobil, Chevron, Texaco and Occidental Petroleum. For example, ExxonMobil was closely tied to Indonesian security forces that committed numerous acts of murder, torture and rape in the oil regions of Aceh. Stewart supported a lawsuit filed by local villagers against ExxonMobil, telling the court, "It'll strengthen our government's campaign against terrorism while furthering our efforts to promote human rights."

Stewart also went after ExxonMobil for human rights violations in Chad, where it was helping to develop the Doba oil fields. "The 650-mile 3.7-billion-dollar pipeline project, the largest investment scheme in Africa, will run from southern Chad to the Atlantic Ocean in Cameroon," Stewart told Rachel. "The pipeline will gouge through Chad's most fertile agricultural region and the Atlantic Littoral Forest, home to the indigenous Bagyeli people and rich in biodiversity. Chad's government has engaged in repression, torture and rape of political opponents and critics of the pipeline. They've diverted oil payments earmarked for schools and hospitals to purchase weapons. The Cameroon government has also attacked environmental and human rights activists."

****

To strengthen the Green Party's formal role in her administration, Rachel met with leaders of the Green congressional delegation every Monday night, along with several of the national Green staff and party officials.

Ray and Sandy were the deans of the Green congressional delegation and chaired the meetings. They usually spent half an hour or so on a formal agenda, with a similar amount of time for informal conversation. The Greens pitched their pet projects and proposals, while giving Rachel an opportunity to try out some of her ideas.

Sophie raised the need to replace some Greens who'd been appointed to various positions within the federal government. "Most of the Greens are doing a great job," she reported. "They're really shaking up some of these agencies, bringing in new ideas. But some are in over their heads. They don't know the issues well enough or they have really poor people skills. Some of the men in particular are loose cannons. They just issue directives without worrying about whether they have the legal authority — or the funds."

McDaniels said, "If they can't do the job, they gotta go. We're not running a patronage mill here."

The reassignment or dismissal of several Greens prompted heated protests. Rosa Perez, the Green peace activist, called Rachel on behalf of Marguerite Rivera, who'd been removed from running the southern California office of Health and Human Services.

"Rachel, how the hell can you fire Marguerite?" Rosa demanded to know. "She's a single mom with three kids who's been a fighter for social justice for years. She's chair of the LA County Green organization. She's an inspiration for lots of women out here. You're burning a lot of bridges."

"I know Marguerite's a great person," Rachel told her "It's just that she's a poor administrator. Someone who's great at organizing a protest isn't always cut out to run an agency. She's overwhelmed by the paperwork. She focuses on a few things that she's personally interested in while everything else grinds to a halt waiting for her to give some direction."

"But her heart's in the right place," Rosa argued. "She knows how the system needs to be changed. She's not one of these bureaucrats who learned about poverty in a college class. She's lived in the trenches."

"I'm sorry, Rosa, she can't do this job," Rachel responded. "We offered her a position helping to formulate policy. It'd be great if you convince her to take it. But she's not ready to be a high-level administrator."

"Rachel, a Green world needs leaders like Marguerite. You can always find paper pushers. What's hard to find is someone willing to speak truth to power. This is a big freakin' mistake," Rosa said, slamming down the receiver.

****

Rachel's inner circle settled into more defined roles after the midterm elections.

"John, I need you to take the lead in dealing with Congress," Rachel told Mumfi, who still had the physical presence of the football linebacker he was in college. "You're our ambassador to the Democrats. I need you to put together a workable majority for our initiatives." Mumfi worked closely with the congressional Black and progressive caucuses, the labor unions and other liberal power players.

On a few occasions Mumfi went further with concessions than Rachel had approved. When Sophie complained, Rachel told her to sign off anyway. "If he's going to be taken seriously, he has to be viewed as being able to deliver on stuff. I'll talk to him about being more careful in the future, but it's not worth undercutting him."

Mumfi played a pivotal role in the election of Congressmember Barbara Wiley of San Francisco as the new House Minority Leader. "We need someone who'll spend more time taking on Baker rather than Moreno," Mumfi argued with his former colleagues. Wiley was friendly with the Greens. Her constituents had recently elected a Green mayor of the city in a nonpartisan runoff with a corporate Democrat.

Mumfi told the liberal Democrats in Congress, "This is an opportunity to move the party in a more progressive direction. We agree with most of Rachel's agenda. She and the Greens are doing most of the heavy lifting, taking the flack. We can keep our moderate base while getting a heck of a lot more of our agenda through than before. So we lose some corporate contributions. The unions and the liberal groups will make it up."

Mumfi's relationship with Senator Majority Leader Deutsche was difficult. "John, can you remind me which team you're on?" Deutsche asked after a heated exchange over the federal budget.

"I'm on the people's team," Mumfi replied testily. "I'm working exactly for the issues the voters in my district originally elected me to work on."

"Not many districts are as liberal as Harlem," Deutsche pointed out.

"Senator, I suggest you focus more on what Rachel is saying rather than on the color or her party," Mumfi responded. "Her agenda plays very well in a lot of Democratic congressional districts. If the party is viewed as placing partisan concerns ahead of the issues, that's going to hurt us at election time. And believe it or not, she does listen to what I have to say. I'd think you be surprised how responsive she'd be to your concerns if you tried a little harder to work with her."

Rachel and Mumfi agreed that he would coordinate three of the Cabinet departments: Housing and Urban Development, Health and Human Services, and Education. HUD and HHS had been starved for funds over the last two decades, as funding for antipoverty programs was diverted to corporate handouts and for-profit private developers. Federal funding as a percentage of the overall education budget had also been declining, and many inner city and rural schools were underfunded and heavily segregated

Rachel told Mumfi that she had three main housing goals: "Eliminate homelessness, make quality housing affordable to all, and promote energy conservation and efficiency as an integral part of new housing construction. By the end of this decade, I want solar hot water units on houses to be the norm rather than the exception."

Mumfi scoffed that Rachel's proposals were the easy part. "All they take is money. The real challenge is to end the de facto housing segregation. Despite decades of public funding, in many ways we're more segregated than when we started. Far too many people of color, and poor people in general, still live in inadequate housing in unsafe neighborhoods," Mumfi said.

Anna continued to coordinate employment issues such as family leave, day care, and unemployment insurance. Rachel's budget proposals included more funding for domestic violence programs and rape prevention. Anna also helped to create economic development policies for women both in the US and in third world countries, promoting the type of small-scale sustainable development projects she had worked on for years.

Anna's personal relationship with Rachel was also a subject of gossip, starting with the tabloids. Anna's sexual orientation was common knowledge, noted even in the mainstream papers, such as the *New York Times* and *Washington Post*.

Anna softened her image a bit, letting her close-cropped hair grow longer and wearing expensive business suits. "Come on, Wynn, cut it out," Rachel said when he teased Anna about her new look. "You're the one who always argues that those who wish to be the most radical must appear to be the most reasonable. What we should be talking about is a makeover for you. Enough of this sixties downtrodden revolutionary look."

Anna pushed Rachel on gay and lesbian issues, such as same sex marriages and transgender rights. "This civil union stuff they started in Vermont is okay, but we want more. We want the right to marry just like anyone else. We don't want to be second-class citizens."

"I know I'm going to sound like a politician," Rachel responded, "but we don't need to debate the merits of this, we have to figure out the politics. We're not going to win without pressure from the grassroots."

"If ya want pressure, sweetie, just propose legalizing same sex marriage," Anna responded. "That'll get 'em out of the closet — so to speak."

"It'll just get us clobbered," Rachel replied. "It's the type of issue that the right is just waiting to jump all over me on. We push it in Congress right now, we could end up with a constitutional amendment banning it. Before I introduce a bill, we're counting votes. I'd rather have the attorney general fight for it in court. Or figure out a way to push it locally, maybe through one of the liberal states like California or Massachusetts."

Local Green officials came up with a strategy. Green Mayors in San Francisco and New Paltz began issuing marriage licenses to same-sex couples. The response was overwhelming, far beyond what they had anticipated. Hundreds of couples rushed to get hitched before the gate was closed., as conservatives rushed to court seeking injunctions.

"I've been living with Millie for ten years now. I want to be her wife," said Harriet, a fifty-year-old librarian. "We want to be able to take care of one another if either us gets sick, not be told by the hospital that we have no say in our partner's medical treatment if she isn't able to decide. I want her to be able to collect my Social Security and pension. I want our relationship to be recognized by society, for us to be treated like normal human beings."

The airwaves were filled with images of beaming, joyous couples leaving City Hall after they tied the knot. They became the poster children of a new civil rights movement.

"Mayor Walsh," asked one reporter of the New Paltz Mayor, "shouldn't this issue be handled by the legislature or the courts rather than you acting on your own? Isn't this act of civil disobedience in violation of your oath of office to uphold the law."

"This is an act of civil obedience," Walsh replied. "Our constitution provides for the equal protection of the law. I take that responsibility very seriously."

A number of congressmen, starting with Senator Branston, introduced a constitutional amendment to ban gay marriage. "The bible says a marriage is between a man and a woman. The government shouldn't bestow the sacredness of marriage upon such an abnormal lifestyle. It is just one more nail in the coffin of traditional family values, a further erosion of our society's morality," Branston argued. He had the strong support of many religious conservatives.

"I've been hearing for years from conservatives that marriage is a solution to poverty, that too many women are raising children out of wedlock," Anna replied. "So why isn't the religious right jumping for joy that at least one community is embracing the idea of marriage? I don't see how allowing two people who love each other to make a lifelong commitment in any way threatens the marriages of heterosexuals. It seems like straight folks were already having too many divorces way before same-sex marriages came long. If Branston wants to defend the institution of marriage, maybe he should call for public funding for marriage counseling."

While the politicians debated — or tried to duck — the issue, a tidal wave of same-sex marriages rolled across the country. More and more local officials began to issue marriage licenses to same-sex couples. Judges consistently ruled that a ban on same-sex marriage violated the equal protection clause of the constitution. Each new step forward in the fight for gay marriage just emboldened the supporters to push ahead even faster.

Rachel said she would veto any law or constitutional amendment that sought to ban gay marriage. "The Constitution is about empowering the American people. This amendment would be the only provision that sought to take away rights from one group of people. It would set a dangerous precedent that I will not be party to."

****

Of the inner circle, Wynn's role was the most difficult to get agreement on, particularly from him. More than once Rachel had received a call from top ranking administration officials, even the Senate Majority Leader, asking for clarification on a recent conversation they had with Wynn.

"Wynn, you can't keep calling up Cabinet members and barking at them. They don't know if you're talking for me or just blowing off some steam or lobbying them. Believe it or not, some of them do know what they're doing. You also have to stop jumping from issue to issue depending upon the morning headlines."

Wynn had been attacked in the press for acting liking a copresident, the male version of Hillary Clinton or Eleanor Roosevelt. Wynn occasionally sat in on Cabinet meetings, though Rachel had insisted that he keep quiet in a chair along the wall. "If you wanna offer your opinion, do it after the meeting, to me, in private. And don't be passing notes or making faces when somebody says something you disagree with." Wynn quickly lost interest in attending.

Despite Rachel's occasional need to curb his enthusiasm he was still her most trusted adviser, her initial sounding board. He drafted several of her major speeches. She relied upon him to keep track of the big picture, to make sure she wasn't sidetracked by the day-to-day details of running the government.

Wynn agreed to focus on the environment and development in Africa. He also teamed up with Pete on transportation issues, pushing for increased public investment in hybrid electric cars, biodiesel and mass transit, and for no-car zones in major cities. He took the lead in coordinating the administration's work on global warming, restoring the ocean's fisheries and protecting natural habitats and biodiversity.

Rachel appointed Wynn to head a task force on environmental justice. For too long, communities of color and low-income neighborhoods, including Native American, had been the favorite siting location for all forms of toxic, hazardous and radioactive wastes and poisons — chemical factories, waste incinerators, garbage dumps, bus depots, oil refineries.

"The Environmental Justice Task Force will look at how to clean up the existing problems, compensate those who have been injured and eliminate such work environments and practices in the future. Environmental justice affirms the need to clean up and rebuild our cities and rural areas, all in balance with nature," said Rachel in announcing the initiative.

Wynn held hearings around the country to solicit testimony. The residents spoke of living with the smell, the fear, the lies and closed doors of company officials and government agencies. They spoke of neighborhoods with high rates of cancer and birth defects. Of miscarriages. Of premature breast development. Reproductive problems. Of rashes that would not go away. Of liver diseases. Of children with stunted growth and learning disabilities. All in the name of profits.

They told about neighborhoods where every young child had am inhaler to help with their breathing problems. "Asthma is the number one cause of childhood hospitalization in most major urban areas," testified Dr. Nora Williams, "sending far more kids to emergency rooms than gunshot wounds or car accidents. African-Americans are two to three times more likely than whites to be hospitalized for or to die from asthma."

"I felt trapped," said Theresa, a thirty-year-old mother from Louisiana. "I knew it wasn't good for me or for my family. I'd wake up in the mornin' and the porch would be covered in this dark kinda soot-like stuff. I knew we was breathin' it in, that the ash was gettin' in our lungs. We all had these coughs that never went away, but we couldn't afford no doctor. We had no place else to move to. We had no money, and no one would give us nuthin' for our place. And then one night it was really bad. We live in a little hollow by the river. It was wicked hot and everythin' just came down on us, you could hardly breathe. When we got up the next mornin', our baby wasn't breathin' too good. She died a week later."

Wynn's task force drafted legislation to regulate the siting of hazardous facilities, ensuring that they wouldn't be concentrated in densely populated areas, especially in those with a high minority or poor population. It proposed significantly higher fees on polluting facilities and manufacturing processes to raise funds to clean up existing toxic sites, and to provide healthcare and relocation assistance to victims.

Some in Congress just laughed when they got together with lobbyists for the chemical industry and other polluters to review the recommendations. "What does Rachel think? That we're going to put these things in rich people's backyards? In suburban neighborhoods where everyone votes? That's political reality. Poor people get stuck with the garbage. It's not rocket science to figure it out."

****

The last straw finally landed on the back of former Secretary of State Darling, convincing him of the need to run for president. It was Rachel's agreement to extradite Henry Kissinger, Secretary of State under Presidents Nixon and Ford, for a trial in Chile for murder of former Chilean President Salvadore Allende.

"Kissinger has long been considered by many to be a war criminal, especially by several countries for his role in political killings and other terrorist activities in South America and in countries around Vietnam," the attorney general announced in a press briefing on the request for extradition from a Chilean Judge. "His role in the assassination of President Allende three years after he was democratically elected has been well documented by the National Archives Project. Kissinger also led Project Condor, in which the US killed democratic reformers throughout Central and South America."

Kissinger had approved the invasion of East Timor by Indonesia, which resulted in numerous war crimes and the death of one fifth of its population. Now that East Timor has achieved independence, they're demanding action against those responsible for war crimes against them, including Kissinger. Kissinger's role for war crimes in Vietnam and Southeast Asia was still too controversial for even Rachel to raise.

Darling considered Kissinger a hero "whose service to his country and commitment to building a better world had been validated by receiving the Nobel Peace Prize for negotiating the United States retreat from South Vietnam" — even though the retreat rapidly led to victory by the People's Liberation Army of North Vietnam. Darling felt that Kissinger was one of the few politicians "who understood what was really going on and had been willing to do the dirty work needed to protect America."

"Extraditing Mr. Kissinger is critical to show that America's serious about being even-handed in prosecuting those accused of terrorist acts," Rachel said in announcing her decision.

"We can't expect other nations to prosecute their citizens for war crimes if we disallow the prosecution of our own. In this case, we're responding to a formal judicial request from a Chilean court. One of our citizens is accused of playing a major role in the overthrow of a democratically elected sovereign government, including assassinating its president and other officials. It's alleged that his signature, and that of our government, are on the bodies of thousands of innocent civilians killed in direct contravention of both US and international law.

"We as a nation must recognize our own faults and mistakes, no matter how painful that process may be, if we want to create a world based on justice," Rachel added.

Most aggravating to Darling was that Kissinger had been packed onto a plane bound to Chile so quickly that his attorneys had no opportunity to block it in American courts. "This is an outrageous violation of due process," Darling charged.

"Such an expedited extradition process was provided for in the antiterrorism package that Congress passed days after September eleventh over my objections," Rachel retorted. "While Congress may have intended it to be used primarily to bring captured individuals to the US, it works in reverse as well. Congress is welcome to change it at any time. Kissinger will get his day in court — it'll just be a Chilean one."

****

Rachel sought to strengthen relations with Mexico, pushing for increased economic aid and relaxed immigration policies. With her Mexican grandfather, she was a national hero there, more popular in many ways than the new Mexican president, Ricardo Torres.

Torres had finally broken the stranglehold of the moribund and corrupt Party of the Institutional Revolutionary Party (PRI), which had managed to hold on to power for 70 years, the longest tenure by a single party in any democracy. He had won as an electoral alliance between the conservative National Action Party (PAN) and the Green Party, though the Greens were a weak partner.

Torres felt the US should open its border with Mexico as part of Free Trade. "NAFTA is helping to eliminate 'borders' between the US, Mexico and Canada with respect to the movement of trade and capital. Surely we should do no less with the movement of citizens. Instead, the US and its border states are wasting billions of dollars trying to block migration."

"Raising the standard of living in Mexico is critical if America wants to stop the flow of Mexican workers across the border," Torres told Rachel. "I hope the US will see the value in funding a 20-billion-dollar-a-year development program targeting the poorest sectors of Mexico." Torres had gotten the idea from the 35-billion-dollar European Union fund to create jobs and raise income in the poorer countries from the former Soviet bloc in Eastern Europe.

Mexico's disparity in wealth and income is one of the worst in the world. More than 40 percent of the population lives on less than two dollars per day, and nearly 20 percent on less than one dollar per day. The income of the top 10 percent of the population is 25 times larger than that of the poorest 40 percent. The gap has been widening since the economic crisis of the 1980s.

Wynn, Sophie, Rachel and Mumfi held a meeting on Mexico and overall immigration policy over lunch one day in early spring. Rachel wanted to discuss what she would say when President Torres paid a formal state visit the next month.

Rachel initially assumed that immigrant reform with Mexico would be easy. "We've gotta stop poor Mexican workers dying in the desert merely because they want to earn a living," she told the others over lunch. "A lotta times they're working the land their forefathers worked on — and often owned — before our government stole it from Mexico. It's about time we acknowledged that much of our country's prosperity has been built by the sweat and blood of immigrants. These are our neighbors, not criminals."

Wynn raised the environmental problems associated with increased immigration.

"Environmentalists who want to restrict immigration aren't just snobs looking to maintain their privileged lifestyle. Immigration poses real threats in terms of depletion of resources. The worst-case scenario isn't that immigration will change our lifestyles but rather that they won't change. More people living in the US means that much more obscene use of fossil fuels, of plastic, resulting in more solid waste, air pollution, gas guzzlers and so on. Immigration already counts for half of our population growth. The world couldn't survive 400 million Americans in 2050."

"Speaking of overconsumption," Mumfi jumped in, "what are we eating? It's delicious but I feel my waistline expanding already."

"Someone gave me a Moosewood Cook Book for Christmas," Rachel replied, "so I'm having the White House chef systematically go through the recipes. This is a cheese and almond stuffed zucchini dish, with a side of artichoke heart and tomato salad," Rachel replied.

"We also got organized labor to contend with," Mumfi added. "Agribusiness, assembly lines, garment factories, you name it, they all use immigrant labor to drive down wages and working conditions. Sure, businesses claim that Americans don't like hard labor anymore, that only the foreign workers will take the really back-breaking manual jobs. But what they really mean is that American workers balk at putting up with slavery. And the downward pressure on wages is being felt not only in traditional jobs taken by immigrants like agribusiness and the meat packing industry, but increasingly among technical workers in the engineering and computer fields."

The immigration debate made for strange bedfellows. Supporters of liberal reforms included the various ethnic groups that had themselves recently immigrated, as well as religious activists and human rights advocates. Other supporters included business interests that profited from cheap foreign labor. Opponents, in addition to some environmentalists and labor, included those who viewed non-European immigrants as a threat to American culture, that is, racists.

Sophie added her two cents, stretching past Wynn to grab a roll. "Yeah, but people who work hard, pay taxes and contribute to society should be given the opportunity to obtain permanent residence. Every human being has a right to make a decent life for themselves. They shouldn't have to worry about the knock on the door or the INS showing up at work. And immigrant women often get turned into slaves for the sex industry. If they complain, they end up being deported and wasting their family's life savings that was used to send them here."

"We're the ones that allow these situations to occur," Sophie continued. "We also have to stop deporting people back to countries where they're going to be persecuted, whether it's because of their politics or just because they're poor."

Progress on immigration reform was frustratingly slow, though Rachel used her administrative powers to make it easier to protect refugees on humanitarian grounds.

Rachel was able to relax the border rules with Mexico, making it easy for Mexicans to work in the US even if they couldn't obtain permanent citizenship. Mexico agreed to the same rules for American workers. She issued an executive order to allow Mexican identity cards to be used for many business and government transactions — a quasi-green card.

She also proposed amnesty — citizenship — for anyone who had been living in America for three years, and to shift immigration quotas to favor applicants from South America rather than Europe. "For two hundred years, we've treated the countries south of us as our colonies, impeding their economic and political development. It's time to make amends." Congress had other ideas.

Rachel convinced Congress to provide an annual fund for economic development, though much less than Torres had requested. Critics complained she was pouring American tax dollars down the drain of political corruption in Mexico. She had mixed success in making sure that the money was invested in sustainable community economic development, rather than going to politically connected American and Mexican businessmen running low-wage factory operations for export to the US and Canadian markets.

In exchange for these reforms, Rachel pushed Mexico to improve its human rights record and environmental programs.

A few months after Torres's visit, Rachel held up payments to Mexico when two environmental activists were jailed on trumped up charges of protecting local farmers growing drugs. Torres called to complain. Rachel said, "I don't know what the problem is, must be something to do with paperwork. I'm sure it will only take a few months to straighten out. By the way, how's your lovely wife, and how quickly will you be getting those environmentalists out of jail?"

"You know, Rachel, just because your grandfather was Mexican doesn't give you the right to be a Yankee imperialist, interfering in the internal affairs of our country. We have laws that have to be followed. And as hard as it may be to believe, judges and prosecutors don't always listen to what we say in Mexico City. I believe that's one of the reforms that you champion in democracies. It's not like the US doesn't have its own history of political prisoners. I'm not the one who put them in jail, but they aren't exactly the boy scouts their supporters make them out to be."

"Mr. President, in our country, we don't torture people to get confessions," Rachel responded. "And while it may be local corruption that put them in jail, someone has got to step in and clean up the mess. You're the one with the power to do it. And I find it hard to believe that the farmers are the ones making the profits from the drug trade, or that they're the ones with the money to buy protection from your police force and military.

"If you want us to treat Mexico as a full partner, then you have to strengthen the rule of law and respect human rights. Please keep my office informed on how the case is coming," said Rachel

Rachel also pushed Torres to step up the investigation into hundreds of cases of "disappearance" of political dissidents in the '70s and '80s during the so-called "dirty war." "You have got to give closure to their relatives," she told the president. "Even if you grant amnesty to those who come forth to speak the truth, it'll make your country stronger. It'll make it far less likely that it'll ever happen again."

****

Anna pushed Rachel to establish a similar fund to support economic development in impoverished third world countries, building upon the principles that her women's development group had followed.

"You think Mexico is bad? A lotta countries are much worse off. Take some of the savings from the military cuts and help the poorest of the poor, particularly women who are the ones rearing the families. A couple of hundred dollars for a family to fix up their house or help improve the local sewage system will have 'em dancing in the streets," Anna pleaded.

The UN had recently approved the Millennium Declaration to combat global hunger and poverty. It set a goal of 2015 to make significant progress in hunger, poverty, education, the status of women, health, the environment and other areas of concern in developing countries. For instance, it had a goal of reducing by half the number of people living on less than one dollar a day, reducing by two-thirds the mortality rate among children under five — one out of ten children dies by the age of five in developing countries — and reducing by half the proportion of people without sustainable access to safe drinking water.

Rachel proposed that the G8 and other industrial countries commit 50 billion dollars annually to support the Millennium Declaration. She asked Congress for 15 billion, hoped for 10, and got 7 in the first year. The UN raised a total of 25 billion dollars the first year.

Rachel also supported the call for the US and other industrial countries to end agriculture subsidies to its farmers. Such supports resulted in American farmers dumping their products in third world states, hurting farmers in those countries.

Rachel held a press conference with Bread for the World. BFW's president, Rev. Harold Cunningham, stated, "The US and other developed countries continue to protect their agriculture by paying farmers more than 300 billion dollars in subsidies annually — six times what they give in development aid. Because such payments encourage farmers to produce more, world agricultural markets are glutted with subsidized crops like corn, cotton, sugar and wheat, resulting in lower prices for all farmers.

"US farm policy enables it to export certain crops and agriculture products significantly below actual production costs. Corn, for instance, is sold at 20 percent below cost. Though developing countries often have the business advantage of cheap land and labor, their farmers cannot compete with these subsidized prices. Unable to sell their products even in local markets, poor farmers and the communities they live in are condemned to a cycle of poverty and hunger," said Cunningham.

Eliminating such subsidies would enable third world countries to triple their annual net agricultural trade to 60 billion dollars — almost two-thirds the value of all development and humanitarian aid provided by industrialized countries.

Rachel added, "I know many in Congress support agriculture subsidies because they want to support our family farmers. But the bulk of the subsidies go to large corporate farms. Besides redirecting subsidies to only small farms, we should use the funds for rural development. This would include job training, infrastructure development, development of niche markets and crops, and direct assistance to poor families."

The congressional members from farm states fought hard to maintain the subsidies. "Our farmers don't get a fair price for the crops they grow," said Senator Paul Hastings of Iowa at a congressional hearing on farm subsidies. "They can't pay their bills. These subsidies are the lifeblood of our rural economies. It's critical to our national security to ensure a strong domestic agriculture system."

"We need to allow families to stay in the farm business and continue to act as stewards of our land," added Senator Mike Osborne of Nebraska. "If you want to continue low food costs for the American consumer, we have to open the global market to our farmers by requiring all countries to cut import tariffs and export subsidies. We'll all benefit in the long run with a more efficient agriculture system."

"We've been handing out subsidies for generations," Cunningham testified at the hearing, "and yet our family farmers are being driven off their land. We have to support America's rural economies without distorting global markets. Let's give money to the small, struggling farmers, but impose an income limit so that the large corporate farms don't gobble up all the subsidies."

Rachel also had USDA issue proposed regulations that mirrored the sustainable, organic agriculture practices that had recently been adopted in Europe. Agribusiness interests immediately filed suit to block their implementation.

TWENTY-ONE

A NEW FOREIGN POLICY

The conflict between Israel and the Palestinians escalated sharply in the spring of 2003. The Israelis launched increased military attacks against Palestinians in the occupied territories. Palestinian suicide bombers responded by killing civilians in Israel. Israeli Prime Minister David Skolnick then imposed military curfews in many of the cities in the occupied territories, along with arrests and executions of suspected militants.

The situation spiraled out of control when Israeli forces launched a massive attack to eliminate resistance in the Jenin refugee camp, resulting in a week of house-to-house combat. Palestinians claimed Israel massacred hundreds of civilians. It was not the first time that charges of leading a massacre had been leveled against Skolnick during his half-century military and political leadership.

Rachel stunned the world when she announced she was going to join the voluntary Peace Keepers in their efforts to separate the combatants. "All my words and prayers have accomplished little so far. Perhaps laying down my body for peace will be more successful. I urge all Palestinians and Israelis, all people, to take to the streets peacefully to quiet the guns and to isolate the extremists who advocate the use of violence."

Rachel hoped her trip would empower the various peace groups on both sides.

One of the peace activists that Rachel had been communicating with was Zinab Sourani, who'd started a Palestinian women's group based on the principles on nonviolent resistance. The Peace Institute had been working closely with her.

Sourani was a charismatic young activist barely over five feet, with an easy smile and intense eyes. Her two younger brothers had been killed by artillery shells fired by Israeli tanks as the boys walked past a Jewish settlement on the way home from visiting some friends. The Israeli tanks used flechette shells, which contain dart-like shrapnel that's sprayed over a large area upon impact. The use of such shells against a civilian population is unlawful under the Fourth Geneva Convention of 1949. An Israeli tank also ran over the body of one her brothers.

"Too many of our brothers and sisters have been buried, and too many are forced to live in poverty and endure a life without meaning or purpose," Sourani told Rachel. "Groups like Hamas and the Islamic Jihad have shown they can kill Israeli citizens but not that they know how to make peace with our foes. We need to learn how to live with Israel, not destroy it.

"We must find a different path, force Israel and the US to confront their own hypocrisy about their commitment to liberty, peace and democracy. We must stop giving them excuses to oppress our people," Sourani told Palestinians as she traveled throughout the occupied territories holding community meetings she tried to keep hidden from the Israelis.

"We need to create a society that no longer sanctions violence as a solution to our problems. Those who have advocated terrorism and violence for decades haven't brought us our homeland, a return of the refugees or an end to the military occupation. It's time to confront Israel with a nonviolent resistance movement, just as Gandhi confronted English rule in his country," she added.

The nonviolent movement initially had many skeptics among Palestinians. "You women are naïve, a tool of the Zionists and American imperialists," charged a young supporter of Hamas at one of the meetings. "For decades the world has watched as the Zionists have stolen our lands and killed our people. The world will watch again as the Israelis drive their tanks over your prone bodies. They won't stop till they kill us all or drive us into the sea."

"We're not asking you to sit back and wait for diplomacy to succeed. We're asking you to take to the streets," Sourani responded, "to confront the Israelis, to confront the military, to say we'll no longer tolerate being treated as less than human beings. We reject the use of violence as a failed strategy that will never bring peace and liberation to our cause. We also ask you to see Israelis as our neighbors with whom we need to make peace. Our enemy is the Israeli government, not Jews."

The Palestinian Alliance for an End to Violence had organized marches to challenge the blockades and tanks, singing songs and offering gifts of food and wine to their oppressors. The marches were led by women and children too young to have yet learned to pick up rocks and guns.

"The Israelis and the American politicians call us monsters for our suicide bombings, but they ignore all the bad actions of the Israelis — their support for apartheid in South Africa, the assassinations, the state-sponsored terrorism — and point to the genocide of the Holocaust. The Israelis say they'll never stand by and allow their people to be murdered again. Well, it's the Israelis that made the Hamas and the Islamic Jihad what they are. It's Israel that's reaping the seeds of hate they have sown," Sourani told Rachel when she called to discuss her visit.

"I know we won't win by becoming like our oppressors. We need to make the Israelis look into the mirror and see what they've become, that what they have done to the Palestinians is wrong, and that they must find the courage to admit their mistakes and to work for peace instead, to end the occupation. Enough is enough," Sourani added.

As the nonviolent resistance movement had gained followers and began to organize nonviolent direct action, reporters asked the Israeli Prime Minister if he felt that the new movement gave hope for peace.

"Israel has always respected the sanctity of human life," Skolnick replied to the media, dismissing the movement as just a publicity gimmick. "We've always sought to avoid bloodshed. If the Palestinians want peace, they need to stop their own people from killing innocent civilians. Groups like Hamas want to kill all Jews. Time and time again we have offered them a just resolution to this matter, only to have them walk away.

"We know that peace will require sacrifices on both sides," Skolnick added, "and we are willing to accept that. The Palestinians, too many of them would rather fight than live in peace. They prefer to die the death of a religious zealot."

The call for peace also grew stronger in Israel. More than a thousand military reservists announced their refusal to serve in the occupied territories. They issued a letter stating, "The price of occupation is the loss of the military's human character and the corruption of the entire Israeli society. We know that the territories are not Israel, and that all settlements are bound to be evacuated in the end. We shall not continue to fight beyond the 1967 borders to dominate, expel, starve and humiliate an entire people."

Peace Now activists in Israel were calling for unilateral withdrawal from the occupied territories, particularly the Gaza Strip and the most isolated of the West Bank settlements.

"Since the Oslo process, the population of the settlements has doubled. We're farther than ever from peace, and Israel is still stuck in Gaza, said Moria Shlomot, the Director of Peace Now. "Unilateral withdrawal is the type of dramatic action needed to convince the Palestinians that Israel really wants to end the occupation. It's time to leave the settlements and stop the terror. The security of ordinary Israelis would dramatically improve once these indefensible settlements are dismantled."

Darling led the howls of protest over Rachel's trip. "The most reckless form of cowboy diplomacy I've ever seen, a cheap political stunt that risks lives on both sides," he said. Most political observers dismissed it as "Rachel being dramatic. She's just trying to get Skolnick and Arafat to come to Camp David for a little arm twisting."

Sophie argued that it was too risky. "All you need is one person to believe that his cause would be better served by killing you, and the whole powder keg could explode." Even Anna said, "I dunno about this one, kiddo. You're too far out on a limb. And these people kill one another at a drop of a hat."

The State Department argued about the need to get a formal invitation from the Israeli government before she visited. "Well they better have it done in the next 48 hours, because that's when I'll arrive," Rachel said tersely. "I've accepted an invitation to visit from a women's peace group representing both Palestinians and Israelis. Find me the nearest airport that we can land Air Force One at, and I'll fly in by helicopter from there. Better yet, the Egyptian president has been asking me to make a visit. We'll fly to Cairo first. Maybe I can ride a camel from there."

"The US bears responsibility for this mess," Rachel told the media as she boarded Air Force One. "We've been arming the Israelis so they can be our proxy army in the Middle East. We've got to rein them in. But we also have to make it clear to the Palestinians that blowing up Israeli citizens is the wrong response. Trying to convince Skolnick and Arafat to make peace hasn't worked. It's time to work with average Israelis and Palestinians to put a halt to this insanity."

Skolnick delayed giving his formal approval until Air Force One lifted off, then demanded that Rachel go first to Israel before proceeding to the occupied territories. "I look forward to setting her straight about what is going on. It is incredible how foolhardy she is. She has no idea what she's doing," he complained to the Israeli Cabinet. "She's encouraging terrorism."

Rachel sent a message to Skolnick that unless he was prepared to make major concessions, "I will visit you after I've completed my meetings and investigations."

Rachel did her best to hide her churning stomach. But once she hit the ground, she felt a wave of excitement, of history, of people's hopes and dreams breaking over her. She created a mini-riot wherever she went, as everyone surged forward to see her, particularly women who felt empowered to pour into the streets to demand peace for their children.

Rachel's visit to Palestine was the proudest moment of her presidency. She felt it was her tumbling of the Berlin Wall, a moment that changed what was possible in the world.

Rachel had a small but significant personal security team surrounding her as she moved through the occupied territories. A much larger Israeli security force tried to establish a perimeter of several hundred yards around her. The security efforts were futile, as a wave of humanity flowed around her in jubilation. Tens of thousands of Palestinians poured into the streets wherever she went, celebrating peace as if the war had been won, a rolling festival of noise and laughter and dancing.

With Sourani at her side, Rachel urged the Palestinians "to reject violence as a response to the occupation. Try to follow the path that Gandhi used in India to throw off the British occupation. If the women of Palestine and Israel work together, you can help your fellow citizens overcome their mutual distrust and anger."

Rachel stayed for four days. Each day the size of the nonviolent protest grew exponentially, until it seemed that the entire Palestinian population was participating. Tens of millions rallied in support of peace in capitals around the world. Other prominent religious leaders, politicians, women and peace activists from around the world flew to join her, though many were barred by the Israeli government from entering the occupied territories. More than 200,000 Israelis marched in support of peace in Jerusalem.

Rachel ignored Skolnick's demand that she depart until he agreed to allow a UN peacekeeping force to take control of the occupied territories. "Anything to get her to leave," he finally said in exasperation. It had also become clear that Israel would have needed a massive deployment of force to reassert control over the occupied territories.

The first small contingent of American troops for the UN peacekeeping operation, which Rachel had ordered assembled several weeks before her trip, arrived before she departed. NATO forces arrived shortly afterward.

Many Palestinians had lost hope as they suffered daily humiliations by the Israeli occupiers, with unemployment and impoverishment universal. Many now believed that peace was inevitable with Rachel and

America on their side and the UN force in place.

The arrival of the UN peacekeepers dramatically changed the dynamics of the negotiations. Now peace was the expectation. The Palestinians felt emboldened, negotiating from a sense of strength. The Skolnick regime felt a sense of urgency for the first time. In addition to the creation of a two-nation state, there were thorny issues like water, jobs, land and refugees to resolve. The women on both sides did a better job than even Rachel could have imagined, negotiating directly with each other, forcing the male politicians to play catch-up.

The Israeli government was forced to call early elections in the summer of 2002, with military hardliners facing off against a coalition of political parties committed to peace. The peace coalition won with a surprisingly large margin of victory. Their success led to calls by the Palestinian peace movement for elections in the Occupied Territories as well. "Let's show the world that we're ready to embrace a different path. Let us empower our leaders to negotiate a final resolution," Sourani said.

****

Colombia represented everything that was wrong with American foreign policy.

The cocaine trade and the existence of oil had made Colombia the single largest recipient of US military aid despite its terrible track record on human and labor rights. Colombia is the world's number one source of cocaine, responsible for 80 percent of the cocaine consumed in the US and half of the heroin.

Rachel used Colombia to highlight her new foreign aid policy, "one based on support of sustainable local development that raises living standards for all and strengthens democratic institutions, rather than one promoting American economic and military domination." It was rough sailing in Congress.

"Colombia is the end product of America's two centuries of colonialism in South America as well as a remnant of the war against communism. It is the latest in the series of countries into which the US pumped billions of dollars to prop up a corrupt government that routinely killed political opponents. That government also routinely sided with American corporate interests against farmers seeking a better life," Rachel told the American people in announcing a halt to the military's role in combating the local drug trade.

"The civil war in Colombia has been going on for 35 years," Rachel explained. "While Colombia is often called Latin America's oldest democracy, civil liberties and the rule of law have been repeatedly suspended over the last half century, replaced by the rule of force and repression. More than 35,000 Colombians have been killed in the last decade alone, with nearly two million people displaced from their homes. More trade unionists are killed in Colombia each year than in any other country in the world. The end result is that more than 20 percent of Colombian residents are unemployed, while more than half live in poverty."

The Clinton administration had justified its Colombia plan on the ground that it would slash drug production and therefore cut abuse here in the US. When Harrington took office, the US was providing $1.3 billion annually to Colombia to help eradicate its coca crops, including the use of dozens of top-of-the-line military helicopters to fumigate the fields. Harrington got Congress to provide 98 million dollars to train and equip Colombian troops to guard the oil pipeline operated by Occidental Petroleum.

Rachel proposed a complete termination of military aid to Colombia. "We have to stop paying people to kill other people. Any funds we send to Colombia should be for land reform and strengthening civil institutions. If we want to stop drug abuse, the solution lies within our own country, not on foreign soil. We have to cut the demand for these drugs, and that starts with education and treatment programs. And we have to stop making the drug trade so lucrative."

In addition to demanding democratic reform in Colombia as a price for US support, Rachel insisted on "funding for crop substitution programs and infrastructure investment to help create a viable legal economy in coca-growing regions. We also need to provide relocation assistance to the millions displaced by decades of civil war."

Her opponents accused her of being soft on drugs and of supporting Marxist rebels over democracy.

"President Moreno promotes nonviolence, but she seems more concerned about a person's politics than about their actions," said Darling on the Sunday morning talk shows. "If they spout leftist rhetoric, she's willing to look the other way when they pick up guns. The government in Colombia has bent over backward to find a peaceful resolution to this long-standing conflict, but the rebels always find some excuse to break the peace. The guerrilla forces are more concerned about protecting the profits of the drug trade than they are about the well-being of the peasants they use for political cover."

The US Greens demanded that Rachel take immediate action when Bridget Pulecio, the presidential candidate of the New Colombia/ Green Oxygen Party, was kidnapped by the leftist Revolutionary Armed Forces of Colombia (FARC) in the summer of 2003. The Greens were a new player in Colombian political circles, with only a small base of support.

The kidnapping of political figures was a common practice in Colombia, with the rebels hoping to trade them for their own members that had been captured by government forces, or for other concessions. Since none of the hostages were Americans, the US media and Congress paid little attention.

Pulecio's kidnapping symbolized the plight of many Colombian citizens. "It's not only about my daughter." said Yolanda, Bridget's mother, "It's about the 4,000 others kidnapped every year, the tens of thousands of dead and the hundreds of thousands who have been displaced because of this war. It's a conflict in which the poor are the main victims. We want a country without violence and an end to this absurd war."

Rachel identified with Pulecio, a young woman confronting the lack of democracy in her country. Pulecio had been very critical of the corruption of her colleagues in parliament. She was also one of the harshest critics of the FARC guerrillas and of the drug lords who were financing their movement — as well as many politicians, judges and businesses.

"Corruption is like AIDS to democracies. It's always fatal, it's the most important disease to fight," Pulecio remarked. "The drug lords buy everyone off. Everyone becomes addicted to the money, so no one wants to cut off the flow. And if anyone tries, the drug lords kill them while everyone looks the other way."

A few years ago, the Colombian government set up "free zones" from which government troops were excluded and in which FARC could operate openly. Recently the government suddenly called off three years of peace talks and revoked the no-troops agreement. President Cossio, the Liberal Party leader, claimed, "FARC has never really been interested in the peace talks. They just used the ceasefire and the free zones to expand the drug trade, increase their kidnappings and launch military attacks." Pulecio was kidnapped after she decided to campaign in the former free zones.

FARC accused the government of using the ceasefire to conduct business as usual, trying to improve their international image, allowing the rich to get richer while refusing to discuss their demands, such as land redistribution, legal reforms and increased democracy.

Three weeks after Pulecio was kidnapped, Rachel sent Anna to Colombia to try to mediate the situation. Anna had worked in Colombia on small-scale, sustainable economic development for women. She had also worked with the Fair Trade movement to help Colombian farmers develop cocoa co-ops to market chocolate, trying to support the traditional, ecofriendly growing practices that maintained the biodiversity of the forest.

Anna found little sympathy for Pulecio's plight among Colombian officials, who also made it clear they were none too happy to be negotiating with a woman. The officials dismissed Pulecio as a spoiled brat and publicity hound.

"She hardly grew up in this country. You Greens treat her as some peasant heroine but her father was part of the elite, a diplomat," Colombian officials complained to her. "She grew up abroad. She doesn't really understand what's going on here."

"With all due respect, her criticisms of, er, the current state of your country, starting with the domination of the illicit drug industry, seem right on target," Anna observed.

"Sure, it's easy to point fingers at the corruption and the drug trade," said Ramon Cancino, the Minister of Foreign Relations. "The hard part is coming up with real solutions that are going to stick."

"Don't you think her outspokenness is what got her kidnapped?" asked Anna.

"She's the one responsible for getting herself kidnapped," Cancino replied. "She shouldn't have gone there. The military told her it was unsafe. It was just a publicity stunt for her campaign. Now she expects us to risk troops to go in and rescue her, or exchange her for dozens of rebels who have killed innocent civilians."

"President Moreno would appreciate whatever you could do to expedite her safe return," Anna said.

"It wouldn't surprise me if she and the FARC staged her kidnapping," Cancino mumbled.

Anna held a clandestine meeting with representatives of FARC a few miles outside of Bogota, arranged by some of local Green representatives. A meeting farther out in the countryside, though safer for FARC, was considered too dangerous for Anna. The FARC representatives rejected her suggestion that they release Pulecio as a goodwill gesture. "We've made plenty of such gestures, but nothing changes. They never want to talk about real land reform, about real democracy," said Mauricio Sandoval, a spokesperson for the governing Secretariat of FARC.

"Would you be surprised to hear that the government says the same thing about you?" Anna responded.

Sandoval spat on the ground. "The politicians and their wealthy backers, they always tell you Americans what you want to hear. They tell you that of course they want to cut off the drug trade, that we're just the muscle for the drug lords. But they make far more money off drugs than we do. They say they want the farmers to stop growing coca, but they never come up with any real money to help the farmers make a living, no matter how much aid your government sends."

"What needs to happen to get Pulecio released?" Anna asked.

"If your president wants to show us she is serious, suspend all military funding to the government. Or send us money for guns so we don't need income from the drug barons. They're crazy anyway. The sooner they're gone, the better."

"You know we can't do that," Anna replied. "But President Moreno is trying to cut off the military aid. Our Congress is being, um, somewhat difficult."

"Your country has been robbing our people for centuries," Sandoval replied. "You're the ones responsible for this mess. You have the power to fix it if you want."

Rachel continued to push Congress to cut military aid to Colombia, particularly for the assault on the poor farmers who grew the coca leaves, the raw fuel of the drug trade.

"The US is attacking those at the bottom rather than where the money is concentrated," Rachel explained to the country. "A farmer who produces one kilogram of coca per hectare annually gets about one thousand dollars for it. By the time it reaches the streets of New York City, it sells for 100,000 dollars a kilo. Since 1996, we've sprayed herbicides on more than a million acres in Colombia to kill the coca plant. But since the payments to farmers are a small fraction of the cost of cocaine, the amount under cultivation has actually tripled to ensure that enough survives to keep the drug pipeline flowing."

Anna met with Gerardo Marquez, a representative of the Colombian Growers Peasant Association. "The planes come and spray everything," Marquez told her. "Kill not only coca, but all other crops. Rubber, sugar, bananas. The spray makes our women miscarry. People get sick, even die. When they spray, you got to grow coca again. Coca grows fast, ready to harvest in six months. You got to support your family. No choice. Other crops take much longer. A rubber plantation, maybe ten years before go to market."

In the fall of 2003, Congress and the American media began paying attention after an American airplane carrying several "businessmen" crashed into territory controlled by FARC. The businessmen were CIA operatives.

"It's time for President Moreno to stop placating these terrorists," Senator Deutsche told the media. "FARC and their allies routinely use kidnapping, torture and murder to intimidate the government and their opponents. When they see our government bending to pressure, they just go out and kidnap more people."

With Congress demanding increased military action against FARC to secure the release of the Americans, Rachel sent Anna and Secretary of State Miller back to Bogota, Colombia's capital.

"I realize that American dollars from the drug trade have contributed to the violence and the conflict in Colombia," Rachel said in announcing the trip. "I will increase efforts to prosecute those businesses and members of the international banking community that are assisting in laundering the profits from the drug trade. I also hope that both sides will allow the Peace Institute to mediate. I'm prepared to support the deployment of international peacekeepers to help enforce the ceasefire and to restore civil law."

Flying in at night, the lights of Bogota's skyscrapers could have been any US city. In the light of day however, it is a typical South American capital, a sprawling chaotic nightmare of choking traffic and smog, and street vendors struggling to make a living. Colonial monuments lined grand plazas while homeless children bedded down in the sewers. Poverty, wealth and violence bred off one another.

The Colombians — along with Congress — were perplexed that Rachel would use the American hostages as an excuse to curtail military involvement. "Shouldn't you be sending in American troops rather than pulling them out?" a miffed President Cossio asked. "It seems like you're giving in to the kidnappers."

"We need to bring everyone — the government, paramilitary, and the rebels — to the negotiating table," Miller responded. "The ceasefire must include an end to all violence."

Anna added, "You're not going to get peace without real land and political reform. Mouthing these words without real follow-through isn't going to work. That includes getting the paramilitaries to return the lands they've appropriated from the farmers." Anna also mentioned Rachel's suggestion that the Cossio administration bring in judges from other countries for a few years to help restore the judiciary's independence.

The Colombian president angrily accused Rachel of siding with the rebels. "Your president, she believes in Robin Hood. She has romantic illusions about the guerillas. She needs to understand that we're the good guys, we're the ones caught in the middle. FARC are terrorists. We've given these groups many opportunities for peace, but they always find some excuse not to disarm."

Miller backtracked a bit. "President Moreno recognizes your personal commitment to peace and the dangers that reformers in your country have faced. She tremendously respects the personal courage of those who have spoken up for change. But she knows that a successful conclusion to these negotiations will require compromise and sacrifice on everyone's part, and that true peace must deal with the plight of the least fortunate, the least powerful, including a respect for human and legal rights."

"The rebels just use the demands for land and human rights as slogans," Cossio said dismissively. "They've become too dependent on the drug lords. Even if some rebel leaders agreed to peace, the drug lords would just kill them and put someone else in place. They've wrecked our economy, and you want us to turn over our land and our government to them?"

Anna brought a private message from Rachel to the FARC leaders. "I hope you will take this opportunity to put the peace talks back on track. I'll ask the Colombian government to resume the ceasefire and I will personally monitor the talks to help ensure progress," Rachel had written.

"Congress wants to send in the marines. Unless we get some action soon, you're going to be facing American troops," Anna warned.

Pulecio, the American hostages and a number of other prisoners were released a week after Anna returned to Colombia — "a good-will gesture" from FARC. The pictures of the hostages being turned over to Miller, Anna and the Colombian vice-president were splashed across the Colombian and international media. However, many other kidnap victims were still being held to pressure the Colombian government to release rebel fighters in their jails.

The negotiations were not easy, lasting another four months.

The rebels were skeptical of laying down their arms in exchange for a promise of fair elections.

"We've heard the same promises before. Nothing changes," FARC spokesperson Sandoval said. "They'll still control the election machinery. They'll still decide who votes, they'll still own the newspapers and television, they'll still have their wealth to buy the election. We need to see real, permanent reforms in other areas before we put down our guns. We need the American president to guarantee our safety once we're disarmed, and we want some of our soldiers and officers integrated into the national army."

Anna argued with the rebel leaders to choose the path of peace. "You're never going to get a better deal, and who knows if President Moreno will remain president after 2004? We can't promise that you're going to be the new rulers. But is war a better answer? A war that kills many of your loved ones and prevents your children from getting an education, from having hope for a better life? We can promise you that we'll make the election as fair as possible and you'll get some of your members elected to Parliament. And if we don't see land reform and protection of human rights, President Moreno will cut off all American funding."

Rachel came to Colombia to be a formal witness to the peace agreement and to reinforce the commitments Anna had made. Not all of the parties were satisfied with the final results. Much of the ruling elite was still opposed to real land reform, though the US offer of money in exchange for land overcame some of the resistance.

Rachel got Congress to agree to shift the focus of US aid to help peasant farmers raise their standard of living, rather than seeking to wipe out the coca fields. It was agreed that international peacekeepers would be deployed to help maintain the ceasefire and to apprehend and prosecute anyone engaged in violence, including the drug lords. The peacekeepers, however, would not engage in efforts to dismantle the drug trade. That was left to the Colombian authorities.

****

Rachel got her first opportunity to make an appointment to the Supreme Court in the winter of 2003. With lifetime terms and its role as final arbiter of the law and Constitution, a Supreme Court appointment is one of the most important presidential decisions.

Wynn argued for an African-American. "We've got to correct the travesty of Clarence Thomas grabbing the Supreme Court's 'black seat' from Thurgood Marshall. What an insult to go from one of the towering legal minds and civil rights leaders of our time to a third-rate attorney best known for his love of pornography, sexual harassment and brown-nosing," Wynn snarled.

Thomas had assiduously positioned himself as the conservative black jurist that would be acceptable to a Republican president if the opportunity to replace Marshall arose. Marshall, who became the first black member of the Supreme Court in 1967, had come to national prominence as the chief lawyer for the NAACP for more than two decades, successfully arguing the historic 1954 school board integration case *Brown vs. the Arkansas Board of Education*. All told, he won 29 of the 32 cases he argued before the Supreme Court.

While Sophie and Rachel agreed about the need for a person of color, they also felt it was time for a third woman on the Supreme Court. "Half the population is women, yet in 230 years we have managed to place a grand total of two women on the court," said Sophie. "I think we should start with the goal of only nominating women during your entire administration. How about the attorney general? Doris is certainly qualified and it would be great to have someone on the court to help redefine the powers of corporations," she proposed.

They had to agree that Doris was too closely identified with Rachel, and would serve as a lightning rod for Rachel's critics. Plus she was doing a great job as attorney general and it would be a challenge to find a comparable replacement. They also debated the politics of the nomination process, which required approval from the United States Senate. In recent years this had often proved contentious, as it's one of the few tasks involving the constitutional system of checks and balances that the Senate and public took seriously. Several nominees in recent decades had been forced to withdraw due to Senate opposition.

"The Senate is going to use the nominee to question many of Rachel's actions," Wynn chimed in, "starting with the issue of corporate crime and prosecuting CEOs for human rights abuses. We might want to put forth a really great candidate who will shake things up, even though she would likely be defeated. The Senate usually gives you your second choice if they defeat the first one. That way we could get credit with the various constituencies that supported our first nominee, while making it more likely that our second nominee, who would be our real choice, would get through," he suggested.

TWENTY-TWO

2004 PRESIDENTIAL ELECTION

It was a foregone conclusion that Rachel would run for reelection in 2004.

The only one with doubts was Rachel.

She longed to get out of the spotlight, to step away from the pressure cooker and regain control of her life.

After they had made love one evening, she broached the subject with Wynn as she slowly rubbed her hand on his chest, lightly reproaching him for the love handles around his waist, the product of not enough exercise and eating food that was too rich since they'd moved into the White House.

"You promised me four years ago that this would only be a few months of making speeches about healthcare and globalization. Now you have me up there pretending to be the leader of the free world, trying to stare down all these generals and politicians and CEOs with their testosterone just popping out of their ears — and other places."

Rachel rolled over on her back, looking up at the ceiling.

"Wynn, I don't want to run again. I've given enough. I wanna go home, have some time to grieve for Tommy. It's time to let someone who enjoys all of this be president, who doesn't mind playing all the games. I'm losing myself, I don't know who I am half the time. I feel like I'm watching someone else inhabit my body," Rachel said.

The words began to come out in a torrent. "There are all the compromises we make, so half the time when we win, I feel like we lost. The rich are still getting richer and the corporations still have most of the power. Everyone wants a piece of you and no matter how much you give, they want more. And when you're tired and your mind isn't working right and you say something stupid, it's front page news."

Wynn leaned over her, giving her a long kiss to quiet her protests, moving his hand along her thigh, cupping her buttocks, moving his lips downward, starting with her throat.

"I love you Rachel, and even more than that, I'm really proud of what you've done in the last few years. It's your decision and I'll respect whatever you decide. I'm happy to go back to Seattle and organize protests, maybe write a book or two, do some Indy Media work, whatever, just hang out with you, serve tea when all the important people come to visit you."

Wynn brushed the hair out of her eyes and gave her one his famous knock-'em-over smiles. "But there's no one else who can keep the dark forces from winning the White House. You're the only Green who can win. If you want a chance for all the things we believe in to succeed, you're the only viable option. I'm sorry."

Rachel pulled Wynn on top on her, holding him close, whispering in his ear. "I know. But it still feels like a prison sentence."

Months before Rachel decided to seek reelection, Wynn pushed Rachel and Sophia to bring in an experienced national campaign manager.

"We need someone who has dealt with 50-million-dollar campaign budgets, who's done national TV ad buys. We gotta move up to a whole new level to win reelection. We need the Greens to have a strong national effort but we have to pull in our own team to focus on you," he argued.

Rachel gave him a green light to find a campaign manager, her major criterion being to hire a woman. "I'm not interested in the old boy's network and smoky backroom politicking. And we need a team approach."

It was Mumfi who first suggested that Wynn talk to Lynne Holzer. She'd been running Democratic campaigns for the last twenty years, often for African-American and women candidates. She was also active with the DC Statehood Party that had recently merged with the DC Greens. She also worked with a variety of national women's, labor and environmental groups when their major bills finally came up for vote after years of work. It was her job to get them across the finish line, and she was unusually good in making it happen.

"She's my miracle worker," said one labor leader in recommending Lynne. "She's pulled our chestnuts out of the fire on more than one occasion."

Lynne largely agreed with Rachel on the issues. Campaign strategy was a different matter.

Rachel and Sophie both got a big laugh when Lynne's first piece of advice was to soften Wynn's image.

"Being the first First Husband would never be easy," Lynn told them. "It's especially difficult for someone who's been protesting all his life. Wynn's life story didn't get the soft-sell from the media four years ago because not only didn't Rachel run for president, you guys weren't married — so the public didn't get to know him before your opponents started complaining he was too involved And an interracial marriage doesn't make it any easier. That's still jarring for a lot of voters, especially older ones," Lynne said.

"We need to put Wynn in some toned-down business suits, play up his law degree. Maybe get him to start wearing some glasses to make him look more professorial," she added. "Have him smile more often." Rachel and Sophie nodded in agreement while Wynn scowled.

It wasn't a foregone conclusion to everyone that she would run as a Green.

Anna raised this subject one Saturday afternoon as she watched Rachel putter around her White House garden.

"Rachel, have ya given any thought to running as a Dem? I know you and Wynn are big on the Greens, but it's going to be a tough haul to get reelected just on the Green line. The Greens hardly exist down South, and they're not exactly a powerhouse in the rest of the country. It'd be a heck of a lot easier as a Dem — maybe a fusion ticket. Darling's an old fart. If you jumped in, there's a lotta Dems who'd climb on your bandwagon," Anna said.

Rachel was on her knees, pulling up weeds, doing what she enjoyed most. She rubbed the back of her gloved hand across her brow to keep sweat from trickling into her eyes.

"Anna, I can't abandon the Greens. They're the ones that got me here in the first place. Plus all the good people, the fun people, are in the Greens. If I jump into bed with the Democrats, then it just becomes personality politics," Rachel said as she planted some seedlings.

"Get real, Rachel," Anna responded. "You're here because of you, not because of the Greens. You're what's important."

Rachel laughed. "Well, now look who's dissin' idealism. I hope the FBI or somebody is taping this so I can play it at your next birthday party. Listen girl, I am the first to say that the Greens drive me crazy but at least they speak the truth."

"The Greens are well-intentioned," Anna replied defensively, "except for the crazies and the men, but they're clueless about how to win a national election. They think writing a treatise is how you change people's minds. They're too isolated from the average person. There are too many people who are counting on you, too many issues that are important, to throw it away on some idealistic dream."

"If this country is going change for the better, we need a group like the Greens to get power, to kick in the door. Gotta keep your eyes on the prize," Rachel replied. "I might be able to grab the Democratic nomination but the corporations are still going to control the purse strings. I'd rather go down in flames doing what's right than have me sell my soul to the company store. Hand me that tray of tomato seedlings, will you?"

****

More than a dozen Republican and Democrat contenders jumped into the presidential sweepstakes. Despite her considerable success on a host of domestic and foreign policy issues, Rachel was viewed as extremely vulnerable, a one-term fluke. All but two of the candidates were male, all but Darling were white. Corporate America lined up to help shove Rachel out the door.

The Republican candidates were highly critical of Rachel's performance. While most Democrats joined in the attacks, a few tried to position themselves as the liberal, responsible alternative to Rachel. "I agree with most of her issues, but she can't govern as a Green. She's trying to move too fast on too many fronts. She needs to bring people together to solve problems, not divide us," said Senator Charles Cummings of Iowa, a boyish-looking former trial attorney.

Darling was considered the Democratic frontrunner. He was viewed as an experienced and steady hand on defense and foreign policy. He was tough on crime — street crime, that it. He was moderate to liberal on most domestic issues. He supported rebuilding inner city communities and strengthening education. Darling was prochoice but opposed same-sex marriage. In public, he was soft-spoken and gracious — except when talking about Rachel.

"I'm just running to make a few points," Darling said during the initial stages of the campaign, "and then I'll leave it to someone younger to carry the party's torch." Darling protested each step of the way that he was a reluctant candidate, past his time, while his campaign operatives broke arms behind the scenes to win the nomination. In private, he told party leaders and backers, "We've got to save the country from that misguided young woman."

The probusiness, promilitary wing of the Democratic Party, which rallied behind Darling, blamed the "liberal, NOW, ecofreak, good-government activists" in the party for Rachel's presidency. "Harrington never should've offered the VP slot to her," complained Reggie McCarthy, head of the Democratic National Committee. "And the party elders should've blocked him from doing it. He was just doing some window dressing, and look where we ended up."

The amount of special interest money raised by the candidates and the two major parties was staggering, surpassing all previous records. Darling led the Democrats in raising corporate donations, but several Republicans raised far more. A third of the candidates, including Darling and the eventual Republican nominee, removed themselves from the primary matching system since they could raise more money by ignoring the limits. It highlighted how little progress had been made in campaign finance reform, as the politicians and special interests drove bulldozers through every little loophole.

Rachel hammered away about the need for full, public campaign financing, Her campaign website provided a running update on how much money had been contributed to her opponents by chemical companies, drug manufacturers, defense contractors, hospital groups and real estate conglomerates. "Government for sale to the highest bidder" screamed the digital banner headline, flashing in red, white and blue, as CEOs and politicians dressed as fat cats danced around holding money bags.

"While I support full public funding, at a minimum we should increase the match for donations in the presidential primaries to four to one, like they do in New York City elections," Rachel said in her weekly radio address. "We should also lower the contribution limit to 100 dollars. We need to provide more incentives, like free TV for candidates who comply with the public funding systems, and more penalties for those who don't — like denying them the right to participate in any televised debates. Candidates shouldn't be free to ignore the public funding system when they want to raise more money."

****

The selection of Rachel's running mate was a contentious issue.

Many Greens assumed they would nominate a Green to replace Mumfi on the ticket. "Mumfi's okay but he's still a Democrat," David Smythe, one of the national cochairs, posted on the national Green listservs. "We need a Green who'll articulate our agenda. There are plenty of Green elected officials to choose from. Any of the Green congressional members would be good, like McDaniels. He has good ties with the unions and the anti-globalization folks. Or Alvarez."

Rachel's campaign manager argued to keep Mumfi on the ticket. "I know that John was the one who got me this job, but he's also the one that most helps you win reelection," Holzer argued. "John gives you a fusion ticket. It makes it a lot easier for the liberal Democrats, especially people of color, to pull the lever for you. It also demonstrates loyalty on your part, shows the voters that you're willing to rise above partisanship."

"Normally the only question about the VP candidate," added Holzer, "is their ability to step in as president if something happens to you. With John, we've already answered that question for most voters."

"That's true," Sophie conceded, "but someone like McDaniels would also fill that role."

"I like Ray, too," Wynn added, "but Lynne raises good points. John expands our base more than any other candidate, including Ray. Or even Barry. And dumping him might cause a backlash among African-American voters. It's already going to be tough pulling them if Darling is the nominee. Though if we went with Sandy, she'd help with the Hispanic vote."

Alvarez and McDaniels made the choice easier by supporting Mumfi. "Why break up a team that works well?" Alvarez asked. "What the Greens should focus on is running as many strong congressional candidates as we can."

"John does a much better job of balancing the ticket," McDaniels argued, "not only among blacks, but with his New York and East Coast base. Besides, with me, there's the little constitutional problem that the presidential and VP candidates can't be registered voters from the same state."

Mumfi had his own concerns.

"I appreciate you asking me to run for reelection," he told Rachel. "You know I support you personally and I agree with most of the Green platform. I'm willing to help build the Greens, because I believe a strong Green Party will move the Dems to embrace more of our agenda. The bigger question for me is how does this fusion concept translate into races lower down the ticket?"

"What do you mean?" asked Rachel.

"If we're a fusion ticket, how do we relate to Democratic congressional candidates?" Mumfi asked. "It's the same dilemma we had two years ago. If they're willing to publicly support us, do we support them? Even if there is a marginal Green in the race?"

"Do you really think many Democrats, particularly incumbents, are going to jump on our bandwagon?" she asked.

"Not incumbents," admitted Mumfi, "at least not at first. They won't want to piss off the party leadership and find themselves facing a primary. But lots of insurgents will endorse you in their primaries, trying to tap into your supporters to help kick out the party regulars."

"But we'll pick up some incumbents during the final few weeks," Mumfi pointed out, "especially if you're doing well in their district. Some will endorse you out of conviction, others to protect their political base. Others may just want to work together on get-out-the-vote efforts."

"How will endorsing these Johnnies-come-lately help us?" Rachel asked. "Or the Greens? Seems like these Democrats would just be riding on our coattails."

"I hate to be the one to break this to you Rachel, but I don't think we'll be coasting to victory in the last week. We'll be fighting for every vote. Picking up the endorsements of Democrats, especially incumbents, in the last few weeks could add a few thousand voters in that district — maybe even ten thousand. That could be pivotal in a state where it's close. Plus it'll show we're picking up momentum."

"It's going to be pretty hard to switch horses that close to the finish line," Rachel said. "It's one thing to get the local Greens to sign on when we've got months to talk it through. I'd be really upset if someone did that to me after I'd been campaigning for six months."

"The best approach is for the Democrat to sit down and work it out with the local Greens." Rachel added. "If they can't reach an agreement, I don't know what we do. Maybe you and I try to get both parties to agree, maybe each of us just work for own candidate. But I can't betray the Green Party and I won't ask you to do that with the Democrats."

"With all due respect, Rachel, that's exactly what you're doing," Mumfi replied. "You know they're going to call me a traitor. They might even try to get my county chair to strip me of my party membership."

"There's always a home for you in the Greens," remarked Rachel.

"I appreciate that," Mumfi replied, "but I've kinda gotten used to a little bigger house. Now, you might just see me moving in sooner than we expect, but I'd like one last chance to shake up the Dems," Mumfi said. "My point is this: If there's a Democrat, especially an incumbent, who's willing to support us in Congress, we should strike a deal. Particularly if the Green is only going to pull a few percentage points."

"John, I'm the public face of the Greens. I won't publicly support a Democratic candidate in a race where the Green Party tells me not to," Rachel told him. "If we can work behind the scenes — share lists, voter ID, literature drops — we can do it. If you need to go campaign for particular candidates, I understand that. But our deal is between you and me. If you want to get the Democratic leadership to sit down to discuss a team approach to Congress, I'm willing to listen and bring the Greens in. But without such a deal, I can't undercut Green candidates just to bolster my own chances."

Mumfi agreed to run with her. "Are you sure the Greens will go along with this?"

Rachel laughed. "Oh, there'll be a lotta screaming, and some rather unpleasant things will be said. Whatever you do, don't give 'em your personal e-mail address. You're going to have to go through a fair amount of questioning. But if they want me, they'll have to take you."

"By the way, I assume you've got the Justice Department working on making sure all the votes get counted this time?" he asked.

"Of course," Rachel said, acting insulted that he raised it. "We've standardized the machines. Made sure there's a verifiable paper trail. Had federal employees write up the computer codes so that it's all public property and out in the open. We've got half the world sending in election observers. We're not going to allow this election to be stolen."

The Green Party was none too happy at the prospect of supporting Democratic congressional candidates. "This is supposed to be about building a long term party and movement, not just helping one candidate, even if it's for president," complained a number of Green organizers. "Supporting Democrats for Congress weakens our point that the two major parties are both corporate parties with little difference between them on fundamental issues."

The possibility of Rachel's campaign working with a Democrat that had a Green opponent was especially controversial. Even the hint of such discussions generated bitter complaints.

"How can you betray us? I don't care if we have no chance of winning. This is about being Green, not running the made-for-tv candidate," argued Scott Cooke, who was managing a Green congressional campaign in Chicago.

"It's your call," Wynn told him. "All we ask is that you involve the local Green supporters in the decision, and that you take a serious look at what is best for the country and the future of the Greens. Look at the big picture. We'll respect whatever you decide."

Rachel, Wynn and Green Party officials spent hours on the phones and in personal visits recruiting strong progressive community leaders to run on the Green congressional slate. "Your country needs you," was Rachel's sales pitch. Even when they were unsuccessful in convincing someone to run, they were usually able to get the potential candidate to agree to help the campaign. As Wynn noted, "Almost no one is insulted when you tell them they'd make a great candidate."

More than one hundred of their targeted community leaders ran. Most were able to raise between 40,000 and 100,000 dollars, some considerably more. This made them at least somewhat financially competitive with the other parties.

The Greens were far ahead in volunteers and ideas. They also invested heavily in mobilizing support in communities which traditionally didn't bother to vote. "These are our people," Lynne told the campaign workers. "They're tenants and young people. They're the poor. They're the ones so disillusioned by the status quo that they've given up on politics. Let's get them to the polls."

Several hundred additional candidates were hard-core Green organizers and supporters who were doing the best they could with the limited resources they could muster. They found significantly more community and financial support than in prior campaigns.

While there was still no public campaign financing for congressional candidates, Rachel had pushed through reforms increasing their access to the television and radio airwaves. The Greens made extensive use of public access on cable television and micro radio stations, small inexpensive systems that could broadcast over a few square miles.

There was a tremendous increase in the number of debates for congressional candidates. "Voters have the right see and hear the candidates in person, not just on slick TV ads," Rachel said in addressing the Citizen Assemblies' national convention shortly after Labor Day. "I urge you to go back and meet with all the candidates, hold them accountable for supporting your proposals."

Rather than being allowed to deliver glib speeches full of platitudes, candidates were grilled on their positions on specific issues. They complained that they felt like they were being interviewed for their first job.

The Green candidates benefited from the ten states that now used preferential voting. Voters were free in those states to vote for the best candidate rather than the lesser of two evils.

Wynn gave Lynne a poll from the 2000 presidential race. "I know this seems hard to believe, but only 9 percent of the voters who supported Frost actually ended up voting for him. Convinced Frost couldn't win, 55 percent voted for Harrington to make sure Prescott was defeated. But what is most incredible is that 37 percent voted for

Prescott in order to beat Harrington. If we can convince our supporters that Rachel has a realistic chance, we should be able to win this."

****

In many ways, Rachel's opponents in the general election were their own worst enemies. They ignored the changed public attitude since September 11. They continued to push an image of a polarized world, with America needing to forcefully strike back to assert its domination.

Senator Jim Johnson from Missouri captured the Republican presidential nomination. Rachel's presidency had shifted the Republican Party even further to the right. Johnson had a strong base among what Anna referred to as the "hate coalition" — the antichoice, antiimmigrant, antiwomen, antiblack, religious right who were NRA supporters. He was financed by military contractors and the most reactionary elements of the business community and was one of the candidates who decided not to seek public funding. Johnson viewed Rachel as an abomination in God's eyes.

"We should've responded to September eleventh with an iron glove to reinforce who was top dog," Johnson said in his stump speeches. "The best way to ensure peace, not only for America but for all countries, is to extend America's military and economic strength to every corner of the globe. Once every inhabitant of the planet becomes part of the same consumer market, there'd be no need for war." Darling echoed similar sentiments, though in more diplomatic language.

"We need to reward those who work hard, the ones who put the rest of the country to work. We need to get these government bureaucrats and know-it-alls that work for Moreno off the back of the working man. We have the world's greatest economy, one that supports anyone willing to work hard," Johnson contended. "Moreno wants to tear the rich man down. I'd prefer to lift everyone up. Even the poor in America have a standard of living better than the middle class in most of the rest of the world. American businesses are doing a good job — and we have to help them do an even better one."

Darling agreed with Johnson's basic premises, though he threw in a few platitudes about helping the middle class. "We need to ensure that everyone has the opportunity to be successful. I'm here today because of the help I received from our government after World War Two. We need to help more Americans become homeowners, and to send their children to college. We have to cut down on regulations that are burdensome for companies and make it cheaper for them to do business. Otherwise, we'll continue to see more of our jobs exported overseas to take advantage of cheaper labor costs."

"We need to apply more of a business attitude to how we run government, cutting waste and increasing productivity," Darling said. "It's a tough world out there and we need to work hard and invest wisely if we're going to maintain our status as the leading economic and military country."

Johnson added, "We need to take advantage of privatization opportunities both here and abroad. The private sector does it cheaper, quicker and better, while cutting down on the corruption. And our foreign policy should aim to assist countries that agree with this approach, including supporting Free Trade to cut down on market barriers and inefficiencies."

Rachel's campaign staff were overjoyed with the nomination of two right-of-center candidates by the major parties.

"The Democratic Party at the national level always take the votes of environmentalists, women's groups, minority groups and labor for granted," Lynne would tell prospective campaign workers she was recruiting. "After all, who else are they going to vote for? Well, Rachel's that alternative.

"With Rachel capturing the liberal vote and the Democrats and Republicans splitting the conservatives," Lynne continued, "Rachel wins if she gets a third of the moderate vote. I doubt that Darling and Johnson can tone down their personal hatred of Rachel and her positions to effectively compete for this vote. It's not going to be easy, but if people like you make a personal commitment to make it happen, we can win. This is the moment we have dreamed of our entire lives."

Rachel's support among women was so strong that traditional Democratic women groups like the National Organization of Women and National Abortion Right Action League (NARAL) were forced by their grassroots membership to endorse her. A last minute compromise to endorse both Darling and Rachel was shouted down from the floor of the NOW convention. Several old-guard leaders resigned in protest.

The Greens' efforts on behalf of same-sex marriage was also paying dividends with strong support from the five to ten percent of the population who are gay or lesbian.

Many of the national labor leaders argued against abandoning the Democratic Party. "It's too risky. Moreno's fine, but the Greens don't understand the needs of the working class. They always put the

environment ahead of jobs. Besides, we've got to defeat Johnson and
the Democrats are our best shot."

The younger union members, the rank-and-file women, and more
progressive unions argued, "We've never had a president who has been
more strongly in favor of labor, and working people, not even FDR.
This should be a no-brainer."

The AFL-CIO, after much internal debate, decided to remain
neutral between Rachel and Darling. "We're going to put our resources
into defeating Johnson." Individual unions were free to make their own
decisions. Rachel picked up the support of unions that represented
government workers, healthcare and the service sector, including the
Communication Workers of America, the UAW and the IBEW. Darling
picked up the support of the construction and heavy industry unions.

Darling had a commanding lead among African-American voters,
but the combination of Rachel's policies and Mumfi's presence on the
ticket was allowing her to pick up 35 percent among this bloc. She was
pulling a majority of the Hispanic vote, now the largest minority group
in the US.

****

Rachel was under a tremendous financial disadvantage in the general
election.

"Even though I'm the incumbent, I receive much less public
funding than my opponents since it's based on the Green Party
receiving ten percent of the vote four years ago," Rachel explained to
reporters. "A party must pull at least 25 percent of the vote to get full
funding in the next election. The Greens will get only a quarter of what
the Democrats and Republicans get. Plus I'm prohibited as an individual
candidate from raising any additional funds to make up the difference,
though the Green Party can compete with the others for funds."

Johnson and Darling received 75 million dollars each for the general
election — the three months left after the August national conventions
— while Rachel received 18 million. The candidates of the other
national parties — Libertarian, Natural Law, Socialist and Reform —
received no public funds. The two major parties also raised far more in
"hard money" donations to support their get-out-the-vote efforts,
though donations to the Democrats dropped precipitously as Darling's
poll numbers became mired in third place.

Rachel did attract media coverage as the incumbent, but the

corporate owned media stove to make it as negative as possible. Rachel and the Greens heavily utilized the internet to create virtual town meetings and rallies. They produced a series of short, MTV-style videos for the internet, anywhere from ten seconds to five minutes, with a heavy emphasis on music and flashy visuals. Progressive media groups helped Rachel master the art of staging events to maximize the visual impact — a picture is worth a thousand words. The campaign ran a number of campaign infomercials, half-hour segments that combined voter education, volunteer recruitment, fundraising and entertainment.

The Campus Greens were Rachel's volunteer core. Green chapters had sprouted on more than 600 campuses during Frost's 2000 campaign. They'd been rejuvenated by Rachel's call for peace after 9/11, and played a critical role in the peace movement. Rachel had made sure that the party devoted significant organizing resources to them ever since. She attended all of their annual conventions and established the Thomas Moreno Internship Program for Campus Greens. Pete recruited many Campus Greens into Green America, helping to establish green businesses and services on many campuses, getting them in on the ground floor of the new green economy.

"We Greens are traditionalists," Rachel told Rob Simpson on Comedy Central's "The Daily Show," her favorite news program. "We campaign the old-fashioned way. We knock on people's doors and listen to what they have to say. And we throw lots of green festivals. We believe in having fun."

Rachel ran a full-out campaign as if she was a dark horse challenger trailing by 30 points. She showed up at an unprecedented number of events for an incumbent president. It was certainly easier to travel with Air Force One ferrying you around.

She used the power of incumbency to her advantage. Sophie and Holzer worked overtime to think of important issues to engage. She intervened in a border flare-up between Pakistan and India, and was instrumental in settling the civil war in Liberia. She visited Haiti to tour some of the new sustainable farm cooperatives started with the UN Millennium Development funds. Rachel hosted a meeting of the Israeli and Palestinian negotiators to help them get back on track, conveniently reminding the country that the ceasefire had held for more than a year.

After Labor Day, Rachel flew around the country attending the openings of community health centers, electric-car manufacturing plants, the Redwood National Forest and a mixed-income public housing project. "Christ," she complained to Holzer, "I'm beginning to feel like one of those plastic politicians I used to despise. Pimping for photo ops with a big smile and a check to hand over."

"Just remember to smile for the cameras," Holzer reminded her. "And remember that you really are doing some good. It'll be over soon, one way or the other."

"Thanks for the pep talk," said Rachel.

Her opponents, of course, accused her of illegally using the power of the presidency to promote her campaign.

Many of her campaign rallies were staged in rock arenas and football stadiums. Ronnie Faith, Pete and Wynn recruited the performers and celebrities to attend, often a nightmare of logistics and egos. Rachel did 50 events of 20,000 people or more. On several occasions she pulled close to a hundred thousand supporters. The events were performance spectaculars, complete with music, videos on issues, political comedy, speakers and exhibits by a myriad of causes. The events provided her with tens of thousands of campaign volunteers.

A presidential campaign had not seen such huge crowds since progressive Henry Wallace bolted the Democrats to run for president against Truman in 1948. Wallace, vice-president under FDR, ran against the Cold War and big business, supported rights for blacks and women, and campaigned in support of the minimum wage.

"Let's make sure we do better than Wallace's two percent of the vote and zero Electoral College delegates," Lynne warned her staff. "Crowds are great, but we got to make sure we get them out on election day — and get 'em to drag their neighbors along."

****

Darling enjoyed hearing himself talk, and the presidential race gave him plenty of opportunity. "Darling's campaign slogan should be Back to the Past," Wynn told Rachel as they lay in bed one night watching one of his speeches on C-SPAN. Darling also made the classic mistake of talking more about Rachel than about his own vision for the future.

"It's good to see a woman being taken seriously," Darling said in an interview with Tom Brothers on "Face the Nation," one of the Sunday morning talk shows. "Unfortunately, President Moreno is leading us in the wrong direction. We need someone who will help the country look forward. We also need to be serious about the challenges posed by foreign interests."

"You don't think that President Moreno's actions in convincing the

UN to pursue bin Laden was successful?" Brothers asked.

"I have no disagreements with the killing of bin Laden," Darling conceded, "other than it was unfortunate that we didn't have the opportunity to question him about his terrorist network. But bin Laden is just one individual. Al-Qaida is still out there. There are many other terrorist groups out there, in Yemen, Syria, Iran, North Korea, and various African and South American countries. We need to be proactive in ferreting them out rather than waiting for the next attack on America."

"President Moreno has this bad habit of always finding fault with America," Darling added. "She should be proud of what our country has accomplished, and the sacrifices that we have made. A lot of American blood has been shed in defense of our country, especially in World War Two when America stepped up to save the world. Far too many Americans have died on foreign soil to hear that we don't care about the rest of the world."

Darling and Johnson parroted similar lines about September 11.

"We have enemies that are coming after us and our loved ones. They don't care how brutal they are or how many innocent people they kill. They routinely torture their opponents; they certainly don't read them their Miranda rights. Our first priority must be to defend ourselves, not political correctness," was a typical campaign speech from Johnson.

"The way we live in the US is a lot nicer than in the rest of the world, and I would like to keep that way. Let's focus on changing the behavior of other countries. Rachel doesn't believe that we have the best country in the world, the best democracy, the best protection of civil liberties, the strongest rule of law, the best in so many things," Johnson added.

Darling constantly attacked Rachel's inexperience on foreign policy, rehashing every disagreement they had while he was secretary of state, "Making sure that history gets it right."

"You don't become stronger by making part of yourself weaker, which is what President Moreno has done," Darling continued.

Johnson concurred. "We can't afford on-the-job training. September eleventh occurred because our enemies thought we were soft, that we wouldn't attack back, and so far President Moreno has done her best to prove them right. She's preaching peace while our enemies are hatching plots to hurt us by any means possible."

"My administration has taken steps to deal with terrorism," Rachel would point out. "We've helped cut off the flow of funds to terrorist groups by cracking down on the royal family in Saudi Arabia. Rather than starting World War Three in the Middle East, as my opponents seem to advocate, we strengthened the rule of international law, helped bring peace to Israel and Palestine, and have created the Peace Institute to help resolve international disputes without the use of force. Sure, there's more to be done, but that's what a second term is for."

"I believe that America is a great country," Rachel added, "but that doesn't mean that other countries shouldn't be respected for their cultures and their values. And no matter how great we are, we can always do more to improve our quality of life and that of our neighbors."

Johnson was also critical of Rachel's prosecution of corporate crime.

"President Moreno is always looking for an excuse to attack business. She views business as the problem rather than an essential part of the solution. She talks a lot about the need for more living wage jobs but then objects whenever a businessman wants to create jobs. We've seen her style of government in the Soviet Union, and it didn't work," contended Johnson.

"No one disputes the need to protect the environment," Johnson added. "The big question is, Who pays for it? Moreno always wants the businessperson to pay for everything. That just gets passed on to consumers in the form of higher prices while making American companies less competitive in the global marketplace. President Moreno has been great for job creation in the third world. We need to focus on creating jobs here in America."

"Senator Johnson seems more interested in protecting his corporate campaign contributors from criminal prosecution," Rachel responded, "than he is in protecting consumers and taxpayers from being ripped off. And why do politicians who profess to support the 'free' market always want the taxpayers to absorb the cost of dealing with the pollution that businesses create? We need ecotaxes on pollution to avoid such cost-shifting."

Darling argued that the best way to help the third world was to allow American businesses to help build an economy that could support an American lifestyle.

"The American government, along with many of our leading commercial representatives, have done a good job in helping to address the development needs of many impoverished countries. We can't be the Santa Claus for every country. Free Trade is going to make things better for everyone in the very near future. We're always willing to sit down with responsible leaders of any country to work out a mutually beneficial plan for development."

"My opponents and I seem to agree that the world will be a better place when we have raised everyone's standard of living," noted Rachel. "The difference is that I believe that the rest of the world should have a say in how we accomplish this. My opponents support a race to the bottom, forcing American workers to take pay cuts or see their jobs exported overseas. I prefer to focus on how we can help lift up the poor, both abroad and at home. I want to create win-win situations."

****

Rachel's campaign staff focused on pulling votes away from Darling, targeting moderate and liberal Democrats whose fear of Johnson was the only thing keeping them in the Democratic column. Darling's aggressive courtship of the right-of-center vote helped push moderate Democrats into Rachel's corner.

Rachel was in many ways a born campaigner, preferring to talk and listen to real people rather than play the political game back in DC. She would escape the White House at every opportunity if Sophie would let her.

Rachel's support was strongest on the coasts. The polls showed her sweeping the West Coast of Washington, Oregon and the big prize of California. But since those states now used various forms of proportional representation to allocate seats in the Electoral College, she wouldn't pick up as many electoral votes there as under the old system. She was doing well in New York, New Jersey, Pennsylvania, Massachusetts, DC, and Rhode Island, as well in the larger Midwestern states such as Minnesota, Michigan, and Ohio. She was doing better than expected in Florida, with strong appeal among senior citizens. While she was lagging in the South, she was holding her own in Georgia, North Carolina and in the Southwest.

The liberal wing of the Democratic Party thought Darling was a disaster. "He's a dinosaur. He lectures rather than listens. We should be trying to take our base back from Rachel, not trying to out-Republican the Republicans," Congresswoman Wiley complained to McCarthy at the DNC. Johnson and Darling were dividing the prowar, procorporate vote, with Johnson picking up the lion's share. Darling's numbers began sinking badly in the closing weeks as it became clear that he had little chance of winning.

While Darling and Johnson were often clumsy in their attacks on Rachel, their campaign commercials were more focused, highlighting the most controversial aspects of the Green program.

Johnson's campaign ads attacked her on welfare and taxes. "President Moreno wants to raise your taxes to pay for more welfare. Ending the old welfare system has been a success, helping people break the cycle of dependency passed down from one generation to the next. She wants to reinstitute it."

Johnson also hammered Rachel for her granting of clemency to Native American activist Leonard Peltier and her support for a new trial for Mumia Abu Jamal. Johnson ran campaign ads that showed the silhouette of large black man holding a gun, towering over a prone police officer laying on the ground in a pool of blood. "President Moreno's idea of justice" read the headline. Another ad featured old photos of Rachel and Wynn at protests, superimposed with pictures of riots and burning buildings.

A cottage industry of personal attacks thrived, financed with millions from corporate interests, right-wing fundamentalists and hate-mongers. Production values ran from crude to state-of-the-art. "You thought the first term was bad. Just wait to see what Moreno does if reelected. She'll make everyone adopt the Green lifestyle — no cars, no meat, no tv except PBS. Big Sister 24 / 7. Paganism will be the national religion. To heat your home, she wants you to chop wood and wrap yourself in blankets. The mobs will rule the streets. Anarchy." The attacks on the internet were pornographic, homophobic, racist and misogynist.

A few weeks before the election, one of the national tv networks aired an hour-long "documentary" on Rachel. "President Moreno has carefully cultivated an image of a hard-working single mom who raised her son, who heroically died in 9/11, while putting herself through school to become a nurse. Our exhaustive investigation has found a quite different story," intoned reporter Jack Fassel.

"The father of her son was a drug dealer. She lived for many years in communes that featured free love and illegal drugs. She's had numerous extramarital affairs, including at least one with a woman. She was involved in counterfeiting. Her main fundraiser got rich by stealing patents from the auto industry. She and her husband have been arrested numerous times, including for acts of ecoterrorism, and her son was suspended from school for drugs. All this and more when we come back," said Fassel.

Rachel called Sophie at home shortly after the show aired. "Get the head of the network on the phone. I want Fassel fired tonight. And tell him were going to have the FCC yank their licenses," she said in a rage. "What they said about Tommy crossed the line. They're dead meat."

Sophie tried to calm Rachel down. "Other than the stuff about Tommy, this is just the same crap your opponents always peddle. It's not going to change anyone's mind. They're just desperate. Don't overreact. Focus on the finish line. We've got less than three weeks to go."

"We'll, we've got to do something," Rachel replied. "They gotta know there's a price to pay if they go after Tommy."

"I'll have our attorneys send them the standard demand for a retraction," Sophie promised, "threaten to sue them for libel — none of which will do us much good. Our best bet is just to ignore it for the time being. Making a big stink will just draw more attention to it. We'll get them after the election."

****

Unlike most incumbents, Rachel willingly accepted opportunities to debate, either with all the candidates or one-on-one. A debate allowed her to force her opponents to defend their positions and accusations, something the corporate-owned media did not do. She demanded that Johnson and Darling provide documentation for the points they made, something they frequently stumbled over. She took great pleasure in lumping them together as the "boys." Many of her supporters preferred to refer to them as "the grumpy old men."

After a few joint appearances during the summer, Johnson and Darling's handlers avoided such events. "Let's focus on a few debates at the end, where we can control the format." Darling's campaign manager told him. Darling had looked particularly bad in a joint appearance on the Oprah Winfrey show. Darling complained afterwards, "Rachel likes to play victim and warrior at the same time. One moment we're seen as picking on a mother whose son was killed on 9/11, the next minute she's Xenia the warrior princess."

Rachel wanted the fall debates to include every candidate on enough ballots to have a chance of winning the election. Johnson and Darling balked at this. They eventually agreed to allow the Libertarian candidate into the first debate. They refused to participate in the debate sponsored by the Citizen Assemblies.

The candidates' contrasting visions of democracy was a central theme of the debates.

"My opponents contend that we need to go to war to defend our democratic values. Before we send more American men and women, along with our tax dollars, to kill and be killed on foreign soil for the interests of some multinational corporation that makes lot of campaign contributions, I would like to get a little clearer sense about what type of democracy my opponents are talking about."

"My vision of democracy involves everyone, not just the powerful. It also includes people who live in other countries. I hate it when we go to war to save some government that oppresses its own citizens, denies basic human rights to women, fails to have free elections and allows a few to live well off the work and sacrifice of many," Rachel said.

"My idea of democracy starts with the president being elected by a majority of the voters, not ten percent," Darling retorted. "I believe in the rule of the majority, not the minority. And I believe in the rule of law. When people and countries violate the law, there need to be consequences."

"Unless the criminals are CEOs," Rachel interjected.

"President Moreno, no interruptions please," said the moderator. "Senator Johnson."

"America's democracy and stability is the envy of the rest of the world. We need to insist that countries that want to be part of the world community adopt similar standards. The world would be a much better place if every country was as democratic as ours," Johnson said.

"We need to fix democracy in our own country, not slap on a few more BandAids," Rachel responded. "Unfortunately, rather than the American people running our country, power is held by a handful of wealthy individuals and corporations. Elections should be decided on issues, not on the volume of cash you can vacuum up out of the cesspool of politics and special favors," said Rachel.

"Welfare for politicians," was Darling's response, "that's all public campaign financing is. President Moreno wants to spend our tax dollars giving every kook a platform. We already have strict limits at the federal level on how much money special interests can donate, much stricter than most states have. I agree that we need to tighten the rules up a bit. But if a candidate has a message that people support, they'll be able to raise money to be heard. The fact that President Moreno is with us today shows that the system works."

The candidates clashed in the debates over issues of affirmative action and racism.

"What about some affirmative action for all the hard-working people who pay taxes and keep this country functioning?" Johnson asked. "Our country will only remain strong if we hire people based on merit, not on the color of their skin. We should help people who help themselves, and too often the hardest working Americans are the ones that find our government slamming the door in their face."

Darling opposed Rachel's support for bilingual education. "We're wasting money with all these special classes to teach people in Spanish. We speak English here in America, and if you want to get ahead, you need to learn how to speak it. President Moreno isn't doing these people a favor by letting them avoid learning English. People become successful by overcoming their handicaps, not by society saying it's okay to be handicapped."

Johnson attacked Rachel for her support of reparations for African-Americans.

"I never owned a slave, and neither did anyone else in this audience," said Johnson. "There comes a point when you have to stop blaming others for your situation, and take responsibility for yourself. Giving away our tax dollars because of some liberal guilt about what happened 150 years ago is just taking the food off your and my table. President Moreno is just trying to buy votes. She thinks government is the solution to every problem and every injustice," said Johnson.

Darling also spoke out against reparations, though he criticized Johnson's lack of awareness of racial injustice in America. "We have to stop thinking of ourselves as victims, and instead focus on empowering one another. In America, if you work hard, you can get ahead. Instead of demanding handouts, we need to organize more tutoring and mentoring, more support for small businesses in our community, help grow the entrepreneurial spirit," he argued.

"Just to clear up any potential conflicts of interest on this issue," Rachel responded, "my husband's ancestors were slaves. In fact, we've discovered that one distant relative was owned by Senator Johnson's family. Nothing personal, of course," Rachel added, turning to Johnson, "but I just felt that full disclosure was needed here."

"Slavery is a dark stain on this nation's heritage, one that our society hasn't atoned for," Rachel added. "Many African-Americans still suffer from economic disparity left over from slavery. There are other legacies as well, including healthcare issues and the disproportionate rate of incarceration of blacks. A simple and just step is for our government to invest in helping black America achieve economic parity with the rest of society. The wealth in our country from the unpaid work of slaves is estimated to be worth about 1.5 trillion in today's dollars. And after we finally freed the slaves, we promised them 40 acres and a mule. After 160 years, it's time to pay up"

"By creating jobs and strengthening the economy, we will be helping blacks enjoy in the economic prosperity of our society and that will benefit all of us," Rachel concluded.

Johnson attacked Rachel on "Christian family values. "I believe in marriage between a man and his wife, raising their children together," Johnson said. "President Moreno supports an anything-goes approach — same-sex marriage, legalized drug use and prostitution."

Darling sought the middle ground on the same-sex marriage issue. The lower courts had consistently ruled in favor of same-sex marriage. The Supreme Court was expected to get the issue in the next year or two. "While I personally believe that marriage is a union between a man and a woman, I believe the prudent thing to do at this point is to leave it up to the courts to decide. And I oppose amending the federal constitution to ban same-sex marriage."

"I am heartened that Secretary Darling is coming around on this issue," replied Rachel. "I hope eventually he will join me in standing firmly behind full civil rights for all Americans, including marriage Less than forty years ago there were still laws on the books in sixteen states that would have prohibited me from marrying my husband because he is black and I am white.

"I am glad that society now views marriage as being primarily about love and commitment," Rachel added. "But throughout most of human history, with a few notable exceptions, marriage has primarily been about property. In many societies, the woman and her dowry went from father to husband. Our country freed the slaves, gave women the right to vote and now it needs to allow gays and lesbians to marry. My administration will do what it can to assist the Supreme Court in making the right decision."

****

Once again, election night ended without a resolution to the presidential race.

Rachel won 41 percent of the popular vote, with Johnson at 32 percent and Darling at 24 percent. The rest was divided between the Libertarians and other parties. She won 231 electoral votes, since 40 percent was usually enough to win in a three-way race. But she was still 39 electoral votes shy of the 270 needed to win. Johnson was second with 188, 82 votes short. Darling held the balance of power, with 119 votes.

The Greens had become the third national party. The Greens won 42 congressional seats, giving them the ability to determine the new Speaker of the House. The Republicans had the largest number of House seats but well short of a majority. In the Senate, the Democrats held a slight majority, though the Greens had won three seats.

"If the Electoral College is unable to pick a president," Brothers told the tv viewers, "it's up to Congress to resolve. However, the decision would be made by the old Congress, not the one just elected. Since the lame duck Congress has a majority of Republicans, they'd pick Johnson. So it makes sense for the Greens and the Democrats to strike a deal, either with each other or with the Republicans."

Darling wanted to inflict as much pain as possible on Rachel, publicly dangling the possibility of throwing his votes to Johnson. The American public and even many Democrats had other ideas.

"Rachel won the election," said her supporters. "It's time to end these political games. This is the third time now in the last four years where the status of the presidency has been thrown into question."

"She hasn't won yet," replied her critics. "This election was primarily a referendum on Rachel and a clear majority voted against her. The Republicans and Democrats should come to an agreement, and get the country back on track."

"Rachel, you've won," Wynn confidently told her shortly after the election. "All that's left is to play out the endgame. The only scenario that makes any sense for the Democrats is to give you the presidency. The Greens agree to support their candidate for House Speaker in exchange. This way they still get a Democrat as VP and they keep the Republicans out of the White House. Plus a lot of Electoral College members are congressmen who either we supported or came from districts where we finished first."

The Democrat's corporate contributors had different ideas. Sandy Clemons, head of the Council of Economic Advisers under Reagan, said, "Our first priority has to be to put an end to the Rachel's presidency. The Democrats will still control the Senate, maybe even the

House. And we'll make sure that President Johnson works with you, gives you a say in the Executive Branch. After all, he's our guy."

"I thought Darling was your guy too," Deutsche responded. "We need a better deal than that. We screw Moreno, the Greens will screw us in the House. Right now we get to control two out of three seats of power. Your proposal costs us power. You want to broker a deal, convince the Republicans to support Darling, and we'll make Johnson VP."

"If we give the White House to the Republicans, we're writing our obituary," argued Congresswoman Wiley. "With Rachel, we'll just have to ride it out for four years. She'll have to deal with us to get anything done. Her appeal won't carry over to the next Green presidential candidate. Besides, it would give me immense satisfaction to replace Baker as Speaker."

As happened four years earlier, Rachel and the Greens were far faster to respond to the election results than the other parties. The first demonstrations were organized at the offices of a few Electoral College members by the afternoon of the day after the election. Tens of thousands gathered at many of the state Capitols across the country the following weekend.

Several million rallied in DC, New York, San Francisco, Ann Arbor and elsewhere the following weekend. "Rachel won. Don't steal democracy." The women's groups, environmentalists, unions and Citizen Assemblies weren't about to allow corporations to steal power back.

By the end of the first week, Rachel had already publicly picked up half of the additional Electoral College votes that she needed. Wynn and Sophia told the national Democratic leadership, "We're going to win this with or without you. The American people know who won. They won't accept Johnson or Darling as president, and we're picking up more electoral votes each day. The sooner you cut the deal, the more you're going to get out of it."

The Democrats' bottom line was they needed the vice-presidential slot, as well as a number of cabinet positions. Deutsche argued that Mumfi was unacceptable: "He's too much in Rachel's corner."

Anna pointed out to Rachel, "If you give them the VP slot, all they have to do is kill you."

Mumfi offered to step aside but Rachel rejected his offer. "Hey, I took a lot of flack from Greens for sticking with you." She then turned to Sophie. "I don't see any need to now take grief from liberal

Democrats and blacks for jettisoning him," Rachel said. "Set up a meeting with Darling. Let's end this. I'll go to his place if he wants."

When the White House entourage pulled up, Naomi Darling, a large, robust woman, graciously greeted Rachel at the door. She had a commanding presence, and was a force in her own right in the social and political scene in DC.

"It was nice of you to come by," Mrs. Darling told Rachel. "I know how much Bob appreciates it, though I know he'll never admit that to you. He knows the score. He just needs to be stroked a bit. He's really a pussycat under that gruff exterior of his."

"I really doubt that, Naomi," Rachel laughed. "I'll do my best."

Naomi, who was much darker-skinned than her husband, escorted Rachel into Darling's study. A fire was lit in the fireplace. Darling was wearing a beige cardigan. The walls and shelves were filled with mementos from his military and political career. After a few minutes of small talk, Naomi left the two of them alone.

"Well, Mr. Secretary," Rachel began, "since we've always been blunt with each other, I see no reason to start playing games now. I'm here to ask for your support for my presidency, not only because it's your only logical option, it's also what's right for the country."

"Rachel, perhaps you might not have caught all my speeches during the recent campaign, but it's not so clear to me that you're the best choice," Darling caustically replied.

"I caught enough to know that we have some significant disagreements," Rachel replied. "But it's in the country's interest to put an end to this stalemate. And I've always respected you as some who tried to do what was best for America."

"Opposing what you wanted was often what I felt was best for the country," Darling retorted.

"I know that, Bob, and I'm sure there will continue to be similar situations in the future," Rachel replied. "But I can promise you that I'll try to make decisions based on what I feel is best for *all* of us."

"You blame America too much for the problems in the world," Darling said.

"I think you and too many other leaders refuse to acknowledge the mistakes that were made," Rachel responded softly. "Including mistakes that resulted in 9/11."

"But it wasn't —," Darling began to reply.

"Bob, we've had this argument before," Rachel interrupted. "I didn't come hear to argue history with you. I came here to talk about America's future. We may differ on the details but, as I said, both of us have always tried to put the needs of the country first. I can't say that about Johnson."

"Johnson isn't just about helping the rich," Darling responded. "He has a much different view of the world than you do."

"That's true," Rachel conceded, "but there's too much hate in his world. Starting with people of color, immigrants and Jews. Women don't fare too well, either. You've always talked about America being the land of opportunity. That's not what Johnson believes in."

"I received by far the highest number of votes," she went on. "If we had preferential voting, I would have won on election night. Bob, I'm going to win in the Electoral College with or without your support. The only issue question is whether John Mumfi stays on as VP — an important issue, of course, for African-Americans. I'd prefer to resolve this with your support. It would show the country that the Democrats and Greens are willing to work together. It would show the country that you're a statesman."

"I would hope that most of the country already knows that," Darling growled. "Including you."

"I do, Bob, and so does the country." Rachel paused. "Bob, this is one of those moments that will define both of our legacies. It's your choice how we write the closing of this particular act. I think it would be better for both of us, and for America, if you're standing alongside me and John when we take the oath of office."

They went out to tell the waiting press that the election was over.

TWENTY-THREE

REFLECTIONS:
THE LAST DAY OF THE PRESIDENCY

January 2009

Rachel looked out of her White House bedroom window for the last time.

The new occupants would be moved in during the inauguration ceremony that afternoon. She had asked her successor as a favor to maintain the vegetable gardens and greenhouses that took up an acre and a half of the White House property. Some of the food was used in the White House, the rest donated to local food pantries and shelters.

Rachel had transformed the White House into a state-of-the-art facility for appropriate technology during her stay, with windmills, photovoltaic and fuel cells and sewage disposal ponds growing fish and vegetables. There was a commercial-size compost facility for food and yard waste. Green America had donated most of the equipment.

A large playground — dedicated in Tommy's memory — was used by the daycare program she'd started for White House employees. If the federal government was going to require businesses to provide on-site daycare, she needed to set an example.

She felt two arms hugging her around the waist from behind. She turned around and kissed her daughter on the forehead.

"Are you sad to be leaving, Mommy? I am. Are you sure my friends can't come along? The president is supposed to be able to do anything she wants," wheedled Latisha.

"You know that's not possible, kitten," Rachel said, stroking her daughter's hair. "They have their own mommies and daddies to live with. Don't worry, there'll be plenty of children for you to play with in Seattle. We'll throw a big party next weekend so you can meet some new friends. But you can e-mail your friends back here every day, if you want. You can still do your internet video games with them, and we'll come back to visit, I promise. Where's daddy?" Rachel inquired.

"He's in his office. He wanted to make sure they packed his computer right."

"Daddy and his computer. I'm surprised he hasn't figured out a way to put a computer chip into his brain yet," kidded Rachel.

Latisha giggled.

"Are you going to miss your friends too, Mommy?"

"Many of my friends live in Seattle, so I'll get to see them more often. But I'll miss my friends in DC," she said. "And this is where we first met you, so it'll always be special."

Rachel and Wynn adopted Latisha when she was four. Olivia, her mother, had died of AIDS.

The public liked to think that the AIDS epidemic was over. After all, people like Magic Johnson were still going strong, and there were these "cocktails" that held the disease at bay. Unfortunately, AIDS was still an epidemic, especially in many third world countries — and in America's third world inner city neighborhoods. Many could not afford the drugs, though the World Health Organization, with Rachel's support, had made significant progress.

In the US, the drugs were now covered by the national healthcare program. But that had come too late for Olivia.

AIDS was especially an epidemic among poor women of color. They often lacked the information about the reality of the disease, not believing what they heard, faced already with too many problems. Why worry about one that wasn't here yet? And too often they were abused both by society and the men in their lives.

"As soon as I realized I was pregnant, I tried to clean up my life," Olivia told Rachel. "I knew that I had screwed mine up. I didn't wanna mess up my child's. I gave up the booze and drugs, and stopped hanging out with all those wacked out guys who just used me."

One of the ways Rachel coped with September 11 was by volunteering a few hours every few weeks, doing hospice with terminally ill individuals, often providing respite to a parent or other caregiver who needed a break. It was part of her campaign to increase community volunteerism. Federal employees were now allowed 40 hours a year to volunteer at nonprofits and schools.

Rachel would show up early in the morning to help someone get up, get them bathed, and help with any medications and therapy they needed. That's how she met Olivia.

Olivia had gone to a community health center when she was four months pregnant. They got her into a drug rehab program. "Then they told me that I had AIDS. I freaked out, screaming and throwing things. I thought I'd killed my baby. They told me that since a baby got AIDS during childbirth and breastfeeding, they could save her. They were real nice, helped hook me up with welfare and got me this apartment." They also put her in touch with a neighborhood community center that provided support for AIDS patients.

Latisha played jump rope on the streets as her mother lay dying upstairs in their apartment.

Rachel met Olivia only a half-dozen times before she died. She lived in a small two-room apartment in a tough DC neighborhood. Boarded up houses and litter-strewn lots dotted the street. People in the neighborhood did their best to survive on government benefits or with jobs that hardly paid enough to cover the rent. Some were recent immigrants.

It was a noisy neighborhood, especially at night when residents bolted their doors and pulled the shades down as the drug dealers took over, hanging out on the front steps waiting for their customers to drive by on the way home to the suburbs. The sounds of sirens and gunshots often punctuated Saturday nights.

Olivia had flowerpots in the window and on the fire escape. Rachel brought a few transplants from her own garden.

Violence and poverty had been recurring companions for Olivia, starting when she was a child. She had moved in with her 25-year-old drug dealer and boyfriend when she was 16. She lasted there two months before ending up on the streets, learning the routine at homeless shelters and how a poor young woman survives on her own. Her body was her most marketable asset.

Latisha's father, at least the assumed father, was part of the drug crowd Olivia crashed with. "We knew that sharing a needle was a good way to get sick, but who cared? We weren't long for this life anyway. Just give me the next high. Sex was just a way to get more drugs. And why waste money on rubbers when you needed it for the next score? It got pretty nasty when we was strung out," Olivia said matter-of-factly.

When the public health authorities finally tracked down the likely father, locked up in a county jail for shoplifting, he claimed he wasn't aware that he had AIDS. "Did that bitch Olivia give it to me?" he asked. When he got released, he kept walking and never contacted Olivia.

Rachel and Olivia were talking as the early morning light tried to break through the grimy windows on the third-floor walkup. Rachel held Olivia's hand, pressing a wet cloth against her forehead.

"The only thing I did right in my life is Latisha," Olivia told her. "Whatever goodness I had I gave to her. Wished I had her sooner. She made me realize all the wrong things I was doin' to myself. She gave me someone to care about, a purpose."

"You've done a good job with her," Rachel said reassuringly. "She's a great kid."

"Thank you," Olivia replied. She gathered her remaining strength. "Please promise me you won't let her got lost in the system. Maybe be her fairy godmother so there's one person in the world that still loves her? I know I'm askin' a lot, what with you not really knowing me or nuthin', but she ain't got no one else. Whatever you can do for her, I'd be grateful. God bless you," Olivia begged, tears streaking her face.

Rachel arranged for Latisha to stay with her for a few days after her mother's death, to help her ease into the foster care system. She never left.

Sophia coordinated the search for Latisha's father. He'd been shot to death in a drug dispute in Baltimore two years after Latisha was born.

****

Rachel's pending departure from the White House had led to a plethora of stories and analyses of Rachel's legacy as president. She had turned down most requests for interviews, calling them a distraction. "I wanna concentrate on getting a few more things done before we depart," Rachel told Sophie. "There'll be plenty of time later to reminisce."

Rachel did agree to an interview with Roberta Sanchez of Justice for All, the national morning news program on the Pacifica radio network.

"What do you want to be remembered for?" Sanchez asked, warming up with a softball.

Rachel had been idly twirling a piece of yarn protruding from her sweater. She was picking up too many of these nervous habits.

"I hope I'm remembered as someone who listened to the people and tried to do what was needed, not just what was popular," Rachel replied. "I'm very proud that healthcare is now a right in the US. We've also made progress on developing a sustainable economy, creating ten million new green jobs that pay a living wage.

"I'm proud that we've made the defense of our planet a national priority. Even our business schools are stressing the importance of not using up resources faster than the planet can replenish them. It's a relief to finally see worldwide action to confront global warming. We clearly waited too long, but hopefully we'll be able to avoid the most catastrophic impacts. I'm heartened the federal government has adopted the Precautionary Principle, that we cannot take action unless we're sure that we won't harm the environment or public health." Rachel noted.

"Our push to develop renewable energy has reduced our military drive for oil," she added. "I love it that solar panels and windmills are sprouting like mushrooms after a rain."

"Some groups, like the trial lawyers, argue that you gave up too much to get universal healthcare. They've brought suit against some of the caps you agreed to on personal injury lawsuits," Sanchez noted.

"The thousands of insurance companies who didn't want to lose all their profits from healthcare pulled out all the stops to try to defeat the single payer system. Congress felt it had to throw them a few bones. Perhaps if the trial lawyers had been more selective in whose congressional campaigns they financed over the years, we wouldn't have needed to make so many compromises," Rachel responded. "The final healthcare package didn't have everything I wanted. Hopefully, as time goes on we can expand the program."

"Some senior groups argue that there are too many restrictions on what surgeries are covered," Sanchez added.

"We're always going to face choices in which healthcare services the government pays for," Rachel admitted. "A significant percentage of a person's lifetime medical expenses — around fifty thousand dollars — are incurred during the last year of their life. Is society willing to pay a hundred thousand dollars for surgery that might extend someone's life for six months? We're going to be grappling with questions like this for years to come."

"One of the central themes of your presidency has been the restoration of democracy in the US," Sanchez said, switching topics. "Do you feel you've succeeded?"

"The Citizen Assemblies have been a wonderful step forward, giving community residents a real voice in government. They've dramatically changed how we make decisions. And we've made public campaign financing the rule rather than the exception. Even the Supreme Court now recognizes the right of the people to stop special interests from buying elections," Rachel noted.

"We've made significant progress in adopting fairer electoral systems like proportional representation and preferential voting. People no longer have to choose among the lesser of two evils," Rachel added. "People are losing their cynicism about government and elections.

"And I'm proud that gays and lesbians have won full civil rights. Though that victory was due to grassroots activism, not me. I'm happy that my administration was able to play a small role."

"Some progressives argue that corporations and the wealthy still have too much power," Sanchez interjected.

"Unfortunately, they're right," Rachel acknowledged. "Our political system too often dances around the fringes of real power. I wish I could've done more to democratize the economy, to put people's needs ahead of corporate profits. We've greened parts of the economy but capitalism still exploits all of us, as well as the environment. At least we now have a democratic International Trade Organization instead of the old WTO. They're trying to make sure the global economy protects the environment and respects local cultures. But it needs more power over multinational corporations. The next decade will be critical.

"A true democracy requires an independent media to keep the politicians, the ruling class, honest," she added. "Corporate ownership of the US media is still a major problem, but at least we've reduced the number of radio and tv stations that one company can own. I'm glad that we have been able to reverse the trend toward privatization of the internet, helping it become the one communication medium that the public actually controls and uses."

"Before you took office, you were a vocal advocate on welfare rights and poverty. That was one of your biggest criticisms of the Clinton administration. Yet we still see soup kitchens and homeless shelters. Have we done enough?" Sanchez asked.

"We haven't ended poverty, if that's what you mean," Rachel responded. "When I took office, one out of every five children lived in poverty — twice the rate of any other industrial country. We've managed to cut that in half, starting with our children's allowance which helps every child with housing, clothing and food costs. And I hope that within five years we'll finally see a universal childcare program."

Rachel twirled the ends of her hair. She was thinking about coloring the gray streaks now that it would no longer be front-page news. "We've passed other critical initiatives for our children, such as increased funding for after-school and prekindergarten programs, as well as for more teachers — and higher pay for teachers and childcare workers. We've banned television advertising aimed at young children, and stopped corporate sponsors from using the education system to hawk their products to students."

"Welfare is always a contentious issue," Rachel added, "because there are conflicting needs and problems. Most people just need a real opportunity; others needs more support. I think we've found a good balance between providing a strong safety net for people and giving them the skills they need to become economically self-sufficient. We've placed the emphasis on empowering people. We've also made welfare for the poor more of an income support program, putting it on the same level as all the other welfare programs for homeowners and corporations and farmers. We've given dignity back to poor people."

"Your administration has experienced dramatic lows and highs in the area of foreign policy," Sanchez observed. "from the tragic losses of 9/11 to bringing peace to the Middle East. You've often said that you hope the Peace Institute will be your most enduring contribution to the world. Are you satisfied with its progress?"

Rachel would always remember the days she had walked through the streets of Palestine. She adjusted the desk photo of her holding a Palestinian baby in the midst of a refugee camp. Next to it was a photo of her and a Jewish child in one of the kibbutzim she visited. She continued the interview.

"The Peace Institute has established a lot of credibility in just a few years, though admittedly more in the rest of the world than here in America. Countries are turning to it early looking for assistance in resolving disputes," Rachel said. "It has already helped prevent several wars."

"The Institute has taught us that you have to build peace, not enforce it," Rachel continued. "Countries go to war because they believe it's the only way to achieve a particular purpose, to get a grievance addressed. We reduce the threat of war when we provide countries with more effective alternatives to resolve their differences," Rachel noted.

"Of course, there are still some who don't want to give up the military advantages they have over their neighbors. But we're increasingly isolating these individuals. The more the world community shows it will not tolerate such behavior, the stronger a deterrence it will be," Rachel explained.

"On several notable occasions when the representatives of the Peace Institute were unsuccessful," said Sanchez, "you supported the deployment of peacekeeping forces to separate the combatants. The peace forces had also been used to apprehend those responsible for crimes against humanity. Is a permanent peacekeeper force still needed?"

"The creation of a permanent Peacekeeping Command allows the world to take collective action without the need to wait for troop commitments from individual countries. They've become an effective deterrence to war, but we need to continue to strengthen them. And to continue to have the Peace Institute train their forces on techniques for maintaining peace and resolving disputes without resorting to the use of guns," Rachel told Sanchez.

Rachel's push for a permanent peacekeeping force had generated considerable opposition within Congress. Baker, now the House Minority Leader, argued, "It's the first step in creating a world army to impose its will on sovereign countries. I'd rather have the US in charge than the UN General Assembly."

Rachel had countered, "The peacekeepers will have one mission — to act as peacekeepers — not to engage in offensive war." The force remained much smaller than she'd wanted.

"What about September eleventh?" Sanchez prodded. "Have you been able to heal from that tragic day, which included the loss of your own son?"

"There are no words to describe my sadness about that day. It's amazing how resilient we humans are, that we've been able to build something positive out of this horror. But there isn't a day when it doesn't stab my heart for at least a few minutes. I continue to beg forgiveness from those who died as a result of my actions," Rachel said.

"I shudder to think what would have happened if we'd responded to September eleventh with military attacks on Afghanistan and the Middle East," Rachel added. "We would've killed thousands of innocent civilians. We would have created ten new terrorists for every one that we killed. We could have ignited a new world war. We could have imposed a police state in our own country, with increased surveillance and denial of civil liberties, and harassment of immigrants. I'm proud to have been a common sense person who was in the wrong place at the right time."

"Your biggest disappointments?" Sanchez asked.

Rachel smiled. She weighed how blunt she could be, now that she would soon be leaving the Oval Office.

"I'm disappointed in how big the military budget still is. I think it was former House Speaker Tip O'Neill who said all politics is local, and that is certainly true when it comes to the military. Every weapon system, every military base, has a Congressman who feels that it's a life or death matter to save it. It's clear that military spending is less about national defense than it is about corporate welfare."

"But you've managed to cut the military budget by more than 30 percent since you took office," Sanchez noted. "I mean, before you took office, the US was spending more on the military than the next ten big spenders combined."

"We've hardly even cut the fat," Rachel replied. "We still spend by far the most in the world. I want a lean, trim fighting machine, one that defends the American people, not corporate profits."

"I'm also disappointed," she added, "that we haven't made more progress on improving the status of women in many third world countries. At least it's a criterion our government utilizes in the annual review of our relationships with other countries. But women are still denied basic rights in too many parts of the globe. They're denied the right to control their own bodies, to obtain an education, hold a job. We have a lot more to do. Starting here at home."

****

After Roberta Sanchez and her crew departed, Rachel reflected on her efforts to make the world a safer place.

She had worked to reduce the conditions that led the US to war. After the end of the Cold War and the policy of containing communism, America's military continued to be used to advance corporate America's drive to create and control a global economic empire. The People's Summit after 9/11 had pushed a different agenda, to create a world that sought justice for all, seeking cooperation rather than US economic domination.

While America was no longer the big bully, Rachel was disappointed with how little progress had been made in improving relations with the few countries powerful enough to stand up to the US.

Russia responded warily to Rachel's efforts to reverse the increasing tensions between the two countries since the departure of Gorbachev and Yeltsin. Rachel persuaded Congress, Europe and Japan to increase their aid to Russia for economic development and environmental restoration. In exchange, Rachel pushed Russia to "strengthen your democratic institutions, including an independent judiciary."

Russia was more concerned, however, about its own internal problems, including the rise of nationalist fervor, crumbling infrastructure and the challenges of governing an essentially ungovernable country.

Rachel made little progress with China. It was a growing economic force, as its huge pool of cheap labor and antiunion actions attracted multinational corporations like moths to a flame. Rachel joined with American labor unions in pressuring China and American companies to improve working conditions for local workers.

China continued to increase its military presence throughout Asia, developing and exporting new weapon systems, including nuclear forces, ballistic missiles and destabilizing missile defenses. The two countries did make some progress in negotiating formal arms- reduction agreements.

Rachel showed her support for the right of self-determination of various cultures under China's control by meeting with representatives of Tibet and other repressed minorities. She also supported democracy movements in China, as well as those who called for stronger environmental protection. Chinese leaders regularly protested what they saw as "undue interference in our internal affairs. Human rights are already guaranteed in China. We also have the right to protect ourselves from subversive forces in collusion with foreign interests."

China and the US almost came to blows over Myanmar, formerly Burma. The location of the predominately Buddhist nation between China and the Indian Ocean made Myanmar strategically important to China.

Rachel had long championed the cause of Aung San Suu Kyi, the Nobel Peace prize winner whom most observers thought easily won the 1991 presidential election that the military dictatorship had voided.

Aung Sun's father had been a general and national leader who was assassinated in 1947. Her mother had been Burma's ambassador to India. Aung Sun had raised her family in England, but returned in 1988 to care for her ailing mother, just as a national democracy movement took root. Soon she was addressing a rally of a half-million, calling for the creation of a democratic government.

Over the next fifteen years her popular support grew despite being subjected to repeated house arrest by the military junta.

Rachel used American diplomatic forces to escort Aung Sun out of the country so she could address the fifth annual conference of the Peace Institute. The military let her go, hoping that her departure would be permanent. The conference was also a celebration of the ratification on the International Peace Treaty — they had picked up the additional fifteen countries needed during the last year. The next step would be to convince Congress to allocate funding.

Aung Sun spoke of the need for peace activists to take action.

By peace I do not mean a life of passivity, I do not mean a life without action because sometimes we have to act a lot to bring about peace. Peace, development and justice are all connected to each other. We cannot talk about economic development without talking about peace. When we talk about peace, we cannot avoid talking about basic human rights, especially in a country like Burma where people are troubled constantly by a lack of human rights and a lack of justice and a lack of peace. The fact is that the present military authorities are in great fear of people power.

Rachel used the ceremony to announce, "I'm extending American diplomatic recognition to Aung Sun as the democratically elected leader of her country." She got the UN Security Council, by a narrow vote, to also extend recognition,, though they balked at Rachel's request to send in the UN Peacekeeping Command to give it effect.

Rachel sent a squadron of American jet fighters to escort Aung Sun and Air Force One home. Aung Sun had declined Rachel's offer to accompany her. "Thank you, but this is something that I and my people must do. It's enough to know that you and America are true friends."

The military leaders allowed the planes to land, but said, "We cannot guarantee your safety if you leave the airport." The troops waited to place her under house arrest. The populace took matters into its own hands, with a million residents marching peacefully to the airport to welcome her and escort her home.

China rushed its troops to the border, offering "whatever assistance was needed to prevent foreign interference." Rachel sent a message to China: "The US is prepared to intervene upon the request of President Sun." Senator Deutsche protested, "The president is about to drag America into a war with China without consulting Congress and where no national interests of the US are involved."

The Myanmar military leaders, however, saw the size of the popular uprising and the quality of Rachel's support and decided to cut a deal with Aung Sun. She agreed to leave the military largely intact if they withdrew from any political involvement and recognized her as national leader.

Rachel had made some progress in reducing the threat of nuclear war.

When she took office, the treaty with Russia called for reducing the nuclear arsenal to 3,500 active warheads each. This still left the US with seven nuclear warheads available for each Russian military target. An additional 1,000 nuclear weapons were "in storage" waiting for deployment.

"My dream is that when I leave office, I'll be able to report to the

American people that we had dismantled every nuclear warhead in the world," Rachel said. She pointed out that Ronald Reagan had made a similar declaration in his second inaugural address, stating, "We seek the total elimination, one day, of nuclear weapons from the face of the Earth."

She worked with House Speaker Wiley to convince Congress to support nuclear disarmament.

"Our arsenal of nuclear weapons makes the world a far less safe place, at a great expense to American taxpayers. The more nuclear weapons we have primed to launch, the greater the risk of an accidental launch. The only ones who will lose when we remove these weapons of mass destruction from their launching pads are the military contractors who build and maintain them," Rachel told Deutsche at a meeting in the Oval Office with him and the Speaker of the House.

The US was spending more than 40 billion dollars a year to develop new nuclear weapon systems and to maintain the existing ones. The US had spent nearly six trillion dollars on its nuclear weapon programs.

"The size of our nuclear arsenal stops many countries from trying to compete," argued Deutsche. "If we reduce our forces too much, stop being a real deterrent, other countries may seek to expand theirs. We could just set off another arms race."

"Jonathan, how can we ask countries like Pakistan and India to step away from their nuclear weapons, from their Hindu and Muslim bombs," Wiley responded, "when a country like ours that faces far less credible threats is unwilling to disarm? This is the type of decision that you look on with pride when you retire, that you did something to make the world a better place."

Rachel began by unilaterally lowering the US number by 1,000. By the time she left office, it was down to 500 nuclear warheads on each side, along with agreements to increase inspections and verifications.

America, Russia and China were not the only members of the nuclear club. Britain and France were longtime members. South Africa had given their nukes up, along with several former members of the Soviet Union. The threat of nuclear war hung over the repeated border crisis between India and Pakistan. Israel was widely believed to possess nuclear weapons as the final veto against an all-out attack by Arab countries. It also threatened preemptive strikes against countries such as Iran if it found evidence of efforts to develop nuclear weapons.

Rachel was able to strengthen the international treaty on nuclear nonproliferation. A number of countries argued that it was hypocritical for the US to push for others not to develop nuclear capability while the US remained the largest nuclear power. Rachel nodded in agreement. "Feel free to convince Congress to disarm," she told the other countries. "I'm doing the best I can."

****

Rachel sat at the president's desk to compose a handwritten note to her successor.

"I've found this to be a place of personal growth. While it presents great challenges and disappointments, it also provides opportunities for great rewards, starting with the satisfaction that you have done your best to help our country and our world. Be willing to listen to your heart and have the courage to choose the true path."

It doesn't matter so much what road you traveled to get here, but what you do once you arrive, Rachel thought as she put the pen down and looked around the room. It was a circle of power, power that had been thrust upon her and a power that changed her. Like the gentle little hobbits in their Tolkien world, she had carried the power into dark places to try to destroy it, to win freedom for the oppressed.

The power was seductive. Many people coveted it and their whispered pleadings to use it on their behalf never ceased. She wondered how it would change her successor. While she had made the world a better place, she worried that she had increased the power of the Oval Office.

She stopped in the corridor outside the Oval Office to straighten several of the pictures of members of the Secret Service who'd been injured or killed in the line of duty. She looked closely at the two agents who'd given their lives to save hers.

****

It was a bleak February afternoon, with the threat of snow hanging in the air. Rachel was battling a cold. Wynn was back in DC in bed trying to shake his off.

She used her speech to the United Auto Workers' convention in Detroit to announce her proposal to give workers more control over their pension plans. The speech hadn't been one of her more inspired efforts.

"Pensions are merely the deferred earnings of workers," Rachel explained. "These plans are the single largest source of ownership of the American economy, including the Fortune 500. Yet the voting rights for the huge amount of stocks owned by these plans are given to the banks, insurance companies and financial wheeler-dealers that oversee the pension plans. These financial managers invariably vote for what's best for the company's top management, not the workers — the true owners."

The overlapping board of directors — interlocking directorates — among the companies and financial institutions conspired to extract as much compensation for themselves and top management as possible.

"If the true owners of American corporations were given control, you wouldn't see your jobs shifted to some foreign country where workers are paid a dollar a day," Rachel stated to boisterous applause.

In a private meeting beforehand, she pushed the UAW leadership to fight for more environmentally friendly cars, starting with increases in the mileage per gallon and production of biodiesel and hybrid electric cars. "These are your future jobs. If American car manufacturers don't do it, Japan or Korea or Brazil will. You've got to make this part of your contract negotiations. Or start figuring out how to use your pension funds to fund worker-owned companies that will do it."

For the drive to the airport, her security detail wanted her to get into the limousine in the hotel basement. She was flying to LA and Portland for appearances, followed by a late-night flight back to DC. Her staff wanted to get out of Detroit as soon as possible; it was sunny and warm at their next stop.

But as usual a crowd of well-wishers was gathered outside the hotel to catch a glimpse of her and hopefully shake her hand. She swore that she'd spend no more than ten minutes working the crowd. Her assistants, knowing that she'd run late, got ready to start pointing at their watches.

The crowd, smaller than usual — maybe a few hundred — was dressed for winter, with large overcoats and scarves. Many had waited more than an hour, bouncing on their feet to keep warm.

As Rachel leaned over the barricades to shake hands and say a few words, a tall, thin, gaunt man with a dark complexion and a short, curly beard, emerged from an office complex across the closed-off street. The building, a few hundred yards way, had been searched several times that morning and was inside the secure zone.

The man walked across the snow-covered lawn in front of the hotel. He briefly locked eyes with a Secret Service agent before glancing away.

The agent began to watch him more closely. When he reached the edge of the crowd, now several dozen deep where Rachel had paused to shake hands, he began to elbow his way forward.

Chang talked into the transmitter on her wrist. "Check out the tall guy with the dark overcoat pushing through the crowd," she instructed a nearby agent. The man noticed the agent approaching, and began to move faster, now thirty yards from Rachel.

Rachel sensed the increasing tension of her security detail and glanced up to scan the crowd. Everything began to move in slow motion. She heard Chang say, "Move, we're out of here, stop him." She felt two agents grab her and almost lift her off her feet, pulling her toward the car. The agents' hands went to their guns inside their clothes. The crowd began to move away from Rachel.

The man made a final lunge toward Rachel just as the Secret Service agents were about to reach him. He shouted, "Praise to Allah" and exploded. Rachel flew through the air, her arms outstretched as if about to hug someone, slamming into the side of the car.

Her collision was cushioned by two agents who had wrapped their bodies around her. The one in front didn't survive, her skull fatally cracked upon impact. Another agent was killed, along with several bystanders. Bodies were scattered everywhere.

Another car screeched to a halt and her security thrust Rachel in. She couldn't understand why Chang kept on asking her, "How many fingers do I have, Madame President?" *Why does my arm hurt so much?* Rachel asked herself. She slipped in and out of consciousness. Chang was yelling, "Rachel, stay awake. We're almost there. Stay with me."

More than thirty people were treated at the scene or taken to hospitals, most suffering from shock, though some had serious injuries.

Rachel snapped back into real time as the convoy was about to reach the hospital designated for such an emergency.

"What happened? My arm really hurts," Rachel moaned. She suddenly became alert, instructing the driver to turn around and return to the hotel. "I've got to make sure that we take care of anyone that's injured." Chang and the driver ignored the order.

"Madame President, we're doing everything that's possible. Your presence would just make it harder to help others," Chang said. "And the last thing we're going to do is put you in an unsecured situation. I'd love to just put you on Air Force One and get outta here, but we've got to get you checked out at the hospital first. We need to take care of your arm, and make sure you don't have any internal injuries."

Rachel insisted on walking into the hospital. "I need to show everyone that I'm all right, that things are under control." Chang decided to avoid a long argument. "You have ten seconds to get out, wave once, and walk through the hospital door. If you're not inside within ten seconds, we're carrying you in."

Even before her arm had been set, the news media was speculating that it was the work of Middle East terrorists. "A suicide bombing is a Middle East tactic. It's likely revenge for the killing of bin Laden. We'll need to act swiftly and decisively in response," was the media line to the American people. A few commentators suggested, "It may be the work of a group like Hamas who've been forced aside by the peace efforts in Palestine. This may be a signal that the accord is dead."

The man who knew the most no longer existed. No group stepped forward to celebrate or claim responsibility. The attack was condemned worldwide, including by several of the "suspected groups" in the Middle East. Corporate America was noticeably quiet. In private, many expressed regrets that Rachel had survived.

The bomber was eventually identified as Yusuf Abu Suleiman. Twenty-nine years old, he'd been born in the US to Iraqi parents who were studying engineering. He had returned to Iraq when he was five. He came back to America to attend graduate school and had taken a job here after graduation. He had visited Iraq a few months ago, allegedly to see his parents.

His coworkers and friends found it hard to believe he was an assassin. "He was very friendly, very outgoing, enjoyed having a good time. He was a hard worker, always on time, never a problem. Sure, he occasionally talked politics but he was far more passionate about sports."

The CIA, however, produced evidence that Suleiman had been active with the Baath Party as a teenager. Baath was the party of Saddam Hussein, the Iraqi dictator. His family told reporters who contacted them, "It was nothing. He joined the youth group so he could play on the soccer team, that's all."

Then came information that his older brother had been buried alive as one of the conscripts on the front line in the Gulf War. American bulldozers piled sand into the trench he was in.

"Whoever did this were professionals," Sophie reported to Rachel. "The bomb was very sophisticated. It could have been triggered either by Suleiman or by an accomplice by remote control. It's much more likely to have been the work of a state agency than an underground terrorist network."

"A government could have supplied a terrorist group with it," Wynn pointed out. "There could be multiple parties involved here."

"That's true," Sophie conceded. "There must also have been a support network within the US. This operation was far too complicated for one man to pull off alone. However, the FBI hasn't come up with anything firm."

The few leads they had led down dead ends: what evidence was available was inconclusive.

The most popular theory within the foreign intelligence establishment was that the killer had been a sleeper agent employed by the Iraqi secret service. They also speculated that the Iraqi secret service might have been compromised by the al-Qaida network.

"It would be a mistake to believe that the Muslim terrorists have given up their war just because Ms. Moreno is president. They aren't interested in what we have done for peace in the Middle East, they just want to wipe us off the face of the Earth, especially women like President Moreno," Senator Branston contended on the Sunday morning talk shows.

A CIA official identified Ahmad Rubai, an Iraqi intelligence officer, as having been the possible contact with Suleiman. Rubai had taken a temporary assignment at the UN a month before the attack. There were several days where his movements were unaccounted for. He returned to Iraq a few days after the attack.

Information was also leaked to the *Washington Post* showing increased cooperation between the remnants of the al-Qaida network and the Iraqi government.

Calls intensified from Congress and the media for Rachel to launch a retaliatory attack to remove Hussein from power.

Rachel was skeptical that Iraq was behind the attack. "Hussein wouldn't have anything to gain from killing me. It wouldn't boost his stature in the Arab world and it would increase the threat to his rule from our government. And a joint operation with al-Qaida is unlikely, since they're not supportive of Hussein's regime, for both religious and ethnic reasons," she told Sophie.

Hussein denied that his government was involved. "I wish to convey my deepest personal regret for this horrendous attack on the person of President Moreno. I would welcome a personal envoy from the president to come to Iraq to investigate."

Rachel had ended the American bombings and embargo on Iraq six months after the September 11 attack. "The embargo has led to the deaths of hundreds of thousands innocent civilians, particularly children," Rachel said in announcing her decision. "I still can't figure out why President Bush didn't finish the job when he had the opportunity. But denying the average Iraqi citizen basic necessities has only solidified the power of Hussein."

Shortly after Rubai was singled out, Hussein reported, "He was killed in a car accident a week after he returned from the US. We are investigating to determine the true circumstances behind his death. I wouldn't be surprised to discover that outside forces arranged his death to cover up their involvement."

Several weeks later, Hussein announced, "While we have not found any evidence linking Rubai to Suleiman or the attack on President Moreno, we have found evidence that Rubai had received payments from American companies with close ties to the CIA. If any orders were issued to Mr. Suleiman, it was done by parties hostile both to President Moreno and the Iraqi people."

Hussein produced documents — allegedly found in Rubai's house — showing that a large deposit had been made to his secret bank account in Lebanon a few weeks before the attack. The documents also showed that Rubai's job had brought him into contact with a number of American defense contractors and intelligence operatives in the Middle East.

It was spooks chasing spooks down unlit back alleys.

"It looks like Rubai sold information to anyone with the money to buy," Sophie reported. "He's quite a piece of work. He did business with lots of people who wouldn't cry over your demise."

"An incestuous little world," Anna remarked.

Wynn and Anna argued that the attack had been orchestrated by her opponents in the business and military communities.

"Someone killed the Secret Service agent guarding the building Suleiman came out of," Wynn remarked. "To get the explosives not only into the country but within the security zone required detailed knowledge of our security operations. It's an inside job."

"Corporate America, the national security establishment, the military-industrial contractors, they all got freakin' motives," Anna exclaimed. "You've put a helluva number of CEOs behind bars. You're challengin' the ruling class's control of the global economy. Who the heck da ya think tried to take ya out? Stuffin' the ballot box didn't work, pull the trigga."

Rachel had brought in her own people to run the CIA and other national security agencies. But there were far too many rogue elements that wouldn't go down without a fight, and they certainly had staunch allies in Congress and the military-industrial companies.

With no conclusive proof as to who was responsible, Rachel decided to proceed against both potential culprits.

"Introduce a resolution for a Special Tribunal to indict Hussein as a war criminal," she instructed the US ambassador to the UN. "Hussein's a nasty, brutal dictator. The Iraqi people, not to mention the rest of the Middle East, would be much better off if he's removed."

While none of the allegations against Hussein were new, Rachel's stature in the UN ensured that the resolution was treated seriously. Many of the abuses that most bothered Rachel were the ones committed against other Iraqis, including the unrelenting torture and ruthless oppression of political dissent. Hussein's political party represented a minority of Iraqis, so he brutally suppressed the two other major groups.

Many of the briefs submitted to the UN by foreign governments in support of Hussein's indictment focused on the 5,000 Iranians killed by chemical weapons between 1983 and 1988. The use of chemical weapons has been a war crime since 1925. It was politically safe for countries to argue over the rules of war rather than over the time-honored tradition of domestic oppression. "We're concerned about what you do outside your borders, not inside," was the feeling of the leaders of many countries.

The UN targeted the use of chemical weapons in 1988 in Halabja, a town in northeastern Iraq where thousands of Kurdish villagers were killed. Iraq had been a major ally of the US in its war against Iran.

"There's considerable evidence that the Kurdish deaths were due to the use of chemical weapons by the Iranians," Sophie told Rachel. "A 2002 report by the US Defense Intelligence Agency found that the deaths were primarily due to cyanogen chloride, which Iran used but not Iraq. However, some Iranian combatants in Halabja were killed by mustard gas. This was probably due to the Iraqis."

The Arab countries took matters into their own hands. Rachel had warned them, "Either you resolve this or we may have to send in American troops or the UN peacekeeping forces to arrest him."

When Hussein was in Egypt trying to rally support at a meeting of Arab nations, the UN suddenly passed a resolution to bring Hussein before an international tribunal for questioning for various war crimes. Egypt announced they would comply with the order. Hussein was killed as he tried to run a roadblock while fleeing to the airport. "An unfortunate development," the Egyptian government announced. "A breakdown in communication."

The Arab Summit quickly passed a resolution creating a peacekeeping force to send to Baghdad. "We need to provide protection against possible interference by outside forces. We offer fraternal assistance in the orderly transition to a more representative government." The Baath party was warned, "Either capitulate and be allowed to participate in the new government, or face attack from a coalition of Arab countries." They decided to smile and welcome their brothers.

The transition to a freer, more open society was a difficult one in Iraq, as religious and regional tribal forces jockeyed for power. The Arab nations, the UN and the Peace Institute assisted with the restoration of civil society, avoiding direct US involvement. "The last thing we'd want is to be a military occupation force. That'd be a nightmare, with body bags piling up," Rachel told Sophie

Rachel also gave orders to purge — by forced retirement, firing or transfer — members of the CIA and other national security agencies who were not on board with respect to the changes she had initiated. She also went after anyone with ties to Rubai or who was less than forthcoming in the investigation. The companies with alleged roles in the intrigue with the Iraqi government had their contracts carefully scrutinized by the Justice and Defense Departments for any possible civil or criminal violations. Investigators found quite a few.

****

Rachel went to spend a few final moments in her favorite place on the White House property.

This was where she came to center herself, to meditate, at the center of her garden, surrounded by trees and vegetables, flowers and butterflies. When it was in full bloom, she could sometimes find her center, coming into tune with something far larger than herself, stronger, peaceful, ancient. She thought of it as Gaia.

The last eight years had often felt like a blur of perpetual motion. It was a luxury to step outside that blur for even a few moments, to slow it down, to sit and contemplate nature, to read a book for enjoyment, not knowledge.

The first year after Tommy's death had been hard. There was no lack of things that wore her down. She found it hard to sleep. She often spent the quiet hours after midnight wandering around her quarters searching for peace, for some type of resolution or understanding, trying to shake her demons lose, praying for forgiveness and guidance and courage. She prayed for the well being of the world, for her son and for her own soul.

She thought of Tommy every day. Of the boy he was, of the man he had become. Of the father and husband he would never be.

****

Rachel's last year in office had been a hectic one. Her political opponents had hoped her lame duck status would hamper her ability to push her agenda. Rachel instructed her staff, "Forge boldly ahead. I wanna do so much that it'll take them a couple of years to even figure out everything we put in motion."

She finally told her staff to close it down two days before the inauguration. Rachel gathered her key staff in the Oval Office for some photos and a toast from a bottle of some very old Scotch.

She was looking forward to stepping off the roller coaster. She welcomed the opportunity to be a mother again, to raise a daughter and help her grow into womanhood, blending strength with kindness, wisdom with courage, trying hard not to spoil her.

It was time for her and Wynn to have an actual honeymoon. The results of the 2000 election had curtailed their initial plans. They needed some time alone to rekindle the passion, to become just wife and husband, not some larger-than-life figures playing on a world stage. "Let's retake our wedding vows on Hurricane Ridge on the Olympic Peninsula," Wynn surprisingly suggested one evening. "Then take a month's honeymoon in Hawaii."

Wynn had his owned mixed feelings about leaving the White House. Unlike Rachel, who looked forward to a time of reflection and disengagement from the political process, Wynn felt he was being liberated to pursue his own agenda, to speak more freely. He had often felt confined in the White House.

Wynn and Rachel's relationship during the years of her presidency had its share of turbulence. On more than one occasion, Wynn had stormed out of the Oval Office or their personal quarters. Several times he took extended trips to get away, going hiking in the wilderness, canoeing down a river or locking himself into someone's house for a weekend with some old friends.

Wynn was not used to playing such a secondary role. Not only was he the first "First Husband," but unlike his predecessors as First Lady, he hadn't had years to grow into the role of supportive spouse. There were times when he felt shunted to the side, not so much by Rachel but by everyone else. Many valued him not for who he was as an individual but for his access to Rachel.

A few of his former colleagues from the antiapartheid movement complained that he and Rachel had not done enough to confront racism. "We've got a couple of centuries of oppression to make up for, and all we are seeing is a token downpayment, despite all the rhetoric and compassion," Dwight Foster told him. Dwight had been arrested outside the South African embassy in DC a half-dozen times at protests Wynn helped organize.

"Yo, bro, you're welcome to do better," Wynn responded. "Just persuade Congress. Rachel did the best she could, you'll be lamenting her when she's gone. Corporate America and their political parties have a different idea about what needs to be done. Unfortunately, they've got most of the real power, and they haven't surrendered yet."

"Precisely," Foster replied. "This progress is an illusion, little more than cosmetic. Okay, a few things got done but they won't last a year after Rachel has departed. Half the rules you guys put in place they figured out how to cheat on before the ink was even dry. The white man keeps getting richer off us. You've got to throw out the whole racist, capitalist system from top to bottom. It's inherently exploitative."

"Duh," said Wynn. "What else is new? As Bart Simpson said in episode 673, it's a whole lot easier to say that you need to cross the traverse than it is to build the bridge across.

"Rachel and I never pretended that we we're going to win everything. We always knew that we had to mobilize people, get them invested in the decision-making, try to give them some power that they'd be able to keep once Rachel's term was over," said Wynn. "You wanna make a difference? Vote Green, organize in your community, speak truth to power."

Wynn had pushed Rachel to move faster on some issues. He argued that she sometimes seemed content to state support for an issue but then didn't do the arm-twisting needed to win. She responded that it was a matter of choosing your battles.

On more than one occasion Wynn unwittingly dragged Rachel into a controversy. One instance was the rape trial of one of the best-known pro basketball players, Henri Sampson. Sampson, from Wynn's hometown of Brooklyn, was considered a quiet, reserved guy who avoided the superstar lifestyle of most players far less famous than he.

It was considered out of character when he was accused of raping a young student he met when he was in Idaho for a basketball camp run by a college teammate. The woman had gone to his hotel room after meeting him at the hotel pool, where she had swum up to him at the poolside bar and bought him a drink.

Wynn was well-known as a basketball junkie, often attending NBA games in DC or New York. He'd met Sampson a few times. A reporter friend asked Wynn what he thought about the case when they bumped into each other at a Knick-Wizard game.

"Sampson's a good guy," Wynn responded. "If it was a white player, they wouldn't even bring this to trial. Sampson can have any women he wants, why would he need to rape someone? I don't see how he can get a fair trial in an all-white, rural county. I've seen reports that this woman had sex with other guys right before and after this all took place. That could account for her so-called injuries. She liked to party, have a good time. What did she think she was doing when she went to his hotel room in her thong bikini? Going to read the Bible?

"It is certainly believable that she couldn't get whatever it was she wanted out of Sampson, so she makes up a story to get some attention, maybe make some money out of it," Wynn continued. "Her story has so many holes in it, you could drive a truck through it. Just another poor black dude getting railroaded," he said.

Wynn's comments were plastered all over the news the following morning. Rachel, Sophie and Anna took turns yelling at him.

"Let's forget for a moment how stupid it was to talk to the press about something you have no personal knowledge of and which *we* have no role in. Don't even bother with the crap about you thought it was off the record. Let's focus on you dissing a woman who has filed rape charges. Not only that, you argued that her sexual history was relevant in determining whether or not she was raped. You want to throw out decades of progress in protecting women against sexual assault because you have a buddy that can throw the ball through a hoop?" Rachel screamed at him.

"Okay, I'm sorry, I should have kept my mouth shut," Wynn admitted. "That was dumb."

"Very dumb," she replied.

"But aren't you forgetting that someone is entitled to a presumption of innocence, even a basketball player? And aren't you forgetting that black men have a history of not getting a fair trial in this country, especially when it involves sex and a white woman?" Wynn responded.

"This wasn't the moment for you to deliver a dissertation on the legal system's treatment of black men," Rachel said. "We've got enough problems without you looking for more. The woman is the victim here and she's been treated shamefully, including by you."

"I'm not talking about putting the accuser's sex life on trial," Wynn said defensively. "I'm talking about specific events that occurred right before and after the alleged rape that appear to contradict her statements both about the physical injuries she got, and about her emotional condition. Sampson has the right to show he's innocent."

"Every woman who gets raped is gonna think long and hard before deciding to file a rape charge because of the way this woman was persecuted by the media," Rachel told him, "her personal life hung out for the whole world to see. I'm gonna have to spend days now, maybe weeks, dealing with your comments. Start writing your apology now. Anna has volunteered to help you."

Most of the time, however, Wynn had been Rachel's bedrock, her source of uncritical support when she was most under attack. He would shore up her sagging morale, soothingly reminding her that she was doing what was right, what was best for the country.

"Don't give up hope," Wynn would tell her as he gave her a back rub. "Keep the pressure up. It always looks darkest before the storm breaks. Congress will back down before you do. They're more interested in covering their butts than anything else. They just need a political solution to keep their funders happy."

But at times he argued that she was too cautious, too boxed in by political considerations. Behind closed doors they continued their debate over the correct balance between revolution and reform.

"You can't support half measures." Wynn argued. "You'll just get of our opponents mad while not actually solving the problem, failing the people we're supposed to be helping. It's the worst of both worlds. Give in now, and you'll lose the opportunity for real change, letting them off the hook. Do what's right, not what's expedient," pleaded Wynn.

"I wanna see a difference in the lives of the average person. Symbolic defeats at this level don't do us much good," Rachel replied, often in exasperation. "It's important that we be seen as winning, it makes it easier for us to win the next fight. If we go down in flames, we look vulnerable. It makes it easier for Congress and our opponents to beat us in the future. Isn't that the lesson you hammered into me when you dragged me to yet another protest for a stop sign back in Phoenix?"

****

One of her staff members who attended the farewell brunch the morning before the inauguration was Jennifer Garcia, the housekeeper who alerted her to the problems with Harrington's death.

Jennifer approached her several weeks after September 11 as Rachel came down the hall to her private quarters. Rachel did her best to offer a smile of greeting. Jennifer surprised her by giving her a hug, telling her how sorry she was about Tommy's death.

"I have two children, a fifteen-year-old boy and a thirteen-year-old girl," Jennifer said. "If something was to happen to them, I dunno what I'd do. I know nothing I say can make the pain go away, but it will get easier with time." Jennifer took a step backward, holding on to Rachel's hands while looking her in the eye. "President Moreno, the people of this country, the real people, the workin' people, we know whose side you're on. We love you."

"Why, thank you very much, Jennifer. That's very kind of you to say," she replied.

After they talked for a few minutes, Jennifer broached an issue.

"Madame President, I don't mean to take advantage of you but I was hopin' you could tell me who to call about a nephew of my sister-in-law? He was workin' in the World Trade Center when it collapsed. He didn't have papers to be in America, so they aren't doin' nuthin' for him."

Many of the individuals killed in the World Trade Center were undocumented workers who did many of the menial tasks, cleaning floors and emptying wastebaskets, working in restaurants and making deliveries of all sorts, from flowers to take-out food. Early morning was one of the peak times for undocumented workers to be in the building.

The initial death count had been 6,000; it eventually dropped to 3,000. One of the reasons for the drop was the failure of many of the undocumented workers to appear on the final official list. Their loved ones were doubly cursed.

Many families had a hard time proving that their loved one were there, as employers often failed to keep work or pay records. Plus they were afraid that if they pursued their husband or son too hard, the INS would show up to deport them and their family.

"My nephew's wife came up from Mexico to look for him. She brought their two young children. She don't have any family in the city. She's at her wits' end. One door after another is slammed shut. She's outta money. The officials don't even treat her as his wife 'cause they didn't have paperwork," Jennifer said. The widow felt invisible, wandering wounded through a great tragedy while everyone ignored her pleas for help.

"Don't worry Jen, we'll take care of it," Rachel told her. "Maybe you can be one of my representatives helping other people without papers, make sure the government is doing the right thing. You can help keep me informed about what's really going on. The last thing we need is red tape for people trying to deal with the loss of a loved one."

Jennifer's present job was as liaison between with White House and the Immigration Naturalization Services.

****

Rachel's final interview was with an Indy Media affiliate. It was broadcast live on their radio, internet and satellite distribution networks.

"How will you cope with your loss of power?" George Macris asked, pushing the buttons on his personal tape recorder nervously, uncertain if it was working. The other Indy Media technicians in the room just shook their heads.

"Leaving the presidency will empower me," Rachel replied. "For the first time in a I'll be free to speak the truth."

"Are you saying you've been lying to the American people?" he asked.

Rachel laughed. "It'll also be empowering to no longer have to watch what you say to reporters. No, what I meant was that as president, I had to be a politician. I couldn't just say whatever I thought, I had to talk about what was possible, what was the best under the circumstances. Every elected official, even the president, operates within limits.

"What I can do now is talk about what is needed. When you tell some members of Congress that we should make decisions based on what is best for the majority rather than on what maximizes the profits of a few, they look at you like you're insane, at best pollyannish. I'm glad that I will no longer by limited by what the politicians and corporations think is feasible.

"I want to talk about a green revolution. About a feminist revolution. About a worldwide revolution for peace and justice. People forget how radically our world has changed in the last century, the last twenty years. We live in a time that has experienced change at an unprecedented rate, but yet our conception of what is possible is rather limited," Rachel said.

"I intend to move beyond these limits. There's no reason why we can't radically change our global political and economic systems in a very short period of time. We have the technological ability to provide everyone on the planet with a decent standard of living while protecting our environment for future generations. If we're willing to spend a little time thinking about how to create a world that we'd all be proud of, where meeting everyone's needs is the first and overriding goal, I think we'd be surprised how quickly and easily we could accomplish this," she added.

Rachel smiled. "It's time to think globally, act locally."

"Some people accuse you of creating a cult of personality around you," the reporter said. "There are a lot of Rachelites who seem to hang on your every word. I'm sure you've heard the joke that the fastest way to end a conversation at a cocktail party is for someone to pipe up, "Well, Rachel says ..."

Rachel laughed. "I guess it depends upon the party. I don't see too many cocktails served at Green parties. Beer, some wine, some organic juice, Free Trade coffee, but not cocktails."

Rachel got serious.

"My message has always been that people need to think for themselves. They need to be willing to ask critical questions and to take action when something's wrong," she said.

"I think Americans have gone through a process of healthy self-examination in the last seven years. It helped heal us from the tragedy of September eleventh. We've defined a new set of goals as to the type of world we want to create. There will always be disagreements, of course, about how to get there, about what type of world is in fact best, but at least that's something that we now openly discuss, and it helps determine what our government does. There are holdouts, naturally, people who don't want to give up their power and privilege. I trust they're dinosaurs who will soon be extinct," Rachel noted.

"But many people say you're a prophet, a beacon to light the way to our future. What do you think about that description?" Macris asked.

Rachel sat thinking of a response for almost a minute. The radio crew and her staff began to panic about the dead air time, wondering what was going on. The reporter began to say something to break the silence. Rachel raised her finger asking for a few more seconds.

"Prophet is a powerful word. I was taught that it was a good word, a holy word, when I was growing up. Mainly I thought it was just some old crazy guys wandering the desert where they were free to scream the truth. But if they came into town to speak, the authorities arrested or killed him."

"I believe that all of us need to be prophets, just like all of us are part of God, of Gaia, of Mother Earth. The world has been sick and troubled. It's time for all of us to lift our voices to save it. I've been privileged over the last eight years to have my voice. Thank you all very much. Keep up the struggle."

She unfastened her microphone from her suit jacket and departed.

****

Rachel took Wynn and Latisha's hands in her own as they walked out the front door of the White House. They would walk to the inauguration ceremony rather than ride. They were joined by many of the White House staff, Green congressional representatives and Cabinet secretaries. As they passed through the White House gate onto Pennsylvania Avenue, they were joined by thousands of Green Party members carrying banners and signs.

They marched down Pennsylvania Avenue chanting, "The people, united, will never be defeated."

APPENDIX A - PROPOSALS FROM THE PEOPLE'S SUMMIT

A. Adoption of the Tobin Tax on Currency Speculation

A major cause of the financial crisis in many countries is currency speculation. Foreign currency exchange exceeds more than $1.5 trillion daily, a sum larger than the combined volume of all the world's stock exchanges. The "Tobin Tax," named after the Nobel laureate economist who originated the concept, would deter short-term or overnight trades by increasing their cost. Reducing the ability to play such speculation games would restore the ability of countries to control their own currencies. The annual 100-billion-dollar annual Tobin Tax revenue would be democratically distributed to support sustainable development projects, such as small-scale agriculture, reforestation, disaster aid and food distribution, health clinics, disease prevention, clean water and pollution control.

B. Creation of a World Economic Parliament

Based on the European model, the parliament would set policy for international economic relations. One of its first tasks would be to develop a Common Agreement on Investment and Society to regulate and guide relationships between countries, businesses and society. Where local forums couldn't resolve conflicts, a "World Economic and Environmental Court" would hear cases. Judges would be appointed by the parliament. The long-term goal would be to have participation, including elections, begin at the community rather than the state or national level.

C. Creation of an International Bankruptcy Court

To deal with the problem of third world debt, an International Bankruptcy Court would oversee debt relief to low-income countries. An International Finance Organization (IFO) under the UN would guide international investment, promoting domestic ownership and control. The People's Summit called for the IMF, World Bank, and regional development banks to write off 100 percent of the debts owed to them by poor countries.

D. Replace the WTO with the International Trade Organization

The Summit supported replacing the WTO with a democratic

International Trade Organization, promoting full employment, environmental protection and sustainable development while breaking up multinational corporations, their global cartels and monopolistic practices.

E. Rules of Conduct for Corporations

The delegates proposed establishing standards for workers' rights, environmental protection and cultural protection. The rules would be incorporated into an International Treaty on Corporations and Investments. Multinational companies could be brought before an international tribunal for violating these standards. Corporations would no longer be viewed as the legal equivalent of a human being, nor would they be able to finance political candidates or lobby for laws. A tax would be placed on the true social costs of the company, so they could not transfer such costs to the public or environment. Companies' charters would be time limited, and they would have to demonstrate that they had acted for the common good for a charter to be renewed. Antitrust measures to control the size and power of multinational corporations were proposed.

F. Adoption of Precautionary Principle for Corporate and Government Activities

If a practice or product shows a possible threat to human health or the environment, it must be restricted or halted until it is conclusively established that such harm does not exist. The Precautionary Principle would immediately apply to genetic engineering. The summit also called for a worldwide ban on the ownership of the genetic structure of living beings, including humans. It called for an end to the practice of biopiracy and bioprospecting, which is the practice of private companies that seek to steal the healing knowledge of indigenous cultures of natural substances — plants, animal or mineral.

G. Protection of Domestic Economies

Contrary to the principles of the WTO and the Free Trade movement, the People's Summit concluded that protection of domestic economies was necessary to promote sustainable development and living wages. The summit supported public subsidies for vital community efforts such as small-scale organic agriculture for local markets or small-scale energy and transportation infrastructure. Corporations would be required to use "site here to sell here" policy for manufacturing, banking and other services. The summit also proposed the introduction of pollution taxes and the imposition of high taxes on the extraction and depletion of natural resources such as lumber, water, and minerals.

H. The Elimination of Corporate Welfare

The summit proposed the elimination of corporate welfare as a violation of both Free and Fair Trade. Public subsidies of corporations, besides often failing to create jobs locally, also gave companies an unfair advantage on the global market, since the government subsidies often allowed them to sell products at a lower price than companies based in countries that didn't or couldn't afford to provide such subsidies. Protecting local sustainable economies was also recognized as a priority. Countries should also have the right to ensure that products reflected their true production costs; many companies sought to pass on their true costs, such as pollution and resource depletion, onto consumers and the general public.

F. Declaration of Human Rights and the Environment

The conferees supported the adoption of a Universal Declaration of Human Rights and the Environment, based on a 1994 UN gathering convened by the Sierra Club. "Human rights, an ecologically sound environment, sustainable development and peace are interdependent and indivisible. All persons have the right to freedom from pollution, environmental degradation and activities that adversely affect the environment, or threaten the life, health, livelihood, well-being or sustainable development within, across or outside national boundaries. All persons have the right to protection and preservation of the air, soil, water, sea-ice, flora and fauna, and the essential processes and areas necessary to maintain biological diversity and ecosystems. All persons have the right to adequate housing, land tenure and living conditions in a secure, healthy and ecologically sound environment. Indigenous peoples have the right to control their lands, territories and natural resources and to maintain their traditional way of life."